D1596211

THE SALT HOUSE

A Max Strong Thriller

MIKE DONOHUE

ALSO BY MIKE DONOHUE

MAX STRONG/MICHAEL SULLIVAN PREQUELS

Sleeping Dogs

The Devil's Angel

MAX STRONG THRILLERS

Shaking the Tree

Bottom of the World

Hollow City

Trouble Will Find Me

Burn the Night

Crooked Prayers

SHORT STORIES

October Days

For my grandmothers –

You didn't get a chance to read this one,
but I'm sure you're handselling it in the next life.

If I cannot move heaven, I will raise hell.

— VIRGIL

THE SALT HOUSE

PART ONE

CHAPTER ONE

Alex Blackburn sat at his desk and read the pages for the third time. It didn't take long. Bad news rarely wasted time. There were only four pages. A cover letter, of sorts, and then three official documents. Each was a copy, but still, complete with signatures, notarized dates, and what appeared to be an embossed seal at the bottom. He recognized all the names listed.

His name and address on the envelope were handwritten. No return address for obvious reasons. He might have dismissed it as junk mail and discarded it unopened if it had been printed, that would have been a very costly mistake, but the handwriting had caught his eye. It had arrived mixed in with the rest of the day's mail and Consuela had placed it in the tray on his desk. It had sat there ticking away like a bomb for four hours until he'd finished a late afternoon conference call and picked up the stack.

The letters were blocky, in black ink. The envelope was cheap, plain white. It was probably one from a box of 50 or 100 and available at any drug or office supply store. The envelope was thin, and it bulged with the folded papers inside. He pulled out the letter and flattened it on the blotter. At this point, he was more curious than concerned. The first time he didn't really read the pages, he'd skimmed them, looking for context, his name, or trigger words that might tell him what it was about. Did he need to tune in and pay attention or could he pitch it all in the trash? He flipped through the pages. Some sort of legal documents. Something related to Rose and the ranch.

The second time, he read each word and became more concerned. By the time he reached the signatures and seal, a cold tightness had crept through his gut. The intent of the letter was clear enough and the documents were short and straightforward. He didn't doubt the originals would hold up to whatever scrutiny was needed. He looked at the names and dates and did the math. His mind rapidly spun out different scenarios and outcomes. None of them ended well for him. Not unless he did something about it.

He weighed his options and then reached for the phone but hesitated. There was the standing meeting, of course. They talked once a week. He didn't like to call or bring anything up outside of that forum. He didn't want to give the man any reason for unease. This would be the first time he'd ever done it. Should he wait? No, the weekly meeting was still four days away. He should call. But should he handle it on his own? That was an option, but it brought its own risks. That type of response was not in his primary skill set. Not anymore. He'd done it before, of course, but he'd been a younger man. A totally different man. To get where he was now, sitting in this office, he'd needed to take certain types of risk. Now, it was different. He needed to keep his hands much cleaner. He didn't need to take those risks, but he still needed to manage risk. What was the best way to manage this specific risk? If he went about it on his own and it went wrong? The man wouldn't react well. But if he handled it quickly and cleanly? Maybe it never had to be mentioned at all. Or, maybe he could position it as taking initiative and being accountable. Was it worth the risk?

He went back and forth for a few more minutes and then picked up the phone and dialed a number. He was never a man to waste time. He always felt better when taking action. *The only way out is through* was a primary rule for him. He hung up the phone feeling a little better. This was unexpected but could be overcome. Perhaps whoever had sent it was actually doing him a favor. If he hadn't known about it, or learned about it too late, he might have lost everything.

He spun around in his chair and looked out the window. The setting sun cast the pool and patio in a soft golden light. Beyond the pool, near the barn, he could see the horses grazing. It was a lot to lose. Most people would see a peaceful and bucolic scene. Not Blackburn. Blackburn saw it as necessary window dressing. It all added up to status and power and money. The three keys to opening up locked doors in this world. Blackburn had already opened a few doors, which was actually impressive for someone with his background, but he wanted more. He knew those doors were just the lowest rungs of the ladder and he didn't intend to settle for that. He intended to keep climbing right out of this backwater town. He intended to keep going until there was no higher rung to grasp and he no longer had to make the sort of phone call he'd just made.

As he turned away from the view and closed the blinds, he had another thought. He picked up the phone again and made another call. He would come at this problem from both directions.

CHAPTER TWO

Raul Ortiz knew how to stretch a dollar. It was a survival skill. One his mother had sorely lacked. She had poured her paychecks down her throat as fast as the bartender could refill the glass. He'd come to an agreement with her when he was seven. He would act like everything was fine if she gave him 40 dollars on payday before she went to Tully's. Forty dollars for two weeks, $2.86 per day, $1.43 each for him and his sister. If they wanted to eat, he needed to make everything last. Back then, he and Elena still went to bed most nights hungry, but they weren't starving.

He adjusted the small fan on the kitchen counter. No use sweating through his shirt before breakfast. His tie sat on the back of the chair. He wouldn't put that on until he was ready to leave. A tie in Texas during the summer should be considered cruel and unusual punishment.

The summers had been the worst part of his childhood. Yes, he was free from schoolwork, but no school meant no free school lunch and those couple of bucks had to extend even further. That frugal mindset was imprinted so deep in him now, he wasn't sure if he'd ever break free. He looked down at the dry bowl of cereal and the quarter full container of milk. He added a few splashes of the milk and then thinned it out further with some tap water before he spooned some into his mouth. It tasted like soggy packing material, but it would fill him up and he wouldn't have to buy more milk until the weekend.

He glanced at the stack of envelopes in a pile on the table near the front door. Maybe it was good that he hadn't ever fully broken his thrifty habit. Things had been good for a time. After his mother had drank her liver out of business, and Elena had gotten a scholarship and escaped to UTEP, he'd felt lighter. He'd gotten a job as a teller at M&P Savings and Loan. For ten years, he'd worked his way steadily up the ladder. Baby steps and half-steps and some might say sheer endurance; he'd stayed while others had left. He rose up until he became branch manager. Then, he hadn't *needed* to watch every single cent, but he'd done it anyway.

In retrospect, it was like his body knew something his mind didn't. His body had been storing up nuts for a rainy day. And now it was fucking pouring. Almost overnight, it felt like Raul was back in that tiny hotbox apartment above the laundromat. Almost all of the mining and petroleum outfits around Tiendas Reales had closed. Business accounts and deposits had dried up. The remaining mining employees were forced to follow or find new jobs, and there were precious few new jobs in Tiendas Reales. Not enough for all the people looking for work in the last few years. Accounts were closed. Loans were defaulted on. Raul spent most of his days dealing with either irate customers or crying ones. The tearful ones were far worse, but neither left him feeling good about himself. After thirteen years of striving, he was the local branch manager of nothing. He was in charge of a paper kingdom where all the chits and receipts were worthless.

And soon, he wouldn't even be that. The modest collection of M&P assets had been bought up by a large east coast commercial bank. The ax that had been hanging over his head for the last eighteen months had finally dropped last month. The TR branch would be closed and consolidated with the other M&P branch in Freer, over an hour away. He'd talked to a woman in HR and had been invited to apply for a job there. She thought with his retail experience that he had a good shot at landing one of the positions. All those years of work and he'd been *invited* to apply. If he didn't secure a job with the bank, she'd said, he'd receive a week of severance for each year he'd been employed and, as a manager, he'd receive two free weeks of career job placement services. Thirteen weeks. That might see him through to the end of the year. *Might*. Loyalty clearly got you nothing. He'd felt like screaming at her, but he'd politely thanked her and hung up. Job placement services. He was almost perversely curious to see what the career counseling person filling that HR requirement would make of the opportunities available in Tiendas Reales.

Thinking back on that conversation now, he wondered if that was the first crack, or had it been there already? Had the eighteen months after the announcement, that time in limbo, built up the pressure so slowly he didn't feel it? Had he been the proverbial frog in the slowly boiling pot? Did it even matter now? He'd made his choice. He'd gone all in.

CHAPTER THREE

The killers both lived in Los Angeles, but not close to each other. By design, they lived on opposite sides of the sprawling city. They rarely, if ever, saw each other unless they were on a job. Even then, they often tried to remain apart until it was time to pull the trigger. At that point, it didn't matter who saw them together. They didn't live long enough to tell anyone.

They had worked together for almost twenty years. They had started young in Iguala and had each killed their first man before turning sixteen. It had been a necessity. They had both come to see their work as a kind of public service. They were defending their families and communities from outsiders. If the outsiders gained control, things would have only gotten worse. The government was not going to help. Their fathers were not around. They had no choice, and they had no regrets. They did it to survive.

Eventually, they each made their way over the border to a new life in the United States, but they didn't seek out a new profession. They were good at what they did, very good, and they were paid well. There was no incentive to find a new job.

There was plenty of work for them on this side of the border. It wasn't much different than working at home. In some ways, it was better. They were now more anonymous. They were also older, savvier, and had a reputation among the people who mattered. They set up cutouts in Detroit and Vegas. If you needed something done, you jumped through the hoops. If you checked out and the money came through, your problem was taken care of in a reasonable amount of time. They typically worked in the southwest, but it wasn't exclusive. They were willing to travel. Sometimes they even went back across the border. They had friends in high and low places.

On the afternoon that the first call came through, the driver was in his back yard trying to stop the spread of citrus blast from spreading through his small grove of orange trees. He had decided the best course was to cut down the sick tree, as much as it would pain him, before it could infect the rest. He had just gone to the garden shed and grabbed an ax when the phone on his hip vibrated. He always carried it, even though it didn't ring often. Just a handful of times each year. Only three people had the number. He slipped it out of the belt loop holster and checked the display. It was the man from Vegas.

"Yes?"

The driver's voice was dry and slightly tremulous. He didn't speak out loud very often. He'd worked hard during his time in the U.S. to lose his native accent. He did it for the same reason he had his teeth fixed, a few prominent moles removed, and his astigmatism corrected. His job required him to be forgettable, to blend in. He wanted nothing about himself to be memorable. Not his dark hair. Not his medium frame. Not his speech. Nothing. In his experience, most people looked out at the world but were only thinking about themselves. This innate selfishness meant he didn't need elaborate distractions. His only disguise was his basic blandness. It had worked for twenty years and he expected it to continue working for twenty more.

He listened now as the man in Vegas relayed the details of the job offer. He'd never met the man in Vegas. He'd only heard his voice, but he had done some research. He knew where the man lived. He knew his name. He could find him if it was ever necessary. This particular job was vague. Typically, he would reject it. He wouldn't even need to speak to his partner, but it also came from an old, very trusted client. He thought about it.

"Hello?" the man in Vegas said as the silence lingered.

"We will take the job," the driver said eventually.

"Okay. Good." The man in Vegas sounded relieved. He likely did not want to call this client back with bad news. "I will transfer the first part of the payment and then contact you with further details when I have them."

The driver disconnected, walked back to the shed, and replaced the ax. When he worked a job, he worked the job and nothing else. The client had his full attention. That was what he was paid for. The tree would live or die according to nature. He would not intervene. Not now.

A minute later, his phone chimed with a notification. The money had been deposited. He walked back up to the house and checked on his mother. She was sitting on the couch watching a telenovela. He stepped back into the yard. It was unlikely that she could or would overhear him, but the driver was always cautious.

He called his partner across the city.

"We have a job," he said when Mookie picked up. His real name was Alvaro, but he'd been called La Muneca, the doll, in Iguala since he was a small child with a mop of dark hair and cherubic features. The nickname had followed him over the border but had been bastardized in translation from Muneca to Mookie and, like any bad nickname, it had stuck.

"Okay."

A twenty-year partnership was built on trust. His partner didn't ask any more questions, he trusted the driver, they were extensions of each other. A left arm and a right arm. He waited.

The driver continued. "I'll pick you up at the San Antonio airport in two days. In the afternoon."

"Okay." Nothing more needed to be said.

Next, he switched phones and called his sister. He spoke in his native Spanish.

"There is a job up in Sacramento. It might be a few days, maybe a week. Can you stay with Mom at night? The nurse will continue to come and check in during the day."

"Claro." Of course, she responded. His sister was more than ten years younger and only had vague, hazy memories of their time growing up in Mexico. She believed her brother was an insurance claims adjuster for a large company and that he was called out on emergencies a few times a year.

Done with his phone calls, he went inside. He kissed his mother on the cheek. She looked at him with milky eyes and little recognition. Some days were better than others. He knew that in certain ways, her forgetting was a blessing. He could keep her comfortable at home and she rarely asked questions. And when she did, she rarely remembered the answers. He left her to her shows and went upstairs for his suitcase and small kit bag. He unlocked the closet and retrieved the bags. He put the kit bag inside the suitcase and left the house.

He drove to the airport and parked in a long-term satellite lot. He took the shuttle to the terminal then walked with his rolling suitcase around from departures to arrivals and lined up with the other harried passengers at the car rental counter.

The car was always a rental from LAX. If things went sideways, good luck tracing the car. LAX had the busiest rental hub in the country, maybe the world.

The agent tried to give him a silver convertible, thinking he was doing the driver a favor. He declined and went for a white mid-size sedan. He filled out the paperwork using one of the IDs taken from his kit bag then walked back outside and took another shuttle bus out to the rental lot. He found the rental car and drove out into the LA traffic. He spent an hour driving aimlessly just to be sure no one was following. Always cautious. When he was certain there was no tail, he drove to a secure storage facility near El Segundo and loaded two heavy black nylon bags into the trunk. He removed the kit bag from the suitcase and put that in the trunk, too. He left the rolling suitcase in the storage unit. He then relocked the padlock on the door, got back in the car, and hit the road. He worked his way over to the 105 and headed east, then picked up 605 North briefly, then turned east again on 60 and settled into the seat for the two-day drive to Texas.

CHAPTER FOUR

Max blamed Davey Crockett and John Wayne for getting him into trouble this time.

Those two and the cop with the broken nose.

Someone in charge of afternoon programming at the local Boston ABC affiliate must have been a transplanted Texan back in the '80s. Both the Disney miniseries and the 1960s John Wayne movie about the Battle of the Alamo played on heavy repeat. For Max, childhood was the sticky feel of Joyce's crumb-laced red canvas couch, the smell of hot Bagel Bites, and the sound of *Dialing for Dollars* on the 20-inch Goldstar in the living room. And it was John Wayne as Davey Crockett and Richard Widmark as Jim Bowie that he most often recalled watching on that perpetually fuzzy television.

Even as a kid, Max realized the movie was probably inaccurate. But as he drove west through Ohio and into Indiana, he saw Illinois looming to the west on the map and he decided to turn south. Max wanted no part of Chicago or Essex County out in Iowa. He had a history in those places and no rational reason to risk showing his face within five hundred miles. He didn't need a bored state trooper deciding to pull him over for some imagined infraction. His ID and vehicle registration would likely hold up, but he didn't want it to get that far. He wanted to stay out of the system, even if his documents were rock solid. It was difficult to disappear in today's digital world, but with a little help, Max had done a decent job. There was no reason to turn up his nose at that. So, he turned left at Indianapolis and started working his way southwest.

Somewhere around Memphis, as he switched over from Route 55 to Route 40 near the Arkansas border, he thought about Davey Crockett. Texas was on the horizon. Despite his recent peripatetic lifestyle, Max still thought of himself as a Boston guy. He'd rarely spent any time south of the Mason-Dixon and he'd never been to Texas. He plugged San Antonio into the GPS and decided to find out just how full of shit John Wayne was.

He skirted the sprawling edges of Dallas-Fort Worth and decided to stop just south of the metro area, get an early start, and hit San Antonio and the Alamo in the morning. He stopped at a roadside motel, checked in, and asked the desk clerk where he might hear some music and get a cold beer and a decent burger. The town wasn't big, but Max figured any Texas town with a crossroads was going to have music.

The clerk scratched at the T-shirt straining against his belly. "Reveler's Hall is your best bet if you're not picky. They got live music most nights, even if it's just open mic. Burgers are average but the fries are always hot and greasy."

"Sounds good," Max said. "How far?"

"Just a mile farther south."

Max left his bags in the car and decided after a day of driving that a mile walk to stretch his legs and whet his appetite would be a good appetizer. Walking was easy. Traffic was thin and the shoulder was wide. But after driving in the climate-controlled SUV all day, Max had neglected to consider the Texas heat. Even at sunset, the road retained the day's warmth and baked up through his shoes. He took his time but was still coated in a sheen of sweat, his shirt stuck to his back, when he pulled open the door to the bar.

The place was dark and smelled of spilled beer and fried food. The wood floors and scattered four-tops were soaked in decades of spilled drinks. There was a stage at the far end with two scarred pool tables to the right. The jukebox was to the left at the end of a long bar and a row of stools. The place could have been a saloon or roadhouse from the 1950s or 1850s, save for the two large flat-screen TVs mounted at equal intervals above the bar. Both were showing the same college football game. From the grainy footage, Max assumed it was a replay of a long-since decided contest.

A bartender and a cocktail waitress chatted at one end. Single drinkers occupied half the stools along the rail and one group of four guys occupied two tables pushed together near the stage. Two other guys were shooting pool. Max figured it was early for a place like this. He took a seat at one of the tables and put his back to the wall. The cocktail waitress wandered over.

"Mind if I take up a table as a single or do you want me to move to the bar?"

"Long as you don't stiff me on a tip, you can sit on the floor for all I care."

She didn't look much past thirty with a figure that probably still pulled in a fair share of tips, and unwanted hand grabs, in a place like this but her tone betrayed a weariness that made her sound older.

"You got food?"

She pulled a slim laminated card from an apron pocket

and handed it to him. It didn't take long to read. Nachos, chicken wings, a burger, steak. Fries or a baked potato as a side.

"Burger and fries and whatever you have on draft."

"Lone Star or Coors?"

"Lone Star." He nodded toward the stage. "Any music tonight?"

She looked over at the stage as if she'd never noticed it there. "Not sure, but someone usually gets up there eventually. Typically around eight or nine."

"Worth waiting around for?"

For the first time, Max felt her really look at him. "You got a lot of questions. Not from around here, huh?"

"Nope. Just passing through. Staying at the motel up the road. Was hoping to avoid watching reruns on HBO and get some decent food. Maybe hear some decent music."

She sniffed. "Maybe you'll get one out of two. Can't promise anything." She turned and walked away.

Max studied the room. The walls were thin, and Max could feel the heat pushing in. The place slowly filled up and the ratty air conditioner couldn't keep up. The waitress brought his food and Max ordered another beer. A game started up on the second pool table but the stage remained empty. Someone plugged in a four-song set of Patsy Cline on the juke. The burger was on the well-done side but the fries met the clerk's description: hot and greasy. Max had no complaints. He paid his check, including a healthy tip, and was about to leave when he saw a skinny guy in jeans and a leather jacket come in carrying a guitar case and a well-used Fender amp. He saw a couple people wave or say hi as he made his way toward the stage. Max had nowhere to be. Not tonight. He gave up the table and wandered over to the bar.

That was his first mistake.

The room continued to fill up. The guitar guy was good.

His playing was above average; he really knew how to work the room and build a set. He mixed in classic country covers, a few originals, a few crowd pleasers. He never let the energy lag. Tables were pushed aside, and people began dancing. The heat continued to build. Max also felt a certain energy begin to rise, like static electricity in a thunderstorm.

"Hey, get down here and get me my fuckin' drink."

Max recognized the guy lacking manners as one of the group who occupied the pushed together tables when he'd walked in. It was certainly not his first, second, or third drink.

"Hey!" He shoved his way through the people waiting for service at the bar. Max watched as he pushed a petite woman in the back. She stumbled and almost went down. She pushed him back, but it had no effect on the drunk oaf. He just kept pushing forward and hit her in the back again. This time, anger replaced the look of hurt and surprise. She swung an elbow into his substantial gut. That got his attention and a smile.

"Oh, I like 'em feisty." He leaned forward and used his bulk to press her against the bar.

The drunk caught Max's eye. "What are you lookin' at?"

"I'm still trying to figure that out."

The man's brow creased. "What did you—"

Before he could finish his witty comeback, a beer bottle bounced off the side of his head. He took a stumbling step back and his eyes briefly lost focus, but then he recovered and looked at the woman still holding the bottle. The blow to his head appeared to knock some of the drunk out of him.

"Oh, sweet cheeks, that was a big mistake."

It had all happened so quickly and unexpectedly that no one noticed other than Max and a few direct bystanders. None of the bystanders appeared willing to step in now. The big man took a step forward, yanked the bottle out of her hand, and then pulled back his fist. He appeared to have no qualms about striking a woman.

Max slid off his stool and snaked an arm around the guy's neck. He kept the guy's momentum going forward and placed his other hand on the back of his sweaty head. The woman slid to the side and another man jumped off his stool. Max brought the guy's head down on the bar with a solid *thunk*. He let up at the last second, so it wasn't a full impact. Still, the sound was weighty and deep. Max was tempted to do it again just to hear it, but other people heard it too and glanced over. He didn't want to invite further interest. He guided the drunk, and now stunned, man to the empty barstool and sat him down. The man looked at him for a moment with a dull expression, or maybe his normal one, before his eyes rolled back and he toppled off the stool and crumpled to the floor. Max checked that he was breathing and his airway was clear. The guy moaned and put a hand to his face. He'd have a headache, a really good one judging by that sound, and maybe a couple black eyes and bruising but he would be okay. The crowd closed around him, eager to get drinks and back on the dance floor.

Max walked out and made his way back to his motel room. He thought about the guitar player and the fries and whether the Bruins were playing that night. He did not think about the drunk guy.

CHAPTER FIVE

Not until the next morning when he happened to look out his window and saw a police cruiser pull into the lot and the guy got out, along with three other cops, all in uniform, probably the same guys from the shared tables at the bar. As predicted, the guy looked like he'd rammed his face into a cement wall at high speed. He had a splint framing his now bulbous nose, a raccoon mask around his eyes, and a shiny red mark on his forehead. Max chastised himself. He was usually very good at spotting cops. Maybe his intuition only worked in the northeast? He was new to Texas. More likely, he had been distracted by the music and his radar was fuzzed by the beer. They looked around and then one of them went inside the office. Either way, he'd whiffed badly this time. Max knew he didn't have a lot of time. The office manager would need to play nice with the locals and he'd give Max up in a heartbeat.

He grabbed his small bag from the second bed. Anything that wasn't packed, he could replace. He went to the bathroom, pushed the window up, and removed the screen. He tossed the bag out and then followed. It was a tight fit around his shoulders and hips but he was motivated. He scraped through and landed on his feet. He reached in and replaced the screen as best he could. No use giving them a clue to where he went.

He looked around for the best way to avoid these guys. There weren't many options. The motel backed onto an open field. There wasn't a shrub or knob of grass higher than his shin. It was miles of open space broken up only by roads, electrical poles, and the occasional low-rise building. There was a gas station and competing fast-food restaurants for half a mile in one direction. He knew from walking last night that there was a desultory half-empty strip mall and a used last-chance car lot in the other direction before Reveler's Hall popped up.

If it was just one-on-one, him and the injured cop, he might have taken his chances, went for his car, or tried to run for it. But four-on-one was too much to overcome. He didn't relish the thought of some trumped-up charges landing him in a Texas jail for a decade. Even if they didn't try to frame him, they were certainly going to take their pound of flesh in revenge, and he didn't like the thought of a long day, maybe more than one, in a quiet back cell.

There was one other option.

He was about to find out just how motivated he really was.

He opened the lid of the dumpster, dropped his bag inside, and then climbed in himself.

He really hoped it wasn't trash pickup day. It was a very long, very hot, and very foul-smelling wait. He was shin deep in trash. On the one hand, he was thankful that he was staying at a small, rather shabby roadside motel. There wasn't too much trash or waste in the bin. On the other hand, it was still a shabby roadside motel. The dumpster was old, crusty, and well used. It had baked for thirty years under this iron forge of a sun. There wasn't a lot of trash, but the combination of fresh garbage and vintage stains was malodorous and memorable. Max tried to breathe through his nose and listen for any signs of his pursuers. He distinctly tried not to hear the sounds of the other critters in the trash bin with him. To be fair, he was invading their home.

The men were not happy he was not in his room. He heard them tossing the place and then going back to the manager and yelling at him. At one point, a guy walked near the dumpster and Max tensed, but he never lifted the lid. It got quiet after that, and Max desperately fought the urge to climb out. He carefully lifted the top up two inches to get a whiff of fresh air.

The slice of the back lot that he could see was empty. Either they realized they were causing a commotion that would attract the attention of other guests or now that they'd busted into his room and not found him, they were at a loss for what to do next. He didn't think this posse had much imagination. If the three others were like their friend, Max didn't rate them high on the evolutionary scale. Still, sometimes stupid came with a certain cunning and it would be bad to underestimate them. He stayed put and waited. Eventually, he heard the static pop of radios and the deep growl of a V8 engine start up. Duty called. Still, some sixth sense told him to be careful. He waited another fifteen minutes before he climbed out. The hot air baking off the dirty blacktop never tasted so sweet. He crept back over to the window and peered through. Sure enough, they'd left one guy behind. He was sitting in the shadows looking out the front window. The room was a mess. They hadn't bothered to clean up.

He walked around the far end of the motel to his SUV. This side of the lot wouldn't be visible from the motel room's window. He checked the tires. All good. It was a shabby, rundown motel but it still had other guests and cars in the lot. He might have told the waitress where he was staying, but he hadn't told the clerk what he was driving. This is where his natural paranoia and years on the road paid off. He never parked close to his room for this very reason. Always have a way out. He put his bag on the passenger seat and climbed in. The stink would likely leech into the upholstery, but he could get the car cleaned later. Right now, he was anxious to put some miles between himself and these four idiots. He drove over the shallow median and into the adjoining field. He went offroad behind the motel until he met the intersecting crossroad. Then he put the car back on the pavement and hit the gas.

He drove two hours south to San Antonio. He checked his mirrors often in the first hour but saw nothing. After he passed a third trooper on the highway without incident, he breathed easier. He found a new motel room on one of the endless ribbons of highway circling the metro area. It was clean enough and anonymous and blended in with all the other rooms in his recent past. He knew he would immediately forget it when he checked out in the morning. He stripped off his clothes and stuffed them in the room's tiny trashcan, then used both small soaps in the shower to get the stink of the garbage off him. He dressed and then headed back out.

He drove around until he found a place to wash and detail the interior of the SUV. He spent the remainder of the hot afternoon correcting his understanding of the Alamo, the Texas Revolution, and what really happened, or likely happened, at that church in 1836. Finally, he collected his now clean car and had an early dinner of steak, polenta, and grilled summer vegetables.

He sat outside on the city's Riverwalk and considered what or where to go next. He'd left Chepstow because it felt wrong to stay. Dangerous and irresponsible to insert himself and his history into other people's lives. At least without them knowing the extent of his past. It felt safer to be on the move. For him and everyone else. If someone wanted to call that running away or cowardice, so be it. They weren't wrong, but they weren't entirely right either. He knew rationally that he wasn't responsible for the choices and violence of other people but his involvement, however tangentially, was harder to distance himself from emotionally. So, he was running, yes, but he was trying to slow down. He was trying to stop. He knew the longer it went on, the harder it would be to ever stop. It was like running through slowly hardening cement; if he waited too long, he'd be stuck.

But he wasn't ready. Not yet. He looked over the patio railing at the dark water flowing past. He'd come this far, why not go all the way? He'd seen the northern border of this country, why not tag the southern one too?

He spent the night at the forgettable motel. He drifted off to sleep watching the Rangers lose to the Blue Jays and wondering if his phone would ring.

It didn't.

He wondered if he should call.

He didn't.

He woke early the next morning and drove three hours straight south to the border. He pulled off the pockmarked two-lane road at a marked scenic overlook and stared across the muddy river into Mexico. He stood there for five minutes in the growing heat. Sweat ran down his back. Max watched two large black birds ride the thermals and circle overhead. Buzzards? Vultures? Was there a difference? He didn't know.

"Not today, birds."

Nothing else moved. The landscape was static. Anything alive out there in the palette of browns and muted greens appeared determined to conserve energy by staying hidden in the shade. His stomach reminded him that he'd skipped the free breakfast at the motel. He climbed back in his car, cranked up the air conditioning, drove another 30 minutes west. He passed two tractor trailer trucks going in the opposite direction and a sun-faded billboard promising new luxury homes on the horizon. He looked toward the horizon and saw nothing but scattered stunted trees, brown grass, and distant rolling hills that never appeared to get any closer.

He stopped at the first diner he found in the next town. He was waiting on his scrambled eggs and short stack, sipping more coffee, when he spotted the girl getting ready to rob the bank across the street.

CHAPTER SIX

Max's friend Lawrence was fond of saying the most dangerous person in the world was a Black man with a library card. Lawrence was the smartest person he knew. But Max liked to think a juvenile delinquent, reform school grad wasn't too far behind. The internet was just becoming widely available when Max was shipped off to RFK outside Worcester for his youthful transgressions, at least for the one when he was actually caught. Max quickly learned, and it was later reinforced at the adult level, that reform was not the primary aim of the juvenile institution. It rarely rehabilitated anyone, but it did supply an efficient vocational school for future criminals. In Max's case, unlike most, it wasn't his fellow boarders who provided the knowledge, but the vast amounts of time and the bored reform school librarian. Bored and mostly ignorant of technology. Max soon discovered that the administration was progressive enough to provide the boys access to computers and the internet but still naive enough not to know that certain restrictions and blocks might be suitable. There wasn't much out there at the beginning to find, but schools and universities were early adopters and Max took advantage of that access to escape the small, outdated library collection.

His time in the library kept him out of trouble and off the radar of the gang recruiters who worked the halls of the school. He stood up for himself if needed, but he tried to avoid confrontation and put off an air of unexceptional harmlessness. He kept his eyes down and head low. He tried to melt into the yellow industrial-painted walls. To illustrate that such a wet blanket wasn't even worth the effort. It mostly worked. He got into a few scrapes but otherwise was left alone. He read far and wide. Fiction, nonfiction, magazines, newspapers, and journals, including one article from the *American Journal of Psychiatry* on the Psychological Observations of Bank Robbery. It was a series of case study summaries drawn from interviews with inmates serving sentences at federal penitentiaries. It was a surprisingly wide-ranging article that covered the underpinnings of the myths of the 1930s bank robber to the robbery as a condensed expression of psychological pressures. There was also a section on the common behavioral stimuli and responses of bank robbers. That was the part that Max remembered best. If he could have made a printout and folded it up to carry in his wallet, he would have. He committed it to memory, and it had served him well in his future career. He'd heard about similar lists later developed by the FBI and Homeland Security for terrorists. Behavioral tics and cues to help law enforcement identify potential targets in a crowd or in an airport. This obscure article that he pulled off the early internet effectively did the same thing for bank robbery suspects. Or, if read another way, allowed a future robber to better hone his craft by avoiding certain things that might draw the wrong kind of attention.

Nervous body language. Unfocused eyes. Busy hands. Bulky clothes.

Max was too far away eating his breakfast to see her clearly, but he'd bet her pulse was racing. The girl across the street was checking every box except one. She was not a male in her 20s with a history of petty crimes. She looked like a high school student cutting class. So what the hell was she doing? The next 30 seconds could determine the rest of her life.

Max dropped a twenty dollar bill on the table and ran for the door.

The diner and the bank were diagonally across from one another at a four-way intersection. The girl was pacing up and down a short stretch of sidewalk out of sight of the bank's front doors. Max jogged across the street against traffic. He saw her check her phone and then slip it into her hip pocket and take one last deep breath, then she shrugged to adjust the backpack on her shoulders. She headed around the corner of the building toward the front door. Max picked up his pace, but he wasn't going to make it. He was still fifteen feet away as she reached out a hand for the door.

"Hey!" Not the best opening line but it got her attention on the quiet street. She jumped like a startled rabbit and turned around, already looking guilty as hell. She took two steps forward as if she were going to bolt down the sidewalk then stopped. Max stopped, too. He was close enough he could almost smell the adrenaline wafting off her. He kept his distance, afraid to spook her further.

He watched her eyes sweep over him and then continue on, scanning left, right, and then the street beyond before coming back to him. There was no recognition. Her eyes jumped away again. They stood facing each other with the morning sun beating down. The silence grew. Five seconds. Ten. Max heard the sparse traffic noise at his back. Tires hissed on the hot asphalt. A car door slammed shut. A dog barked.

He risked a step closer, but she took a corresponding step backward and Max watched panic fill her eyes. Her back was now almost up against the bank's glass door. Anyone coming out, pushing the door open, would run into her. Max glanced over her shoulder. Little chance of that. There was just one customer inside, her back to the street, hunched over the check writing stand, maybe filling out a deposit or withdrawal slip. Farther inside, he could make out a teller standing at her window.

His attention returned to the girl but he kept his distance. "You don't have to do this."

Her eyes, dark brown, almost black, no longer skipped away. Now, he had her full attention. "Do what?"

Strands of dark hair stuck to her face and neck. How did people live in a place this hot? He could see her pulse now jumping at her neck, a metronome ticking fast. Her eyes might be calmer, but she was still way out on the edge.

"Whatever you're thinking of doing? It's not worth it. Not this way. You go in there and you'll come back out, if you come out, a different person."

"Do you know me?"

"No."

"Then you don't know my business, right?"

"I don't know your reasons, but I think I know a bit about your business. I've been in your shoes. Or a pair like it. And I know what comes next and I don't think you want to go down that road."

The woman inside had finished her business and pushed open the door.

"'Scuse me, honey." The woman was older, wearing faded jeans and a loose white shirt with a turquoise and onyx necklace. She had on an eggshell-colored cowboy hat with the wide brim pulled low. The girl jumped and blushed and stepped to the side. The woman slipped past and continued down the sidewalk and around the corner to the bank's parking lot. A moment later they heard an engine start up.

The girl turned back to Max. The woman's interruption seemed to have broken the fever that had gripped her. Her shoulders came down a few inches. The vein on her neck stopped jumping.

"Sounds like you think you know me, old man."

Her tone now was less aggressive and more sarcastic. Max would take whatever progress he could get, though the old man jab stung a bit. But everyone looked old to a teenager, right? "Maybe I don't know you, but I know a version of you. Hell, I might have *been* you way back in Colonial times."

Her lips twitched at that, but she wasn't ready to give in. Not yet. "Oh yeah? And what do you think a damsel in distress like me was going to do?"

"Walk inside that bank and seriously mess up your life before you really even started." Max saw that hit home as the girl swayed slightly on her feet. Max glanced at his watch. Just after 9:15. "Shouldn't you be in school?"

"Not in the middle of July." She gave him a withering look that said he was a dumbass for even asking.

"Right." He didn't think he'd completely convinced her, but he appeared to have stopped her from going inside, at least for today. But he'd feel better if he could get her away from here. The heat was soaking into the cracked pavement. He shifted his feet. He wouldn't be able to stay here long without getting a new pair of boots. Something with thicker soles. "Okay, so school's out. Anywhere else you need to be? I'm happy to give you a lift."

"Okay, now I get you. You're either a child molester or a murderer who looks for young girls about to ruin their lives, only you step in and save them. But, spoiler alert, you aren't saving them, you're actually kidnapping them off the street, right in broad daylight. Very ironic. Very postmodern."

This time it was Max that felt the blood rush to his face. "No, that's not ..." he stammered.

Then she smiled and swiped at the strands of hair sticking to her forehead. "You got air conditioning?"

"Yes."

"Let's go then."

CHAPTER SEVEN

She sat in the passenger seat with her backpack on her lap. She leaned in toward the dashboard vents and let the rapidly cooling air blow across her face. Max pulled the SUV out of the spot at the curb and drove two blocks until he hit a red light. The town was small, but not a backwater. This wasn't the only traffic light in town. The commercial strip appeared to run another four or five blocks with busy side streets branching off east and west before giving way to residential neighborhoods. He'd driven in on a state road past ranches and isolated homes before coming to the town proper and finding the diner.

He eyed the street now. There was a national drugstore chain, another bank, two competing liquor stores, a combo gas station/convenience store, a dry cleaners, sandwich shop, hardware store, and tack shop all within view. In the distance, on the left, he could see a larger two-story brick structure with multiple flag poles out front that he guessed was the local government seat.

"Take a left at the next light," the girl said.

Max nodded, drove to the next light, and waited to make the turn behind two dusty Ford pickups.

She sat back in her seat now, looking out the passenger window, backpack still in her lap, an arm hooked through one of the straps. The backpack was dark pink with small white polka dots and a picture of a Japanese anime character with large eyes and a tiny waist. Without the bag, standing outside the bank, he would have put her age at seventeen or eighteen. Closer now, with the childish backpack, he could still some baby fat on her cheeks, he thought she might be younger, closer to sixteen, maybe.

She must have felt his eyes on her. She shifted away from him, closer to the window, and asked, "What are you doing in the TR?"

"TR?" Max made the left.

She rolled her eyes. "Gringos," she muttered. "Tiendas Reales." She waved a hand. "The bustling metropolis you see outside the window."

"Nothing."

"That sounds about right. Not much brings people to town anymore. Not since the mines closed."

"How do you know I'm not from around here?"

She ticked the points off on her fingers. "It doesn't take Sherlock Holmes. Your skin is chalky white. You haven't been here long. You've got leather seats." She turned around and inspected the back seat. "And a very clean truck. Also, you've got Massachusetts plates. I'm surprised no one's shot you yet, but the day is young." She gave a crooked smile. He'd found the people in Texas to be welcoming so far, but maybe they hadn't been as observant as this girl.

"What's your name?"

"Angie."

The houses were dwindling now on each side. Max squinted

into the sun. The road continued arrow-straight off into the
distance. Telephone poles lined the left side of the road so,
presumably, something else was out here. They drove on and the
landscape flattened and simplified. There were dwarf bushes
and creeping chaparral, plus a natural drainage ditch carved by
flood runoff on the right where the camber of the road sloped
slightly. Otherwise, the landscape was open and very empty. A
faded roadside billboard broke up the monotony. This one had
lost a corner panel and stated: *elcome Home. Woodland Estates.
Coming Soon* and provided a URL to learn more details.

"Why would leather seats be a giveaway?" he asked
eventually.

"Huh?"

"Your inductive reasoning on why I'm not from Texas. Or
at least a stranger to these parts of the state. Mass plates, no
tan. I get that, but leather seats?"

"Try this. Park this truck for about 10 minutes in the sun
today and then hop in and try to drive. Even with jeans on.
it's going to give your pink parts a little sizzle." She pointed at
the leather-wrapped wheel. "You'll probably get third-degree
burns if you try to actually steer. Most folks will get tinted
windows or buy a good sunshade for the dash, or get seat
covers."

He nodded. "Makes sense. Not something I ever
considered."

"Yankees never do."

"Last place I lived it was more snow tires, chains, and all-
wheel drive."

"Never seen snow except on TV."

He liked this girl. At least the version sitting in the
passenger seat. She seemed transformed from the manic,
edgy, young woman he'd approached outside the bank. This
girl was smart, observant, and a little sarcastic. Not afraid to
give as good as she got. He tried not to but he couldn't help

it. His thoughts turned to Kylie. So long ago now, yet it still hurt so much if he let it. Kylie would have been a similar age and he thought he wouldn't have minded if she had turned out a bit like Angie. He felt his throat tighten and pushed any more thoughts of what-ifs and what-could-have-beens away and locked them back up. He focused back on the road.

"Where are we going, Angie?"

"Just keep going straight. I'll tell you where to turn."

It occurred to Max to wonder how she'd gotten into town in the first place, but he didn't want to push it with the questions. He was putting miles between her and that bank. That was good enough for him. He'd drop her off and be on his way. He had few illusions that he'd saved her, maybe he'd only delayed the inevitable, deflected the universe for a time, but that was worth a few gallons of gas in his opinion. Maybe the delay would give her time to think. The mind of a teenager was restless and fickle.

They drove in silence for five minutes through the flat, brown landscape. Max liked to look at maps. Not just on his phone. He'd bought a big book of maps at a Barnes & Noble back in Vermont. It was a spiral bound Rand McNally atlas that covered the entire U.S. He'd looked at Texas in the hotel room last night. He knew the Rio Grande was curling around toward them from the west. They were in the river basin. Prehistoric waters had once washed over this road and scoured the land clean. No sign of water now. He glanced up. The sky was pale blue without any clouds. The heat waves shimmered and danced on the road ahead. It was the only thing moving out there.

Finally, Angie broke the silence, reached over, and turned on the radio. "You got satellite in this rig?"

"No, I usually just plug in my phone or play radio roulette."

She flipped quickly through the FM band, pausing briefly when something broke through the static.

A man preached, his voice a sonorous lamentation: *Take heed to yourselves, that ye go not up into the mount, or touch the border of it: whosoever toucheth the mount shall be surely put to death* before it faded out. Max didn't recognize the verse, but it sounded like the Old Testament. You did not want to mess with the God of the Old Testament. He had an angry and vengeful temperament.

Angie moved the knob. A voice as dry as sandpaper read a commodities and weather report before switching to a story on the upcoming change to border security to include enhanced scanning of trucks and other commercial vehicles. The technology promised to both speed up commercial crossings and also cut down on border smuggling.

Angie twitched the knob. Max noticed the majority of her fingers were covered in rings. A few were dotted with turquoise and looked Native American to Max's uneducated eye. Others were simple bands of silver or steel. One was a wider band of gold with a pattern of sun, moons, and stars.

A guitar cut through the static in double or triple meter with Spanish lyrics too fast for Max's rudimentary under-standing. He might have lingered but Angie didn't. A call-in talk show came through strong and clear, maybe it was local; Angie, maybe bored or tired, left it, sat back, and stared out the window. They listened to the host's rant about land mineral lease rights and closed mining operations and what recourse the local citizens might have to hold the companies accountable or to buy back the rights.

"Won't make a lick of difference," Angie said. Max glanced over. He hadn't thought she'd been listening. "The land out there is rotted or hollowed out. It's a picked-over carcass. If it weren't, those companies would still be here. Do you think those vultures would leave a cent in the ground? No fracking way." Angie sighed and snapped off the radio. "Nothing worth listening to. Even the radio doesn't want to visit TR. No one wants to come here and no one ever will. Even those desperate enough to risk a border crossing immediately move on to somewhere else. Best to leave the whole spoiled plot to nature and see if she can do anything with it. Check back in a few hundred years."

Max wondered if her brittle nihilism for her hometown was spun from experience or a show of typical teenage angst. It didn't feel put on or fake. There was an edge to it. He'd heard genuine anger in her voice. He was about to ask why when he saw the cop's lights in his rearview mirror.

CHAPTER EIGHT

He was the only car on the road that he could see in either direction. The cruiser was either coming for him or it was passing through. He took his foot off the gas and drifted toward the narrow shoulder.

Angie picked up on the change in his mood or the change in speed. "What's going on?" she asked.

"Police with his lights on coming up behind us."

She twisted in her seat and looked out the rear window.

He tried to keep his tone light. "You a wanted fugitive?"

"No. Are you?"

Suddenly, his question didn't seem like such a joke. He took a breath and ran through his options. He couldn't run. The SUV could hold its own against what was likely a big V8 in the police cruiser, but where was he going to go? The ribbon of road in front of him ran dead flat to the horizon. Probably didn't deviate all the way to the border. He'd be a sitting duck.

He took another steadying breath and kept his hands at ten and two. Rash decisions wouldn't help. The SUV's registration would hold up. So would his ID. He trusted Lawrence.

They were rock solid. Certainly for a small-town cop. But why was this guy coming after him? He mentally replayed the last half hour of driving. He doubted it was his speed. He was always careful to keep that reasonable for this very reason. And he was rarely in a rush to get anywhere. Some local law or ordinance he'd violated without knowing?

He couldn't run. But he also couldn't pull over. There wasn't much of a shoulder before the road fell off sharply into the drainage ditch carved by the runoff. He didn't want to risk getting the SUV stuck. They hadn't passed a car in either direction, so, in the end, he just pulled over as far as he could and put it in park. He didn't want any confusion about his intent to stop. He needed more information first and then he could figure out what to do.

The police car did not veer into the opposite lane and blow past as he hoped. It slowed and pulled to a stop directly behind the SUV. Max kept both hands very visible on the wheel and watched the side mirror. The sun reflected off the patrol car's windshield. He could see little besides the vague outline of a shape behind the wheel. The shape didn't move. Probably running his plate.

After a long minute, the door opened and a woman stepped out. She was tall, with silver aviator sunglasses over high cheekbones. She wore a dark khaki uniform with blue piping on the shoulders and down the seams of the pant legs. Blonde hair was tied into a tight bun at the nape of her neck. As Max watched, she reached back into the car and put a matching khaki hat on her head before approaching the SUV. She kept one hand on the gun in her equipment belt but didn't unsnap the holster.

Max took one hand off the wheel and lowered the driver's side window. It was like opening an oven door. Dry, hot air quickly filled the car. He felt sweat instantly bead across the nape of his neck. He glanced over at Angie; if she felt the jump in temperature she didn't acknowledge it, just continued to stare out the passenger side window. He put his hand back on the wheel.

The officer stayed a pace back from the door. Max kept his body still but turned his head to look at her. He only saw his own reflection in her glasses. Up close, her face was thin with hollow cheeks and a slightly upturned nose. There were pale lines at the corners of her eyes and mouth, and Max wondered if they were from smiling or frowning. She wasn't smiling now.

She took another half-step forward and looked across Max into the SUV's interior.

"That you, Angie?" the officer asked.

She was close enough that he could read the nameplate on her chest: *R. Serrato*. If she was uncomfortable standing on the hot tarmac in that uniform, she didn't show it.

Angie ducked her head and looked out. "Yeah, it's me, Beca."

"You okay?"

"I'm good. Just getting a lift home."

"Who's this? Friend of yours?"

"Uber driver."

Max saw the cop's lips twist just slightly then return to a flat line as she turned to him. "You got some ID?"

"Yes, can I ask why you pulled us over?"

"Sure." She remained silent and Max took the hint. He took his wallet out and handed her his license.

"Maxfield Parish. Like the artist?"

Max was impressed and made a mental note not to underestimate this woman. The few times he'd used his latest name or identification, no one had picked up on that. Maxfield Parrish had had a wildly successful career in the twentieth century, including the popular print Daybreak, but few people appeared to remember him now. Parrish had been born in Philadelphia and Max had come across his works in more than one local museum during his time there. He'd always been struck by the saturated colors and classical imagery.

"Just a coincidence. The artist spelled his last name with two R's."

"Car has Massachusetts plates and is registered to SCP, Inc. out of Delaware."

"That's right. It's a company car."

SCP was one of the many holding companies Lawrence used for his various business interests.

"Long way from New England. What are you doing in Texas?"

"Visiting the Alamo."

He watched her mouth twitch again but this time it was not in amusement.

"I'm not joking, Officer." Max continued, "I was in San Antonio yesterday. I've got the hotel receipt here somewhere. Drove down this morning on a whim to check out the Rio Grande."

"What did you think?"

"Of the Rio Grande?"

"Yes."

"Not that impressive, if I'm honest."

"Muddy trickle of warm piss."

"Not the exact description that came to mind but pretty accurate, yeah."

"That sounds like a fine few days of vacation, but it doesn't explain how you ended up with Angie in your passenger seat."

"She was walking on the sidewalk. It's gotta be close to a hundred degrees, even this early in the morning. I wasn't in any hurry. Figured she might need a lift. She took me up on the offer."

Officer Serrato leaned in again. "That right, Angie?"

"That's about the shape of it. Who called it in? Debra?"

"Adriana. Claimed she just saw a guy kidnap you in a black SUV with Yankee plates."

"Did she really say Yankee plates?"

"She actually said foreign plates."

"Well, she got the basics right. But the intent wrong."

"You sure you're okay?"

"I'm sure."

"I assume you're headed to the ranch?"

"Yeah," Angie replied.

"Mr. Parish with one R, do you mind if I escort you up to the Double R?"

"Fine by me." Max was sure she intended to escort him right over the county line immediately after that, too. Still, if that's all that came out of this, he would consider himself lucky.

"Okay, then. Let's have a little parade." She rapped her knuckles against the SUV's roof before she leaned in again. "Oh, Angie, are you carrying?"

"Of course." Angie pulled her hand up out of the backpack's pocket to flash a small silver .22.

"Good girl."

"Turn at the gate up here," Angie said.

It had been almost ten minutes since Serrato had pulled them over. Neither had spoken since she'd walked back to her cruiser. Max had waited until Serrato had climbed in, then he'd pulled fully back on the road and started driving.

At first, Max didn't know what she was talking about. They had been driving past cattle fencing on the left for a couple of miles with Serrato trailing in their wake and Max had yet to see any livestock that needed to be fenced in. Just more brown dirt and scattered parcels of tough green scrub. The barbed wire and fenceposts were bent and weathered but largely intact. Someone somewhere was doing maintenance on the border.

Now, as he looked, he saw a taller structure resolve itself on the horizon. Distances out here were tricky. Just because you could see it, didn't mean it was close. It was another three miles before he could make out the structure as a set of tall wooden pillars. He slowed to a near stop. A wooden sign with branded letters, Double R Bar Ranch, hung from a thick wooden crossbar between the pillars. A lone tree stood just inside and to the right of the gate. It was stripped and stunted. Its bare branches reached into the sky like broken fingers.

"You got the safety on?" Max asked, looking at the pitted dirt road that led off into the distance. The worn but mostly smooth pavement they'd been on was one thing, but he didn't want a hole in his leg, or anywhere else, simply because the SUV's suspension took a hard jolt over a rock and her finger slipped.

Angie smirked. "I'm Texas born and bred. Rattle in one hand. Gun in the other." She smiled, took her hand out of the backpack, and zipped up the front pocket. "I know what I'm doing."

"Clearly."

"Oh, don't be sore, old man. I wasn't planning on shooting you, but did you really expect me to get into a stranger's car and not be armed?"

Max shrugged. "Since I had no plans other than to give you a ride, so you didn't die of heat stroke, I hadn't really considered it."

She shook her head. "You are clearly not from around here."

The gate was open. Max made the turn and settled the

SUV into the rutted tracks. Serrato flashed her lights once then K-turned across the road and accelerated back in the direction they'd come. Max took it slow as they bumped along the road to nowhere. He could see nothing else. No ranch. No house. No outbuildings. No animals.

He glanced over at Angie. She chewed a fingernail and tapped a foot against the floor mat.

He watched the heat ripple and distort the dirt track, like a fun house mirror as it disappeared over the edge of the world.

Ten minutes later, everything changed.

CHAPTER NINE

Raul Ortiz sat in his hot kitchen and stared at the peeling paint on the wall. His talk with that damn corporate HR woman had been almost three weeks ago but he couldn't get her voice out of his head. *With your history in retail banking, I think you might have a good opportunity with us.* Despite the cutting words, her voice never lost a grating sing-song quality that made him want to reach through the phone and rip out her vocal cords.

"Box 239," he'd said.

He and Millie were in the M&P's small safe deposit box room. There were only three employees left. Millie and Vanessa were the last tellers. Foot traffic was so slow that he typically only needed one to work at a time but today he needed both. Part of the consolidation was inventorying the bank's remaining safety deposit boxes. Customers had been informed but some box leases had lapsed or been forgotten. Those had to be tracked and inventoried before the move.

Millie ran her finger down the printed list on her clip-board. "Box 239, Robideaux, no access in 52 months."

They had been at it all day and he was tired. Millie's voice washed over him. She said 52, he heard 62. That was over the limit. Five years and the box was considered abandoned according to the rental agreement.

"I'm going to run to the bathroom, Raul," Millie said.

"Uh huh." He drilled the box lock and popped opened the lid.

He read the document inside. He frowned and then read it again. It took a moment for him to understand what the document said. To recognize the name at the bottom. Robideaux. There was more paper. He flipped through it. He didn't understand all of it, but he suddenly saw that yes, he might have a good opportunity in front of him.

It just hadn't been with the bank.

He finished his watery cereal and instant coffee, then rinsed his bowl and mug along with the spoon and placed everything in the sink before standing in front of the fan again. He wiped away a single bead of sweat that ran down his cheek and then did up the top button on his shirt. He grabbed his tie off the chair and looped it around his neck. At least he could look forward to cool air during the workday. The devil did his best to air condition hell.

Before he could tie the knot, there was a knock at his door.

CHAPTER TEN

The driver stopped for gas twice on the first day, paying cash each time. He looked for older stations a few miles off the highway that didn't have as many cameras. After the second fuel up, he stopped for dinner at a steakhouse chain and then drove into a nearby industrial park. He pulled to the side of the road, deep in the complex and away from any streetlights, and swapped out the license plate on the rental for a Utah one from one of his black nylon bags. He got back in the car and out onto the highway again. He drove for another hour and then stopped for the night at a motel at the bottom of a lonely exit ramp in Demings, New Mexico. He checked in, paid cash, showed a Utah ID, and gave the desk clerk the number off the Utah plate. He slept for six and a half hours without any dreams that he remembered, woke up, used the room's small coffee machine and small shower stall, and was back on the road by 6 A.M.

He drove straight through the rest of the way with two more fuel stops. His breakfast and lunch were pretzels, candy bars, and sodas from the gas stations. An hour west of the city, he pulled off on a deserted stretch of road and put the rental plate back on the car. He pulled into the San Antonio airport complex a little after 3 P.M. He used his last remaining can of soda and spilled it across the passenger seat and floor mat. He returned the car to the rental company and apologized for the spilled drink. The check-in clerk glanced inside and just nodded. The driver knew the rental company would now have to run the car through some extra cleaning cycles and it would erase any microscopic traces that he had left behind. He took his bags and a shuttle bus back to the terminal and used a different rental agency for his last and final car. This time he used a clean Nevada ID for the forms. He reversed course again, rode the bus out to the lot, found the new car, dumped his bags in the trunk, and drove around to arrivals where he found his partner waiting. His partner's luggage was a single small carry-on with nothing inside to excite any airport sensors. He put it on the back seat and then climbed into the passenger seat. They drove to a hotel near the airport and waited for the next call.

The driver's partner was also on the move. Mookie was shorter and wider, bulkier through the shoulders than the other man. After a childhood mostly without enough food, he liked to eat and he liked to lift weights. He no longer resembled a doll. He had been halfway through a chest set in the garage space he'd converted to a weight room when his partner had called. He'd listened briefly and agreed, hung up, and finished his set. Then he'd showered and drove across town to a coffeeshop with free Wi-Fi. He'd bought an Americano and sat down. He took out one of the disposable mobile phones that he bought in bulk. It was basic but even that included a web browser these days. Each time a new batch arrived, he loaded two apps. The first was a private VPN to hide his IP address and the second was a secure browser. He made sure the shop's Wi-Fi was running through the VPN and then he used the browser to purchase a redeye ticket for the next day, arriving in Chicago at 9:55 in the morning, with an open-ended return. Then he went to a different airline and bought a new ticket with a different name that had him leaving from Chicago and landing in San Antonio at 2:35 in the afternoon. That done, he took his time and enjoyed his Americano and then left. He took the battery out of the phone and tossed it in the trashcan on the way out. In the car, he snapped the remaining parts of the phone into pieces. On his drive home, he stopped at a busy fast-food restaurant and dropped the broken pieces into different trash bins. He had no intention of ever going to prison because he was careless or lazy. It had worked so far.

CHAPTER ELEVEN

Max had to slow to under twenty miles per hour, then fifteen, to be confident the SUV's steering wouldn't get wrenched out of alignment or break an axle shaft. The road, and Max used that word pretty loosely, bent hard to the right after a slow mile and a half and snaked between two long, narrow hillocks that had risen out of nowhere. Each one climbed close to fifteen feet in the air and was covered in tufts of dry desert grass. As he drove through, it felt like driving into a box canyon. Or being funneled into a slaughter chute. An involuntary shiver ran between his shoulder blades.

"By the pricking of my thumbs," Max mumbled.

It was something his Aunt Joyce used to say when he was a kid. He turned in surprise when Angie finished the other half of the Macbeth quote.

"Something wicked this way comes."

She gave him a half-smile. "I might carry a gun, but it doesn't mean I can't also read a book."

As they passed the sloping end of the hillocks, the road turned again and the SUV's front wheels bumped up onto a black and buttery smooth macadam. Max hit the brakes. The two grassy berms of earth had hidden the Double R ranch and its outbuildings. Max took it in now.

The now paved road made a curving approach to the ranch. The house itself was extensive and sprawling, made from light-colored stone and buttressed in places by thick weathered beams of wood similar to the gate. Distinct wings on each side fanned out from the large, two-story main building. It appeared to have been added on to and renovated over time. Max could almost read the boom and the bust economic cycles in the patchwork construction. But it somehow hung together and didn't appear in danger of going bust any time soon. It looked solid and settled on the land, a natural feature of the land, like an immense boulder that had been there for a long time. Movement off to the right caught Max's eye and he saw a barn set farther back slightly behind the house with a small grain silo, outbuildings, and a paddock where two horses galloped around a ring.

"Welcome to Double R," Angie said but her tone was flat and had lost any of the teasing playfulness of earlier.

He drove up and stopped short of a columned portico by the front entrance. A navy-blue Chevy Malibu sedan was parked to the left in the shade under the portico. When Max had first spotted Angie on the sidewalk, he'd thought of trailer parks or efficiency apartments. A living situation that led directly to the distress he'd seen on her face outside the bank. Max felt a flush color his cheeks at his assumptions. He had not expected this. If this was home, then why had she been outside that bank? Why had she looked so desperate?

Before he had time to ask her, the big front doors swung open and a man in a suit stumbled out, slipped down the steps, and fell to his hands and knees. Another man followed him out and stood looking down at him from the top step. The second man was small, thin, and wiry with weathered skin that spoke to a life lived mostly outdoors. His clothes reflected the same. Well-worn jeans, broken-in boots, a long-sleeve light technical shirt with a logo on the chest pocket.

"Stetson Hull. My stepdad's foreman. Complete asshole in case you didn't catch the scent yet."

"A man named after a hat has got an uphill climb in life."

"That man is dumber than a hat but meaner than a snake."

Hull started down the steps when he noticed that he was not alone. He turned to look at Max and Angie in the SUV. His face was all sharp planes and angles with small, dark eyes. He flashed a smile that was a gash of crooked, yellow teeth.

"You mind driving around back?" She indicated a pocked but still paved branching side road to the right that likely led to the barn.

Max hesitated. He had the sense that Hull was not the type you willingly turned your back on.

Hull came off the steps and directed his attention back to the guy in the suit. When the man had tripped, he'd dropped a folio and the papers inside had scattered across the driveway. He was scrabbling around trying to gather them up and stuff them back in the folder. Hull hopped off the last step and kicked the man in the ass. The man toppled over again, the folder skittering away. He moved to pick it up, but Hull put a foot on it. Max cracked his door, ready to intervene if it continued to escalate. He didn't know the particulars of the situation, but he recognized a schoolyard bully.

"Uh-uh. I believe that's Mr. Blackburn's property."

"Those are my personal notes," the man replied. "I delivered a report to Mr. Blackburn."

Hull slid his foot back and the folder skittered away to the bottom of the steps.

"I believe Mr. Blackburn said your business relationship was complete, right? You got ten seconds to get in your car and drive outta here before I consider you a trespasser. And, in the great State of Texas, I've got free rein to do just about anything I like to trespassers on this land."

The man stood and brushed himself off. He was not a big man. His hair was neatly combed. His suit was pressed and clean, at least before he'd landed on his hands and knees. He hadn't smiled but Max would bet his teeth were in a lot better shape than Hull's. But Max would also wager that he was a man who spent most of his time indoors behind a computer screen or around a conference table. He was used to a different kind of fight. Maybe one made up of words and data. But he was in Hull's territory now and he was smart enough to know it. He'd get the short end of the stick, or worse, if he pushed it any further. He'd retreat, but he wasn't going to beg. He didn't slink to the car. He brushed the last flecks of dirt off his pants, Max respected him for that, then climbed in the Malibu and drove off.

Stetson took the folder, glanced over at the SUV again, then went back up the steps and inside the house.

Max closed the door. "Any idea what that was about?"

"Probably about money."

"Money?"

"If I had to guess. It's one of the few things I've seen that gets Stetson motivated. Money, free beer, and big hair."

"Huh," Max replied. "I'll keep that in mind. Still want to go around back?"

"Yes."

They drove around back and parked near the barn doors.

Angie climbed out and walked toward the paddock with the two horses. Max followed.

She leaned on the rail and watched as a man led one of the two horses around the paddock on a long leash.

"What's he doing?" Max asked.

"Basically, he's taking the horse for a walk. That lead is called a lunge line. It's a good way to exercise the horses."

The second horse had seen or smelled them and wandered closer. Max took a step back. Up close, he hadn't realized how big and powerful horses could be. The animals weren't something he'd come across growing up in South Boston.

"This is Bonnie," Angie said. The horse lowered her head and nudged at Angie's shoulder. "You are shameless," she said. Max was happy to see her smile had returned. She walked over to the bucket hanging by a water trough and held out a carrot for Bonnie. "The other one is Clyde. They were my mother's. If I thought my stepfather had an ounce of humanity in him, I'd say he kept them around as a reminder of her, but I really think he keeps them as a way to keep me in line. A carrot for good behavior, you might say. Behave Angie or it's off to the glue factory for Bonnie and Clyde."

"He'd do that?"

She shrugged. "Wouldn't bet against him."

They both looked up at the sound of a screen door slapping closed. Hull exited the back of the main house from a side door on the far left and headed in their direction. The back of the house was dominated by a fenced-in pool and patio with an outdoor living space complete with kitchen, bar, and scattered chairs around the pool deck. A waterfall gurgled from an artificial rock formation at one end of the pool. The only other prominent feature was a striking creeping vine spotted with multicolored flowers that appeared to have started on a trellis on the right side of the house before slipping its bonds on the second floor and spreading out at will.

He turned to ask Angie about it but found that she was gone. Bonnie had moved off, too. It appeared that everyone but him was smart enough to clear out when Hull was around. The man stopped a few feet away. Max saw how discolored Hull's teeth were from chewing tobacco and could see a wad tucked into his cheek now.

"Who are you?" His voice was high and thin. The question came out sounding like a whining complaint.

"Just someone who gave Angie a lift," Max replied.

"That right, Yank?" A bully trying for a rise with a cheap nickname. He spit a dark stream of tobacco through his teeth that landed near Max's feet. A dog marking his territory. "That all?"

"What's that supposed to mean?" Max didn't like the insinuation. The question cemented his dislike for the man.

"You're not exactly Angie's type but she's got a wild streak, so you never know."

"She's just a kid."

The man shot him another ugly smile. "Not for much longer. Birthday coming up."

Max just stared and the man dropped the yellow smile. "Mr. Blackburn would like a word."

Max wasn't inclined to take orders from this guy, but this whole situation felt off and he wanted to make sure Angie was safe before he cleared out. Another phrase his Aunt Joyce used to say popped into his head. Had he delivered Angie out of the oven only to drop her into the frying pan?

He followed Hull up to the house and inside.

"Wait here."

Hull disappeared down a hallway. Max walked farther into the room. The side door where they'd entered led into a small mudroom before opening into a huge living room or great room that dominated the first-floor space. Three rooms without walls. The entire first floor was open and airy with exposed stone and beams and light wood. It held a collection of chairs, sofas, tables, and two separate fireplaces. Two tall glass vases sat on matching coffee tables and held fresh bouquets of light blue delphiniums. When he was younger, his aunt had been an avid gardener. She always had a backyard plot and, some years, she signed up for an additional community plot as well. All three kids had been enlisted to keep the soil weed-free. It was a necessary but thankless task, but he did learn a lot of flower varieties.

He could see another spray of larkspur and delphinium on the kitchen table. The kitchen itself was almost in a separate zip code, to the back and the right. He could just make out the gleam of stainless-steel appliances and an island with chairs. There were a lot of windows to showcase the view and let in natural light. Everything was designed and coordinated and flowed. Even someone like Max could tell that much. It was big but still managed to be inviting. Some interior designer had done a good job.

He walked across the room to a floor-to-ceiling window that gave an unimpeded view out the back. Far in the distance, almost like a heat mirage, jagged mountains broke up the infinite flatness. Adjusting his gaze, he could see from this side that a hot tub was concealed in a little grotto behind the waterfall. He spotted a gardener working along the fence and watched as he leaned over and pulled a weed from a pristine, mulched flowerbed. Beyond the fence was the barn and more outbuildings. Now Bonnie was on the lead being led around the ring. No sign of Angie.

He put his back to the window. Inside, the house remained as quiet as a library. The tabletops were clean. The throw blankets were neatly folded. If he went into the kitchen, he was sure there would be no dishes in the sink. He wondered if there was anything in the refrigerator. All the neatness felt unnatural. Nothing was out of place. Like the patio outside, Max had a sense he'd walked into a showroom or onto a stage where real people didn't live.

He was about to walk back outside, try to find Angie and say goodbye, screw Hull's order to wait, when he heard footsteps.

CHAPTER TWELVE

Max studied the man who emerged from the hallway and approached him from across the room. He was in his mid-50s, an inch or two over six feet tall with short, styled salt-and-pepper hair. He was slightly thick through the middle, but it didn't spill over his belt. It suited his barrel-chested frame and wide shoulders. He wore a blue button-down shirt with a dark blue patterned tie pulled slightly askew. The sleeves were rolled up to his elbows exposing brown forearms that matched the tan on his face. The overall effect was of robust health, confidence, and money. Max had the sense this was not an accident. The look might not have been contrived exactly, but it did feel cultivated.

The man smiled, with straight teeth too white to be anything but cosmetic, and held out a hand as he reached Max. "Alex Blackburn."

"Max Parish."

Max noted he didn't recognize the name like Officer Serrato. Not an art fan. His grip was firm and dry. Max caught a whiff of saddle leather and black coffee.

"Thank you for giving Angie a ride. That wasn't necessary. I could have sent Stetson or Jorge or another staff member to collect her," Blackburn said. "I hope it didn't take you too far out of your way, Mr. Parish."

Collect her seemed like an odd phrase to use for one's daughter.

"Not a problem. The heat out there looks like it could be dangerous. My daughter would be about Angie's age, and I hope someone would do her a similar favor."

"You have a daughter, too?"

"She passed."

Blackburn gave a polite but surprised smile, caught off guard perhaps, and paused, but Max didn't offer more. He rarely talked about Kylie with his few friends, never mind a complete stranger. After a few seconds, Blackburn continued. "Stetson said your car has Massachusetts plates. Don't see those tags much in Tiendas Reales. What brings you down here?"

"Just passing through."

"On the way to anywhere in particular?"

"No."

Blackburn flashed that polite smile again. Max could tell he was used to being in charge. He was used to being able to quickly read a room and size up the people in it. But Max was giving him nothing.

"Just passing through, huh? You sound like an old train hobo." He punctuated the remark with yet another smile, not the awkward polite one, but a big, toothy one to show he was joking. "A little unusual in this day and age."

Max gave a small shrug. "Maybe. I decided I wanted to see the country. I didn't want to see more chain stores and big cities. Small towns and small roads seemed like a better option. I stopped for breakfast this morning and saw an opportunity to do some good." Max held out his hands. "Ended up here."

Max watched Blackburn absorb the story and something flashed through his eyes, maybe a calculation or a decision. "That sounds interesting, Mr. Parish. I wish I had more time to do something similar. Small towns and small roads are the true arteries of this country. You listen to the news these days and you'd think this entire country was a cauldron of hate, guns, and craziness. But that can't be right. Why would everyone be clamoring to get in if it was so bad? Right?"

"I think if you really look, most places have light spots and dark spots."

Blackburn nodded his head. "Well said. A good outlook to have. Do you have a few more minutes? C'mon back to my office."

He didn't wait for an answer, just turned on his heel and started back down the hall. Definitely a man used to having his orders followed. Max thought about walking in the opposite direction, getting back in the SUV, and driving away but thought again of Angie. What had put her on that sidewalk outside the bank? Nothing good came to mind so he followed Blackburn toward his office. He paused briefly at a series of framed photos on the wall. Stark black-and-white prints that Max recognized as various parts of the ranch. The rest were portraits and family snapshots. He watched Angie grow up as he continued down the hall. A different man in the first two, then Angie and a woman alone, obviously her mother through the shared facial features. Blackburn showed up when Angie was likely 10 or 11. There were no photos from the last couple of years. Maybe stuck in a camera phone. Or waiting to be framed. Max glanced over his shoulder again and took in the empty room and the quiet library-like atmosphere. Or maybe for another reason.

. . .

At first glance, Blackburn's office had the same design aesthetic as the rest of the house. There was an openness to the space like the great room and kitchen. It was sparsely furnished with just a wide desk, a pair of paper-thin monitors and keyboard, plus two slim chairs opposite the desk, and inlaid bookshelves along one wall. The back wall was another single seamless sheet of glass similar to the living room. A brass telescope stood in one corner and a large, framed map hung on the other wall.

But closer inspection showed it all appeared to be slowly eroding. There were heavy curtains pulled to the side now, but ready to cover the window behind the desk. The desk chair was picked for comfort and utility rather than as a set with the rest of the furniture. The bar cart in the corner was a reflective silver metal that clashed with the warmer wood. Whatever interior decorator had been consulted originally had not been asked for an opinion on these add-ons.

Blackburn went around the desk and sat, then stood up again. "Can I offer you a drink?" He took a step toward the bar cart. He noted the look that must have passed across Max's face. "No, no. Of course, I can offer you something stronger, but I do realize the time. I also have water, juice, and club soda. I could have Consuela make a pot of coffee. It's no trouble."

He thought it might be trouble for Consuela but maybe she was used to that. Maybe trouble was part of her job, but Max wasn't going to add to it. "No, thank you."

"What do you do, Mr. Parish?"

"This and that," Max replied.

Blackburn nodded as if that made complete sense. "Just passing through. This and that. Let me be blunt. Do you need a job?"

"Not particularly."

Another slight hitch as Max's answer again wrong-footed Blackburn.

"Let me put it another way. Do you want a job?" He held up a hand. "It pays well and it's nothing illegal, I assure you."

"In my experience, a guy says that, maybe things aren't illegal but they might skirt up against that line."

"Would that bother you?"

"Not particularly."

In fact, he found Blackburn's offer only made him more curious. Accepting it would give him a legitimate reason for sticking around and allow him to keep an eye on Angie for a little longer. First, the bank, then Hull, now Blackburn and this big, empty house. It all gave Max weird vibes. His friend Lawrence would tell him to just get the hell out of there. Anything that aroused Max's curiosity usually led to bad luck and trouble. Blood and injuries weren't far behind. He rubbed his fingers over the messy pink scar on the back of his hand.

Blackburn gave him a big smile, maybe sensing things going sideways. "It won't be necessary this time. Truly. I need help finding someone. Is that something that might fit your skill set?"

"It might."

"I thought so."

"I take it I'm not the first guy you've asked."

"No. That's true."

"What makes you think I can do any better? You know nothing about me. I could be a mechanic or an accountant."

"Precisely. You saw the gentleman leaving as you came in?"

"Yes."

"A private investigator. He came recommended and with impeccable references. He did not live up to his reputation. Nor did the previous firm I employed. Now, suddenly, you show up. An outsider. A stranger. Someone just passing through. I'm a rational man. It's how I've made money and turned this ranch around. But I also trust my instincts and go with my gut. Do you believe in God, Mr. Parish?"

"We have an ongoing conversation. Still trying to figure each other out."

Blackburn gave a short bark of a laugh. "An ongoing conversation. I like that. I might steal that line. I'm not one to sniff at the thought of higher powers at work in this world. You showing up just as I was looking for someone to help feels like God, or the universe, or someone giving me a shove. Who am I to ignore that?"

"Let me be clear, whatever you might think, I'm not a former cop or trained private eye. I don't have any experience or background in finding missing persons."

"Exactly. That's exactly what I'm saying. It might sound irrational but maybe those other people I hired were *too* professional. Maybe they all followed the same rules and protocols and ended up in the same place. Let me tell you it wasn't very far from where they started. No, maybe I need someone who will come at this from a different angle. Someone who will ask questions those guys never even considered."

"It's hard to stay missing for very long today. If these guys, with their access and tools, and databases, couldn't get a good lead, I'm not sure there's one to find."

"You might be right and maybe you will be my last desperate attempt, but I have to try."

"Why? Who am I supposed to find?"

"My wife."

"Your wife is missing? Why are you using private investigators? Why aren't you calling the cops?"

"It's a little more complicated than that."

"Really?"

"My wife is dead."

CHAPTER THIRTEEN

Max checked his watch. Not yet 11 A.M. but the heat continued to ramp up. By afternoon, he thought it would top triple digits and be like a physical punch to the gut. A person could die in this heat. He looked around, out past the artificially manicured grounds close to the ranch house. It was low, featureless country. The only thing rising higher than a couple feet were those weird earth berms that made up the approach to the house. The rest was just unbroken vistas of sandy soil, bleached grass, and wizened trees. Heat like this, you'd expect a storm but the sky was a searing blue with no clouds in sight.

He stood in the shade of the portico, almost hesitant to make the short walk to what promised to be a very hot car, when he heard a sound. He turned and found Angie sitting on a small stone bench. She didn't seem bothered by the heat.

He took a few steps in her direction. "I'm going to be sticking around for a bit."

"Alex paying you?"

"I expect to earn it."

"Okay."

He wouldn't be around forever, maybe not even a week, but, while he was here, he was determined to help her.

"Promise me something."

Her eyes showed a sudden wariness. She'd heard promises before and they'd left her alone on a ranch with no family. But hope was a stubborn thing. Or maybe she'd been taught enough manners to hear a stranger out, no matter the request.

"What?"

He could almost hear the eye roll in her response, but he wouldn't be deterred. Sometimes it was important to say the words.

"Promise me that while I'm here, if you're in trouble, you'll call."

She tilted her head and considered his request.

"And then what?"

"I'll come running."

Max bumped off the smooth road and took his time navigating the rutted dirt before he reached the state road that had led him to the ranch. He passed under the tall wooden pillars and then hit the brakes and paused. Left to the highway. Right to town. Did he want to do this? He thought of Hull kicking the guy down the stairs. Max hated bullies. He thought about Blackburn's false smile. He thought about Angie pacing by the bank and then later the flash of panic on her face when the ranch had come into view. Could he save everyone? No. Could he save her? Maybe.

He turned right.

Three miles down the road, a shape shimmered in the distance out of the heat. Serrato's cruiser was parked on the opposite side of the road in the middle of the lane. She was a dot of color in the muddy palette of brown that extended in all directions. Her elbow hung out the window and she burped the lightbar as Max approached, but he was already slowing. He stopped in his lane, the drivers' windows now facing each other, and lowered his window. He squinted as the dry heat hit his face.

"Easier to hook up with the highway in the other direction," Serrato said.

"That right?"

"Yup. Big interchange about 20 miles north. You'd get your pick of the compass points."

"Thought I might head back into town and finish my breakfast."

"And then?"

"Might take your suggestion and head north. Might not. A lot can happen over breakfast."

"That right?" she echoed and studied his face. She didn't seem particularly surprised to see him again.

"You care to join me, Officer?"

"I'm on duty."

Max glanced around. "Not even the armadillos are out in this heat. I can't imagine any local criminals can muster the energy."

"You'd be surprised," she replied. Max was about to ask her what she meant when she continued, "Just breakfast and then you're on your way?"

"Let's find out."

The Tin Roof Cafe was mostly empty, the breakfast rush over, if it even existed. One white-whiskered guy sat at the counter and read the paper. A coffee cup and half-eaten piece of pie sat at his elbow. A row of booths ran along the wall opposite the counter. Scattered tables filled in the space between. A small stage with a battered upright piano sat at the far end. Old concert posters and handbills were stuck one on top of the other in a makeshift wallpaper behind the stage. Breakfast joint, cafe, bar, music venue. It appeared The Tin Roof filled a lot of niches in Tiendas Reales.

Serrato led him to a booth in the back corner. It was now late morning and just the short walk from his car to the diner had beads of sweat running down Max's back. Two dusty, old AC units worked hard inside to push the temperature down into the low eighties, it wasn't cold, but it felt like stepping into a freezer after the kiln-like heat out on the street.

Serrato slid into the booth, putting her back against the wall. Max would have preferred that seat and the view of the diner's door and other patrons. Then he reminded himself he was with a cop. What was going to happen? He pushed down his paranoia and long-held habits and slid in opposite her.

A waitress approached with a pot of coffee. She turned over the cups that sat on saucers on the table and filled them without being asked. It was the same waitress from when Max had been in that morning. She was middle-aged with thin, blonde highlighted hair falling to her shoulders. The nametag pinned to her starched shirt read Adriana. She gave a quick nod to Serrato but didn't meet Max's eyes before retreating behind the counter.

"That Serpico?" Max asked, tilting his head toward the waitress and simultaneously referencing the 70s crime drama starring Al Pacino

Serrato smiled. It was a good smile and transformed her stoic and serious face. "I'm not sure that analogy fits exactly but yes, she called it in this morning. Better to have a vigilant populace than an apathetic one, right? If you see something, say something."

"Not the first time she called something in though, right?"

Serrato played with a sugar packet. "That's true."

"It's a fine line between vigilance and vindictiveness."

"Can you be vindictive toward someone you don't know?"

"That's the problem. She thought she knew me, or made assumptions about me, and then called the police."

"Do you think what she did was wrong?"

Max started to respond then stopped. Would he have done differently? He likely would not have called the police, but he might have followed up if the situation felt wrong to him. Wasn't that what he was doing right now? He'd taken Blackburn's offer, but it was really just an excuse to stick around and make sure Angie was okay. Did that make what he did any different from what Adriana did? He was profiling, maybe not a person, but the situation, in the same way.

"No, I guess not," he eventually conceded.

Serrato picked up one of the small menus stacked against the napkin dispenser, glanced at it, then put it back. "Not sure why I bother. I know exactly what's on it. It hasn't changed in ten years."

Max picked up a menu even though he too remembered most of what was on it from that morning.

"Ten years, huh? Lazy or just good at what they do?"

"I'll let you decide."

Most places like The Tin Roof were the same. A menu was unnecessary. You could smell it when you walked in the door. It wasn't noon yet, but he felt like he'd done breakfast already even if he hadn't gotten to finish. He flipped the menu over. Burgers and different variations of burgers or beef. He was in Texas after all. He put the menu back.

"You lived here long?" he asked.

"Most of my life."

"But not all? That feels like it might matter around here."

"It does to some. I was born here but went to A&M for

college then joined up with the Rangers for a few years before I ended up back here."

She stopped there but Max could tell there was more to the story. How do you go from being a Texas Ranger to a deputy in a border town? Tiendas Reales wasn't a dusty, one-horse town, but it wasn't approaching a mid-sized city either. The opportunities in law enforcement here would pale to a career in the Rangers. He didn't push it. It was her story to tell. Or not.

Adriana wandered back over. Serrato seemed to be on the same wavelength about lunch. She ordered something called an onion burger with fries. Max doubled the order and asked for a glass of water.

"What about you?" Serrato asked after Adriana had jotted down their order and retreated through a swinging door to the kitchen. "You were a little cagey out there when I asked."

"Didn't mean to be cagey." Max took a sip of coffee. It was hot and strong. "What do you want to know?"

"Did you really come down here to visit The Alamo?"

"Wasn't the only reason, but it was *a* reason." He briefly told her about his Saturday afternoon history with John Wayne and Richard Widmark on Channel 5.

"That was a terrible movie."

"Not to a ten-year-old kid who had never been outside of South Boston. But yes, I did rewatch it a few years ago and it didn't hold up so well. Then, I visited and found out just how inaccurate it all was. Terribly disappointing."

That got another smile. "So you kept driving south to deal with the trauma?"

"When in doubt put some open road in front of you."

"That a life philosophy?"

"It's worked so far."

They covered some more small talk until Adriana brought

the burgers and fries and refilled their coffees. They each took a moment to tuck into their meal. Max had thought the heat had dulled his appetite, but the fries were crisp and the onion burger was thin and delicious. He'd never tasted anything like it.

"Pretty good, huh?"

"What the hell is that?" Max asked forcing himself to slow down and not inhale the patty in three bites.

"Can't take credit for it. We stole it from Oklahoma. The story is that it came out of the Depression. A small ball of ground meat smashed together with a huge portion of thinly sliced onions. Topped with cheese on a soft bun. So simple, it's genius. Like a peanut butter and jelly sandwich. You cannot improve it."

"I don't want to improve it. I just want to keep eating it."

"Glad you got something out of your trip to the TR."

Max took another couple of bites, it really might be the best thing he'd eaten in a long time, before he responded. "I got a job, too."

Some of the open friendliness that Max had seen in Serrato's eyes dimmed. It didn't disappear completely, but her face and demeanor shifted back to cop mode. He could see her suspicion take priority.

"I figured," she said as she wiped the grease from her fingers and pushed her plate back.

"That's not just your usual speed trap spot?"

"No."

"You knew I would be coming back that way?"

"I wouldn't say that. I just had a hunch that when I left you at the gate to the Double R that it wasn't the last time I was going to see you."

"Why?"

She shrugged. "Can't explain a hunch, can you?"

"I'm not the first guy to get this job from Blackburn, am I?"

He knew the answer, Blackburn had told him as much, but he was interested to know how much Serrato knew.

"No. Far from it."

CHAPTER FOURTEEN

"That going to be a problem?" Max asked.

"Depends on you. I don't care if you take Blackburn's money. He's got plenty of it. I care if it starts bleeding over into the town," Serrato said.

"In other words, don't make waves."

"Might be hard to get the job done without making waves but try not to break any laws."

"I plan to just ask a few questions. Look around. I'm less concerned with the money and more concerned with making sure Angie is all right."

Serrato's eyes jerked up from her coffee cup. "What do you mean? What's wrong with Angie?"

"I'm not sure anything is wrong. Just my own hunch. But if there is? Well, she seems like a good kid. I have the time, why not see if I can help out?"

"Why the interest in her?" No friendliness in that question. It was all cop.

He picked up his own coffee and sipped to buy some time. It had gone cold while he ate. He felt he did owe her an explanation. From the outside looking in, Max could see why people would be suspicious. People like Adriana. Or Serrato. A man his age. A girl Angie's age. Everyone has been primed to assume the worst nowadays.

He decided on the truth. Serrato would sniff out anything else and he needed her help. "My daughter would have been about her age."

She was smart enough to note the tense and smart, or polite enough, despite being a cop, not to push further. She appeared to accept his explanation. At least for now.

"Okay, so you're a stranger with a heart of gold. Not the typical type that Blackburn employs."

"What can you tell me about him?"

"He did not grow up here. He moved here when he married Angie's mom seven or eight years ago. Took over the ranch and then slowly took over the rest of the town."

"How did that happen?"

"What? Taking over the town or marrying Rose?"

"Let's start with the town."

"I can't really help with either one. It all happened during the time I was with the Rangers so I don't know the particulars, but it doesn't take a genius to figure it out. Even in boom times, this town lives on the economic edge. It's nobody's destination. We used to have the mines just to the west. That was the economic engine for a while, but those days are over. Mines are all closed. Now, the TR is just a place on the way to somewhere else. Blackburn came in with cash. To most folks, at the time, he was a savior. They had bills. He had a solution."

"And now?"

She shrugged. "They took his money, what can they say?"

"Did you take his money?"

"No."

"So what do you say?"

"I can't argue that his money kept the town, and a lot of the people in it, afloat. But he didn't do it out of charity. He's making money."

"Plenty of people outside of Tiendas Reales do the same thing. What makes him different?"

"That's the million-dollar question. Is he on the side of the angels or ..." She trailed off.

"Or is the devil already here."

"Exactly. You can be on the side of the angels without being one yourself."

"Lucifer was once an angel."

"The wicked angels," Serrato said.

"What is Blackburn getting for all that money? You said it wasn't charity. So, what?"

"That's the question I keep asking myself. Is he squeezing the last drop of blood from a stone or is he breathing new life into this place?"

"And how do you answer yourself?"

"I don't. Not yet. Jury is still out."

"But?"

"I don't trust him."

Adriana cleared their plates and refreshed their coffee for a third time.

"Tell me about Angie's mom."

"Rosalind Robideaux. Everyone called her Rose."

"You knew her?"

"Sure, I knew her. We weren't tight, not best friends. But TR is not that big. You're going to run into people, especially when you're younger. She was two years older than me. We went to the same schools and crossed paths a few times. She was popular enough. Not a cheerleader. Not a mean girl. But not an outcast. She was smart and social, friendly with most of the cliques. She survived high school and adolescence better than most from what I remember.

"She was an only child, so she gradually took over the Double R as her parents aged. Married a local guy. Had Angie." Serrato paused and Max could sense the all-American story was about to take a turn. "Things sort of went pear-shaped after that. Chuck, her husband, died in a freak accident on the ranch. The ranch wasn't going great before he died, but they were getting by, sort of treading water, but things went downhill after that. Rose struggled without him. The ranch and that land have been in her family for generations. They can trace the Robideaux name all the way back to the first families that arrived with Stephen Austin. Years before Davy Crockett had even heard of The Alamo. But the rumor was that she was scraping bottom and the bank was losing patience. It looked like she'd have to sell most of it or risk defaulting and losing all of it."

"Blackburn didn't just save the town. He saved Rose and the ranch, too," Max said.

"He saved the ranch, at least," Serrato replied.

"Rosalind Robideaux. Double R Ranch."

"It was a tradition in their family. The name thing."

"But not for Angie?"

Serrato gave a brief smile. "No, for Angie, too. She was Roxy for a long time. Roxanne Angela Robideaux. She started going by her middle name after her mother ... disappeared. She was 11. That's a tough time to lose your mom. Fuck," she rubbed a hand over her face, "any time is tough, but 11? Probably explains the name thing."

"What happened to her? Rose, I mean."

"No one knows. It's an honest-to-God unsolved mystery

and, as a cop, I know how that sounds and how rare it is. Even if you can't prove it, you usually know who did it, right?" She took a sip of water and gathered her thoughts. "It was six years ago. Rose's car was found on the ranch. The working part of the ranch is smaller these days, but the Double R as a whole is over 10,000 acres. Her car was found in a remote corner near where the old family house was. There was a lot of blood, but no body."

"Definitely her blood? How much?"

Serrato took the questions in reverse order. "Enough to make them question if she could have lived. The coroner said yes, it was possible. They also had the blood checked by two different labs. It was hers. No doubt. This all happened when I was still with the Rangers. I didn't move back until a few years later, but I've read the reports. It was all done by the book. The area, while remote, was searched competently and thoroughly. No remains were ever found. No trace of anything was ever found outside the car. She vanished."

"Blackburn?"

"He called it in. He was also pretty much the only suspect seriously considered. They couldn't come up with any other names to even check. She led a very solitary life out there. Solitary but, by all accounts, happy enough. They dug into the marriage and didn't find much. Blackburn was given the third-degree but was cleared. Three people vouched for him that night."

"Hull?"

"Hull, the housekeeper, and two other employees." She held up a hand. "I know. Those people could be persuaded or pressured to lie for Blackburn, but he was also on his own security cameras the entire night. Whatever happened to Rose, it wasn't him." She paused. "Not directly."

"You think he hired someone?"

"I don't know. A complete outsider would make some

sense. He certainly had the cash for it. And they looked there, too, but didn't find any unusual withdrawals. Still, as a cop, you usually know even if you can't prove it."

"You got a feeling?"

"When you have eliminated all which is impossible, then whatever remains, however improbable, must be the truth."

Max smiled. He liked this woman. "Sherlock Holmes, really?"

"Might be a cliche for a detective, but I'm just a lowly flatfoot."

There was a pause as Adriana dropped off the check.

"Sometimes it's hard not to resent Blackburn for his money and ambition and ..."

"Personality?" Max said.

She smiled. "You saw it, too?"

"I saw what he wanted me to see."

"Exactly." The spark was back in her eyes. This case, for whatever reason, had its hooks in her. Maybe it was just the local angle. Or maybe it was more. "There's something else going on, right? It's not just my personal jealousy or his own outsider status."

"I'm not ready to go there, I met him for 10 minutes, but I do agree; there is a whiff of conman about him. He presents one face to the outside world, and I'm not convinced it's the same face when the door is closed. Angie hinted at that."

"What did she say?"

"Not much, just a passing comment about how he could be cold. How he might be capable of sending the horses to the glue factory."

"Huh."

"And that was definitely not the impression he tried to make on me. He was in gladhanding, best buddy mode."

She tapped a finger on the edge of her cup. "You don't know how good that is to hear. I thought I was going crazy."

"No one is looking at Blackburn anymore?"

"Hell no. Not for a long time. This is all ancient history. Money and influence can pave over a lot of sins."

"Even murder?"

"Absolutely. Isn't that the best antidote?"

CHAPTER FIFTEEN

They paid and walked outside. Serrato handed him a card as they reached their cars.

"Mobile number is on the bottom. Let me know if you find anything useful."

Max could feel the heat radiating off the black steel of the car's door as he reached out a hand to open it.

"You should pick up a dashboard sunshield if you're going to stick around for a bit," Serrato said.

"So I've been told."

"Will's Hardware is just up the road." She nodded in the direction behind Max.

"Thanks. Listen, any chance I can get a copy of the official report on Rose's disappearance?"

Serrato slid her sunglasses on and looked away. "Maybe. Might take a little time to come up with an excuse to look again. Chief keeps a tight grip on that one. He wasn't happy the last time I asked but I was new and could claim I needed to see it as it was the biggest open unsolved we had. This time I might have to be more creative. He's very keen to keep Blackburn's support."

"Is the chief here elected? Like a sheriff?"

"No, he's appointed. But he's appointed by the town council and the town council positions are elected."

"They're owned by Blackburn?"

She waggled a hand. "Maybe? Probably? He's in the background of everything here. Crept in like an invasive weed. If Blackburn wanted a different police chief, I'm sure it would happen."

"Or a different flatfoot walking the beat? I don't want to cause you any trouble."

She shrugged and smiled. "A little trouble might be what this place needs."

He watched Serrato drive away. There was a radio on her belt but, in the entire time he'd been with her, he hadn't heard it chirp with any reports or requests that might require her attention. The criminals and armadillos were both laying low. He wondered what she did all day. Just from their brief chat, she was obviously intelligent. How was she not bored out of her skull? Why had she given up a career with the Rangers to come back to this town?

A car horn interrupted his train of thought. He looked up and watched two kids lazily cruise across the next intersection on a couple of skateboards. They either didn't see or didn't care about the traffic. They made it across and disappeared down a side street.

Max left his car and walked up the street. By the time he'd made it around the corner, the two skate rats weren't in sight and his shirt was sticking to his back. He was about to turn around when he heard a shout. He crossed to the shaded side of the street and kept going for another block until he found a small park. There were two tennis courts, a playground structure, and a set of swings. Max noticed a plaque posted near the entrance next to the waist-high fence that surrounded the space. *Revitalized and made possible by the Blackburn Group.*

The park was empty save for the two kids. Max imagined the colored plastic of the play structure suffered from the same problem as his car. Just too much heat, especially for little kids, to use in the middle of the day. The skaters were rolling and turning on the smooth surface of the tennis courts.

Max approached and stopped on the other side of the fence.

"Hey," he called when one of the kids missed a trick and the board rolled close to the fence.

"Fuck off, old man. We don't have any drugs and we're not into touching your dick."

The kid grabbed his board and pushed off but not before flashing Max his middle finger for good measure.

Max felt his face flush with embarrassment, even though neither suggestion was close to what he wanted. He went to the gate and entered the court. There was another gate at the opposite end and the two boys moved in that direction. They were big men with loud mouths when they were separated by a fence, or maybe a phone screen, but pop that bubble? They ran for the hills. Typical teenagers.

"Hey," Max tried again. He stopped walking and held up his hands. "That's not what I want. I just want to ask you a question."

One kid continued through the fence and disappeared behind a high line of shrubs, but the other one, the one that had spoken up and flipped him off, stopped.

"Twenty bucks."

"What?"

"Whatever you want to ask us, it'll cost you twenty bucks."

Blackburn could afford it, Max thought. "Sure. Twenty bucks."

"Money first."

Max took a bill from his wallet and held it out. The kid skated over, but Max pulled the money back as he went to reach for it.

"Hey," the kid said, now sounding exactly his age.

"I might be old, but I'm not an idiot. Information first, then the money."

The kid circled away on his board but then ground to a stop and faced Max.

"Do you know Angie Blackburn?"

"She doesn't go by Blackburn."

"So, you know her?"

The kid had shaggy dirty blond hair that hung down into his eyes. He was lanky and bony with almost cartoonishly big hands and feet. A man suit waiting for the teenage body to catch up. He absently brushed his hair to the side. "Sure, I know her. She's a year ahead of me and Toby at school." He looked over his shoulder but the other kid, Toby apparently, hadn't reappeared.

"What's she like?"

"What's she like? Fuck man, she's a chick. If I knew what made chicks tick, do you think I'd be out here skating in this sauna? Hell no."

"Does she have friends?"

"I guess. She's a little weird but she gets by."

"A little weird? Like skater weird?"

The kid smiled at that. "No, not quite that much of an outcast, but she's not in the popular crowd either. Pretty smart, I think. She'll say hi to us in the halls or whatever, which is more than some of them will do. Just mostly keeps to herself. Lives way the hell out there on that ranch."

"She ever get in trouble?"

"Trouble? Like what?"

"Don't know. You ever heard anything?"

"No, nothing like that. I mean, I've seen her at a few parties, but she's not big into that scene either. She sort of floats along. You know about her mom, right?"

"Yes."

"There you go. My old man left when I was three but he's up in Fort Worth. Got himself a new family. He's a prick but at least I know where he is. Having your mom disappear like that? That'll mess anyone up. I think she's doing all right, all things considered."

Max didn't know what else to say. The kid was right. It backed up the impression he'd gotten during their car ride and from Serrato, but it was good to have it confirmed by a peer. Of sorts. He held out the bill; the kid grabbed it and skated off toward the exit.

CHAPTER SIXTEEN

On the walk back to his car, he noticed a sign pointing down a side street for the town library. The internet was great, easy, and almost always available now in his pocket, but it often lacked context, especially for a smaller local story like Rose's disappearance. He had a rough idea of who he wanted to talk to or at least the type of people he wanted to talk to. Serrato had been a good start, but he knew there would be other lines of inquiry that he could pursue. There would be other people with different parts of the story or opinions that the police might not know. He followed the sign and turned left. Maybe by visiting the library he could kill two birds with one stone.

The Tiendas Reales Public Library was a low-creeping building with two wings split by a central lobby entrance. The outside walls were painted in a variety of pastel colors that had faded under the harsh climate. There was a line of cabbage palms separating the parking lot from an apartment complex across the street. An American flag and the Texas State flag flew from a pair of poles near the entrance.

Max walked past an after-hours book deposit box and

went in. The bathrooms were off the lobby just inside the doors and he ducked into the men's room and wiped his face and neck down with cool water. Feeling slightly more human, he exited and found his way to the circulation desk.

A woman looked up from the pile of books she was scanning before putting them on a rolling cart for reshelving and smiled at him.

"Good morning, can I help you?"

The woman was in her late twenties, small and petite with brown hair. If she hadn't already been standing in a library, Max would have said she looked like the type most at home in a bookstore or sipping a cup of tea.

"Old copies of the local paper?" Max asked.

"How old?"

Serrato had told him Rose had disappeared six years ago. Blackburn had come on the scene two or three years prior to that. He gave himself a buffer. "Ten years, maybe."

"Okay, that works perfectly actually. The *Tiendas Reales Tribune* is digitized and online for the past ten years so you can just pull it up on one of the computers using a library account. If you need to go back further than that, we have it on microfilm."

She came around from behind the desk and led him to a separate room on the right. There was no one else inside. He'd spotted a few cars in the parking lot but other than the librarian, he hadn't seen anyone else inside. The computer room was square, 20 feet by 20 feet, and hummed quietly with the sound of cooling fans. There were two broad wooden tables with a dozen desktop computers, six on each table, three facing one direction, three facing the other. The librarian moved the mouse on the nearest one and the screensaver disappeared.

"Are you a local resident?"

"No."

"Okay, I can sign you in using a guest account. It will be limited but includes newspapers and journal database access." She typed a username and password into the box then navigated through a series of menus before she stepped back. "Works pretty much like any other search engine. Type what you want in the box and hit enter. If you click here," she moved the mouse and clicked on a link under the box, "it will give you some hints and examples on ways to narrow the search with the date or exact terms. Things like that." She met his eyes and smiled. "Sound good?"

"Yes, thank you."

"No problem. If you need anything else, my name is Merry. I'll be at the front desk."

"Thanks," he said again then thought of something. "Wait." If Merry was in her late twenties, she'd likely be too young to have known Rose personally and was too old to know Angie, but it couldn't hurt to ask. "Did you know Rosalind Robideaux?"

He watched something flicker across her face. Anger? Disappointment? Curiosity? It was there and gone too quickly to pinpoint.

"No. I was at school getting my master's when all of that happened. Why are you asking?"

If he was going to poke around in this town, he was going to need an answer to this question. Telling people he worked for Blackburn might not be the best way to go. Not for everyone. It was already clear that Blackburn's influence cast a long shadow. It might make some people hesitant to talk. What to say? A journalist? Documentary filmmaker? He didn't think he'd get too far with either of those lies. They would come apart too quickly. Too easy to check.

"I'm a private investigator." That felt closer to the truth.

"Oh?" This time he could see excitement spark in her face. "Who are you working for?"

"That's confidential." He'd let her draw her own conclusions. "Did you grow up in town?" he asked, pushing to get back on the front foot with this interview.

"Yes."

"Did you know the Robideaux family?"

She shook her head. "No, not really. Everyone knows the ranch, of course. It's the biggest around for miles, been around forever, maybe since before the town itself, but I didn't know Ms. Robideaux or the family. Mr. Blackburn is in town quite a bit on business; he actually donated most of the money to renovate the library's children's room. It's named after Mrs. Blackburn." She paused then continued. "I was trying to remember any other times I might have seen Rose or Roxy in town." Max noticed she slipped into using Angie's childhood name. "I was away at school when Rose disappeared, so it would have been before that, almost ten years, but I was in high school. They weren't really on my radar." She paused again, almost as if considering whether to stop or continue. Max kept quiet and she eventually continued. "They didn't socialize much in town other than Mr. Blackburn's business trips. All business. Otherwise, they tended to stick to the ranch."

He had the sense she had picked her words carefully.

Merry left the room and a moment later Max heard the intermittent beep of the scanner as she continued checking in the returned books. Max sat in the padded chair. The AC blew down from an overhead vent and he felt the sweat on his back begin to cool. He thought about what Merry had said about Blackburn paying for the children's room and naming it after his missing wife. Was it a monument? A living appreciation? A reminder? But to whom?

He put the cursor in the search box and thought about

where to begin. He entered Rose's name, and the results came
back as he expected. The entire first page was related to her
disappearance. It had generated a lot of local interest and a
lot of stories. He skimmed down the headlines. They spanned
from the initial disappearance, the discovery of the car, the
follow-up search, then slowed to a single five-year anniversary
story. He noted that most were written by one woman.
Melinda Carson. He found the filter option and sorted the
results chronologically. The name Rosalind Robideaux only
appeared three times prior to her disappearance. Twice it
showed up in notes for meetings of the town's library trustees
and once as part of a public notice for the sale of a parcel of
land. Max thought back to what Serrato had said about the
ranch struggling in the wake of Rose's husband's death.
Maybe she'd had to sell a slice of land to keep the creditors
at bay.

He clicked on a few of the stories about the disappearance itself and skimmed the details but didn't learn anything
that Serrato hadn't told him already. There was some background on the Double R Ranch and the Robideaux family, the
death of Rose's first husband, and later remarriage to Alex
Blackburn. The stories did include some quotes and reactions
from friends and townspeople. But to Max, the quotes all felt
generic and cribbed from what others had said during similar
tragedies. He jotted the names down on a slip of paper just in
case. In all, it painted a picture of a woman that was
respected and liked but not very well known.

Max cleared the search box and tried Blackburn's name. If
his wife liked to keep a low profile, her second husband more
than made up for it. There were hundreds of stories across
multiple pages of search results. Max again scanned down the
headlines. The vast majority were about business deals,
mostly announcing a new venture or opportunity coming to
TR. He'd have to read through these more carefully. He

wondered how many of the announced plans actually came to fruition. Most stories mentioned that Blackburn owned the Double R Ranch but there was little other personal information.

Max opened a new browser window and did a general Google search on Alex Blackburn. The name was fairly common so not all the results in the list were relevant. There was an Alex Blackburn who was a prolific YouTuber and another Alex Blackburn who had been drafted by the Minnesota Twins in 2017. An Alex Blackburn had married Lidia Sandoval thirteen years ago in St. Paul, Minnesota. Max didn't click on the wedding announcement but did briefly wonder if the couple were still together. He rubbed his eyes. Probably not. If you believed the census data, most marriages stalled out after eight years.

He focused back on the screen. More than half of the results were the right Alex Blackburn. Max read through the top headlines. Some were repeats of the *Tribune* stories he'd just seen. A few of the stories had been picked up by the larger San Antonio papers. Others were self-promotional press releases or pages from various Blackburn Group websites. Others were from various Tiendas Reales town meeting minutes which were posted, like the library trustee notes, on the town's website. He went six or seven pages deep before the algorithm broke down and the results really started to diverge. He noticed something though. He went back and checked a second time. There was a lot of information about Blackburn and his local business interests but that's where it ended.

Like Alex Blackburn didn't exist before he set foot in Tiendas Reales.

CHAPTER SEVENTEEN

Max stood up from the computer and walked back to the front desk. The small lobby entrance area was still empty. Merry had finished processing the returned books and was sitting at the counter reading a book. Max figured it was probably one of the few jobs where reading was encouraged while an employee was on the clock. Not bad work if you could get it.

"Find what you were looking for?" she asked.

"Maybe too much."

She nodded. "That's the problem these days. It used to be finding any information was the challenge, but now it's all turned upside down. The challenge is finding the *right* information."

"The signal in the noise."

"Exactly. If you're looking into the Robideaux case, you should talk to Margit Callenbach, the children's librarian. She might be able to help. She's been around forever and probably knew Rose and Roxy."

"Is she here now?"

"She is, actually." Merry indicated the hall just past the

circulation desk leading off to the left-hand wing of the library. "Just follow the yellow brick road."

Max had thought she was being cute with a literary reference, even if the movie was more well known than Baum's series of books, but it turned out she was actually being literal. A carpet printed with a yellow brick pattern led off the main lobby down a hallway with walls painted with scenes from Oz to the dedicated children's area. *The Rosalind Robideaux Blackburn Children's Reading Room* was spelled out in gilded gold letters above the arched entryway. Here, finally, Max saw some activity in the library. At the far end of the large rectangular room, in an open area in front of a large picture window, a gang of preschool kids was sprawled in a semicircle on a colorful rug around a woman reading aloud from a book. Parents, nannies, and strollers ringed the outside of the rug.

The woman reading briefly looked up and met his eyes as he entered. It was a story about dragons and tacos. The woman's voice easily carried throughout the space. She changed her pitch and tone to the characters. Not in a silly, showy way, but just enough to differentiate the characters and keep the children attentive.

Max wandered through the low stacks filled with picture books, past a messy craft area and wooden train set. He knew a solitary man roaming the children's area of a library could bring unwanted attention. He stopped at a matching window on the opposite side of the room, far from the group of kids, that gave a view out to the parking lot and the surrounding grounds. There was a small fenced-in grassy area with a modest playground and benches just below the window. A separate entrance was also available from this side directly to the children's area. A number of minivans, large SUVs, and other family cars were parked nearby. That explained why

Max hadn't seen or heard anyone entering while he was using the computer.

The playground was empty at the moment, as was most of the main parking lot, save for a small, rusting green hatchback parked near the cabbage palms, peppered liberally with bumper stickers and slogans. Max pegged that one as Merry's. Next to that was a blue Toyota sedan and an old, boxy, pale-yellow Mercedes. The only other car in the lot was in the back, partially obscured by the palms, a late-model, gray Chevy Equinox. Max couldn't see if there was anyone inside.

He turned away from the window and sat in a rocking chair, appreciated the air conditioning, and listened to the woman finish the book. Turns out dragons and tacos don't mix very well. At least not indoors. The kids cheered and clapped when the book ended and then began to disperse. After sitting quietly and listening, most of the kids headed outside to the playground. A swing was a swing even in this heat. A few wandered through the aisles and picked out books. The librarian didn't waste any time. She gave a couple of the children hugs and pats on the back and then headed straight toward Max. He stood as she approached. She was tall with a long face, aquiline nose, and upright bearing. Her hair was gray trending toward white, but Max didn't think she was much older than 60. Maybe it was because she was surrounded by children's books, but he thought of Miss Clavel, the teacher, from *Madeline*.

"Can I help you?" Her speaking voice, unlike the one he'd heard when she was reading, was patrician and had an edge of authority. Like Blackburn, she was someone used to giving directions or feedback.

"My name is Max Parish. I'm looking into the disappearance of Rose Robideaux. Merry, at the front desk, suggested I speak to you."

The woman's mouth tightened, her eyes hardened. He

wasn't sure if this reaction was in response to the Robideaux case or because of Merry's loose tongue. "You're with the police?"

"No. Private."

"Who are you working for?"

"Sorry, that's confidential."

She sniffed at that. "He's still trying to clear his name, huh?"

"Who?"

"Alex Blackburn, of course. All his money can keep mouths shut but it can't stop people's thoughts."

"You think he killed Rose?"

She looked around. The room was mostly empty and they had this half of the space to themselves. "Yes, I think that's the most likely outcome, don't you?"

"I just started this morning. I don't have many thoughts yet."

"Well, you will by the end of the day and, if you have an ounce of intelligence, Blackburn himself is going to be at the top of the suspect list."

"That's what everyone in town thinks?"

"Those with a brain, yes."

"Why would he do it? What do people think?"

"Why do people usually do it? For the land. The ranch. Take your pick. But ultimately for the money."

"I've heard the Double R wasn't doing that well."

"I don't know too much about that sort of thing, but I do know that Blackburn appears to have plenty of money now. The land itself, even way out here and with most of the mines closed, still has to be worth millions."

"But if he was married to Rose, why would he need to kill her? He could just divorce her and get at least half."

"Maybe half wasn't enough for someone like Blackburn, but that's a good question. Maybe you do have something going on up there. You might make it further than the others."

"I'm not the first PI to talk to you?"

"Oh, you're the first to come to see me, but it's no secret that other people have been poking around lately."

"Why do you think that is? If Blackburn did it or was involved in some way, but was cleared by the police, why do you think he keeps pushing it? He got away with it. Isn't it better to just let it fade out?"

"Have you met the man?"

"Yes."

"Then what do you think?"

Max thought about the smile, the handshake, the convivial attitude. "Ego or more power. He wants to run for office and can't have this murky situation in his past."

She smiled like a teacher would when a student had the correct answer. "I'm not sure about the political part. I've never heard anyone mention that type of ambition. I've always had the impression that Blackburn likes to use his power to manipulate from the shadows, but I think you're spot on with the ego. He can't stand that us townspeople, us peons, hold him in such disregard. He already fancies himself the savior of our town, but he needs to be the white knight too, not the black knight."

He didn't know Blackburn well enough to say if Margit Callenbach was right. Though he'd bet she was right about things more often than not. Max needed to think about it some more. It all made a sort of oblique sense but didn't feel totally right. He had one more question. "Why did Blackburn name the children's room after his wife? Was it just more community service? Spreading the money and influence around?"

Callenbach's face softened for the first time since they'd been talking. "No. Maybe that was his own motive, but in this case, there was a reason. Rose loved books. Absolutely adored them. She came here as a child and read through the stacks. Then when she became a mother herself, she continued to make the trip into town multiple times a week to bring Roxy."

"You were friends with Rose?"

"Friendly. We talked about books but weren't friends. Not really. There was the age difference, but Rose was also quiet. An introvert. She was a good mother and doted on Roxy, but she seemed happier in the company of books rather than people. Rose was a trustee on the library's board. And not because of Blackburn's money. She was on the board even before her first marriage." She paused and then made a decision. "If you want to talk to one of her friends, then you should talk to Leslie Halford. She owns a jewelry shop just outside town. She's another board member. In fact, I think Rose actually nominated her for the position. They seemed pretty close."

Callenbach walked over to her desk along the wall and Max followed. She flipped through an old Rolodex and wrote down a name and phone number on a piece of paper and handed it to him.

"Good luck, Mr. Parish. I hope you find some answers, if only for Roxy's sake."

Max thought it was interesting how some people used Angie and others used Roxy. It was like her life was split in two. Then he realized it probably felt like that to her, as well. Before and after. Maybe Blackburn didn't deserve answers, maybe he already *knew* the answers, but it was hard to argue that Angie/Roxy was better off not knowing what became of her mother.

Max turned to leave but then remembered the byline on so many of the local newspaper stories. "Do you know Melinda Carson?"

Callenbach surprised him by laughing. It transformed her face. The lines became less aristocratic and more open and gentle. "You definitely are not from around here. I mean, I could sort of tell." She waved a hand and Max was afraid to ask what she meant, maybe it was just the chalky-white skin. "But that question cinched it."

"Local celebrity?"

"Are newspaper reporters ever celebrities?"

"Woodward. Bernstein."

"In this century?"

"Fair point."

"Mel is less a celebrity and more an institution. She's run the paper almost singlehandedly for as long as I can remember."

"Do you know where I can find her?"

CHAPTER EIGHTEEN

The *Tiendas Reales Tribune* building was on the commercial strip, a ten minute drive from the older downtown section where he'd spent the morning. The strip butted up against Highway 35 that led north to San Antonio. The proximity to the highway didn't appear to be helping. A slowly deteriorating shopping mall sat across the street with only a few cars in the acres of available parking. Like much of the rest of the town he'd seen, it appeared to be slowly eroding under the white-hot sun.

The newspaper building itself was a low, long rectangle. He spotted two delivery trucks parked on the right side toward the back. One had a cracked, flat tire. The building was likely pulling double-duty as an office and a distribution space. Max turned into the lot and parked next to a dusty Subaru Impreza hatchback. It was the only other car currently in the lot. The building had a vaguely Spanish-style facade tacked onto the front on top of whitewashed cinder blocks. Arches and columns framed the entrance doors. *Tiendas Reales Tribune* written in a traditional Gothic newspaper font hung over the doors and clashed even more with the building's confused architecture. It all gave Max a headache as he climbed out of his car and headed toward the building. Or maybe the headache was from the heat, but in this case, he doubted it.

A bell rang quietly as he opened the door. Inside, the building was divided, as he suspected. The public space he now stood in included a small, tiled lobby area with a reception desk. A pile of newspapers sat to one side of the empty desk. Beyond that, a series of high cubicles, presumably for the reporters. Blown-up pages of the paper and archival photos were mounted and framed on the outer walls. There was a glassed-in conference room, also empty, at the far end. He spotted a set of large metal doors in the back corner, with a red 'Authorized Personnel Only' sign prominently plastered on the front, which likely led to the back half of the building, the printing press, warehouse, or distribution space. Max guessed they at least did some of their own printing here as the building, even this front space, smelled strongly of hot paper and ink. He could feel the slight vibration in the floor of heavy machinery running.

He walked over to the reception desk. The chair was pushed in, and the space was neat and tidy. No coffee cups, no pink message slips. It didn't appear to be staffed. He paused. Other than the low background drone of the equipment, the entire front section was very quiet. Even at a biweekly paper like the *Tribune*, he expected the newsroom to be a little more lively. He wandered past the desk into the rows of cubicles. The first four were abandoned, like the reception desk. As he moved past more empty cubicles, he caught the scent of cigarette smoke.

He walked to the end of the row and found a burning cigarette perched between the space of two crooked clay teeth in an ashtray that was presumably supposed to resemble an open mouth. This cube's desk and walls were adorned with paper of all shapes and sizes. Printouts, notes, scribbled words on scraps, message slips. It was a firetrap with a laptop, beat-up iPhone, and an old multiline desk phone at the center.

He was reaching to put out the cigarette when he heard a voice from behind.

"Whoa, wasn't expecting visitors today. Who are you?"

He turned to find a short, wrinkled woman with a square jaw, vibrant eyes, and a frizz of white hair that probably hadn't seen a comb since the '80s. Her matching dark pink Velour jacket and sweatpants also would not have been out of place in the '80s. She carried more paper in one hand and another burning cigarette in the other.

Before Max could answer, she moved past him, dumped the paper on her desk, and sat in the chair. She pulled the ashtray closer and tapped some ash into the mouth.

"My grand-niece made that," she said nodding at the lurid clay mouth. "I'd think she was trying to be ironic, but she was seven at the time. It was probably more literal." One cigarette had burned down, she stubbed it out and picked up the spare. "Of course, I'm not supposed to smoke inside, but," she waved a hand around, "who the hell is going to complain? Barb comes in twice a week," she said indicating the cube behind him which featured far less paper and many more cat tchotchkes, "to do the accounts and general office mainte-nance." The woman shrugged. "I try not to smoke as much when she's here but I'm not sure she notices with the stick so far up her ass. Anyway, I'm violating the number one rule for a reporter. Talking too much and not listening. And you," she focused those blue eyes fully on Max now, "look like you might have a good story to tell. So, who the hell are you and why are you here?"

"My name is Max and I'm looking for Rose Robideaux."

Hmph. "I was sort of hoping you'd have something more

interesting to say. You a reporter? Please don't tell me you're a podcaster."

"Private investigator."

"So, you're working for Blackburn."

"My employer is confidential."

"Please, honey, don't insult my intelligence. No one else in this town besides Blackburn has the resources or a reason to hire a private dick to look for his missing wife." She waved a hand in front of her face dismissing Max's objection. "Let's forget all that. It's a slow news day. Hell, it's been a slow couple of years around here as you can see. I got time. How'd you end up here?"

"Margit Callenbach at the town library pointed me in this direction. I'm looking for Melinda Carson."

The mention of Margit's name seemed to pique the woman's interest.

"Well, you found her, I'm Melinda, and if Margit sent you over maybe you're more interesting than you look. What do you want to know about Rose?"

"I read your clips about the case at the library." He pulled over the chair from Barb's cube and sat down. It took three more cigarettes to tell Carson what he currently knew about Rose's disappearance.

When he finished, she was quiet for a moment, then reached under her desk and dragged a bulging cardboard box out, then dragged out a second matching box and patted the top. "My notes and background materials. It sounds like your time at the library was well spent. You've got the facts down. I'm not sure what else I can tell you, but you're welcome to dig through my notes."

"You had those handy."

"Just did a retrospective recently. To be crass, it moves papers. It's the biggest thing to happen in TR since they found coal on the banks of the Rio Grande." She nudged one box back under her desk. "But, truth be told, the Robideaux case never goes too far. I probably think about it once a day."

Max knew what she meant. He could already feel it working its way under his skin.

"Anything you didn't put in print?" he asked.

"Of course. As I'm sure you're learning, or soon will, everyone in this town has a theory."

"The same theory?"

Carson smiled. "You mean Blackburn? He's certainly high on the list and, if you made people vote on the most likely, he'd probably win in a landslide despite all his influence, but he's far from the only theory I've heard. It runs the gambit from secret lover to crazed illegal psycho killer to wild coyotes dragging her from the car."

"Any of them seem likely?"

She gave it a moment's consideration but then shook her head. "No. If I've learned anything in 50 years of doing this job, it's that, despite our human need for mystery, we tend to overcomplicate things."

"So you think Blackburn did it?"

"I'm a reporter. I'm impartial. I selfishly root for the story."

"Do you have an opinion?"

"Yes." She reached into her handbag and pulled out a pack of cigarettes, shook one loose, and lit it. "Have you ever been married?"

Max felt a thin spike of familiar pain deep in his chest. "Yes, once."

"Did you love your wife?"

"Very much."

"Did you have a perfect marriage?"

"Of course not."

"You fought?"

"Not physically, no, but we argued and bickered."

"Bad arguments?"

Max thought back. "Sure, there were a few bad ones."

"Would your friends and neighbors say you had a good marriage?"

"I think so."

"But they didn't really know, right? Just like you wouldn't know about their relationships."

"You think Blackburn and Rose had a troubled marriage?"

"I don't know. I honestly don't. That was my point. And I didn't hear any rumors or whispers, either. I've looked at this case from every angle for more than five years. That is one corner of it that I could never shine a light on." She paused to tap ash off her cigarette. "How much do you know about Alex Blackburn?"

"I know what you put in your stories. Moved here about 10 years ago. Married Rose. Helped get the ranch back in the black and then some. Seems to want to help get the town back on its feet, so to speak. He's spread his money and influence around."

She nodded. "That's all true. As far as I know. But what do you know about Alex Blackburn *before* he moved to Tiendas Reales?"

Max thought back to his brief searches at the library. He hadn't looked very hard, but he'd still found remarkably little. "Not much."

"Well, if you found not much then you found more than me."

"What do you think that means?"

"The man has secrets."

CHAPTER NINETEEN

Max left Melinda Carson as she lit up another smoke. If he hit a dead end, he'd return and risk lung cancer from the secondhand smoke and read through her boxes of notes. For now, he looked up the police station's address on his phone and let the GPS guide him back into town. The station was situated just a few blocks from the bank and the diner where this all started that morning. It took up most of a corner block and shared space with the town's fire department. It was a bunker-like building with few windows and an ugly, rough stucco exterior that looked like furry, toxic mold was covering the outside. He drove around the block. The police station entrance fronted the main street. The two garage doors for the fire department were around the corner. A fenced-in lot took up the remaining quarter of the block. He pulled to the curb and parked with a view of the police entrance and the parking lot.

Max checked his watch. It was close to 5 P.M. He could see four cruisers in the lot and a newer SUV with 'Chief' marked on the door. Five official cars. Was this a shift change or were they just idle cars? He wondered how large of a force a small city like this required? Did they run three shifts around-the-clock or two with a skeleton crew on the third shift, relying on the highway patrol or county sheriff to pick up the slack? It was clear Tiendas Reales was in an economic downturn, but he hadn't seen that much evidence of higher crime during his brief time here. He remembered Serrato not getting a single call during the hour he'd spent with her at the diner. Probably too hot. Maybe crime spiked in the winter.

He watched a woman, not in uniform, maybe administrative staff, exit the building and immediately light up a cigarette. Maybe she was related to Carson. She exhaled the smoke toward the sky. She looked around briefly, saw no one in the lot, and continued down the sidewalk. He watched her walk a block south and then flick the cigarette in the gutter and enter a place called Lotus Lounge.

He took out his phone and tapped a contact.

"Guess what I did this morning?" Max said.

"Slept in an anonymous motel room and ate breakfast at a diner while reading a paperback?"

"Very funny."

"And I'm wrong?" Lawrence asked.

"Well, no, but I also visited the library."

"Ah, my favorite thing to do other than making money or making love," Lawrence answered, affecting a deep voice.

"Your Barry White impression needs work."

"Good thing I was going for Isaac Hayes. You white boys have no taste." He dropped the jocular tone and asked, "You okay?"

"I'm good."

"I don't hear no sirens, so I assumed as much, but I always have to ask with you. What do you need?"

"The library didn't have all the answers. I was wondering if you could do a little digging for me."

"Why not? I haven't been shot at or threatened by any

lunatics in a few months. I was getting too comfortable in this skin."

"Lawrence, if you don't feel comfortable help—"

"Stop right there. You know I've got your back. You call, I answer. That's my choice. That's how this works. You'd do the same for me. Plus, you know I hate feeling comfortable. It's boring. You are the spice in my life, my friend. So spit it out; how can I help?"

Max smiled. He'd spent so long watching his own back that he was still adjusting to having people ready and willing to help. His smiled faded slightly. Still, ready and willing or not, he realized his friendship came with a price. He wondered if this strange quest for redemption he appeared to be on was just two steps forward and one step back? Was he a sinking ship and taking down everyone with him?

"Max? You there?

"Sorry, yes. I need all the information you can find on an Alex Blackburn, most recently of Tiendas Reales, Texas."

He spent five minutes filling Lawrence in on his day and his unexpected new employer.

As he spoke, he watched two men exit the rear of the building. Both in identical uniforms to what he'd seen Serrato in earlier. One was shorter with gray hair and matching mustache. The uniform was snug on his paunchy frame. The second guy was thin with a buzzcut down to the scalp. They paused at the end of the sidewalk and spoke briefly, then parted, the older one going to the chief's SUV and the younger walking to a gray extended-cab pickup among a row of civilian vehicles.

"All right, I'll get Eddie on it," Lawrence said when Max had finished. "Even if this guy has had some data scrubbed, he likes a challenge. We'll get back to you as soon as we can."

. . .

Max pulled Serrato's card out of his pocket and tapped in the mobile number. She picked up on the second ring.

"Hello?" She sounded hesitant. He could hear background office noise and a man's voice.

"It's Max Parish."

"I didn't think I'd hear from you again so soon." The background noise dropped away suddenly.

"It's been a productive day."

"Is that right?"

"I'd like to keep it going and was hoping to see that report now."

"Now? I told you it might take a bit of time."

"I don't need a copy or anything official, I just need to read it. I just saw the chief leave. Maybe I could come in and take a peek? You could have the file back in its place before Mrs. Chief is serving dessert."

"You're outside?"

"I'm around back. I could always come in through the front and make an official request."

There was silence and Max did feel bad about squeezing her, but then he thought about Angie outside the bank, Hull kicking the PI down the stairs, and Blackburn hiring a total stranger. It all stank of pressure, maybe desperation, and told Max that maybe time and proper manners were luxuries he could not afford right now.

"All right," Serrato finally answered. "Meet me out back in twenty minutes."

CHAPTER TWENTY

"You got one hour. And don't leave this room," Serrato said. She backed out and shut the door. He heard the lock engage. He felt a static buzzing flare up at the back of his neck. Her tone had been short and curt. This was a risk for her, but it was no picnic for him, either. The door lock probably engaged automatically as a precaution when questioning suspects.

He hoped.

His eyes scanned the room as he searched for exits and weak points. An old habit. It didn't take long.

He was in was a small, nondescript box, maybe eight by ten. The walls and ceiling were gypsum board painted light green. The ceiling was plain white. He guessed the walls were reinforced with concrete behind the gypsum board, both for security and soundproofing, but he knew that the light green was supposed to make the place less threatening if a recording was played in court. There was likely mesh wire in the ceiling. It would be bad form to have a suspect escape by crawling into the ductwork. The floor was concrete with an

easy-to-clean epoxy over top. There was a table with two
office chairs positioned on one side and a single chair bolted
to the floor on the other. He guessed there were microphones
and recording devices he wouldn't spot unless he really
looked. It was all clean and professional and a bit higher
grade than he would have expected from the outside looking
in. Any budget clearly hadn't been put into the building's
exterior, but it had been put to good use on the interior.
More of Blackburn's money? A quid pro quo for clearing him?
Still, any money couldn't cover the smell of sweat, coffee, and
nicotine.

A slim gray folder sat in the middle of the table. Max sat
down in one of the office chairs and pulled the file closer. If
this was all the paper they'd generated in an official investigation, he didn't think he'd need the whole hour.

The initial crime scene reports were as dry as kindling and
only verified what he'd learned at the library and from
Melinda Carson. He took photos with his phone as he read.
Rose's car had been found on a remote part of her own ranch.
Blackburn himself had called it in via 911. The blood was definitely hers. Best guess from the techs was that she'd been
missing for less than six hours. Long enough to get lost if she
was confused or disoriented and she might have been with
that much blood loss, but likely still alive when the search
started. But no trace of her was ever found. No clothing. No
bag. Nothing.

The initial focus had been on search and rescue with the
subsequent reports carefully worded but Max could read
between the lines. The crime scene, if it was one, had gotten
screwed up or potentially contaminated with a lot of people
coming and going in the search effort. The car and blood
were kept pristine, but if there were tracks or impressions to
be found in the immediate area, those were compromised.

Max remembered the brown, hard-packed landscape as he drove up to the Double R Ranch and wondered if, even in the best of conditions, they would have found anything.

But they didn't. No one else's blood. No signs of a struggle. No other DNA that couldn't be explained. Rose Robideaux Blackburn had driven her car off into the night, bled profusely, then vanished and stayed that way for weeks, months, then years.

The interview transcripts were more interesting. Carson and Serrato had told him that Blackburn was the primary suspect, even Margit Callenbach, the librarian, had considered this common knowledge. The logic was obvious, he was the husband and the primary suspect given the very limited pool of possible and probable suspects. Random attacks by strangers are typically too rare to consider. Normally, you don't have to look beyond the spouse.

He read the transcripts, and Max realized he had assumed the department had used kid gloves, cowed by Blackburn's reputation and influence in the town. That was not the case. To his credit, whatever money Blackburn had spread around, it hadn't stopped the detective in charge, Tom Wilson, from going after Blackburn hard.

At the time of Rose's disappearance, Blackburn was in tighter financial straits than he let on. Max wondered if that was still the case today. He made a note to find out about Blackburn's current financials. Everyone assumed he had money, but did he? And, if he did, where had it come from? He wasn't flush six years ago. The ranch was treading water and they were overextended on a vacation property in Mexico, plus they'd pushed their credit cards pretty high. It was a precarious balancing act but, Max knew, not that unusual for the upper class. There were still plenty of assets to borrow against and plenty of places that would give it to them. Still, it likely led to some hand wringing around the dinner table. The stress that came with scraping up change to pay the bills didn't change whether you were rich or poor.

Husband and wife also each had a million-dollar life insurance policy. Again, not all that unusual. But there would be no payout until proof of death and Blackburn was cleared in the investigation. The more he read, the more Max became confused. Surely, if Blackburn needed the money from the insurance, he would have found a way to have the body discovered. But that hadn't happened, and the insurance company was content to let the situation stay that way. And so was Blackburn, until recently. What had changed?

He heard footsteps approaching the door and a moment later Serrato came through the door.

"Coming up on an hour. You good?"

"Does the file turn into a pumpkin if I need more time?"

"Gimme a break, Parish," Serrato said. "You're putting me in a tight spot. I'm trying to play nice because, for some reason, I think you might actually be able to do something about all this."

"Okay, I hear you. Five more minutes?"

"Five minutes." She let the door close and leaned against the wall.

Max flipped through the last pages. They were the interviews with the ranch staff. All of them were short and perfunctory. He scanned one and got the gist. "Nothing from the hired help?"

"See no evil, hear no evil. Can't say I blame them. They probably really didn't see anything and if they said anything they'd likely lose their job, and those are hard to come by around here."

He closed the folder. "Then I'm done."

"Learn anything?"

"Maybe. The department really held Blackburn's feet to the fire."

Serrato nodded. "Wilson did a thorough job."

"He still around?"

Serrato shook her head. "Retired to Arizona, then dropped dead six months later after a massive coronary."

"Damn, would have been good to pick his brains."

"I know. According to the guys here, that case bugged him right up until the day he pulled the pin."

"You'd probably know better, but it appears he did everything right. He certainly asked Blackburn all the tough questions."

She nodded. "You could argue that he could have secured the scene a little tighter initially, but that's a tough call in that situation where the missing person might still be alive but hurt. I think most would have made the same call, especially when you consider Blackburn's weight in this town."

Max tapped the folder. "Blackburn is essentially cleared in here, but you get the feeling that if her remains were found tomorrow, he'd be right back in the hot seat."

"I don't think you'd have a problem getting a warrant, no."

"Still, I see the problem Wilson had. If you read between the lines, something hinky is going on. The pieces are not lining up like you'd expect if this was a run-of-the-mill husband kills wife scenario. Something's missing."

Max stood and held out the folder for Serrato but then pulled it back. "Hold on." He flipped open the front cover where a chronology report was pinned to the cover. "There should be a note of when Blackburn last requested an update."

"He hasn't."

"Not once? Since he was cleared?"

"Nope."

His wife goes missing, her car is found dripping with blood, and he never followed up with the police? Not once in five years? How was that possible?

"So why did he hire me this morning? Why now?"

CHAPTER TWENTY-ONE

He left Serrato at the station house's back door and she scurried back inside like she was afraid the sky was falling. Her nerves had rubbed off on him and he tried to shake it off as he walked to his car. He opened the door and a wave of heat boiled out at him. Even close to six in the evening, the Texas sun was set to perpetual boil. He put the windows down, cranked the air conditioning, and tried to ignore it. It appeared to work for the locals. It didn't work as well for him. He navigated back to the crossroads near The Tin Roof where this day had begun and spotted the Will's Hardware store sign on his left. He U-turned in the middle of the street and parked in front just as someone was exiting and locking up.

"Excuse me, do you sell those dashboard sunshields?" Max asked as he got out of the car.

The man turned around and looked Max over. He was older, slightly stooped with gray hair and a bulbous nose. The name embroidered on the shirt pocket said Lou. Max briefly wondered how many Lou's lived in Texas. It just didn't seem to fit. Eventually, Lou made a decision. Maybe it was the sweat dripping off Max's forehead. Maybe it was pity. Or maybe Lou was just a true champion of retail and couldn't resist the opportunity for one more sale. He nodded. "Yes, we do." He held the door open for Max. "Aisle four, on the right."

Max found a sunshade and carried it up to the register. He added a bottle of sunscreen from a display and a pair of black sunglasses. He might as well make it worth Lou's time. He almost added a Snickers bar but stopped and asked Lou, "Where would you go for dinner in this town?"

Lou scanned the three items and then paused. It was becoming clear to Max that Lou didn't make any decision rashly. "What are you in the mood for?"

"No preference, really. Just something decent that won't tie me up in knots three hours after I eat it."

"Well now, that eliminates any Tex-Mex for me. Tastes fine going down, especially with a cold beer, but my stomach can't handle it anymore. You got just about every cuisine under God's sun off Route 35 but that's mostly fast-food catering to the travelers who want to get back on the road in a jiffy." He bagged the items and made change from the twenty that Max had handed him. "Couple good lunch places I could recommend, but those are closed up at this hour. Tell you what, your best bet is probably The Tin Roof just up the block a piece. Good burgers and steaks. It's a diner masquerading as a cafe, but the food is solid."

Max put the new sunshade on the dash, then walked north two blocks. The bell over the door rang out his entrance for the third time that day. Adriana was no longer on duty. A different waitress smiled at him and told him to sit where he liked. The Tin Roof must rely on breakfast and lunch to survive. He had his choice of tables. An older couple sat at a two-top in the back. Two overweight guys in stained blue jeans and bent trucker hats had their guts tucked up under the counter, trying to chat up the younger version of Adriana as she filled their water glasses. Max watched one exchange. He was too far away to hear the words, but he could guess the intent. They both struck him as people you instinctively avoided having conversations with if you could, but this waitress didn't have that luxury. She had gas and electric, and no doubt rent or a mortgage to pay, so she gave them both a tight, polite smile, just enough to keep her tip, but not enough to invite more attention before moving on.

Melinda Carson sat in a front booth overlooking the street, drinking coffee, and looking like she wanted a smoke. He walked over. Various sections of *The New York Times* sat scattered across the tabletop mixed with the slimmer *Tiendas Reales Tribune* tabloid.

"You're a news junkie, aren't you?" he said and nodded at the papers.

"Well, if it isn't our own Philip Marlowe."

"I'll take that as a compliment."

"You do?"

"Sure, he got the job done. I'm surprised you don't like him. The man had a sharp tongue and liked to smoke."

"Don't forget the whiskey, chess, and poetry."

"Never learned chess and, while I enjoy a beer and the occasional bourbon, I'm sure Marlowe would have drunk me under the table. I will cop to enjoying the Elliott Gould version. Overall I think I prefer Jessica Fletcher and *Murder, She Wrote*, if I needed a PI."

"That nosy bitch?" But she smiled as she said it.

"Mind if I join you?"

"Sure. I already read most of this rag." She moved some of the paper aside as he slid in across from her.

"I read your clips. They're good. You ever think about trying for a bigger paper?"

"Thank you for saying that, but I don't think I was cut out for the east coast or big-paper politics. Probably wouldn't have lasted a week."

Max wasn't so sure about that. He thought Melinda Carson might have some hidden claws.

She picked up her coffee, took a sip, then continued. "When I was young, I thought about it, but ultimately, I stayed. I don't know if that was the right choice or the coward's choice. Depends on which day you ask. I'm not Nellie Bly but I hope when I'm gone that my work stands as an archive of a certain time and place. Maybe it'll have some value to someone. Maybe that's also just the rationalization of an old woman."

"I don't think so. The universe tends to have a way of putting people in the place they need to be when they need to be there."

Hmph. "Now that sounds like someone who's drifting through life without a real purpose." But she cut the comment with another grin.

"I was going for a classic Hollywood quip."

"Keep trying."

Max picked up the menu, even though he still remembered most of it. "What do you recommend?"

"Finding another restaurant."

"What if that's not an option?"

"The burgers or the chicken fried steak won't kill you."

The waitress wandered over and put a glass of water and set of silverware wrapped in a napkin down on the table and then looked at him expectantly. He was tempted to go with the onion burger again but decided to go for some variety and something green.

"I'll take the hamburger steak with green beans and mashed potatoes."

The waitress nodded and then turned to Melinda. "Anything else for you, Miss Carson?"

"Vera bring in any pies today?"

"Yes, ma'am. Pecan and some apple dumplings."

"I'll take a slice of the pecan."

"A la mode?"

"Is there any other respectable way to eat pie, hon?"

"No, ma'am. Not in Texas."

The waitress nodded and walked away. The two truckers watched her. This time, the other one tried a comment leading with 'sweet cheeks.' She ignored him and continued through the swinging doors into the kitchen. Tips were only worth so much. The guy muttered something under his breath. Again, the intent was clear. Both guys were drinking sodas but as Max watched, the first guy dipped into his pocket and pulled out a flask and dumped a hefty measure into his glass before he offered it to his friend.

Max turned back to Carson and tapped a finger on a large color advertisement taking up the lower corner of the *Tribune*. "What can you tell me about this?"

"That," Carson responded, "is a large reason that I'm still able to publish a paper twice a week."

"Blackburn?"

"Yup. I'll say this, the man definitely puts his money where his mouth is. He has a lot invested in this town."

Max glanced out the window and could see three empty storefronts within a stone's throw. What did Blackburn see in Tiendas Reales that was worth so much time and investment? "Is this the same place I keep seeing billboards for on the outskirts of town? I assume that is also Blackburn?"

"Right on both accounts. You can see the billboards are getting a little faded. I checked in two weeks ago. He's got a dedicated PR person for all his non-ranch business interests, woman by the name of Jill Cresidien, and she insists they are still on schedule to break ground on phase one in two months. She says that every two months when I call. It's like talking to an obstinate chatbot."

The waitress reemerged from the kitchen at the far end of the counter. The men stayed quiet. She collected the check from the couple in the back booth. They gathered their belongings and left. Max looked at the advertisement; it was a similar architect's rendering or stock photo that appeared on the larger billboards. He read the accompanying text. "Who's going to buy these?"

"All part of Blackburn's grand plan according to Cresidien and her press releases. He's going to siphon off talent and wealth from the coasts. Lure them here with gentlemen ranches at discount prices. A discount from New York or California but still a nice tidy profit for Tiendas Reales."

"Where are they all going to work?"

"I presume they'll still work in New York or California."

"But live here."

"The new world order. I've heard he's been talking to some of the big internet companies too, trying to get some dedicated high-speed lines built like Google did for that town in Kansas. That would be a perk for the ones that still work. Ideally, they would have cashed out already and can put that new money to work in TR."

"Seems ... optimistic."

"It does. And he has a backup plan, of sorts. Not all the developments look like this." She tapped a finger on the advertisement. "These are just the show ponies. He has more modest plans, too. And he built a big warehouse just south of here that he says will provide jobs even for locals."

"Warehouse for what?"

"A shipping and receiving depot. It's up and running now and he says it will only grow larger."

Before Max could follow up on that, the waitress delivered their food.

"You all right, Gemma?"

She gave them a sunny smile as she set down the food, but it didn't reach her eyes. "Of course, Miss Carson." She lowered her voice. "Those guys are all talk. Just part of the job." But Max could see the tension in her shoulders and the worry on her face, and apparently so could Carson.

"Joe working the grill tonight?"

"No, it's Tommy."

Carson tsked. "He's still in high school."

"Enjoy your food," she said brightly and walked off to clear the back booth.

They took a few minutes to dig into their food and then talked about innocuous things. She'd lived in Tiendas Reales her whole life, and they compared growing up here versus Boston. The hamburger steak was a juicy slab of ground chuck and brisket topped with sweet grilled onions and a fragrant brown gravy that mixed well with the green beans and mashed potatoes. There was a side of spicy jalapeno cornbread that he used to clean his plate.

He hadn't realized how hungry he was. Maybe the heat also amped up one's metabolism. He was considering a slice of pie, Carson hadn't let hers go to waste, when there was a commotion by the kitchen. Max looked over and saw one of the men holding Gemma's arm and pulling her forward so she was leaning over the counter. Her face had gone white and her eyes wide. The kitchen door swung open, and Tommy stood there holding a baseball bat. Tommy was thin with a buzzcut and acne. He looked just as scared as Gemma.

CHAPTER TWENTY-TWO

Carson moved to slide out of the booth, but Max put a hand on her arm. He was a little curious to see what her plan was, to see what it looked like when her claws came out, but he also didn't want her to get hurt. The two men were well oiled up now from whatever was in the flask and even an accidental blow or push could do significant damage to someone Carson's age.

"I got it."

He stood and walked over. The one he'd seen with the flask had a grip on Gemma's upper arm from across the counter. "Your boyfriend here going to take a swing at me?" he asked as he glanced at Tommy and his baseball bat. "Billy, take care of that boy. Gemma and I are going to have a chat in back."

"It doesn't look like Gemma has anything to say to you," Max said.

Both men turned around. They hadn't heard him approach and seemed surprised anyone else was in the diner. They both had slightly glassy eyes and slack-jawed expressions.

"This has nothing to do with you. Go sit back down with your grandma," the one holding Gemma said. He seemed to be the talker.

Max leaned between them and placed two twenties on the counter. "Dinner's on me. Maybe take off. Better yet, sleep it off."

The men looked at each other. "Maybe we're not done quite yet." He eyed Gemma. "Maybe I'd like some dessert."

"Maybe the three of us could talk outside then. If you still want to talk with Gemma after that. You're welcome to."

Billy and the other man smiled. Apparently fighting was a close second to sexual assault on their list of enjoyable post-dinner activities. The man let go of Gemma and she stepped back and rubbed at her arm.

"Just remember when you wake up in the hospital that you asked for this."

"After you." Max held out an arm toward the door.

Carson had come up to stand behind him during the exchange and put a hand on his arm. "Are you sure about this?" she whispered.

"A little exercise after you eat is supposed to be good for digestion," Max replied.

He smiled down at her, but she seemed unconvinced. He watched the men exit. They each outweighed him by a hundred pounds. He dropped the smile and shook out his arms. He felt the adrenaline leaking into his limbs. The next few minutes promised blood and violence and mayhem. A part of him felt ashamed that it felt so good. Carson didn't know him. This would be a slaughter, but he wasn't the lamb. He turned back to her, and she took an involuntary step back. "I'm sure but lock the door after me if it makes you feel better."

He followed the men outside. The thing he kept locked up in his chest banged against its cage. It had cooled into the nineties. Both men were standing together in the empty street, already sweating. If they'd been smart, which they clearly weren't, they'd have spread out and come at Max at the same time from opposite sides. Even big and stupid, one of them would have gotten in some good shots. Maybe they would have had a chance. But no, they were big and stupid and drunk and overconfident. That was a lot to overcome. Too much.

The one that had been holding Gemma smiled and put his fists up. Billy kept his hands down, took a few steps back, content to watch. "Get 'em, Lenny," he said.

Max had a fleeting thought about Lennie from *Of Mice and Men*. He'd read it in Vermont last winter. He wagered that Novel Lennie's IQ might have been higher.

Texas Lenny shuffled forward a step.

Max didn't wait. His rule for fights was simple: hit first. Firsthand experience from his many bouts on the ice during hockey games or in the streets of South Boston taught him that the winner was almost always the one who landed the first punch.

Max took two quick steps forward to get inside the bigger man's reach and snapped off a jab to Lenny's nose. He felt the cartilage crunch against his knuckles. It wasn't a hard shot, he didn't want to break his hand, but it stunned the man and caused him to drop his guard and put his hands up to catch the blood now pouring down his chin.

Max's second rule was that there were no rules. No gentleman's agreements. No manners. No civilized behavior.

He stomped down hard on Lenny's instep, followed that with a sharp knee to the groin that bent him forward and then scythed an elbow around that connected just above Lenny's ear and swept the rug out from under his equilibrium. Lenny took two shambling steps to the left, then tipped over backward. Max doubted the fall hurt. Lenny had ample padding in the rear. The whole incident took less than five seconds, and Billy was still smiling and looking at the space where Lenny had just stood. It took another two seconds for his brain to catch up to the new reality.

"Hey," he blubbered, "you hurt him. You really hurt him."

Max didn't think his statement really needed an answer but he replied anyway, "Yes, I did. Maybe you should consider that the next time you try bullying people or worse."

Billy took a step forward then stopped. He seemed caught between defending his friend or walking away.

Max gave Billy credit for having some balls. It wouldn't save him, but there was some valor in going down with a friend, even a piece of crap like Lenny. Billy squared himself up and appeared about to bull rush Max, a strategy that might have worked better than Lenny's, when they both heard the wail of approaching sirens. They each turned to look down the street as two patrol cars blew through the intersection at fifty miles an hour. A fast flash of blue and red. There and gone. They were responding to something, but this altercation wasn't it.

Max kept one eye on Billy, but the sirens had sobered him up. He helped a dazed Lenny get to his feet and they walked off. Or limped off in Lenny's case. Max could see two tractor trailer cabs without trailers parked in an empty lot down the block. Max watched until he was sure they wouldn't change their minds then turned back to The Tin Roof. Gemma, Timmy, and Carson stood in the doorway. Carson unlocked the door and stepped out.

"Well, you've got a better jab than Jessica Fletcher, I'll give you that."

CHAPTER TWENTY-THREE

"You have a car?" Carson asked.

"Sure. Parked down the block by the hardware store."

"Good. Let's go," Carson replied and started walking in that direction.

"What?" Max said and followed in her wake. An ambulance and a third police car, also with their sirens and lights on, went past the bank and through the intersection. "Where?"

"Wherever the police are going."

They reached the SUV and Max unlocked the doors. They each climbed in, the new sunshade helped a little with the suffocating heat, and Max backed out, made a left, and followed the sirens. Dusk was falling and traffic was light. Once they'd cleared the meager downtown, the road was a straight shot, and the flashing lights made the line of emergency vehicles an easy beacon to spot in the growing dark. Soon, the last houses and traces of Tiendas Reales fell away. Max slowed and kept the SUV a steady half mile back. There was nothing else on the road, save a lone tractor trailer that blew past in the opposite direction, shaking even the heavy SUV in its wake.

A familiar billboard flashed by and Max realized he was ending his day in much the same way he'd started. This was the road that he and Angie had driven almost twelve hours before.

"What else is out here besides the Double R?" Max asked.

"Not much. Past the ranch, you run into Route 78 which runs east-west along the border. You keep going south on this road and you hit Mexico. Other than some stray mining rights that are all abandoned now, Blackburn and the Double R own the land right up to the border."

"You think we're heading to the border?"

"No, TR police wouldn't respond to that. That would be the Border Patrol out of Laredo. That's Federal. Given all that's gone on at the border in recent years, or not gone on, depending on your perspective, the Feds would have to be on fire to call in the locals."

"Maybe an accident on the highway?"

"That would be state, the highway patrol, and they might ask for help."

"But not likely."

"No, but it could be."

"You think we're heading to the Double R, don't you? You thought that back at The Tin Roof."

"Like I said, not much out here in this direction. Plus fifty years as a reporter gives you a certain sixth sense about these things."

"You had a hunch."

She smiled. "Call it what you want."

"Well, thanks for including me."

"The least I could do after what you did for Gemma back there. That was headed in an ugly direction." She paused, maybe waiting for him to respond, but when he remained silent, she continued. "Plus, I hate driving at night. You were convenient."

"There's a lot to be said for convenience."

Five minutes passed in silence. Another tractor trailer rumbled past in the opposite lane on the narrow road. They continued to follow the emergency lights south.

"Can I ask you something?"

He knew what she was going to ask before she said it. Fifty years as a reporter meant she was used to asking questions and pulling at threads.

"You want to know if I enjoyed it, right?"

She shifted in her seat. "Your face looked ..." She trailed off.

He glanced over and gave her a thin smile. "Animated? Happy?"

"No, it wasn't happy. I don't think that's what you were feeling. Not exactly. You looked plugged in. As if someone had turned up the volume." She huffed out a breath. "You looked alive."

"Turned up the volume," he repeated. "I haven't thought about it that way, but it's a good description. In those types of situations, things do get heightened, sharper. The world feels prickly and dangerous. It feels like everything matters a bit more. And, if I'm honest, that does bring a certain rush, a sense of being very much alive, but I don't enjoy it."

He stopped. Did he? That was the question he kept running into like a brick wall as he drove all those back roads. Did he put himself in these situations on purpose? Did he enjoy that rush a bit too much? Was it walling him off from stable relationships and a more normal life?

He continued. "At one point, maybe I did enjoy it. It can become an addiction."

"And now?"

"Drugs. Alcohol. When you're an addict, those things never stop feeling good. I've done some bad things." He thought of Michaels and a deep hole in Iowa. "Very bad things. Maybe put myself in situations where I knew it would come to violence. I'm not proud of that but I did make those choices. I'll own that. But I don't crave it. I don't need it." He stopped. He sounded like he was trying to convince himself.

"And the diner?" Carson asked.

"Did you think those two were going to listen to either of us and come to a peaceful solution?"

"Did we even try?"

"Yes. There was a choice. They could have walked away. I even tried to pay them to walk away."

"But you had a choice, too. I won't argue that a man has two sides. That's been said before by people much smarter than me. We all have the capacity for violence, and we all have the capacity for peace. It's our choices that determine the type of person we are."

"I agree with you. I had a choice and I shared it with them. Fight or flight. Trying to reason with them any further would have been like giving medicine to a dead body. In my experience, sometimes violence is the answer. I do my best to limit it to self-defense."

If he had rationalized his other answer, this one felt closer to the truth. She didn't respond. He glanced over at her, but it was now full dark and he couldn't read her expression.

"Sometimes you need to add to the suffering to stop the suffering," she said quietly.

Up ahead, the line of flashing lights continued into the dark.

. . .

Ten minutes later, they passed the entrance to the Double R. The tall wooden pillars stood out as a darker outline against the stars like an oversized door. What was behind that door? A broken family struggling with the loss of a wife and mother? A revived and thriving business? Or something else? It flashed past in the rearview mirror before any answers came to Max.

"Not heading for the Double R."

Carson sniffed. "Not to the house."

Max looked out across the vast open space. "How does the Double R make money?"

"On paper, they do what most ranches do. They raise cattle and horses. Dabble in farming with wheat and sorghum, where irrigation is possible. There might still be some mineral and oil lease rights for additional income."

"On paper?"

"You've been to the house. You see a lot of activity?"

"I saw Stetson Hull and a gardener and maybe another ranch hand. Is that the entire staff?" Max didn't think that could be correct.

"The ranch is a private company so it's not like I can pull up annual reports. I mostly have to go by whispers and rumors. He does bring in seasonal help but most of Blackburn's focus appears to be on his other business concerns. The real estate development and the holdings he's bought in town. The ranch now seems more like an afterthought."

"He's got money coming in from somewhere. That house is a pretty nice afterthought."

"Follow the money is never a bad strategy to get some answers."

"Let's finish with these cars first." He motioned through the windshield. The line of emergency lights had slowed and turned off the main road. "That still Double R's land?"

"Can't tell for certain in the dark, but it has to be. If it's not, it's unincorporated. Can't belong to anyone else."

He turned and followed. The SUV bumped off the road and onto a dirt path more fit for cows than cars. There were deep ruts that kept the SUV locked in like train tracks. They bumped along slowly, staying far back from the leading cars. The convoy stopped after half a mile where they met up with a waiting police car. The trailing cars clustered around it. Max stopped the SUV two hundred yards farther back and turned off the headlights. In all the commotion, no one had noticed them yet.

Max studied the scene. He could feel Carson taking in the details next to him, as well. He could make out a small, rough shack in the glare of all the responding cars' headlamps. The structure wasn't large enough to qualify as a house or cabin. It was roughly a square with a slanted roof, once red, now faded to a pink. It was simple, probably a single room, like a child might have drawn. The door was open. The only thing missing from the drawing were any windows. At least on the two sides that Max could see. All the official personnel had exited their vehicles and gathered near the first police car. Even from this distance, Max could read their body language. There was a charge in the air, the excitement of a change to the usual quiet weeknight, but no frantic energy. No rush to action. Whatever had happened was already over.

Max and Carson continued to watch from the SUV, and it became clear that the cars were blocking something nearer the house that they themselves couldn't see. There was an animated discussion going on that they could see but not hear. The people stood in a rough circle and turned occasionally and indicated at something with an arm or a hand. They walked closer to the shack, then retreated back to the circle. Max had a good idea what lay out there in the dark. He didn't think a dead horse or cow would bring this type of response. Not even in Texas.

Finally, someone in the group noticed them. One of the officers broke away and started walking toward the SUV. Max recognized the gait.

"Looks like we're about to get the bum's rush," he said.

Carson straightened in her seat. "We'll see about that."

As he watched Serrato get closer, he asked, "You recognize this area?"

"Yes."

Max turned back toward her. There was something in the way she said it. Quick, with no hesitation.

"It's the old salt house. It's where they found Rose's car. And all that blood."

CHAPTER TWENTY-FOUR

Max didn't know what a salt house was. Salt*box* houses were common in New England, but this certainly didn't look like that. Before he had a chance to ask, Serrato was at the window.

"Mr. Parish. You keep showing up in the most interesting places today."

She wore a wide official hat and her face remained inscrutable in the shadows of the brim. Was that teasing or suspicion?

"Interesting must mean something different to the police."

"Interesting doesn't have to mean good," she replied. "Crime scenes are always interesting. And not just for cops." Serrato leaned over and peered in the car. "Miss Carson, that you?"

"Yes, dear, it's me. Who died?"

"Who said someone died?"

"You did. You just said crime scenes are always interesting, so unless the town's response to littering has changed, I'm guessing there's a body out there."

"We on the record?"

"I don't do chitchat at crime scenes."

"Yes, there's a body. No use denying that. You and everybody else will learn that soon enough. Male, late twenties, maybe early thirties. Hispanic. I don't recognize him."

"Coming over the border? How far are we? Gotta be close."

Serrato stood up and squinted over the roof of the SUV. "You're right, not far. Less than a mile, give or take, but he's not a migrant, or he's the strangest one I've come across."

"Why's that?"

"Dressed well. Suit, collared shirt. No tie, but nice enough shoes. All still in decent condition. Mostly clean. I can't see him hiking across the border in those clothes."

"No ID on him?" Max asked.

"Don't know. Rodriguez was first on the scene. He checked for vitals and when he found nothing, he backed off and didn't touch anything else. COD is a gunshot wound. We won't know much more until the state crime scene unit gets here and that's at least three hours from now."

"I haven't heard of any missing persons reports. How did you find him?" Carson asked. "Someone from the ranch?"

"No. Anonymous call to the station."

"Huh," Carson said. Just then a new pair of headlights appeared on the road in the distance. Serrato tapped the top of the roof with her hand. "That'll be the chief. Do me a favor and get out of here. You're not going to get anything else tonight, and none of us need the hassle if he sees us being chummy."

"I'll call you later," Carson said.

"I don't doubt it," Serrato replied and walked back to the group.

Max started up the SUV and took a wide turn heading back to the road. The chief might wonder about the car that was leaving but he wouldn't get a good look and hopefully had more important things on his mind. Plus, Max was beginning to get the sense that Serrato would be prepared with a very good story if he did ask.

As they drove back toward town, Max realized he didn't have a place to sleep. "Can you recommend a hotel around here?"

"Sure, could recommend several. A couple of independent places still hanging on as well as one or two chains out by the highway that haven't closed down along with the mines. Mostly clean."

"Mostly?"

"You particular?"

"Not really. I'll stoop as low as musty and thin walls. I draw the line at stains and bedbugs."

Carson scratched at her chin. "Actually, I have a better idea."

"What's that?"

"Better if I show you."

"Is it near town?"

"Yup."

"Okay then."

They drove in silence for a few miles before Max said, "What's a salt house?"

"Pretty much what it sounds like."

"I'm a city boy."

"Before easy refrigeration, salt was the best way to cure and preserve meat. A salt house was typically where ranchers and farmers kept salt and minerals. They'd use the space to salt and dry the meat or sometimes make a heavy brine and store it in wooden barrels. The brine would keep the meat moister than the drying. Some homesteaders preferred that even if it was additional work. Either method would keep the meat from spoiling for months."

"Why is it way out there? So far from the ranch?"

"The Double R wasn't always in its current location. That salt house was set up for the original ranch house that was nearby. You can see the foundation in the daylight."

"Why leave that building standing?"

Carson shrugged. "Not sure. You could ask Blackburn. I don't remember it coming up in Rose's case. The Double R is so big, he might never have laid eyes on it before that night. Might be more trouble or cost than it's worth to tear it down. Easier to just let nature take its course."

As they continued back toward town, a truck rolled past, then the darker shape of Blackburn's housing development billboard, and Max thought about the type of man who owned so much he might not recognize what he actually owned. If that was the case, did he actually own it? That was a logic knot he was too tired to try to untwist. He did, however, decide that he wanted to go back out and get a look at the salt house in the daylight.

Carson turned on the radio and nimbly flipped the AM band to pick up an all-news station.

"You really are a news junkie, huh?" Max said.

"Keeps me young."

They listened to a story about Congress's push to increase the scanning technology at the border to slow the cartels from flooding the country with fentanyl and whatever the next deadly, addictive drug of choice turned out to be. It was similar to the story he'd heard earlier when Angie had sat next to him. Another surreal moment in a day full of them.

"You don't find the constant bad news demoralizing?"

"I stick to this station mostly," she nodded at the radio. "Don't watch much television. Don't need those images or the sensationalism. I'm good at compartmentalizing. Plus, I have other alternate strategies if things start to get out of whack up here."

Max glanced over and she tapped the side of her head.

"Like what? You knit?"

"No, I smoke."

"I noticed but that seems like fighting a grease fire with olive oil."

"I don't always smoke cigarettes, hon."

CHAPTER TWENTY-FIVE

Carson guided him through a series of lefts and rights until they were driving through an older residential neighborhood north of The Tin Roof and east of the commercial strip with the *Tribune* building. The houses were low, mostly single-story, a mix of stucco and brick in muted shades of yellow and brown with the occasional splash of deeper red. A facade painted in a bright pink flashed through the headlights just to prove the exception. The neighborhood was quiet. Max could see the occasional glow of a television behind closed curtains and lights on in bedrooms. The parked cars were a mix of older pickup trucks and low-cost sensible sedans. The yards were close together.

"It's the last house on the left."

Max pulled into the driveway. A motion-activated light clicked on and illuminated a short driveway leading to a closed garage door and the surrounding front yard. "You don't have to put me up. I'm fine at a hotel. Really."

"I don't live here." She paused. "It's hard times for most folks in TR and likely to get harder unless Blackburn actually pulls off whatever it is he's planning. Even then ..." She didn't finish the thought, but Max could read it on her face: would the deal be worth the cost? Carson continued. "A lot of people are having a tough time getting ends to meet. I thought this might be a small way to help out. The room is clean and neat. A guest room out back, separate from the main house. You'll have your privacy. You can pay, right?"

"Sure. That's not a problem."

"Good." She opened the door and slowly climbed out and walked toward the front door. Max followed and took in more of the surroundings. The house was a brick variant of the ones they'd passed on the surrounding streets. It gave off a slightly ramshackle feel with assorted potted plants and decorative fountains and lawn ornaments filling the front yard under the wide, spanning branches of an old white oak.

The door opened as they approached and a woman in a green fuzzy robe and white slippers stood on the threshold. "Mel, is that you?"

"Yes, Dee. It's me."

"Who's that with you?"

"This is Max. He's going to stay in Daniel's old room for a few days."

As she took a step into the light, Max saw a woman who looked like a diminutive Carson with slight but noticeable differences. She had larger ears under downy gray hair, full cheeks, and a slightly upturned nose. She extended her hand formally with a big, wide-mouthed smile. "My name is Dorothy."

"Max, meet my sister," Carson said.

"Do you like flowers?" Dorothy asked.

"I guess," Max replied.

"What kind? What's your favorite?"

"I'm not sure. I'd have to think about it. My aunt liked peonies and calla lilies."

Dorothy nodded and smiled. "I'm glad you didn't say

roses. Roses are pretty but also the most popular flower in the world. Don't tell anyone, but I get bored with roses."

"Okay, Dorothy. It's late. I'm going to show Max to his room."

"Nice to meet you, Max. I work at The House of Flowers. We have peonies but no calla lilies because it's summer and not spring, but come visit anyway."

Max smiled. "I will."

They walked past Dorothy, down a short hall and into the kitchen. Carson took a key off a hook next to an old rotary phone and then used the slider to exit out into the back yard. "You don't need to go through the house. You can enter around the side, but Dorothy has so many plants and fairy houses and knickknacks scattered about the yard that you'd be risking death by gnome if you attempted it in the dark."

She led him to a small separate outbuilding to the left that may have once been a garage. As if reading his mind, Carson said, "Originally, this was my father's workshop. He was a carpenter. Later, we had it converted to a living space for Daniel. Daniel was my brother, Dorothy's twin. He's since passed."

"I'm sorry."

Carson waved a hand. "More than five years ago though Dee sometimes still talks about him as if he's coming home any time now."

Carson unlocked the door. They walked inside. The air was stale and hot, but the space was neat and clean, almost spartan. The tour took 10 seconds. It was a single room, discounting the bathroom framed into a corner. There was a small galley kitchen to the left, then the bathroom with a small upright shower in the back corner, a single bed and nightstand on the opposite side, and a small loveseat facing an older model flat-screen TV.

"There's a window AC unit." She looked around the space. "Any questions?"

"Dorothy lives alone?"

Carson leaned against the wall. "You ever heard of Williams syndrome?" Max shook his head. "It's rare. Not many people have. We hadn't heard of it until Dee and Dan were almost thirty. Not that there's much we could have done. It's a neurodevelopmental condition characterized by many symptoms. You might have noticed some of the physical features, but it also contributes to delayed development, cognitive challenges, and cardiovascular abnormalities. Still, we, my parents then me, have tried to give them both as normal a life as possible. She's mostly independent. Works at the flower shop in town, as you heard. Has worked there for years. She never forgets a customer or an order. I mean never, literally. Whatever other problems Williams-Beuren syndrome dropped on her, it boosted her memory for names and faces. A home health aide comes by three times a week to check on her. She remembers faces, but sometimes forgets dinner, so the aide helps keep the fridge stocked and makes sure she's eating. Taking care of herself. Things like that. I live across the street. We get by."

It seemed like a practiced speech, a soundbite she'd perfected over the years, but telling it also appeared to wring her out. She suddenly looked tired and deflated and just as small as her sister.

She held out the key and Max took it. "Long day," she said.

"Interesting day."

"The best kind at my age. Too many are long and boring."

With that, she left. Max watched through the window as she walked back to the house. Dorothy was waiting in the kitchen. Carson gave her a hug and then took her gently by the arm and led her out of sight. A minute later, the kitchen light went off and the house went dark.

Max turned the AC unit on high then sat on the bed to unlace his boots. He glanced at the clock mounted on the wall over the kitchenette sink. Late, but maybe not too late.

He took out his phone and checked the Bruins schedule. He smiled. They were out west in Edmonton. She'd be awake. She still held a deep grudge against those 1980s Oiler teams that kept Bourque and Neely from winning a Cup in Boston. He tapped the number from his short contact list and imagined it going up in Texas bouncing off satellites and relay towers before beaming back down into the woods of rural Vermont.

Vic was definitely not asleep. There was no hello or any formalities.

"What's the exchange rate right now? You'd think if these maple leaf loving yahoos were going to cheat and pay off the refs they'd at least find ones that were more subtle about screwing us."

"Not going well?"

"It's tied at two but that's only because we've had one goal called back and they've scored both of theirs on the power play. Two of their six power plays, I might add. Do you know how many we've had?"

"None?"

"That's right. None. Not one. It's like the normal rules of hockey don't apply north of the border. It's the third friggen' period, Max. Do you really think not one weasely Oiler has committed a penalty all night? Fat chance."

She blew out a breath and he knew it had gone to a commercial or she would have continued her commentary. He loved that she still was able to get so invested in a game.

She'd loved hockey as a girl and played at a high level. It was a small piece of their past that they had in common and right now one of the fragile threads that tethered them together. If she'd been born now, or had a few breaks go her way, maybe she would have gone a lot further, but it didn't work out that way. Not all wishes are granted, no matter what the life situation or talent involved. Yet, despite a bitter end to her own playing days, she still loved the game and rarely missed watching her beloved Bruins.

"How's Bailey doing?" Max asked.

Bailey had been severely injured in an attack last year and Max still felt a sense of guilt for bringing it on, even though Vic had long since told him to stop apologizing and trying to take responsibility for other people's actions. Especially the actions of demented psychopaths. Still, seeing visions of Bailey's blood all over the motel's office floor every time he walked in was one of the reasons he left Vermont.

If running kept the blood at bay, how was it the wrong choice?

"He's okay," Vic replied. "Still moves a little slow sometimes in the mornings, but if you didn't know better you probably wouldn't notice. Vet says he's fine."

"Good. Give him a scratch for me."

Max heard the gentle rattling of the dog's tags. The dog had long since forgiven him, he knew. A dog's biggest strength was their large heart and short memory. If only relationships with people were as simple. When he'd left Chepstow, he thought it would be for good. Like all the other times. It was how his life had gone in recent years and seemed destined to continue to go in the future. Max seemed to draw trouble to him like a magnet, and the results often spilled over and hurt innocent people. It was not something he consciously sought out or wanted, but it kept happening and he could not deny his part in that. The easiest and simplest answer was to turn his back, move on, and try again. It was a reaction. Easy and simple. But was it right? These were the questions he kept wrestling with as he ran. Was he just expanding his field of personal destruction? Was he like a tornado that rarely looped back and hit the same place twice but continued to wreak havoc as it moved forward? Was that any better than staying in one place?

He didn't know or wasn't yet ready to look difficult truths full in the face. He was still running but something was making him look over his shoulder this time. It was brittle and delicate, but it was there.

He called and she kept picking up.

"Where are you?" she asked.

"In a small, flat town where the temperature is still in the nineties after dark."

"See anything interesting today?"

"A little." He told Vic about Angie and the bank, then Blackburn and the ranch, then Rose and Carson, and finally the body out by the salt house.

"That's a full day," she said when he'd finished. "You really think you can find this woman? Rose?"

"No. I think she's gone. For good."

"But you're going to stick around for the girl, right?"

"Yes. At least for a few days. Something isn't right. I don't feel good about just walking away."

"Could be nothing. Teenagers are strange creatures."

"True but could be something too."

"Could be," she said and yawned.

He'd told her before about his own daughter. Chepstow, Vermont could be a quiet place and they had had long, rambling talks about many subjects, including Max's past. The good, the bad, and the very ugly. Vic knew the painful costs of those past actions. She didn't bring up Kylie now and he appreciated it.

"Can't hurt to hang around and ask a few questions."

"Be careful, Max."

They said goodbye and Max lay back on the bed.

He hadn't mentioned the fight with the two truckers. A lie by omission? Or was he still hiding parts of himself? And from whom? Before he could answer he fell into a rare deep and dreamless sleep.

Even his ghosts didn't want to deal with the Texas heat.

CHAPTER TWENTY-SIX

Max woke up in his clothes, but the window AC unit had done its job. The small room was ice-cold and he savored the chill, knowing he might not feel it again that day. He stood and stretched. His back was kinked up from too much driving and the old, spongy mattress. Or from approaching forty. No, he decided it was definitely the mattress. He walked outside and retrieved his suitcase from the SUV. It was approaching 6 A.M. He could see the thin orange line of dawn just starting to crease the horizon. He changed into some workout clothes and dug his sneakers out. It was already warm, but it was still pleasant without the direct glare of the sun. He knew if he waited any longer, a run would just be inviting heat stroke and wild rumors of the northern gringo who was stupid enough to try to go for a jog after the sun came up.

He ran the streets of Carson's neighborhood, looping around the cul-de-sacs and dead ends. The streets slowly came to life. People in bathrobes and old cotton T-shirts retrieved newspapers. Lights and televisions were turned on in living rooms. Dogs were let outside. He could almost smell the coffee brewing in the kitchens.

He ran until his shirt was soaked, his back looser, and his legs ached. He walked back toward Dorothy's house and found Carson smoking a cigarette and drinking coffee on her front stoop. He walked up the driveway. The house was the mirror-image of her sister's but with a yellow door, newer roof, and far less plants.

She pointed at him. "I don't trust people who run."

"That right?"

"You know you don't have to do it, right?"

"Helps me think."

"You ever tried these?" She waved the hand holding the cigarette. "Wonderful vice and they also help you think without getting soaking wet. You look ridiculous. Or insane. Maybe both."

"I appreciate the life advice."

"You should. I'm 80 years old and haven't broken a sweat since Eisenhower was in office. And I feel great."

"Good genes?"

"My father was dead of a heart attack by fifty and my mother beat cancer then got hit by a drunk driver, so don't tell me I have good genes or good luck."

"What's your secret then?"

"I'm stubborn and I like my job too much to die."

"We have that much in common then."

She squinted at him. "I was under the impression that up until yesterday you were unemployed."

He turned and started back toward Dorothy's house. He needed a shower and some water. "Okay, we share the stubborn part then."

"Good enough," he heard her say as he went past the garage, through the side gate, and into the back yard.

He hung his shirt on the small fence that bordered a rock

garden. The back yard was full of different plants, shrubs, trees, and garden ornaments. He took off his shoes and socks and left them near the fence. He figured everything would be baked dry by the time he finished shaving.

Inside, he stood in front of the air conditioner and drank three glasses of tap water and checked his watch. He was pretty sure Lawrence only slept a couple hours at night. He called despite the early hour.

Lawrence picked up on the first ring, sounding wide awake. "Despite my affinity for libraries, and librarians I might add. Hey, did I ever tell you the story about what this librarian and I did—"

"Lawrence."

"Right, right. Family show. Where was I?"

"Your affinity for libraries."

"Right. I am not a call-in answering service like a public library."

"I know that. I don't have a question this time. I was just calling to check in on any progress."

"Eddie and I are making progress. Of a sort. This Blackburn guy is proving to be unique."

That got Max's attention. "Oh yeah. How so?"

"I'm not quite ready to say. Give us a little more time. But he is not your Average Joe."

"Take your time on that. I lied before. I do have a question."

"I knew it."

"Can you look up an address based on a license plate?"

"Don't even need to get Eddie for that." Max heard Lawrence moving around and the sounds of keys being tapped. "Okay, give me the plate."

Max recited the Texas plate from memory.

More keys tapping. "Hold on. Okay, got it. That's a rental from Avis."

"Can you get more information? Specifically looking for a name and address."

"I could, but Eddie will be faster. I doubt he's gone to sleep yet. Let me go up there. I'll call you back in ten minutes."

Max showered and shaved and changed into his old jeans and a fresh T-shirt. It was closer to fifteen minutes. He was eating a granola bar from a box he kept in the car and searching the cabinets, without luck, for coffee when Lawrence called back.

"A guy by the name of Reece Kelley rented it for two weeks, returned it yesterday, a week early, with the gas option. The address on the profile is 174 Atlantic Avenue, Suite 8. And before you ask, I looked it up. It's a storefront on the fringes of San Antonio. Suite 8 is home to Key Investigations. It's incorporated as a partnership. One of the partners is Reece Kelley. And before you ask, at the time he founded the business, he lived at 44 Washington Circle in Beaverton, 10 miles south of Atlantic Avenue and just outside the city limits."

"That's perfect, Lawrence. Thank you."

"You're welcome. Do I want to know what you're up to somewhere in Texas?"

"Not yet."

He dropped the joking tone. "You call me if you need me."

"I will."

"Promise? You don't need any more holes in you."

Max glanced at the scar on the back of his hand. "Promise."

"All right then."

. . .

Max put on his boots and retrieved his workout clothes from the yard. They weren't completely dry, the morning was humid, but not too far off. The Texas sun didn't mess around. He looked at the bleached rocks and stone ornaments in the yard and then marveled at how any greenery at all was able to survive. Give nature a crack and she'll find a way, he thought.

He glanced at the small porch and sliding door leading to the main house. The drapes were open, but he didn't see anyone inside. He wanted to say thank you to Dorothy for her hospitality, but it would have to wait. He walked through the side gate. Carson was also gone from her front porch. Max thought about knocking on her door, but presumably she had other ways of getting around town and didn't need him as a chauffeur. He climbed in his car and drove to town. He looked for other options but wasn't surprised when his stomach led him back to The Tin Roof.

Adriana was working and she either didn't recognize him or pretended not to. The place was half full. More guys with the heavyset trucker physique, though none that sent Max's radar pinging. One family in a booth and then scattered singles who looked like local shopkeepers or ranch hands. Adriana led him to an empty two-top table. He didn't need a menu. He ordered coffee, a short stack, scrambled eggs, and a side of bacon. Caffeine, carbs, protein, and fat. The essential macro nutrients in Max's book. He finished his food, plus three cups of coffee, and was on his way out of town before eight o'clock.

He plugged in the address for Key Investigations and followed the directions north. Just as he was about to leave TR in his rearview, he braked and then slowed to such a degree that he caught a few horns from the light traffic. He pulled to the side of the road and let two cars and a pickup truck pass. He mentally replayed the last few minutes and tried to figure out what had snagged his attention. He had been on autopilot with the GPS, letting his thoughts wander. Nothing jumped out at him but something had definitely made him hit the brakes. He'd learned to trust his instincts.

He waited for two tractor trailer trucks to barrel past, one in each direction, then pulled across the two-lane and drove back in the opposite direction. The GPS screeched he was going in the wrong direction, but he ignored it. He drove back two miles and U-turned in a vacant lot and started back in his original direction. The GPS was mollified but his mind wasn't. He swiveled his head to both sides and tried to see everything at once. What had it been?

He drove past competing dollar stores on opposite sides of the street, then a long low building with a red sign that said simply 'Market.' That wasn't it. He drove past a dusty park with a broken set of swings followed by The Sagebrush Inn and then an RV park. He was about to shake off the feeling and continue on toward San Antonio when he passed a cinderblock building painted a bright aquamarine with yellow window frames and a red door. A hand-painted sign out front read Halford Original Jewelry & Unique Gifts. He swung the SUV into the parking lot and stared at the sign. It wasn't the garish building but the sign that had caught his attention. Halford. The name was familiar. Where had he heard it? It took a moment, but it came back to him. Margit Callenbach, the children's librarian, had mentioned Leslie Halford. She was another library trustee and a friend, possibly, of Rose Robideaux.

He pulled out his wallet and found the loose scrap of paper Callenbach had handed him. The phone number matched the one painted on the sign, though the hours were not listed. It was early but maybe Halford was inside. He called the number and it rang ten times before going to voicemail.

Maybe Halford Original Jewelry & Unique Gifts was a by-appointment type place. Or maybe it was just open when it was open. It seemed more like the latter. Maybe the majority of its sales were online now and storefront hours didn't really matter. Max didn't imagine there was much walk-in traffic out here. Other than tractor trailers and smaller work trucks, he hadn't seen much traffic this morning. In fact, during his time in TR, he hadn't seen anyone he might consider a tourist or casual shopper. He wondered how the store survived. Maybe Halford owned the building? Or lived there, too?

He got out of the car and peered through the glass panes in the front door. He could make out some waist-high display cases arranged along one wall and other taller freestanding glass cabinets scattered in the middle and then open shelves along the opposite wall holding knickknacks he couldn't really make out. Large, over-sized prints of the desert hung on the walls. The store was dark and quiet. He walked around the back but other than a matching red door, this one solid with no panes of glass and a heavy-duty deadbolt, and a couple garbage cans, he found nothing of interest. He stood in the shade and tapped to redial the store's number. This time he left a message identifying himself, dropping Callenbach's name and the library, and asking her to call him back. He hoped the vagueness piqued her interest.

He made his way back out front, got in the SUV, and pulled back onto the road and followed it north. He passed electrical wires, rusting cattle fence, and brown grasses that mixed with the occasional tufts of green sage, bee bush, or taller fiddlewoods. Traffic continued to be sparse and consisted mainly of single- and double-barreled long-haul trucks that shook the SUV as they ripped past.

He turned on the radio to break up the silence and listened to the all-news station Carson had turned on the previous night until it turned to static and then he found another AM talker to keep him awake. The run and the big breakfast had left him a little drowsy. The second station had more talk of upgraded border security, but this program wasn't taking callers, rather debating the risks to truckers' health with the larger broad-beam scanners. Based on what he'd witnessed in Tiendas Reales and The Tin Roof, Max thought their diet and sedentary lifestyle more of a risk than any radio or scanning waves. He doubted the program was going to solve the complex border security issue in ten minutes, and he flipped over to the FM band until he found an outlaw country station and Merle Haggard singing about how mama tried.

Two and half hours later, on the outskirts of San Antonio, he pulled into the small shopping center that housed Key Investigations. He hadn't had to make any turns since getting on Route 35 outside TR. The long, single-story building was right off the highway, on a frontage road. Half of the building was taken up by a tile and flooring outfit. Various banners hung off the side advertising different prices and specials. The other half of the building consisted of Key, an injury and accident attorney, an insurance agent, and a dentist. Key Investigations was sandwiched between the dentist on the far end and the insurance place.

Max pulled in and parked alongside two other cars by the dental office. He got out and stretched and looked around. He was still south of the city proper. He could see the taller buildings and urban density in the distance. Maybe Key Investigations had a San Antonio address for their business cards but this was still the far fringes. Max bet Reece Kelley talked to most of his clients over the phone and met them at a place of their choosing. He watched and waited for a few minutes, but despite the lot being half full, nothing happened. When he felt the sweat start to run down his back, he walked to the door of Key Investigations and went inside.

Even though the address was on the fringes, Kelley, or at least someone, had made an effort inside. Max was slightly surprised. Maybe he'd underestimated Reece Kelley. There was a waiting area, a reception desk, and two doors, now closed, presumably to offices in the back. The space was small, but the furniture looked new and matched. The gray carpet was clean. A large plant stood in the corner and some magazines were fanned out on a table by a couch.

A woman that Max judged to be in her late forties sat behind the reception desk and smiled as he came inside and blinked in the dimmer office space. "May I help you?" she asked.

"Is Mr. Kelley in?"

"Do you have an appointment?"

Max glanced over at the empty couch, and she continued, "I meant, is he expecting you?"

"No, I don't think so."

"Unfortunately, Mr. Kelley isn't here right now. I'm sorry, if you had called or scheduled something ..."

"Do you expect him back soon? I don't mind waiting."

"No, I don't think he'll be back soon. If you want to leave your name and number and any other details, I can pass them along to him or you can set up a day and time to come back."

Max thought about it and thought about what he'd seen outside Blackburn's ranch yesterday. Did he want to give Kelley his name and number? Did he want to give the man a heads up? No, he didn't want Kelley rehearsing or editing his answers. He didn't necessarily think Kelley would try to mislead him, but Max found it was typically better to get people talking naturally, on the spot, than give them time to prep.

"That's all right," he replied. "I was just passing by and

thought I'd stop in. I go by a lot. I'll just try again another day."

She gave him another smile and told him to have a good day.

He went back out to the SUV and started the ignition for the air conditioning but didn't leave. He kept his eyes on the front door of Key Investigations. Max thought there were now two possibilities. First, Kelley really wasn't there and the woman was telling the truth. In which case nothing would happen. Maybe she'd make a note and pass it along, but he doubted it. What would she say? He hadn't given a name or reason for coming by. Second, Kelley was inside one of the offices with the closed doors and had either been listening or she was now telling him about the walk-in stranger. If the latter were true, it would likely provoke a reaction. Someone might come to the door and look out.

He gave it five minutes. Nothing happened. A third possibility was that Max was overthinking this. The woman was probably in there trying to decide what glossy magazine to read next. She likely had already forgotten his face. He plugged in the second address from Lawrence and then pulled onto the frontage road and back onto the freeway. He crossed an east-west interchange and Route 35 became Route 10. Five miles later, the GPS directed him off the freeway onto surface streets. The neighborhood appeared solidly middle-class. Single-family homes, fences, yards, some in better shape than others. Reece Kelley's was tan brick on a corner lot. The grass was spotty and shaggy in places, but otherwise the house looked well maintained. He parked on the street and got out.

There was a navy-blue Honda Accord in the driveway. A tricycle was tipped over by the side door. As he walked up the driveway, he could see the edge of a patio around back with a grill and lawn chairs. All the shades on the street-facing windows were pulled low. He could hear a window unit air conditioner running somewhere. A big, leafy oak provided half the house some shade. He glanced up and down the street. Everything was quiet in the midday heat. He stepped up on the stoop and knocked on the screen door. He stepped back and listened. He heard nothing over the rattle and hum of the air conditioner from the back of the house. It sounded like a real beast. It would have to be, to keep up with the Texas heat. He stepped up and knocked again. This time he heard, or felt, movement inside the house.

The door swung open, and Max found himself staring into the ugly black eye of a pump action shotgun.

CHAPTER TWENTY-SEVEN

Max forced himself to look away from the gun barrel to the face behind it. Reece Kelley looked both wired and exhausted at the same time. His eyes were rimmed with red, and his hair was matted and oily. The man he'd seen wearing the suit at the Double R just the day before was long gone. Max forced himself to remain still. A blind nun could hit him with that gun from six feet. The screen door would be as effective as notebook paper in shielding him. Reece Kelley might look disheveled, but he also looked like he knew how to handle the shotgun.

"Who the hell are you?" Kelley asked in a hoarse voice. "Do you work for him?"

"Who?"

"Blackburn." Kelley squinted out at him from the gloom of the house. "You do, don't you? I recognize you. You were at the ranch. Tell me why I shouldn't just blast you back into the street. You're trespassing in my yard. It's within my rights."

"Slow down. My name is Max. Yes, I saw you yesterday at the Double R."

"So, you do work for him?"

"Not exactly."

"Speaking in riddles isn't helping your case. Do you or don't you?"

"Can I get something out of my pocket?"

Kelley nodded. "Real slow."

Max dipped two fingers into his front pocket and pulled out the piece of paper. He unfolded it and held it out so Kelley could see it. It was the check Blackburn had given him yesterday. It had already been made out to cash and was sitting on the desk while they talked. "I believe this is yours," Max said. The man now had a choice. Open the door and take the check or ignore the money and keep threatening Max. He stood there and Max could see his mind running through the various probabilities. "A man should be paid for an honest day's work, right?"

"Why are you here? How did you find me?" Kelley wasn't ready to give in yet.

"I'm here because even if I didn't take the money Blackburn owed you," Max waved the check, "I can tell something hinky is going on and Blackburn is in the thick of it despite what he claims. And I don't want any of it affecting his daughter."

"Angie."

"That's right. Angie. You were working this before me. If you're done, I thought maybe you could at least fill me in and give me a leg up."

Kelley shook his head. "Shit, man, you have no idea what you've stumbled into. Hinky doesn't even begin to describe it." He lowered the gun and looked out at the street. Not just a glance. A good look in both directions. "You better come inside."

"You want coffee?" Kelley asked. "I just made a fresh pot."

The blinds were drawn and the kitchen was dim, just a single overhead fixture illuminated the dated cabinets and patterned linoleum floor. The man's nervous energy made the room feel even smaller and darker. Max thought coffee was probably the last thing Kelley needed. He looked at the man's dancing eyes and wondered if caffeine was the only thing he'd taken.

Still, Max would prefer a cup of coffee in the man's hands more than the shotgun. "Sure, I'll take a cup."

Kelley leaned the gun against the cabinets, still within reach, and opened a cabinet to get two mugs.

Max looked around some more. He glanced into the family room that led off the kitchen. Or tried to. All the shades and blinds were pulled in that room, too. He could make out the sliding door that led to the patio. A sofa, two chairs, and a corner filled with children's toys. The air conditioner he'd heard from the street hung from a rear window. He turned back to the kitchen as Kelley brought the mugs over to the table, then he brought the shotgun over and set it against the chair next to him. The one with a child's booster seat strapped to it.

Max sat opposite and nodded at the shotgun. "What happened?"

"What do you mean?"

Max didn't know if the man was being deliberately obtuse or was just too shook up to think straight. "I saw you yesterday at the ranch. It wasn't a good situation, but you weren't like this. Last I saw, Hull was kicking you off the property. You'd been fired, I assume, but I didn't get the sense that it was so bad that you'd answer the doorbell with a Mossberg."

"That's true. I drove out of there with a bruised ego and a dirty suit, shorted on some cash too, but I thought that was the end of it. I was actually relieved. I took the job because it paid well, and the business is still getting established. We can't really afford to turn away any clients, especially ones who put up the retainer and clearly have deep pockets."

"So what changed?"

"I got home and found my wife frantic. Almost out of her mind. And that is very much out of character for her." He turned and took a phone off the counter from behind him. He unlocked it, flipped to a screen, and then slid it across the table. Max picked it up and looked at it. It was a direct message on Facebook. The sender's avatar was a horse head. The name was SmartyJones75. The message showed a photo of a young girl, maybe three or four years old, on a swing at a playground. A woman with blonde hair was smiling and pushing her in the background.

"There's a second photo," Kelley said, his voice cracking.

Max swiped and felt a pit in his stomach and now understood why Kelley had the shotgun close at hand. The second photo was shot through the kitchen window. Max recognized the wallpaper. The same girl was sitting at the table smiling and eating grapes while the woman sat next to her. There was a caption in all capital letters below the second photo: DO NOT PUT YOUR FAMILY IN ANY MORE DANGER. STAY AWAY FROM TR. There was a link, too.

"Don't click the link," Kelley said in a tired voice. "You don't want to see it. It's one of those narco videos. It's graphic."

"This is your wife and daughter in the pictures, I assume."

"Yes."

"Your house obviously."

"Yes."

"They're safe now?"

"I don't know about safe, but they are a long way from here. Even I don't know specifically where they are. I didn't want to know. In case ..." Kelley trailed off.

"In case they come back."

"Yes. It's why I've been up all night. And why I'm carrying around the shotgun. Part of me wants them to come back, you know? Just sitting around and waiting? Doing nothing, but imagining things? That's worse."

"You said them. Who's them?"

"I have no idea. The whole thing makes little sense. If Blackburn or his goons are trying to scare me off, then why hire me in the first place? Why try to stiff me on payment and humiliate me in the driveway? If they wanted me to stop and just put the whole thing aside, why not just pay me and send me on my way?"

Max shrugged. Kelley had a point. "You said the link is a narco video. Did you find any evidence that Blackburn was mixed up with the cartels or gangs or drugs?"

"No, nothing like that. Nothing that even hinted in that direction other than his ranch's proximity to the border."

Max picked up the phone again and tapped on the horse head avatar. The profile was private but there were ways around that. But then Kelley spoke up. "The profile is garbage. A dead end."

"You got a look at it?"

"I'm pretty good with tech stuff. It was just set up recently. Fake information. No followers. No friends. Just a cutout. The equivalent of a burner phone."

Max thought Kelley was probably right, but he thought he might have Lawrence or Eddie double-check. There might be some digital fingerprints somewhere that might be helpful. "I got some guys. You mind?" Kelley shrugged. Max took out his own phone and snapped a photo of Kelley's screen then put the phone back on the table and tried to make sense of the threat. Kelley was right; it didn't make a lot of sense. "I think we're missing a piece of the puzzle. Or one of the players. How long did you work for Blackburn?"

"A week, give or take. Eight days."

"That's a week longer than me. Do you have a file or notes that you don't mind sharing?"

Kelley thought about it for a minute and then nodded. "If it gets me out of this nightmare, it's worth a try." He stood up and walked out of the room. He left the shotgun behind. Max took that as a sign of progress. Kelley returned a minute later carrying a laptop and a file folder thick with papers. He opened the laptop, and they spent a half hour going through his case file. Most of it jibed with what Max had learned from Serrato, Callenbach, Carson, and Blackburn himself. The one place Kelley had more information was Blackburn's various business interests.

They spent the next thirty minutes going through the financial information Kelley had accumulated. Max was comfortable with numbers, but this was next level. It was approaching forensic accounting. He asked as many questions as he could, and Kelley took him through some spreadsheets two and three times. "Sorry. I used to be at Pinkerton before I went into business for myself. Financial and computer crime."

"Don't apologize, just don't expect me to completely follow this trail. It's like reading a foreign language."

"That's exactly what it is. Numbers are their own type of language."

"And Blackburn is fluent?"

"Blackburn or someone working for him."

"Blackburn hired you to find Rose, right?"

"Yes."

"Why so much background on Blackburn and his businesses?" Max felt Kelley studying him.

"You think he killed her, don't you?" Max eventually said.

"I wouldn't go that far. But everyone else even close to this thing is an open book. Everyone except Blackburn. Even if he was the guy who hired me, as strange as it sounds, Blackburn himself seemed like the best lead to pursue. Like the social media threat, I don't know why he'd do that, but I checked out everyone else. He was the only one left."

"You're not the first person to say that." Max thought back to Serrato and her Sherlock Holmes quote. *Whatever remains, however improbable, must be the truth.* "He was cleared by the police. No one was looking to reopen this."

"I've thought about that, too. The only thing that makes any sense to me is politics. Blackburn wants to run, and he thinks the ambiguity over Rose's disappearance is going to hurt him. He wants to say he was cleared by the police and he did everything possible to find her, including putting up his own money and hiring private investigators. My other thought was that he's pressure testing his old alibi and having PIs look into it. Like a vetting process before the press gets after it."

Those were solid theories. Blackburn was either truly innocent or very confident. "Did you find any indications of him running for office."

Kelley's face fell. "None. But that doesn't mean that angle is dead." Max watched Kelley's eyes brighten again as a new thought occurred to him. "Maybe he's not the candidate. Maybe he's the money."

"What do you mean?"

"You've seen how he's insinuated his way into Tiendas Reales, right?"

"Yes."

"He owns or influences just about everything that goes on there and surely reaps the benefits. Money, respect, power, control. Maybe he's looking to scale that approach. If there is one thing that drives modern politics, it's money. It's so out in the open now that it's been normalized for most people. It used to be that contributions to political candidates or

campaigns were severely limited and included a lot of disclo-
sures. That's no longer the case." Now Kelley's eyes went
distant as he thought this new angle through. Then he pulled
the folder closer and started rifling through it again. Max
kept quiet and let Kelley follow whatever was twisting his gut.
After a minute of searching, Kelley started talking again.
"What if Blackburn is now giving money to politicians or offi-
cials outside of TR? You don't contribute money without
expecting something in return."

"Aren't there laws against that?"

"If you have enough or give enough, I don't think the laws
apply to you."

Max could feel them veering off into different waters.
"But what does he ultimately want? And how does this relate
to Rose's disappearance?"

Kelley shrugged. "I have no idea. They might not be
connected at all. Which might be why I got fired."

"None of Blackburn's companies are public, right? How
did you even get any financial statements on them?"

"You're right, as a private company, they have no obliga-
tion to share most of this financial information with the
public. This is just the tip of the iceberg on Blackburn and
just the bare essentials the company needs to disclose to
investors or potential buyers in his real estate venture. You
saw the billboards going in and out of town?"

"Yes, I've seen them."

"This is a prospectus for anyone looking to invest."

"How did you end up with it?"

"A little social engineering with the business office."

"Find anything useful?"

"Might depend on how you define useful. It shows Blackburn, or his real estate subsidiary at least, is on very solid
financial footing with a lot of liquid cash."

"Has he pre-sold a lot of the lots?"

"No, none as far as I can tell."

"He hasn't sold any?"

"No."

"So where is the cash coming from? Investors?"

"I don't know. I can't tell that from these documents."

"I don't think the Double R is throwing off any profits."

"No, not enough to fund all of this. He does have this other shipping and receiving depot. I couldn't get anything on that, not even a phone number, but that could be the source of the cash."

Max remembered Carson telling him about Blackburn's grand plans including the new warehouse. He needed to follow up with her and get more information. "I'm not sure any of this helps us find out what happened to his wife. It might just be a distraction."

"I don't know if we can say that for sure," Kelley replied.

Max thought about that. Was that true? Did knowing more about Blackburn's business help them get closer to finding Rose? Or was it just Kelley trying to convince himself that all this paper was worth something. "It's never a bad idea to follow the money. Maybe Blackburn's not ultimately responsible for her disappearance but maybe he or his business did something that led to it," Max finally said.

Kelley stood up and refreshed their coffee.

"Did you find out anything about Blackburn before he came to Texas?" Max asked.

"That's a very good question and I don't have a very good answer. I traced him to Oklahoma in the late nineties and then the trail goes very cold. He was a ghost before coming to the TR."

Max knew something about ghosts.

CHAPTER TWENTY-EIGHT

"Millions of people are ghosts in this country," Lawrence said.

"By choice?"

"Some by choice. Some inadvertently."

Max had left Kelley to dig through the spreadsheets to try to follow Blackburn's money. It was both something Kelley would be better at than Max, and it would keep him away from Tiendas Reales. They both hoped that a few days of what appeared to be normal activity from Kelley and away from anything that appeared to be the Blackburn case would convince whoever was behind the threats that Kelley was off the case.

Kelley had also promised to get some sleep. He was practically out on his feet despite the coffee when Max left. If Kelley came up dry on the financial angle, Max could always ask Lawrence to take a look. Max had no doubt that Lawrence knew a few tricks to moving money.

Max was driving south again and called Lawrence. Kelley might be working the money, but Max still wanted to know more about Blackburn's background. The fact that he appeared to have no past, or was trying to conceal it, made Max uneasy. No one went to those lengths without a reason. Maybe it wouldn't explain Rose's disappearance, but he thought it might explain something about Blackburn's motivations.

"How do you inadvertently start living under a different identity?" Max asked.

"Probably as a child. And you probably have no idea. Maybe you're adopted and never go back and update the original birth certificate. Maybe your parents raised you under a different name."

"Why do that?"

"Probably to game the government somehow. Get extra benefits."

"Which then leaves a lot of genuine identities laying around that no one is using."

"Now you're catching on. It is possible to fabricate an identity from scratch, you are proof of that, but it is not easy. Building all that documentation so that it's reliable is difficult, expensive, and time consuming. It is far easier to assume the identity of a real person. Someone whose birth is documented."

"That makes sense, in theory, but how do you go about finding these phantom identities that no one is using?"

"I've never done it, but I can think of two ways. One, the easiest way, is that you know someone who is in the position of growing up under an assumed name. You can take their original name. Second, you can try searching for birth records without corresponding death records and no further history. It's not foolproof, but it would probably give you a good place to start in order to find a person who's not using the name on their documented birth certificate."

"So, if Blackburn did something like that, it will likely be next to impossible to trace him back to his original or true identity."

"That's right."

"Damn. It was a Hail Mary, but I was hoping that there was something in his background that would help explain both what and why he's doing all this."

"If you can't know a man's thoughts, know the total of his experience."

"Exactly."

Max and Lawrence both shared a keen appreciation for research and preparation when doing a job.

"But listen, I didn't say that was the only way to create a new identity. It's just one way. If you can't assume the identity of a living person, the next best thing is to assume one of the dead. The online records make the old graveyard trick of paper tripping harder, but not impossible."

"Paper tripping?"

"The old identity swap method where you walk a grave-yard and find an infant who died in your same birth year. You then obtain a new identity by using that name to get a birth certificate and build the rest from there. Pre-internet it worked well enough but today it's more risky and not quite as effective."

"What would *you* do?"

"Now you're asking the right question. If I didn't have Eddie or access to some world-class forgers, I would look in a couple of different places. First, the childhood friends, like I mentioned. Going with someone's history that you know is the best and safest bet. Even better if the childhood friend is deceased."

"Jesus, that's dark."

"Listen, the type of person who does this is usually not on the up-and-up."

"What about battered spouses? Aren't they on the up-and-up?"

"Okay, they are the exception that proves the rule. But if your knickers are getting twisted over the dead childhood friend, you're not going to like my other ideas."

"All right, I'll keep my morals in check. Go on."

"Okay, the paper tripping thing can still work but I wouldn't waste time combing through cemeteries, too creepy and time consuming. Instead, I'd focus on small rural towns with a lower likelihood of computerized recordkeeping. I'd go through the obituaries of the local newspaper and see if I got lucky with a person close to my age, gender, and ethnicity."

"Makes sense. Anything else?"

"One more method comes to mind. I'd check natural disasters, specifically those that occurred outside the country. Plane crashes, train derailments, unfortunate accidents. That sort of thing. If the death happened outside the U.S., it would be rare if the record systems tied the birth and death together. If the person fit the profile, it wouldn't be too hard to assume their identity."

"I feel like I need a shower."

"You know what they say about wrestling pigs in the mud."

"You get dirty and the pig likes it. I know. But, while I appreciate your insights into the criminal mind, I'm not sure it gets us closer to Blackburn. If this is even what he did. We don't know for sure."

"Eddie and I are both pretty sure he grabbed this Blackburn identity. If not, we would have found at least a trace of him somewhere. Your Alex Blackburn just pops up wholesale about fifteen years ago. At a glance, all the numbers, social, DOB, demographics fit but go a layer deeper and there is very little backing it up. There's no history."

This, Max thought, was the biggest hole in Kelley's politics theory. Blackburn's past, or lack thereof, was easily checked by any reporter.

"So we're back to the question of who he was before Alex Blackburn. Is it significant to this case and is it possible to even bridge that gap and find out his true identity?" Max said.

"It's a big missing piece, so it will likely tell you something. He is who he is now because of his past. You don't go through this much effort for no reason."

"What do you think? Can we dig him out?"

"I think we have to try."

"How?

"I think we start with a couple assumptions, otherwise it's a needle in a haystack. First, we know Alex Blackburn appeared in Oklahoma; we know the year and we know his approximate age. That will all help backtrack him. Finally, I'm guessing here but it's what I would do, and this guy doesn't seem dumb, he likely picked someone whose secondary characteristics were similar to his in some major ways. All of that should help us cut down on the search pool."

"It sounds like you already started."

"Eddie likes a challenge almost as much as his Red Vines."

CHAPTER TWENTY-NINE

Max disconnected with Lawrence and dropped the phone in the cup holder. He spent the empty highway miles thinking it all through again. He liked to think of this as his gathering lint phase. It was what he used to do when he was researching and casing a potential job. He just sucked up as much information as he could. Some of it would ultimately be irrelevant and some of it would ultimately be critical. He was never sure which would be which at this phase. He just took it all in and sorted it out as new information came to light.

He was so deep in his head wondering about Blackburn and his motives that he almost missed the truck. He was thirty minutes north of Tiendas Reales and traffic had once more thinned to a trickle. He'd gone ten or fifteen miles and only passed a handful of other vehicles. He'd exited the highway and was now back on the familiar two-lane state road. The pavement was worn and cracked. The painted lane markers were faded and mere suggestions after years of expanding, contracting, and baking in the heat. The tractor trailer was approaching from the opposite direction. The land was flat, and the road spun out like a ribbon into the distance. Max could see the truck coming a long way off. The sun glinted off the cab's chrome. As it came closer, he could make out more details. It was an old, red Peterbilt with that distinctive cab shape and exhaust stacks on each side with a square upright grill between flared headlights. It was a beast of a truck that dwarfed Max's SUV.

It was also driving on the wrong side of the road barreling directly at Max.

It was still a mile or more down the road and Max assumed that maybe the driver was distracted and had drifted over the barely visible double yellow. He tapped his horn a few times, but the truck didn't deviate or show any signs of moving over. Max frowned and hit the horn again. This time, he held it down longer. No response. Maybe the driver was disoriented or running on too little sleep, or too many stimulants, to hit a delivery deadline? The sun was at Max's back and was shining directly into the cab. Max couldn't see the driver through the windshield. Maybe the driver couldn't see the SUV he was about to squish like a bug? Maybe he didn't even realize he was in the wrong lane? Both vehicles were moving quickly and the distance was closing fast. Max let up on the gas and glanced in his mirrors. No one behind him. Max steered the car into the opposite lane. The big Peterbilt followed. Max's hands tightened on the wheel. Maybe his lane change had cut through the guy's fog. No harm, no foul. Max steered back into the correct lane.

The truck followed.

Clearly, this wasn't a case of highway hypnosis or a careless, distracted driver. This was deliberate. This truck wanted to run Max off the road, or worse, and Max now had just seconds to figure out a way to outmaneuver the truck and not end up as Texas roadkill.

He checked the mirrors again. Still empty. That would

help. More cars would just mean more potential victims and more obstacles to avoid. His biggest advantage was the SUV's handling and responsiveness but much of that was negated by the narrow road and the quickly closing distance. There was a steep drainage ditch to the right, so he didn't think he could bail out to that side and keep the car upright. He also didn't think he'd be able to slide by on the road before the truck could react in some way and possibly clip the SUV with the trailer. That left only one viable option. When in doubt, go with the unexpected. He punched the gas and the SUV leaped forward. He tried to time it in his head.

Three.

The key was not to oversteer. Max knew the SUV had all sorts of driver-assist technology to keep the car on the road.

Two.

He probably could disable it, but not right now.

One.

If he tried to override or fight it, he guessed he'd only make it worse. He was out of time.

He nudged the steering wheel left and let the car do its job. The SUV cut across the road. The truck tried to match his movement, but the SUV was moving too fast now. The SUV's left wheels went off the road and kicked up a huge plume of dust and visibility quickly shrank to just feet. Max heard rocks and shrubs bang and scrape off the undercarriage, but the car held steady. The big tractor loomed out of the dusty haze and passed so close it might have skimmed a layer of paint off the SUV's exterior, but it didn't make contact. Max gripped the wheel tight and fought the instinct to turn the SUV farther away from the threat. The car was buffeted up briefly onto the two left wheels by the punch of rough air trailing in the truck's wake. Max took his foot off the gas pedal as the SUV settled back down on all four wheels and then rolled to a stop. The dust cloud rolled over the car. Max let out a shaky breath and looked in the rearview mirror. He could barely see through the murky air but could just make out the fading twin red dots of the trailer's taillights. The truck hadn't slowed. It kept on speeding away in the opposite direction, now in the correct lane.

Max put his head down on the wheel and tried to catch his breath. The adrenaline made him feel loose and light-headed as if his brain was free-floating outside of his skull. He sat up and stared at his hands until they stopped shaking. What the hell had just happened? A bored trucker playing a dangerous game with a random driver or something else? Movement behind him caught his attention. The dust cloud was clearing and settling as if nothing had happened. Something on the horizon. A flash in the mirror. Something was coming. He watched it come into focus.

It was a truck. A different one. A blue one. But it was coming on just as fast. Coming for him or just coming down the road? Max had an eerie sense that it was not a coincidence. He felt as if the steel grill of the approaching truck was grinning at him, an apex predator that has spotted its prey. Maybe it was just paranoia or maybe not. Either way, he didn't feel like taking the chance. Max also did not like how vulnerable he felt sitting in a stationary car. He pressed down on the gas pedal to get the SUV back on the road. The car rolled forward and then stalled out. Max hit the start button on the dash. The engine coughed but didn't turn over. Damn. He quickly scanned the dashboard gauges. Gas tank was half full. Engine wasn't overheating. Nothing was beeping or blinking.

He glanced up at the mirror. The truck was still coming, resolving more by the second through the settling dust. Maybe a mile, Max judged. Less than 60 seconds. Wait. The dust. The dirt and dust must have clogged up the SUV's air filter or thrown off the fuel mix sensor. Not a difficult problem to solve, time would mostly fix it for him, unfortunately time was the one thing in short supply right now. He tried the ignition button again. It didn't catch but it almost did. Max punched it again. He didn't dare look up. He didn't need to, some primal instinct told him to run, that his life might depend on it.

This time, the engine caught and held. Barely. It was weak and sounded like it might give out any second. Max feathered the gas and the car responded. But it was agonizingly slow. If he could find some clear air that would help and the engine should recover. He steered the SUV back on the road and put the pedal to the floor. He didn't have the luxury of being gentle any longer. The engine whined in protest, but didn't stall, and eventually the car picked up speed and kept moving.

The noise increased to a thunderous pitch before Max realized it wasn't inside his head or from the SUV. His eyes flicked up. The sharp teeth of the truck's grill filled the mirror completely. There was a loud bang and the SUV lurched violently forward. Max gripped the wheel and just managed to keep the SUV under control and on the road. The truck struck him from behind again.

The steering wheel was wrenched out of his grip and Max felt the SUV slide to the right and onto the dirt shoulder. Time slowed and inched forward in tiny increments. Max watched the truck leap forward again. Its big grill and bumper clipped the back panel of the SUV. The weight of the car shifted. The SUV hit the edge of the drainage ditch, the tires lifted, and the SUV started to roll. Max tried to let his body go limp. He felt the seatbelt bite hard into his shoulder and then his world went upside down. Then right side up again. He watched a crack spread across the windshield before it shattered into tiny fragments. Heat and glass and dust filled the cab. The airbags exploded. He felt a hot pain sear his arm. He sucked in a huge gulp of dusty air. Then he was upside down again. He heard the metal shriek as it bent and crumpled. Then more glass breaking. A sharp pain sliced across his scalp. The SUV rolled a final time, rocked up on two wheels, and then miraculously settled back down on all four.

Max unclipped his seatbelt and tried to open the door. He couldn't find the handle through the deflated airbag. He pushed the material aside until he found the door latch. It was jammed shut and wouldn't budge. Then he noticed the driver's side window was gone. The window looked smaller somehow. He cleared a few remaining shards of glass and carefully pulled himself through the window and climbed out. He looked around. The second truck was now almost gone from sight. He looked in the other direction. The road was empty. He turned back around. The SUV was totaled. The back and side panels of the car were smashed in where the truck had hit it. The roof was crumpled from the rollover. *That explained the smaller window*, he thought, then he turned and threw up. His head felt heavy. He needed to flag someone down or call for help. He felt in his pocket for his phone, but it was gone. He suddenly felt very cold. Then felt sweat pop on his forehead. *I'm in shock,* Max thought. He took two steps toward the road and then found his cheek pressed to the hot dirt. He watched an ant carry a piece of food up and into its nest. Max sat up and immediately regretted it. He felt like he was still in the rolling car. He needed to get to the road. He tried to get to his feet a second time but fell over again.

This time he didn't get back up.

PART TWO

CHAPTER THIRTY

He swam back to consciousness. Or was pulled. The dark nothing was soft and inviting. It was a warm bath that invited him to linger. He was reluctant to open his eyes. He wanted to stay in the simple comfort of the void. When he finally relented and allowed himself to be pulled to the surface, there was more darkness. A shadow stood at the foot of the bed. The shape looked familiar, the slope of the shoulders, the neck, the hair, something, but the harder he tried to focus, the less he saw. It was a dark shape in an even darker room.

The inky shadow moved closer. Max tried to lift his arms to protect himself, but he couldn't. He strained, desperate to move, but his arms and legs wouldn't respond. A spike of panic shot through him. What was happening? He looked down, a blanket covered his body.

The shadow moved closer. There was a buzzing, static. The shadow was saying something, but Max only shook his head. Or tried to. He couldn't understand. His mind felt slow and cloudy. His only thought was to get away from the shadow. He needed his arms and legs to respond. He willed them to listen. There was no response. He felt sweat run into his eyes. More static filled his ears.

The shadow moved closer still and then there was a burst of white. A lightning bolt cleaved his head in two and made him squeeze his eyes shut and turn his head away. The light was worse than the shadow. He tasted blood in his mouth. He tried to scream, anything to escape, to distract, or bring help, but there was something in his mouth. No sound came out.

He struggled harder. He heard more static, more noise, but the light was still there. He could feel it trying to wrench his eyelids open. He shook his head, the only thing he could move, and tried to burrow down into the softness below him to escape. But he was held fast. There was no escape. Nowhere to go. Just when he thought he couldn't bear it any longer, he felt warmth quickly spread through his body and push the pain back. Behind the heat, he felt the comfortable water roll back in and cover him up. He slumped back in relief and drifted off into the dark sea.

The next time he woke, the shadow was gone. The searing pain from the light was gone. His mind felt clearer. He felt sluggish and very sore, but more like himself. He instantly knew he was in a hospital. He looked around. He was alone in a small room. Beeps and soft hisses of monitors came from his left. The blinds covering the windows to the right were closed but he could see sunlight poking between the plastic slats. An armchair and small bedside table were squeezed into the space between the bed and the windows. A pink plastic water pitcher and matching glass sat on the table. He lay back on the pillow. The smell of solvents and disinfectants came from everywhere. He remembered the panic of being unable to move earlier; he wiggled his toes and fingers and felt a flood of relief. All good there. He lifted his arm and saw scrapes and abrasions covered in antiseptic goo. He still had a headache, quite a good one, but the soft overhead lights didn't feel like someone was jamming an icepick into his eye.

Okay, he was in a hospital with injuries. What had happened? How had he gotten here? He remembered The Alamo. He remembered San Antonio and then driving down to the border and looking at the Rio Grande. He remembered the blistering heat and the circling vultures and ... then things started to get choppy. His memories became a stuttering slideshow of places and faces that he didn't understand. It all felt vaguely familiar but just out of reach, like a film he'd seen years ago but now only remembered scattered bits of the plot.

The door opened and a small woman in navy scrubs walked in. She wore no makeup and her light brown hair was pulled back in a tight ponytail that lifted the edges of her forehead.

"You're awake."

Max didn't know if that was a question or a statement. She didn't look like she was waiting for an answer as she bustled around his bedside, checking monitors and IV lines, but he replied anyway to fill the silence.

"Yes." His throat was sore, and his voice sounded raspy.

She glanced at something on his head that he couldn't see then picked up his arm and checked a pad of gauze and bandage there. Satisfied, she straightened the sheets and blankets around his legs before she turned back to him.

"Are you in pain?"

Max thought about it. He ached but he wasn't in any acute pain.

"No."

She nodded. "The doctor will be in shortly."

"Okay."

They made quite a conversational duo.

Ten minutes later, a thin man who looked like a marionette dressed up in a doctor's coat came into the room. He was all pointy arms and elbows with sharp facial features to match. He carried a tablet, Max assumed it was his hospital chart, read it as he walked. He gave off the air of a man who was always in a hurry to be somewhere else. Maybe it was a symptom of the job. Too many patients, too little time.

"I'm Dr. Collato," he said. He didn't look up, or make eye contact, but stopped near the bed.

Like the nurse, Max wasn't sure how, or if, he was expected to respond.

"Max." For a moment, he couldn't recall his current last name then it popped into his head. "Parish."

Collato dropped the tablet on the end of the bed and looked directly at him. His eyes were pale blue. "You are a very lucky man, Mr. Parish."

"What happened?"

"You don't remember?"

Some things had come back just in the time between the nurse's exit and Collato's arrival. He remembered meals at The Tin Roof. Seeing Angie by the bank. Then Blackburn and his ranch. Serrato. Carson. But whatever happened to put him here remained mostly opaque.

"Things are patchy. It's like seeing snapshots without context. I remember a truck. A tractor trailer, I think. Coming up behind me. Very fast. Too fast." Max paused then shook his head. "The rest is gone."

Collato nodded his head. "How about further back? Can you remember anything from say, last week?"

Max nodded. "Yes, I remember that. I remember my name obviously and I remember driving south through

Kentucky and Tennessee." He had gone around Nashville but stopped on the outskirts of Memphis, lured by the barbeque and live music, rather than the crowds of Nashville. He'd been rewarded. He'd stopped at Annie's Hideaway. A small place that cultivated local and regional acts on the edge of east Memphis. He'd had a plate of shatteringly crispy fried chicken with a side of spaghetti and listened to an instrumental duo, a fiddler and a guitar player, that was more West Virginia hills than Memphis soul, but he didn't hear anyone complaining and saw more than one foot tapping. There was a reason that type of music had endured as long as it had and with those two, Max had thought, it appeared to be in good hands for at least a little longer, but he didn't think the doctor wanted his opinion on that. He looked like the type of self-serious man who might only dance at gunpoint.

"Further back? Last year?" Collato asked now.

He thought about Vermont and Vic. "Yes, I can remember that."

"Okay, good." He took out a small penlight and shined it in both of Max's eyes. "That's a fairly common symptom with car crashes. And you were in a doozy, Mr. Parish. I'll let the police fill you in on the details, if you wish, but you were lucky to escape with as few injuries as you did."

"But not my short-term memory."

"Those memories might return in time. That type of memory loss after head trauma is called retrograde amnesia. It's the partial or complete inability to recall the recent past, but it leaves long-term memories prior to the trauma intact."

"Why does it happen? Do I have a concussion?"

It wouldn't be the first, Max thought, and he felt an uneasiness thinking about the long-term cumulative effects head injuries might have on his health, but then the doctor was talking again.

"To answer your second question, yes, you have a concussion, grade 2, I'd say. The car's safety features did their job, or it would have been much worse. As to your first question, we don't really know why it happens. How the mind creates and stores memories is still largely a mystery to modern science and not well understood."

"Will I ever remember the accident or the last few hours before it?"

"I can't say for certain, each person is different, but yes, typically memories do return given time and proper recovery."

Max felt a sense of relief. There was something about not having control over his own mind that scared Max more than any physical injury.

Collato continued the exam and looked at Max's arm while he spoke. "I saw some of the photos in the newspaper about the accident. It really is amazing that you are in such good shape. You're either very lucky or have a very good car."

"Maybe a little of both," Max said. He thought about Carson and wondered if she wrote the story Collato had read in the paper. Maybe she could help fill in the blanks.

"Other than the concussion, you appear to have sustained only superficial abrasions, basically cuts and scrapes. You avoided any real penetrating injuries." He checked the bandage on Max's head before moving down to his legs. He pulled the blanket back. "Move your toes for me. Okay, good." He picked up the tablet again and made a few notes with a stylus. "The head wound you have is what we were really worried about. Initially, we thought it was more of an impact injury. We had you restrained and heavily sedated for the first 24 hours. We did a few scans of both your head and torso to check for any internal injuries. Those came back clean. Bottom line, you're bruised, both head and body, and need rest and time to recover."

Max thought back to the first time he woke up and saw

the shadow at the end of the bed. The restraints would explain his feeling like he couldn't move his arms or legs. But something else the doctor said also caught Max's attention. "First 24 hours? How long have I been here?"

"Two days. This is the third morning."

CHAPTER THIRTY-ONE

Two days gone. He'd gone to see Kelley on Thursday. That made it Saturday now. Collato left, telling Max he would be back in the evening and to try to rest. No television, no reading. Just let his brain recover. Before he left, Collato fiddled with the IV out of Max's sight then, as the door swung shut, Max felt the familiar cozy warmth of whatever opioids were in the drip spread throughout his body. Any further concerns and questions just melted away. He remembered a similar feeling of contented security while going to bed in the childhood room he had once shared with Danny in Joyce's Southie walkup. After a long, sun-soaked day at the Big E state fair, he had laid in bed, full of carnival food and exhausted from the rides, and tried to make the day last as long as possible. It had been pure childhood bliss. He held on tight to that memory now as the darkness came for him again.

He woke up to find Serrato sitting in the chair next to the bed. She was in uniform, and her big hat sat on her lap as she scrolled through her phone. Max could still see light through the blinds, but it was dimmer now.

"Maybe I should have taken your advice and got out of town, huh, Officer?"

"Maybe."

She put the phone down and filled the plastic cup with water and handed it to him. Max carefully took a sip.

"Might have saved you some paperwork."

"Oh, there's no paperwork on my end."

"Not your case?"

"There is no case, Max. There was an accident report, but that's it. I'm not here officially. I'm off duty. I thought I'd swing by and check on you before I went home."

He came halfway up out of the bed and spilled some of the water. "I was run off the road by a tractor trailer truck. And not just one truck, but two. How is there no case?"

Serrato didn't react to his outburst but plucked the cup from his hand. "Two trucks, huh? That skinny doc says you can't remember what happened."

Max slumped back into the bed. "That's true. To a point. I don't remember much, but I remember some things. It's like trying to sort out a jigsaw puzzle. And I keep finding new pieces. But there were definitely two trucks. I remember that now."

"So, you remember two trucks." She sat forward in the seat. "What kind of trucks? Any distinguishing marks? Did you see the drivers?"

Max shook his head. "No. I don't know. I mostly remember colors. One was red and the other was blue, I think. I remember seeing the front grill, you know, just strips of metal filling the rearview mirror, then—" He stopped. Then what? He tried to see past that moment but there was nothing. It was like pulling the plug in the middle of watching a TV show. One moment vibrant Technicolor, the next, nothing but a blank slate.

Serrato filled the silence. "Maybe I should say there is no case, yet, but I wouldn't hold my breath. The chief likes a closed book. He's the type of man to always look ahead, not back, especially after he's made a decision."

"And his decision was what?"

"You were traveling at a high rate of speed and lost control of your vehicle."

"On a dead straight section of road in the middle of the afternoon?"

"You might have been distracted. Checking your phone. Swerved to avoid an animal."

Max suddenly wished the IV would beep and give him another hit of bliss. He didn't want to think about this. "And what do you think?"

"I think I'm off duty and stopped to check on you before going home for dinner."

"That it?"

"I wanted to hear your story. Even unofficially."

So, she was skeptical too. That made him feel a little better. He took a moment to put it together as best he could in his mind and spent the next 15 minutes recounting his stop at Halford Original Jewelry & Unique Gifts, his drive to San Antonio to visit with Kelley, the strange social media threats to Kelley's family, and then his return trip to Tiendas Reales and his run-in with the tractor trailers.

"Alleged run-in, I guess I should say." As he finished up.

"I believe you, but that's not going to carry much water with the chief."

Max shrugged. "I don't care much about that, but I do care that you believe me."

She shifted in her seat and then continued. "You don't think this was random?"

"It's possible that it was two psychos picking on the first car that came along, but I doubt it. This felt too coordinated. Too planned. They were waiting. For me."

"That means someone was tailing you at least from Kelley's place. Maybe from the time you left TR."

"That sounds right. Could be either one."

"So, who? Could it be the same people who sent those pictures to Kelley?"

Max thought about Lenny and Billy from The Tin Roof. The drunk pair who had threatened the waitress. Could they have done something like this? They didn't seem the sort. He guessed they were licking their wounds and rewriting the history of that encounter to fit their egos. Would they take another pop if they saw him on the street? Maybe. If his back was turned. Would they track him down and try to ambush him on a highway? He didn't think so. His gut told him this was someone different but, like everything else so far, he was left with more questions than answers.

"Possible but that would be an awfully quick reaction. I show up at Kelley's house and barely two hours later they know who I am and decide I'm enough of a risk to try to take me out? Does that sound reasonable?"

"Okay," Serrato agreed, "it sounds possible but not probable. What you described doesn't sound all that complicated, but it did take some timing and coordination. If we think time is the primary factor, then they were already following you before Kelley."

Max nodded. "But even then, that's not a lot of time. I must have hit a tripwire really early. I'd only been in town for less than two days."

"So what was the tripwire?" Serrato asked.

They were each quiet for a moment before both saying at the same time, "Blackburn."

· · ·

Max pulled the blankets and sheet off his legs and swung his bare feet down onto the cold tile floor. He pushed himself to a standing position and the room immediately began to tilt. He sat back down.

"What are you doing?" Serrato said, standing up herself. She made it look easy.

"I'm getting out of here."

The room righted itself and Max tried again. The room shifted sideways again. He felt Serrato grip his arm. After a moment, everything settled into place. He pulled the IV out of his arm and detached the monitoring strips from his chest. The machines howled in protest. He ignored them and took slow shuffling steps into the small bathroom in the corner. He shut the door and looked at himself in the mirror. There was still a line of dried blood along his hair, neck, and jawline. A yellow-stained bandage covered a patch of shaved hair over his ear. A larger slice of gauze and tape covered part of his arm.

He dampened some paper towels taken from the dispenser next to the sink and wiped the blood off his face. He looked tired with deep hollows under his eyes, but otherwise his face was unmarked. The back of his head was tight, and he could feel the muted bass drum of a strong headache pounding away. He let the hospital gown fall to the floor. His body was a map of multicolored bruises, scrapes, and contusions. When the painkillers wore off, he knew he would be in for a world of hurt. He peeled up a corner of the bandage on his forearm. The arm was angry and abraded by shallow scrapes and cuts.

He put the bandage back in place and then called out to Serrato through the door. "Did they leave any of my clothes laying around out there?"

He heard her moving around the room, a drawer opened and closed. "Yes and no. I don't see a shirt, but your jeans and boots are here." The door opened a crack and she handed them through. He picked the johnny up off the floor and used it as a shirt then slowly and carefully put his remaining clothes on before opening the door.

"I don't think this is a good idea. You look as steady on your feet as a baby deer."

"I feel about as strong, too."

"Then what's the rush? It's already getting late. At least stay the night. See how you feel in the morning."

"I already know I'm going to feel like shit in the morning and I wish I had that luxury, but think about it, if these guys set this up like we think, what makes you think they're going to stop there? Maybe it was just a warning shot like those photos for Kelley, but maybe it was something more. I don't have a family they can leverage. I'm just a guy who showed up in town. In their eyes, maybe that might make me more of a threat than Kelley. And, if that's the case, I don't want to be just lying here in a morphine haze. It will be safer, for everyone, if I get out of here. I'm surprised they haven't tried something already."

"It's a small clinic. Strangers would be noticed." Max nodded. Security through scarcity, he'd take it. "Where will you go?" Serrato continued. "I'm assuming you're not leaving town."

Max looked at her, his eyes flashed, and Serrato caught a glimpse of a different man. "Would you?"

"Probably not, but this is my home. You have no ties here. Why risk another run-in with whoever is doing this? Why not just take off? Put TR in your rearview."

"I don't even have a rearview anymore. They totaled my car. My reasons are complicated, even to myself, but it comes down to choices. Do you let someone take advantage of you? Or do you stand up for yourself? I'm not talking about some macho, testosterone bullshit over things that don't matter.

Getting cut off in traffic. Bumping shoulders in a bar. I'm talking about things with weight. Things that, if left unattended, will have consequences. Whoever ran me off the road and threatened Kelley? They are not going to stop. Not until they get what they want. And people who will do what they did? Threaten a child? What they want is usually not in the best interest of most people."

There was a manila envelope on the bed. Serrato must have taken it out of the drawer with his clothes. He picked it up and found his wallet, St. Christopher medal, and phone. He tried the phone. The battery was dead. He picked up the medal and let it dangle by his fingers. His mother had given it to him before she passed. The patron saint of travelers. "And who is my brother?" he murmured.

"What?" Serrato said.

"Do you go to church?" Max asked.

"My parents made me go as a kid, but religion like that really isn't my thing anymore," Serrato said.

Max waved a hand. "That's okay, you've probably heard the parable of the Good Samaritan at some point."

"Sure. Guy helps a guy he hates on the side of the road. You're not Jesus in this scenario, are you?"

Max smiled. "No, but I like to think it shows that sometimes we cannot choose who we need to help. We are all on this rock together."

"Very neighborly of you."

"I also really hate bullies. And getting sucker punched with a tractor trailer."

"Very Old Testament of you."

"I am a man of many contrasts."

CHAPTER THIRTY-TWO

I t had taken over an hour to get checked out of the clinic. Dr. Collato hadn't liked it and the discharge papers clearly stated Max was leaving against medical advice, but there was nothing they could ultimately do to hold him. Once they accepted he was serious about leaving, they were happy to have the bed free and the bill paid.

After he'd cut through the last of the red tape, Max walked, or rather hobbled, out the front doors. They'd made a quick stop at the small gift shop in the lobby and Max bought an orange T-shirt with 'Tiendas Reales Health Center' printed in navy blue on the front. It wasn't pretty but it was better than the cotton hospital johnny. Standing on the sidewalk, Max dumped the discharge papers in the trashcan. Two days in the hospital hadn't changed the weather.

"Is it always this hot here?" Max asked.

"I remember one time when I was a kid it got into the seventies at Christmas."

Max couldn't tell if she was joking or not. "I'm going to need to grab some clothes," he said eventually. She had offered a ride. He felt another kick of the bass drum at the base of his skull. "And some Tylenol. Maybe a lot of it."

Serrato's personal car was a red extended-cab Jeep Gladiator. She pulled into a driveway in a dense residential neighborhood behind a red Chevy Malibu. Max eyed the second car and, as Serrato put the Jeep in park, he asked, "Are you sure this is okay?"

She smiled. "I'm sure. You were right about Carson and her sister. I'd feel terrible if anything happened to them. You can crash here for a day or two, then we'll see what's what and make a better decision." She left it at that and climbed out of the car. He had told her about his previous arrangement with Carson and Dorothy and his concern that if he continued to stay in the little guest house he'd put them at risk, too.

He slowly climbed out of the car and tried not to groan. The hospital painkillers were wearing off. To Max, it felt like a dam slowly springing leaks. Serrato's house was on the west side of TR's meager downtown, within a mile or two of the police station. Max figured she could probably walk to work if necessary. From the outside, the house appeared similar to Carson's. It was a single-story, shaped like an L, and made of light bricks. It sat on a small lot close to its neighbors with a mature tree in front to provide shade in the morning. Several bright pots of red flowers lined the front walk.

Max opened the rear passenger door and took his small bag from the back seat. After being sure that they weren't being followed, they'd driven to Dorothy's house. No one had been home, nor at Carson's across the street. They also hadn't seen anyone obviously watching the place. Max worried whoever had attacked him had picked up his tail there on Thursday. That didn't appear to be the case. Or, at least, they weren't watching now. He'd gone around the side and quickly packed his things and left Carson a short note along with some cash and the key. He knew Carson was aware of his situation, Serrato had said she'd stopped by his room at one point, and he didn't want her to think he was running out on her. They made one last stop at the local drugstore for an economy-size bottle of aspirin, some extra gauze and bandages, along with a tube of antibiotic cream.

Max followed Serrato up the front walk to the door. Serrato had her keys out, but the door was unlocked. She made a noise under her breath and shook her head. If the exterior of the house had a homogenous and slightly dated feel that fit a neighborhood built in the 1960s or '70s, the inside was a different story. Max walked into a narrow entryway with bright white walls and light wood floors. Serrato set her keys and phone in a bowl on a table inside the door and kept walking. Max followed. Halfway down the hall was a laundry room with a stainless-steel washer-dryer combo. A small powder room sat opposite. The aroma of fresh bread and slow-cooked meat filled the house. Max's stomach rumbled. After two days of being drip-fed through an IV while he was unconscious, he'd probably eat a boiled shoe, but this smelled much better. The house opened up at the end of the hallway into the kitchen with a large island to the right and a dining area with a long farm table to the left. The living room was to the back of the house with white sofas and armchairs and a flat-screen mounted on a wall. A sliding door led to a fenced-in back yard. Small, colorful pieces of art hung on the walls and added splashes of color to the predominantly white design.

A tall, slim woman with ash-blonde hair that fell to her shoulders was standing at the stove stirring a pot and singing along to Otis Redding's version of "Tennessee Waltz." Two bowls sat on the island with a crackling loaf of cooling, rustic bread. An open bottle of red wine was also on the table.

She half-turned and said, "Ready in five. Why don't—" and stopped when she saw a stranger in her kitchen. "Oh, I didn't know we were having guests." She put the spoon down and wiped her hand on a towel that hung from the oven's door.

"Sorry, it was a late-minute decision," Serrato said. "Max Parish, meet my partner, Sam Kennedy. Max is going to take the guest room for a day or two."

The two shook.

"Pleasure to meet you, Ms. Kennedy, and sorry to intrude. Serrato, I'm more than happy to take a room at a local motel. Might be safer for you, too."

"Oh, now that sounds intriguing. I've spent the day up to my armpits in very boring briefs and motions," Kennedy said. Her cheeks were flushed from either the wine or the heat of the stove.

"Sam works as a local federal prosecutor," Serrato added.

"And she could use a little more spice in her life," Kennedy chimed in, then leaned over to give Serrato a peck on the cheek. "Just kidding, hon. There is plenty of posole. More than enough for three. And an empty bed. I wouldn't wish any of the local establishments on my most guilty client. You are welcome to stay, Max, and you can pay for your room and board with this dangerous story."

Serrato showed him the guest room where he plugged in his phone and dropped his bag. When he returned to the kitchen, Kennedy put him to work making a salad while Serrato showered and changed. They talked about innocuous things: weather, jobs, family, Texas. Or, what should have been innocuous things. Max told her what he could, keenly aware of her job as a prosecutor, and deflected where he couldn't. He tried not to lie. When he was stuck, he asked about Texas. Everyone in Texas appeared to like talking about Texas. Fifteen minutes later, Serrato was back. Sam had moved the place settings from the island to one end of the farm table and added a third set for Max.

"I know it's not exactly soup weather, but neither of us are gourmet cooks and it's quick and easy. If I actually waited for soup weather around here, I'd starve," Kennedy said.

"Not originally from around here then?" Max asked.

She shook her head. "Nope. Grew up in Ohio. Went to school in Kansas. Somehow ended up in Dallas after that. It appears I'm rolling downhill. The older I get, the farther south I end up."

"Not a bad life skill," Max said. "Maybe better than rolling uphill." Even though most days he liked the snow and cold.

"I don't know. Sometimes I miss the seasons," Kennedy said.

"You'd miss the seasons right up until the first snow," Serrato said.

"Not true. I'd be okay with the first snow. It would be the morning after the first snow and all the shoveling that I'd hate. No, you're right," she reached out a hand and grasped Serrato's briefly, "going south has worked out all right so far."

They each took a few minutes and ate from their warm bowls of red pork posole and cut thick slices of bread, washed down with red wine for the women and ice water for Max. Finally, Kennedy pushed back her bowl, looked over at him, and grinned. "So tell us your story, sailor. What calamity has washed you up on our shores?"

Max recounted his brief, but turbulent time in TR starting with his first breakfast at The Tin Roof, spotting Angie Robideaux by the bank, Blackburn's job offer, the body by the salt house, his trip to San Antonio, and finally waking up in the hospital after the accident. Serrato contributed background and details where she could. By the time they were done, the remaining soup was cold and Kennedy was no longer smiling.

"You've been holding out on me, Beca." She had also come to the same conclusions and the same set of questions. "I don't understand the motive. I know Blackburn a little. You can't *not* run into him at some point if you live and work in this town. If Blackburn's guilty, why hire these other PIs or you? If he's not guilty, why set up this accident to scare you off? Something's missing. Why volunteer yourself? He has to know that anything you or the police dig up will put him right back in the hot seat. The husband is always a suspect."

"Until he isn't. But I agree. We're missing something. Maybe I was seeing things with Angie outside the bank, maybe not. Even putting that part aside, I think there is something missing that ties Rose's disappearance, Blackburn's behavior, and this latest body together."

"It's too much not to be related," Serrato said.

They talked about it for another twenty minutes, trying to find angles or theories that would fit what they knew, Kennedy had a good knowledge of the local lowlifes through her job, but ultimately, they came to no firm conclusions. They finished the wine and moved on to other less gruesome topics. Max found himself a little envious of their easy intimacy and camaraderie. It was nice to sit near the glow of it, but it also made him very aware of what his current lifestyle might be costing him.

CHAPTER THIRTY-THREE

"How're you feeling?" Serrato asked as she came through the sliding door and took a seat on one of the patio chairs next to Max.

The back yard was a simple rectangle of scrubby grass surrounded by a white shiplap fence. Serrato carried two Lone Star bottles. "It's medicinal," she said as she handed him one. Kennedy had retreated to her office to finish up some paperwork for a morning deposition. Max had retrieved his battered phone from the guest room and was looking over the call log. Serrato had said it had been found 300 feet from the wreck. It was cracked and scratched, he'd need to replace it at some point, but, after charging while they ate, it appeared to be working. There were a number of missed calls. He put the phone aside.

"Like I got hit by a truck."

"Very funny."

"But true and I've had worse Saturday nights."

"Head okay? You don't want to mess with those types of injuries. Who was Harry Truman's vice president?"

"Are normal people supposed to know that?"

She laughed. "Sounds like cognitive function is okay."

Max didn't want to tell her he had more experience with concussions than he should. "Yeah, head's good. Still can't remember the accident completely, but my vision is okay. No nausea. No halos or stars. I'm mostly just really stiff and sore. But I'll brush up on the presidents to stay sharp."

"Presidents are easy. Vice presidents really get the ladies."

Max laughed; they lapsed into silence and looked up at the stars.

"Did they clear the scene by Blackburn's salt house?" Max asked after a minute.

"Yes, last I heard Garcia was waiting on forensics."

"Garcia's your detective?"

"That's right."

"You guys are keeping it then? Not calling in the Rangers or the state police?"

"We're keeping it. Rangers wouldn't get involved over a local citizen's death unless it was high profile or tied into something bigger. The chief and the state guys don't really get along so he wouldn't call them unless he thought he could screw them somehow, or if he was really desperate."

Max nodded. It lined up with what Carson had told him before about the local pissing matches and it wasn't an unfamiliar story in law enforcement circles. "Blackburn isn't big enough for the Rangers?"

"He might be, but he was at a big fundraiser for a senator in San Antonio that night. Stayed until almost midnight. Fifty people vouched for him. Then he was driven home. Arrived just before 2:30 in the morning, verified by the driver. Medical examiner put the time of death between 11 P.M and 1 A.M. Body was outside so the insects gave us a pretty tight window on when he died. Blackburn's clear."

"Yet people keep disappearing or dying around him."

Serrato tipped her bottle in his direction. "True, but

circumstantial as Sam would say."

"Who was the victim?"

"Raul Ortiz. He worked as a bank manager in town. Been around TR since he was a kid but still a bit of a loner. No next of kin nearby. We're trying to get a hold of his sister in Arizona. No one seems to know why he would have been out there."

"Mind if I take a look?"

"At the scene? Be my guest. It's on Blackburn's land and I guess you still work for him, right?"

"Haven't checked my messages yet, but I think so."

"So you have as much right as I do to be out there."

"Okay then."

Max realized he was now stuck in the big state of Texas without a car. He'd have to figure that out. Look for a car rental place or a cheap used car lot in town.

As if picking up on his thoughts, Serrato said, "My shift tomorrow isn't until the afternoon. I can drive you out there, if you want."

"Thanks. That would be great."

They went back to sipping their beers and listening to the insects' chirps and squeals. A screech owl let out a loud trill.

"Is Sam the reason you left the Rangers?" Max said.

"She's one of the reasons." Serrato paused. "The big reason, yes, but even if I wasn't in a relationship with a woman, I'm not sure I would have stuck it out for the long-term."

"That bad?"

"Actually no, not really. Toward the end, most guys knew how to at least play the part. Say the right things to my face. But then it just came out in other ways and that was worse for me. I could have stayed with the Rangers, but I would have hit the ceiling real fast. I was never going to have a real career there."

"So you came back."

"That's right. Better the devil you know. It's a smaller department, a couple of the guys are assholes, sure, but I can deal with them. I'm not fighting a whole bureaucracy."

"But you're not always at work."

"Ha. Tell that to Sam."

"You know what I mean."

"Maybe it's because I've lived here most of my life and people actually see me, Rebeca Serrato human being, not Rebeca Serrato lesbian cop, but most people appear okay with it. Or at least do a good job pretending. We don't get hassled in town."

A shadow crossed the porch; they both looked back and watched Kennedy walk across the living room. She smiled and waved and mimed going to sleep.

"She seems worth the hassle," Max said.

"She's worth fighting for," Serrato agreed.

Before he went to sleep, he checked his phone messages. There were two numbers he didn't know, likely spam. Carson had called twice. One from Kelley yesterday with a quick update that he continued to work the financials but had made little progress. The last one made him sit up straight. It was from Blackburn. He double-checked the time of the call. Also yesterday. He'd been in the hospital for almost two days at that point. Was he creating an alibi of sorts? The message only said he'd like a report written but also an in-person check-in by the end of the week. He asked for a return call to set a time. Blackburn sounded normal over the phone to Max but that might be harder to pull off face-to-face. He looked forward to talking to Blackburn. He had plenty of questions. Maybe he'd even have some answers by the end of the week.

He slowly unlaced his boots and kicked them off, then

wriggled out of his jeans and slipped under the sheets. The bottle of Tylenol was next to the bed; he dry swallowed four and lay back. No calls from Vic. That wasn't unusual. She always answered but she never called. It was coming up on midnight. They had not gone four days without talking since he'd left Vermont. He didn't check the Bruins' schedule. He decided he didn't need the excuse. He wanted to talk to her. He picked up his phone and tapped her number.

If he woke her up, she did a good job of hiding it. "Is there a difference between serendipity and coincidence?" she said as if they were in the middle of a conversation. Maybe they were.

"I think serendipity usually has a happy ending."

"Ah, okay. Maybe it was more a coincidence then."

"What?"

"The day after last time we talked and you told me about your crazy day in Texas, I went to the Countryside for breakfast. Nothing unusual there. Someone had left a paper in a booth. I was about to read it when Rob showed up. I tossed the paper aside. Didn't read it."

"Nothing unusual there."

"Very funny. Listen, I did end up reading that paper. Later, after work, I was at The Night Owl and Cindy was working. She asked for help with the crossword. Right next to the crossword was a story about this woman on trial in Wyoming for killing her husband. They lived way off the grid. Nearest town was like a hundred miles away. Very much on their own. Ran a subsistence farm. One day she woke up and shot him in the chest with a shotgun as he ate his breakfast."

"Okay," Max said, not sure where she was going with this or how it could possibly be serendipitous.

"Right, sadly, nothing too unusual about the story. You could probably come up with any number of explanations or defenses for the wife. Abusive husband. Alcohol. Drugs."

"Mental illness."

"How about prairie madness?"

"What is that?"

"That is what most of this article was about. The woman's lawyer is saying she did it because of the landscape of where the couple lived. Insanity brought on by the isolation and bleak conditions of their farm. There's this creepy line in the story from her initial police interview, so creepy, I still remember it word for word: 'I've come to hate the wind and I know it hates me with a hate just as deep. Every night, it hisses and jeers when I try to sleep.'"

"So not just the loneliness but the soundtrack of being alone, too."

"Yeah. I know that wind. I've heard it here. Not like that poor woman," she paused, "but sometimes, you know?"

Max had spent just one winter in the mountains of Vermont, but he'd spent plenty of time in the last few years alone. "I know what you mean."

"It made me think of your missing woman. The mother. You said that ranch was out there a ways. That she was a new mother without a lot of friends. It got me thinking, I guess. Maybe she had a touch of prairie madness."

"Maybe. It makes about as much sense as anything else down here."

They talked for a few more minutes. Max deliberately moved the topic over to the Bruins until he could hear the usual spark return to her voice. He didn't like how she sounded when she was talking about the wind. They said goodnight and he lay in the strange bed in the quiet house and thought about living somewhere so still and secluded that even the smallest sound, like the rustling of sheets or the beating of your own heart, became impossible to ignore.

CHAPTER THIRTY-FOUR

"Why here?"

Max stood near the door of the salt house and turned in a full circle. There was little to see other than the small shack. Blackburn's ranch was a mile away and out of sight. Fifty yards to the left, there were a few bent trees near the crumbled stone remains of the original ranch house's foundation, but otherwise the surrounding landscape consisted of rusted fencing, scrub grass, and different shades of brown dirt as far as the eye could see. "It's desolate."

Sunday morning. Hot, dry, and indistinguishable from every other morning he'd spent here so far. He glanced back at the way they'd driven in. The passing road was just visible on the horizon, but anyone driving past would be hard-pressed to make out much detail. At night, you'd be invisible. "Nobody to hear you scream out here except the coyotes."

"Maybe that's the why. Makes it pretty much perfect for killing someone."

"He was killed here then?"

"Yes. He had an apartment in town. It was searched."

"Can we go there?"

She looked uneasy at that suggestion but eventually nodded. "Since they've released it, the sister might be there by now. We could knock."

"The ME is sure about Garcia being killed here?"

Max wiped his brow and tried to figure out what led to Ortiz's body being left here. It would have been risky taking someone captive in a vehicle and driving them way out here. Far easier to kill them in the house if they already had control of the situation and then move the body. A dead body can't scream or run.

"That's the ME's best guess based on the amount of blood on the ground. Gunshot wound to the head. Visible powder burns. Close contact. They didn't find any indications of a crime scene at his place." They both glanced at a spot fifteen yards from the salt house's front door. The scene had been cleaned and released but it was still obvious from the disturbed ground where the body had been. "But the report also noted some other trauma. Bruises on the wrists and ankles. It's likely he was tortured, maybe here, maybe somewhere else, before he was ultimately killed. The report didn't make note of any defensive wounds."

Max nodded. "They wanted information. Tied him up."

"Probably."

"Garcia found no connection between Ortiz and Blackburn?"

"Nothing but the body's proximity to the Double R. We're waiting on a warrant to double-check financial accounts and phone records, but Blackburn says he didn't have any dealings with the bank that Ortiz managed. He used another one in town."

"Probably not lying about that. Too easy to check."

"And, if they communicated, they likely used burners."

"Sure. Same result, nothing to pin Blackburn down with." Max indicated the building. "House itself is clean?"

"Yes. No blood. No fingerprints. It appears all the action happened outside. Nothing of any value inside, really."

Max studied the building again. He walked around the exterior but didn't see anything of note. Nothing that might make it a destination for murder. It was a plain rectangle, slightly deeper than it was wide, made of rough bricks with a pitched ceramic tile roof. There were no windows, just the single door centered in the front. The bricks had been baked and blasted by the constant sun exposure. He could see the roof had missing and cracked tiles, but otherwise the building appeared to be in decent shape. It was in no danger of collapsing.

The door was made of weathered wood, a half dozen vertical slats connected and strengthened by three shorter horizontal ones across the top, middle, and bottom. If it had once been painted, the color had long been bleached out by the sun. It was now a muted gray. He stepped up to it and then paused. He could see some black fingerprint dust on the knob. He looked back at Serrato. She gave him a go-ahead gesture. He expected some resistance, but the brass knob turned easily and the door swung open.

Inside, the small space was hot and smelled like brick dust and mildew. The mustiness might have been from the warped floor. It was made of plank wood that looked like it might have come from the same tree as the door but hadn't aged as well. It was swaybacked in the middle. There were five other items inside. First, a simple wooden table and two chairs. One chair was broken and missing the back. Max didn't see the missing pieces inside. Maybe scavenged for some reason. The second item was a large metal structure with twin wing doors. The doors were open and almost brushing the ceiling. It reminded

Max of the old iron lungs he'd seen in the science museum when he was a kid, only standing vertical not horizontal. The smell of mildew was stronger by the metal monstrosity.

"Blackburn isn't sure, but he thinks that is a homemade smoker that Rose's grandfather or great-grandfather jury-rigged up from some welded oil barrels."

"What about the refrigerator?"

The fifth item was a pale-yellow fridge in the corner. It was likely from the'80s, maybe early '90s, but it looked almost futuristic in comparison to the other items in the room.

"Blackburn says his father-in-law used to keep cattle and horse medicine out here for emergencies or convenience."

He walked over and pulled open the door. The shelves were gone, and the fridge was empty. "Without power?"

Serrato shrugged. "Maybe there was power at one time. Or maybe he had a battery or generator. Maybe he didn't need power, just a place he could store them. Maybe lock it up, if necessary."

Max nodded. Sweat began to run into his eyes. He felt a little lightheaded as he walked back out into the sun. He paused to let his body catch up. The four aspirin he'd taken at breakfast, coffee and toast standing with Serrato at the kitchen island, were working overtime to keep the aches at bay. He felt like a walking bruise. It had taken almost ten minutes to get out of bed and into the shower. But the hot water and aspirin had helped and a body in motion tended to stay in motion. He planned to do his best to keep moving and ignore his aches for the time being.

He took a last look at the salt house and then began to walk back toward Serrato's Jeep. Then he walked past it. He studied the ground while he walked. It was hard but not completely dry. He could make out the Jeep's tracks pressed into the earth. He stopped and followed them back toward the road with his eyes.

Serrato came and stood next to him. "Anything?"

"What do you make of these?"

He knelt. There were other tracks besides the Jeep's. It was a unique pattern and pressed deeper into the dirt than the Jeep's.

"It had to be something heavy to leave that type of impression. And recent." He rubbed a hand in the dirt. "I doubt this dust holds tracks for long."

"Not one of ours from the Ortiz scene. We don't have anything that would leave those kinds of tracks. I'll check the report, see what the state might have brought in."

He nodded then took out his phone and snapped a few pictures. He stood and brushed his hands off.

Was any of this connected to Angie or Rose's disappearance? It seemed too weird not to be connected, and also weird enough to be the type of random horrible event that happened sometimes. Despite their conversation at dinner, life was full of weird, unexplainable shit.

"Let's go," he said.

CHAPTER THIRTY-FIVE

They drove back past the wooden gates of the Double R headed toward Raul Ortiz's apartment in town. They saw nothing moving as they went past, save a lonely armadillo lumbering along the shoulder, maybe searching for some long-lost shade. That changed five miles past the ranch. Three tractor trailers went past in quick succession, each heading the opposite direction, away from Tiendas Reales, and each towing a white unmarked trailer. A fourth, a tanker, was pulling out onto the road from the left. Serrato slowed, then braked to a stop as the rig swung into the opposite lane before straightening out and heading off in the same direction.

"Where does that lead?" Max asked. The road branched off at a crisp 90-degree angle from the state road. It was a smooth strip of black asphalt with bright white and yellow painted lines.

"Blackburn's warehouse."

"Carson mentioned that. What is it?"

Serrato shrugged. "It's a warehouse. That's all I know."

"Mind if we check it out?"

She shrugged. "No." She made the turn. The new road appeared to disappear into the horizon.

"It's in TR? You guys do drive-bys?"

"Yes, it's technically part of TR. It's actually the site of the original town settlement. It was the railroad depot back in the 1800s. It was never very big. It was just too desolate. There were cattle ranches back then but not big enough to support a train line by themselves. Cotton never took off down here. Not the right climate. Or, maybe just better climates nearby. Still, from what I understand it was an important waystation early on. The trains could stop and take on water and supplies."

"On their way to somewhere else."

"That could be TR's official motto. As the trains got more modern and could travel longer distances, the need to stop here dried up. It made a brief comeback with some early mining efforts but then that dried up, too."

Max watched as shimmering dark shapes began to resolve through the windshield.

"They have their own security and it basically dead ends past the warehouse," Serrato continued. "Only one way in or out. Not a lot of reason for us to go out there. I drove past when it first opened but have never gotten a call."

"And you don't know what Blackburn is keeping in the warehouse?"

"No."

"Let me guess. The locals are happy with the jobs and no one in power asks too many questions."

He could feel Serrato bristle slightly at the insinuation. "No reason to rock the boat on this one. It's a warehouse. I assume things get brought in, stored, then shipped out. Not everything is a conspiracy, Parish. Does Carson know?"

"No, and I could tell it bothered her."

Serrato smiled. "She likes to have answers."

"Do the trucks ever come through town?"

"A few come in for meals, but their routes keep them out of town. I think that's by design. No one wants 18-wheelers barreling through their neighborhood every day."

Ten more minutes of driving brought the buildings into more focus. Max was reminded of the warehouse district back in West Adams but in miniature. There were various crumbling outbuildings on either side of the road, and Max could see crumbling foundations and other infrastructure that had been used and discarded over time. It was clear which parts had been renovated and restored. Everything else had been left to rot. The new pavement continued straight as an arrow to a complex of three buildings surrounded by a chain link fence. A guard shack was positioned next to an opening in the gate. They watched the guard look up as they approached. Serrato braked the Jeep to a stop about fifty yards short. There was no way to drive past. The road led directly to the gate and then into the complex.

"This is it."

Max took it in. The three buildings inside the gate were lean, long affairs that were parallel to each other and perpendicular to the gate itself. Each building was spaced out to give the big trucks room to maneuver. Each one stretched at least as far as a football field and had docking bays evenly spaced down their lengths. Six trucks were parked at various spots. Max could see cameras hanging from the corners of each building. They were all pointing inward, but he also noted two at the gate. One pointed at the guard shack, and one pointed out toward the road.

"What's he building in there?" Max whispered.

"What's that?" Serrato said.

"Nothing. Old song lyric. That's a lot of space. And no one knows what goes on in there?"

"I'm sure someone knows but I don't."

"You know anyone who works here?"

The scene was oddly quiet. No trucks were moving and other than the guard, who now seemed to be taking more interest in them the longer they sat on the road, Max didn't see anyone moving inside the complex.

"Not me personally, but I'm sure some people in town do. I can ask around, if you want."

"If you don't mind." The guard came out of the booth, carrying a clipboard, and started toward the car. He wore a dark quasi-military uniform with black boots. He walked with the upright bearing of an ex-soldier.

"Time to leave."

"Yeah." Serrato bumped off the road to make a U-turn and then gave the guard a friendly wave, just two lost tourists, as they headed back out in the opposite direction.

"You notice the guard?" Max asked.

"I saw."

Besides the clipboard, the guy also had a holster clipped to his hip.

"Nothing illegal about having armed security. This is Texas after all."

"Heavy-duty for a warehouse in the middle of nowhere."

Serrato steered them back into town. They passed a small church with smooth white stucco walls and a red roof with a matching red steeple. There were 20 or 30 cars parked in the lot. Half a mile later they passed another church. Another small, simple building with peeling white paint. Brick steps led up to the entrance with simple columns and two doors on either end. There were no crosses or imagery. It was identifiable as a church only by a sign out near the road, Free Methodist Church of Tiendas Reales. About the same amount of cars populated the dirt lot.

Serrato caught a whiff of his interest. "Everything else might be struggling, but God still seems to be doing steady business in TR. We got a variety pack around here. Catholic, Baptist, Methodist, and some non-denominational. Take your pick, however you like your preaching. Light, medium, or well-done."

"Which one were you?"

"Southern Baptist. I went every Sunday until I left for college. It was so ingrained in me that for a long time I didn't think attendance was optional."

"And now?"

"Now, I generally believe God exists and the Bible has something to say about her. I think a lot of people in more rural communities feel the same way. They go to church and believe in God, but the church is also a social center. Or provides assistance during tough times which is most days around here."

"Stability and support. In God's kingdom less is more."

"That's right. When I look at these buildings when I'm on patrol, I don't see a church, I see the people and the lives of those who sat in the pews with me and cared about me. They were as much a part of my life as any blood relative."

"'For he looks to the ends of the earth, and sees everything under the heavens.'" Serrato glanced at him. "There was a period in my life where I had a lot of time to read the Bible. A couple of things stuck."

"I don't know about heaven, but TR definitely qualifies as the ends of the earth."

CHAPTER THIRTY-SIX

Raul Ortiz's apartment was on the ground floor of a brick building just a few blocks from the library and the park where Max had spoken to the two skate kids about Angie. The buildings were part of a constellation of identical brick rectangles, each housing four apartments, two on the ground floor, two above, around a pool and a central courtyard. Various grills and lawn chairs were scattered around the outside of the pool fence.

Raul's apartment was number six. The second building on the left. There was no sign from the outside of the violence that had taken place inside. No broken locks, busted windows, or flapping yellow crime scene tape. A gray Kia Forte with a navy and orange UTEP Miners bumper sticker was parked in the spot closest to Ortiz's door. Serrato stepped up and knocked. They heard movement from inside and a moment later the door opened to a young woman wearing jean shorts and a UTEP T-shirt with the same logo as the bumper sticker on the Kia. The woman's eyes were red and her hair disheveled. There were rings of sweat under her arms and a dark smudge on her cheek. Dirt or eye makeup. Warm air wafted out.

"Elena Ortiz?" Serrato asked.

"Yes."

"I'm Officer Serrato with the Tienda Reales police. This is Max Parish." She left it at that. Not a lie necessarily, just an omission.

"Yes," Ortiz responded. Max could see the grief that still enveloped Ortiz in her dull eyes and flat tone.

"I'm very sorry for your loss. I was wondering if we could have a quick look around. It will only take a few minutes."

Confusion clouded in over the grief. "Uh, Detective ..." The name escaped her. "The detective in charge said he was finished. That I was free to start ..." A sob wrenched loose. She left the door open, but retreated back into the apartment through a door on the left, just past the galley kitchen that was directly inside the entryway. Serrato and Max stayed by the entryway. A moment later, they heard her blow her nose before reappearing. The smudge on her cheek was gone. She waved them inside and continued down the hallway into the living room. Serrato and Max followed.

Max glanced into the small kitchen as they passed. Dishes and cups had been taken from cupboards and piled on the counter, but it wasn't destructive. It was orderly. A small fan also sat on the kitchen counter. Max stepped over to the refrigerator and pulled open the door. It wasn't very full, just a few staples. Milk, condiments, a package of lunch meat, a block of cheddar cheese. But it also didn't appear to be disturbed. He opened the freezer. Carton of ice cream. Two bags of frozen edamame. A package of frozen hamburgers. A tray of ice cubes. He closed the door and joined Serrato in the living room.

"I'm sorry," she said. "This is all such a shock. It still doesn't feel real. I keep expecting Raul to walk out of the bedroom or through the door and start complaining about work." She turned and looked around. The living room was a mess. Drawers were pulled out and dumped on the floor. Sofa cushions pulled off. Books pulled off shelves. "I didn't expect anyone else. I've started to pack things."

She waved her hand at a number of half-assembled cardboard boxes scattered around the room. It didn't appear that she'd made much progress, packing or cleaning. Max knew it would take time for her brother's violent death to sink in, but he doubted very much it would ever feel real.

"You can sit ..." Elena Ortiz trailed off, then picked up one of the cushions from the floor and placed it back on the couch. She picked another one up but then paused, apparently overcome with grief or the enormity of the very unwanted task suddenly thrust on her.

Serrato stepped forward and placed a hand on her arm. "It's okay. We don't need to sit right now." She glanced at Max who gave her a small nod. She had more experience in these situations.

"I'm sure Detective Garcia spoke with you and some of our questions will be repetitive, but we've found sometimes the second time through or some additional time can provide a different answer."

"Okay," Elena said.

"Did your brother have any enemies? Anyone he mentioned having trouble with recently?"

"No. Not that he told me. He never mentioned anyone by name. I've wracked my brain trying to think of anything he said that might have indicated he was in trouble, but I can't think of anything."

"Did you talk to your brother often?"

"We texted back and forth pretty regularly and probably

spoke once a week, definitely once every two weeks. Our mother's gone. Never really knew our dad. Raul remembers him more. We are all that we have left."

Max could see her words hitting her now. She was the only one left. He saw the grief rising in her eyes and this time he thought it might swamp her, but Serrato stepped in with another question that redirected those thoughts.

"Did Raul ever mention an Alex Blackburn?"

The name didn't appear to mean anything to Elena.

"No, I don't think so. Is that someone from the bank? He talked about his coworkers sometimes. Lily. Janeane. Rachel. The tellers and other employees, but I don't remember an Alex. They were mostly female. I would have recalled an Alex."

"Did he work at the bank long?"

"Yes, almost 15 years. He was very proud. We didn't grow up with much. Less than that and our mom liked the bottle more than she liked us. We always had to watch the money. Once he got that job, things were a little easier. Not easy, but easier. He worked his way up to manager. He was proud of his career and proud of his job." Max watched something flit across her face. "At least until recently."

"What happened recently?"

"The bank was bought out or merged or something and the TR branch was going to close."

"He was going to lose his job?"

"He was told he could apply for a position at another branch in Freer, but it would be a demotion. A sales position, not management. He thought it was insulting after all the work he'd put in. He was pretty angry about it."

"Angry at anyone specific?"

Elena shook her head. "No, and I think that was part of the problem. Maybe confronting someone and blowing off some steam might have helped, but this was just nameless, faceless bureaucrats. There was no real target for his anger."

"I understand," Serrato said. She glanced at Max. He shook his head. "We'll look around for a few minutes and let you know if we have more questions."

Ortiz nodded and drifted back toward the kitchen.

"What are we looking for?" Serrato asked quietly.

"Not sure," Max responded. "I figure we'll know it when we see it."

"If we see it."

"Right."

"You want the bedroom or the living room?"

"I'll take the bedroom and then we can switch. See if either of us catches anything the other didn't."

"All right," Serrato said, and she moved off toward the stack of discarded books in a pile near the television.

The bedroom was small and barely fit the furniture. There was a queen size bed centered in the middle of the room. No headboard, just a box spring and frame. An Ikea bedside table was on one side. A bureau that matched the table sat at the foot of the bed. A small air conditioner sat in the window next to the closet on the left.

This room had been searched, as well. The bureau drawers were pulled out and the clothes were piled on the bed. The bedsheets had been stripped and the mattress moved. There were slits along the mattress and stuffing poked out. Max pulled open the bedside drawer and found two paperbacks, a magazine, a bottle of sleeping pills, and disposable earplugs.

He stepped around the bed to the closet. He could only open the closet door a little more than halfway before the mattress got in the way. He glanced inside. The clothes had been removed from the rod and tossed on the bed with everything else. Various pairs of shoes were still lined up on the floor. Max picked each one up but found nothing hidden in them. Two cardboard boxes were pushed to one side. He leaned in and pulled them out. He pulled up the flaps on the first box and ran a hand through the contents. It appeared to be old photos and various family papers. He put it back and opened the second. More papers. Documents, report cards, certificates, awards. All about his sister. Max picked up a yellowed newspaper article about Elena Ortiz and her valedictorian speech at high school graduation. He glanced at the byline. Melinda Carson. Who else? He put the box back and wondered why the boxes hadn't been dumped like the clothes and books?

Before he closed the closet door, he glanced up but didn't see any hatches for a hidden crawlspace or attic storage. He went to a knee and peered under the bed. He pulled out a framed photo of a younger Elena and Raul at a pool, maybe the one outside, Max couldn't tell, both smiling and sun-kissed. It was a good photo. He hoped Elena would keep it and remember her brother that way. He placed the framed photo on the bedside table and walked back out the living room.

"Anything?" Serrato asked. She stood and wiped her brow.

She had finished with the books and had moved to the desk in the corner and was going through the drawers.

"No. You?"

"He was very organized, very detailed, going by the state of his desk. Kept his tax returns exactly seven years. But I'm not finding anything connecting him to Blackburn or Blackburn's businesses. Nothing else very suspicious either."

They swapped rooms and repeated the process but came back with nothing.

"Okay. Thanks for helping. It was a worth a shot," Max said.

"Only wasted a little time."

Max glanced around. He wasn't sure it was wasted time. Raul Ortiz had not been killed at random. Someone was looking for something. Had it been Blackburn? Or Hull, working for Blackburn? Max didn't know. If they hadn't killed Raul, then who did and why?

CHAPTER THIRTY-SEVEN

They left Elena Ortiz to her grief. The glaring sun felt like a rebuke as they walked outside and climbed into Serrato's Jeep.

"One benefit to being a small-town cop is that you don't have to do notifications as much. Never gets easier."

"If it gets easier, it's probably time to find a new job."

"You're probably right, but it doesn't make me feel any better."

"Good, means you're still human."

They drove away from the apartment building with the windows down and let the air conditioning catch up. It was still hot, but bearable. They rolled the windows up and Serrato asked, "Where to?"

"You mind driving out to the *Tribune* building? Carson has a couple boxes of notes I'd like to go through."

"Sure, I have time." She made a left and headed out toward the newer commercial strip. "Looking for anything in particular?"

"Nope. I can tell we're missing a piece, but I feel like we're close. Feels like this persistent itch that I just can't reach, so I'm going to try to get as much information in my head as possible and hope it sorts itself out. I'll keep talking to people, but Carson's notes seem like they might be a nice shortcut."

"Sifting the paper."

"What's that?"

"My first boss when I was with the Rangers. That was his pet phrase. Sifting the paper. There's a body or a crime, of course, but a case is mostly paperwork. Forms, notes, reports. That's what an investigation comes down to—a pile of paper in a file."

"Makes sense. I tend to think of it as gathering lint. Any big problem, I like to collect as much information as I can. Ninety percent won't be used, but at the start or in the middle, you don't know which is which. You just need to stuff it all in your head."

"Be careful, I used to think that half the time the guy was buried in facts, he couldn't see the forest." Serrato pulled into the lot and parked next to Carson's old Subaru. "They leave all the dull parts out of movies for a reason."

"Sure, but the boring bits are how most people make a living."

"That's kind of depressing."

"Yup."

They went inside and followed the smell of cigarettes to Carson's cube.

"I told you exercising would lead to no good," she said.

"You were right. That morning five miler really beat me up," he replied.

She dropped the smile. "I'm glad you're all right."

"Thanks. I know it did nothing to improve my looks, but I feel pretty lucky and physically don't feel half bad."

"Dot gave me the note. When this one kicks you out, you're welcome back any time."

"Thanks, appreciate it. I just didn't want to—"

"I get it. So, what brings you to my humble cube?"

He nodded toward the space under her desk. "I was hoping I could borrow the boxes of notes you have on Rose's disappearance."

"Got the bug, huh?"

"Someone ran me off the road. I'm going to find out why." He watched Carson flinch back and realized he might have put a little too much snap in his voice. He continued a little softer. "I have my own notes, but they won't hold a candle to the five years of scribbling you've got. I'd like to read through them and jump the line if I can."

She pulled them out. "Have at it. Probably healthier for me to get them out of here. Stop obsessing over them so much."

"Be healthier if you gave up cigarettes."

"I was talking about realistic goals."

They left Carson to her addictions; they each carried a bulging box out to the Jeep and put them in the back seat. Serrato drove Max back to her house and let him in.

"Feel free to setup on the dining room table," she said before leaving to start her shift.

He placed the boxes on the table and then filled a glass with water from the tap. He'd noticed the constant heat made him almost paranoid about his hydration. He didn't fight it. He drank the glass down, refilled it, and carried it over to the table and sat down. He opened the first box and was relieved to see that, despite the chaotic nature of her workspace, Carson was meticulous about her files. At least these files. She had everything she'd dug up on the Robideaux case sorted and filed in folders. Four hours later, he had a sore back and bloodshot eyes, but he wasn't sure if he'd learned anything new. He'd gone through official case file reports, newspaper clippings, Carson's and some of the stories from the larger dailies, credit card statements, business documents similar to what Kelley had shown him, a lot of transcribed interview notes, and it all jibed with what he knew already. The only curiosity was a Post-it note attached to the folder with the credit card statements. Carson had written the words 'Ask Mavis' in her now familiar cramped handwriting.

He pulled the credit card statements out again and went over them a second time, and wondered again where and how Carson had gotten half of the stuff. He read through the last four months of Rose's statements: gas, groceries, feed, tack, Amazon purchases, Walmart, florist, dry cleaners. Carson had made pencil marks, little backward checks, beside one merchant he didn't recognize where Robideaux had made repeat purchases, not regular, but regular enough that they showed up every two or three months, BHPV, but when he plugged it into Google, it turned out to be a big photo and video store out of New York. Given her photography hobby, specialty store purchases made sense and didn't trigger the suspicion needle.

He pushed back from the table. He felt antsy. Now he had too much trapped in his head. He had to get out of the house. He used the bathroom and thought about going for a run and then remembered that outside was similar to the surface of the sun. He forgot about running but thought maybe a walk might help. He went out the backdoor and crossed the street to the shadier side; it was still hot, he just didn't need his sunglasses. He slowly walked the neighborhood and saw very little. A dog under a porch, Max checked to make sure the water bowl was full; two kids splashing in one of those flimsy plastic tubs they sell as pools; a landscaping crew decked out in loose clothes, neck gaiters, and wide-brimmed hats. Not much else. Everyone else was inside waiting out the heat. That was fine. He just walked.

He thought about cause and effect. Rose disappeared.

That was the effect but what was the cause? It usually took something specific to trigger a murder, if she was murdered, not always, but usually. Money, sex, drugs, alcohol ... something. Something he was missing.

Max had also never heard of a wife going missing where the husband didn't play some part. Maybe Blackburn wasn't guilty, didn't actually do it, but he was somehow tangled up in it. He was part of the cause. On the other hand, Max had never heard of a husband putting himself in the spotlight as the main suspect which is what Blackburn appeared to be doing. Unless he was telling the truth. Unless he was innocent. Something he was missing.

He walked until the sweat began to roll into his eyes and his shirt clung to him in the front and the back. He let it go and returned to Serrato's house. He'd let his subconscious continue to work on it for a bit. He showered, changed into fresh clothes. In the kitchen, he found Sam drinking a glass of red wine and flipping through the file folders.

"Figure it out yet, Kolchak?" she asked.

He filled his water glass and sat across from her. "Was he a detective?"

She wrinkled her nose. "I'm not sure. He might have been a reporter, but he definitely poked around in mysterious events. I think this qualifies, but I don't think a werewolf took Rose Robideaux."

"Me either, but I didn't find any new clues in there. Just a headache and some eye strain."

"Had to be done. If there was a clue and you didn't do it ..."

"I know." Then he thought of the Post-it. "Hey, who's Mavis?" He picked up the file and turned it around so Kennedy could see.

She looked at the paper and then her eyes drifted up as

she thought. "She was the mail—I was going to say mailman. Mail carrier, I guess."

"Any reason you can think of that Carson would have a note? Or leave it on there all these years?"

"No, not really. She was a bit of a gossip, if I remember. Beca used to complain any time she ran into her that she would press her for details that weren't in the police blotter."

"Used to? What happened?

Kennedy smiled. A big, toothy grin.

"What?" Max asked.

"I think that's the reason you're going to crack this thing, Kolchak."

"What are you talking about?"

"The second question. Any detective or PI would ask the first question, but you're interested. You're curious. You asked a second question."

"I'm just going around talking to people."

"Yes, you are." She refilled her wine glass. "Mavis eloped with the dog catcher."

"Oh, come on."

"I'm serious. It was quite the town scandal. Mavis was single. I think everyone sort of assumed she was a lesbian. Older, single woman, sort of had the look, you know. The dog catcher, his name was Elvis, I kid you not, was married. One day he filed some paperwork and they took off for Vegas. Screwed up the mail for a week. Last I heard, they were living in Arizona."

He put the notes and folders back in the boxes and moved them out of the way and then helped Kennedy prepare a simple dinner. Green salad, thin strips of marinated flank steak she took from the fridge, with fresh corn tortillas and lime wedges. Serrato stopped by briefly and they all sat down and ate. Max was again struck by the easy camaraderie between the two.

"You'll like this one, Beca," Kennedy said. "It went through the courthouse like wildfire today. There was a divorce case before Cranuck this morning. It was a mostly amicable split. The couple had reached an agreement on custody, child and spousal support, division of marital property—the works, everything *except* for one issue. They both wanted the *waffle iron* and were refusing to budge. A waffle iron. I think everyone assumed it had become symbolic or had some significance beyond, you know, cooking waffles." She turned to Max. "Cranuck has been on the bench since about the Taft administration. I'm not sure I've ever seen him smile. I can't imagine he was happy the couple was wasting the court's time with a waffle iron dispute. He calls for a recess. Tells them they have 15 minutes to figure it out or he's seizing all their property and having a garage sale on the courthouse steps and splitting the proceeds 50-50 so they can buy as many waffle irons as they want. So, they go off and at the end of the recess they tell the judge they've reached an agreement. He says great and bangs his gavel." Kennedy paused and took a bite of her steak taco.

Serrato asks the obvious question. "So, who ended up with the waffle iron."

Kennedy smiles. "That's just it. Cranuck didn't ask. He didn't care in the least. No one knows!"

"The mystery endures," Serrato said. "You can have the waffle iron if things go sour between us."

"We don't own a waffle iron."

"Won't be a problem then."

They ate and talked. Serrato told a story about a foot pursuit when she was with the Rangers. She chased a subject for almost a mile, through alleys, over fences. The guy juked and jived. When he finally gave up and was gasping with his hands on his knees and Serrato slipped on the cuffs, he asked, "How'd you follow me so easily? I can always outrun, y'all."

"That right?"

"Uh-huh. Always."

"Let me ask you something. You buy those shoes recently?"

Guy looks down at his sneakers. "Yeah, couple days ago. Why?"

"Watch your feet and do a little jump for me."

The guy did and the LED lights in his heels flashed red.

"Didn't have to be as fast as you. Just didn't have to be blind."

CHAPTER THIRTY-EIGHT

After they finished their meal, Serrato left to go back on patrol and finish her shift. He and Kennedy cleared the dishes. She then retreated to the small office at the front of the house to review case files for the morning. Max went into the bedroom and lay down. He'd spent most of the day moving but now he had nowhere to go and only his aches and pains for company. He picked up the phone and called Blackburn, but the man didn't pick up. He suggested meeting up on Thursday at the ranch, a week into the job, for the status report meeting and then disconnected.

He dug in his bag and pulled out a paperback. He was currently on a kick of 1970s Travis McGee novels from John D. MacDonald. He read a few chapters of *The Dreadful Lemon Sky* before he set it aside. Typically, he would drift off while reading or think about God for a while, but tonight he stared at the ceiling with a line of crackling static running through his mind. He picked up his phone again.

"You keep calling," Vic said.

She sounded slightly tipsy, maybe drunk, which would be

unusual for a weeknight for her. He could picture her now back from The Night Owl and slouched in the recliner in her mother's old house with Bailey at her feet.

"This a bad time?" he asked.

"No."

"Your number's in the phone book," he said trying to nudge her out of her funk.

"No, it's not. Phone books don't even exist anymore."

"Sure they do, check the library."

"Do libraries still exist?"

"Fine, it's on the side of your truck."

"There you go. That's practically an invitation," she replied, but he could hear her smile just a little.

Boots unlaced, maybe kicked off by the door, maybe not. Hair in a loose ponytail, no makeup, work jeans, T-shirt. He was suddenly filled with the desire to be in the same room as Vic. He would untie and pull off the boots if needed. Feed the dog. Help wash the dishes.

Before he could keep it rolling, she continued. "Something happened today."

"What?"

"I lost that bid to scavenge the demo site of the old mill building off Route 6. Pretty sure I only lost it because I'm a woman. The guy said all the right things but the way he said them, like he was always on the verge of saying 'missy' just got my goat, you know?"

"I know." Vic owned and operated the Chepstow Motel but also did a variety of odd jobs. "But that's happened to you before." Her fierce independence and stubborn refusal to be pushed aside or bullied were two of the things Max liked most about her.

"I know. That wasn't the bad thing. That's just some context on why my blood was running hot."

"Oh." He'd seen the result of when Vic's patience was pushed into the red.

"Yeah. I was driving back to the motel, stewing on it, when this yahoo comes flying up behind me in a Boxster. Really pushing up against my bumper. Remember, Route 6 is tight. No shoulder. Trees right up against the road. I can't count how many deer and other animals I've seen jump out there. He tries to go around once but catches a car coming the other way. Almost causes an accident right there. That backs him off for all of 30 seconds and then he's right back chewing on my bumper again. I slow down. That appears to piss him off some more. He adds some headlights and a horn to the mix. Eventually, after a mile of this, we hit the straight by the bridge and he zooms past with a one-finger salute. Max, I reached out and opened the glovebox. I wanted to shoot him."

"I know."

"I looked it up on my phone when I was drinking it off at the Owl. The term for it is disproportionate force."

"You didn't shoot him," Max said.

She continued as if he hadn't spoken. "I think if I started, I might have kept going. One bullet wouldn't have been enough."

"But you didn't shoot him. You let him drive off. It's over."

"That's what I kept telling myself at the bar. All through the first drink, then the second, and into the third. But is it over? I mean, Max, I really wanted to shoot him. I didn't. But what about next time?"

"You'll do the same thing. Maybe the anger will come just as hot, but you'll control yourself."

"How do you know?"

"Because you are an ethical and principled person."

"Is that enough?"

"I think so. It should be."

"But can't you be ethical and principled and still do the wrong thing?"

There was the faint crackle of static on the line.

"Max?"

"Yes. You can."

CHAPTER THIRTY-NINE

Max sat in the shadows and watched. He was looking for a way in. And more importantly a way back out. The gatehouse and the front fence line were bathed in a perimeter of light. It didn't actually extend inside the fence, which Max found curious. Each docking bay was subtly lit, enough to allow the drivers to back up efficiently without crashing, but that was it. The branching roads within the complex were unlit. Maybe the trucks' headlights were enough. Maybe there was a light ordinance. Or Blackburn was just cheap. But maybe there was another reason. Maybe too much light made it too easy to see what was going on. Max was determined to get inside and find out for himself. Would it lead him to Rose? Almost certainly not. But it might help him better understand what was going on with Blackburn and this strange town. And that might then lead him to Rose. It was an indirect route, at best, but it was all he had.

He stood near the wall of one of the surrounding buildings. It was one of the old buildings that hadn't been renovated. It sat diagonally across from the gatehouse and outside the ring of light. Max wondered if the ring of light was helpful or not? Certainly, any guard paying attention would be able to see someone approaching the gatehouse or fence but beyond that they'd likely be blind. Max wasn't being casual about it, but he was confident he couldn't be seen.

He'd waited until 1 a.m. when he was sure Serrato and Sam were asleep, then he'd taken her keys from the bowl by the door. He thought briefly about her gun. He'd watched her lock it up in a small safe in the hall closet and thought he could have gotten it open, but ultimately decided to leave it. If he ran into enough trouble that he needed a gun, he was likely in over his head and the gun would only make things worse. He needed a vehicle and didn't want to drag her into this adventure. Stealing her car was enough. Taking her service weapon would likely get her fired. He didn't want that.

He slipped out the door and let the Jeep roll back into the street before he started it up. He waited until he was three streets away before he turned on the headlights. He saw the taillights of one truck pulling out onto the state road but nothing else as he approached the town center. He made the turn onto the new approach road without seeing anyone else, cars or tractor trailers, the rest of the way. He killed the headlights early and took it slow, thankful that the road was straight and smooth. When he could see the lights of the warehouse, he bumped off the pavement and drove off-road, thankful for the suspension in Serrato's Jeep. He hid the car behind what appeared to be the old railroad depot building, judging by the shape and nearby water tower, then walked the rest of the way in and took up his spot against the wall to watch.

He'd been watching for fifteen minutes now. Unlike the afternoon, the warehouse was alive with activity. Max thought that was both good and bad. Plenty of activity meant there was a good chance he could figure out just what was happening in the warehouse. The trucks coming in and out also provided a lot of movement and distractions but also a lot of eyes. In the time he'd been watching, he'd seen three trucks go through the gate. Two going in and one coming out. There'd also been one roving guard patrol; two men in a black golf cart went past the front gate and continued along the fence line. Max watched and waited but had yet to find a practical way he could get inside. Not tonight. Not alone.

And not through the front.

He walked back into the remains of the railroad town and then, when he'd judged he was far enough away from the gate to be invisible, he turned right and walked into the desert. He took a wide looping route, keeping the lights of the warehouse on his right. The moon was waning but provided just enough light to see objects a few feet in front of him. He was lucky the terrain was mostly flat and empty. But not completely. There were still rocks, small plants, and divots. He had to fight against the urge to go faster. Twisting or breaking an ankle out here would not just be dangerous, it could be deadly when the sun came up.

Occasionally, he heard the big diesel engines of the semi-trucks inside the compound turn over and roar to life. He walked, slow and steady. At one point, he heard a squeal and a cry off to his left and realized that maybe he should be less afraid of twisting his ankle and more afraid of rattlesnakes. He knew they could hunt at night, and he just had to hope his heat signature was too big to take on.

It took close to a half hour to put the warehouse lights at his back. He judged he'd walked a slow two miles. He turned now and walked toward the light. This time looking for a back door. There were no big sodium lights in the back. He stopped a hundred yards away from the fence and tried to see if there were any cameras. He didn't think so, but he couldn't be sure. If there were infrared cameras, he'd probably already been seen. He stood and waited. If he'd been spotted, there would have been a response of some kind. He counted to 500 in his head but nothing happened. Maybe they were patient. Or maybe there were no cameras. There was no road behind the complex. There was really nothing behind the complex but empty desert for miles. Why spend the money on cameras to watch that? Max planned to take advantage of that oversight.

He walked right up to the fence and realized his plan wouldn't work.

The rear fence was topped with barbed wire. Someone wasn't completely asleep when it came to security. Max studied it. It wasn't angled inward. That would have been even more of a challenge. It stuck straight up as a three-foot extension to the 10-foot high fence. He went right up to the fence and looked straight up. It was taut and sharp. Max could see that much, even in the low moonlight. It was more than capable of shredding his skin. He walked the fence line for half a mile in one direction, toward the center, but found no breaks or weak spots. The complex was still new, and the fence had not had time to deteriorate. He walked back in the other direction until he came to the corner and found no gaps in that direction either. The barbed wire continued off unbroken toward the front and the big spotlights. It did not extend across the front of the complex, but he chided himself for not spotting it earlier. It was now going to cost him at least an hour of walking. He glanced down at his watch and then back up at the horizon. Time he might not have.

He retraced his steps back into the dark and swung

around until he was again shielded by the abandoned buildings that surrounded Blackburn's warehouses. He tried to move more quickly and had to check himself from breaking into a jog. At one point, he heard two or three coyotes calling to each other but they never came any closer. He made it back to where he'd parked Serrato's Jeep.

He'd disabled the interior lights so after he opened the rear door, he needed to use his phone to search the Jeep's storage area. He was dismayed but not entirely surprised to find that Serrato kept a very clean car. But she was also practical. Or he was just a little lucky. There were no bolt cutters or extension ladders, he wasn't that lucky, but he did find a jack, a portable air compressor, a first aid kit, and a thick, folded, outdoor blanket. He grabbed the blanket and set out walking again.

As he approached the fence for the second time, he heard a low whine and the crunching sound of tires on gravel. The guards doing their rounds in the golf cart. He quickly retreated and lay down flat on the ground. There was no time to find more concealment. Earlier, when he'd seen the cart drive past the gatehouse, he'd noted a spotlight attached but it hadn't been turned on. They'd only used the weaker front headlights of the cart. Was that because they'd been in the front, the lighted area, and didn't need the spot or was it because the spot was only used occasionally? He had to hope it was the latter and that the guards were lulled by routine. The spotlight would easily pick him out in the emptiness. It was now close to 3 a.m. and Max hoped the guards were thinking more about the end of their shift than searching and securing the complex. The crunching grew louder. He pressed his face into the dirt. As the noise crescendoed, he felt, maybe imagined, the headlights sweep over him. He tensed, ready to stand and bolt. Then the noise moved away. He waited another thirty seconds and then glanced up. The cart was almost out of sight. He felt his heart rate tick back down. This was only the second time he'd seen the roving patrol. He guessed they made one, maybe two rounds per hour. It had been a close call, but he could now use it to his advantage. He looked at his watch. He gave himself twenty minutes. A healthy buffer before the cart circled back again.

The fence was still new, and the lack of holes or disrepair mostly worked against Max, but it conversely helped in one respect. The fence was sturdy and still well anchored. When Max grabbed it, it hardly moved. He stripped off his belt and used it to bind the blanket. He was then able to climb and grip both the fence and the belt. At the top, he carefully unwound the belt and draped the heavy, wool blanket over a section of barbs. He tested it by pressing his hand into the wire. He could feel the barbs poking against the blanket but was confident he could get across without ripping up his flesh. He dropped the belt to the ground and then threw one leg over, balanced for a second, then brought his other leg over before climbing to the ground and retrieving his belt. He looked up. The blanket looked stable, and he had to hope it would remain in place and allow him to reverse the process to get back out.

He crouched in the dark and turned his focus on the warehouse.

CHAPTER FORTY

He'd landed fifty yards behind the final warehouse. The light remained dim back here with little spillover from the warehouses and trucks themselves. The first forty yards were empty scrub before the pavement picked up. Closer to the rear of the buildings, he could make out dark shapes of various pieces of equipment and a few doors scattered along the back, but couldn't make out much more detail than that. It remained quiet and nothing moved. So he did. He ran at a crouch.

He slowed near the warehouse's rear wall. Up close, the equipment resolved into various kinds of discarded junk. A metal door. Piles of bound cardboard boxes. Various tires. A lawn chair. A rusting barbecue. A light pole. Max navigated around them and tried the first door. Locked. He skirted more junk and tried the second door. Also locked. It wasn't going to be that easy. The warehouse was long, and the doors were scattered regularly. He didn't want to waste the little time he had left before daylight checking them all. It was likely they locked automatically when they closed. He back-tracked to the rear corner and turkey peeked around the short side. No one. It was empty as far as he could see. He jogged to the next corner.

The length of the warehouses was equal to a football field, maybe slightly longer now that Max was closer, but the width, the short side, was less than half that long, but in his current condition even the brief jog left him winded. He paused at the next corner to catch his breath and then peeked around. This time, he was looking down the active side of the warehouse. He could see at least three trailers idling at docking bays, but there might have been more. The trailer closest to Max blocked most of his view. Their headlights were off but various white and yellow running lights gave off a soft glow. He couldn't see anyone moving near the closest cab. For such a large facility, it appeared to be sparsely populated with actual workers.

He thought about his next move. Check the truck or check the interior of the warehouse? He glanced over his shoulder. Still dark, but he thought he detected a faint gray line down low on the horizon. Not a lot of time either way. The truck would be faster and expose him less, but he didn't see a way to get into the trailers. Each truck he could see was backed up tight against the loading dock bumpers. There was no way to get into the trailers to check the loads.

There was a short stairway and door next to each dock. Max crept along the side of the building to the nearest door. It was next to an empty dock with the roll-down door closed. The nearest active dock was three bays further along. He went up the stairs two at a time and gently tried the door handle. Locked like the back doors. He'd give it one more shot. Maybe the active dock's door would be open. He came off the step, with one eye on the idling truck cab as he made his way forward. He took it slow. Slow and steady. A fast-moving object is more likely to catch the eye. He went up the steps and reached for the handle but then noticed a seam of light on the steps. Someone had stuck a chunk of wood, a makeshift doorstop, in the gap to keep the door from closing and presumably automatically locking. Convenience always trumped security.

He put an ear to the door and heard the beeps of a forklift backing up, but it sounded far away, maybe the opposite side of the building. He slipped inside. The warehouse was broken into rows, with tall rows of pallet racks reaching almost to the ceiling. Not every aisle was filled to capacity but more than half were. Max heard the forklift approaching and quickly ducked between the rows and around a wrapped pallet. The forklift went by carrying a pallet and Max heard it slow, then a more hollow sound, followed by a clanging thud, then the recognizable sharp beeps of the forklift backing up.

Max slid between the pallets and returned to the loading dock. The trailer was almost full of wrapped pallets. He stepped inside and tried to make out the markings on the individual boxes. He recognized the universal symbol for hazardous, but the rest were difficult to make out. The light was dim in the trailer and thick, overlapping plastic wrap bound and covered the boxes. He pulled at the plastic wrap and took some photos anyway, then he heard the rumble of the forklift approaching again and retreated into the stacks.

He moved away from the active loading dock to the opposite side of the warehouse and took out his phone again. The pallets were already wrapped but he continued to take photos. In a few instances, he could make out the shipping or freight label, but it didn't list an address or the contents. It was just a barcode and a fragile icon with jumbles of letters and numbers that meant nothing to Max. He slid between the rows and took more pictures, but he didn't find any more information to help identify the cargo. He came to the end of a row and could see an office at the opposite end in a more well-lit area. He thought about trying to get inside and search any paperwork he might find but ultimately dismissed the idea. Too risky. It was time to go. He wasn't sure what he'd found, if anything, but he'd add it to his lint pile and sort it out later. He started back for the door where he'd entered but heard the forklift coming and changed course to the next door farther along.

He opened it and immediately knew he'd made a mistake.

The smell of cigarettes hit him first. His brain was ahead of his body. He almost tripped over the guy taking a smoke break on the dock steps. The guy glanced up and was about to say something when he saw Max. More importantly, he saw Max and didn't recognize him. He started to stand, and Max kicked him in the stomach. The air left the guy's lungs with an audible whoosh. He didn't want to hurt the guy. Not badly, but he needed time. Or at least a head start. He couldn't have the guy raising the alarm by shouting for his buddy on the forklift. He grabbed the guy by his shirt and pulled him down to the bottom of the stairs. The man stumbled but didn't trip. Max didn't want him falling and hitting his head. He wanted the guy out of commission for a bit, not permanently brain damaged. The guy was struggling for air but tried to put up his fists. Max quickly stepped left and hit him with a quick hard jab to the side of the head, just behind and above his ear. He knew it was the one place guaranteed to ring someone's bell and leave them dizzy and disoriented. The man went to one knee, his mouth opened and closed like a fish out of water, then he went all the way to the ground. He was out. Max checked his pulse and breathing, both fine, and then dragged him into the shadows near the warehouse wall where he wouldn't be seen easily.

He had exited farther down the length of the warehouse and would have to run around, or crawl under, two tractor trailers before he'd reach the fence. He opted to run around. It would be longer, but faster. He ran to the end of the first one and paused to check for any roving patrols. Nothing. He stepped around the front of the truck, and it was like being hit flush in the face with a two-by-four. He hadn't actually been hit with anything, but he still staggered back a step. Memories flooded back. It was like unlocking a rusty door and shining a spotlight inside. He shielded his eyes and raised his head, almost afraid to look, as if the light would blind him, but it was still dark. There was no bright light. The truck's cab roof lights and side marker lights cast the surrounding area in a soft orange glow. It had only been in his head.

He dropped his hand and stepped closer to the truck. He reached out his hand again, this time toward the truck's grill. The Peterbilt logo was cracked and faded. Only the Peter was still outlined in red. The paint had chipped or faded off the end. This was one of the trucks that had tried to run him down. He took a step back toward the unconscious guy. He might be the driver. He might be one of the guys who had put him in the hospital. On his second step, an alarm started inside the warehouse. He could hear it through the walls.

It might not be for him.

On his third step, a set of floodlights lit up the outside area around the warehouse.

It was for him.

He could duck back inside and try to hide, try to wait it out, but while there were a lot of pallets inside, there didn't appear to be a lot of good places to hide for an extended period of time. He'd only be prolonging the inevitable. Should he go for the fence? That might also be prolonging the inevitable, especially if he didn't get back to the car by first light. Both options were risky and likely to end in failure, but Max decided the fence was the better of two bad choices.

He ran straight down the aisle, no use being sneaky now, and then turned left toward the back corner. He briefly ran through darkness as the lights didn't extend to the short ends of the warehouse and then he was back in the light. He heard shouts behind him and then the sound of engines, not the low whine of golf carts, but bigger, faster fuel-injected ones. He risked a quick glance over his shoulder as he neared the fence. There was no one chasing him. Not yet. They knew something was wrong. That someone was inside but had not yet pinpointed him. Max knew that would change soon. There weren't that many options.

On cue, he heard a shout. "He's heading for the fence. Northwest corner!" Then a spotlight lit him up. He hit the fence and scrambled up but the frantic effort to climb shook the blanket loose. Luckily, it fell toward the inside. He flashed a hand out, mostly from instinct, and just managed to grab a corner. He threw the blanket across the top, put one hand over, threw his right leg across, and then moved to put his other hand across when the fence shook and the blanket fell. Max looked down. A black-clad guard had started climbing in pursuit. Max lifted his left leg over and felt the sharp bite of the barbs in his thigh. He didn't stop. He felt the barbs dig and scrape and then he pulled his leg free. He carefully moved his other arm. He was over the top. He lowered himself a few feet and jumped the rest of the way. He looked up. The guard was alone. He'd been in one of the golf carts. Max could see other vehicles approaching. The guard was near the top and was hesitating. Max reached back and shook the fence hard. The guard yelled. Max had to hope it would make him pause in trying to play the hero. He turned and raced into the dark.

CHAPTER FORTY-ONE

He sprinted hard for 200 to 300 yards, risking the loose stones and divots in order to put distance between himself and his pursuers. He tripped twice and felt blood running down his leg from the barbed wire cut. He ran until his lungs burned and then slowed to a walk. The vast openness of the desert was striking and might have been starkly beautiful in a different context. Max knew the emptiness was just a lie now. He felt all alone but knew it wouldn't take them long to mobilize a response team and come looking. Then it was just a matter of time.

He wouldn't make it easy for them. He glanced around and oriented himself to the town ruins and then began to run again as he retraced the path he'd already walked twice that night. Maybe he'd get lucky and slip through their net and make it back to Serrato's Jeep. On his left, he could now see three sets of headlights leaving the warehouse compound through the front gate. He watched as they turned toward him. The headlights jittered as they bumped off the paved road and onto the surrounding scrub. He noticed the vehicles didn't slow much on the unpaved terrain. He picked up his pace as best he could, it wasn't much, and tried to simultaneously see any obstacles in his way and watch the headlights. The situation got worse. All three vehicles turned on bright, mounted lightbars and lit up the surrounding night even more. The pursuit vehicles appeared to be pickup trucks. There would be no luck involved. Finding him would be like shooting a fish in a barrel. He briefly thought about just going to his knees and putting his hands up. If there were two guys per truck, six total, bad odds, even worse if they were armed, which was likely given the guard this afternoon. But, if he took the first pair by surprise, got a weapon ... no, he didn't envision any scenario that didn't end up with him bound, shot, or even in a shallow grave.

He kept running.

The trucks spread out; they hadn't spotted him yet, but they kept coming. The halogen lights brightened big swaths of the desert. Strong search lights punching out holes in the dark. Only a matter of time. He veered left and right, zigged and zagged to try to increase the time he'd stay hidden. He watched in dismay as the pickups slowly organized themselves, they must be in contact on radios, and began covering the terrain together in a logical pattern. They were sweeping in quarter-mile grids, going east and then north, before reversing west and then north again, guessing correctly that he was heading for the ruins. Anything else was virtual suicide. Max judged they were a half mile behind him. He had maybe sixty seconds until they lit him up and this was over. The nearest building was still over a mile away. The math wasn't on his side. He put his head down and tried to go faster. His mind was willing, but his body had nothing left. Not after three days in the hospital. Adrenaline had gotten him this far, but he had emptied the tank. His legs shook, dark spots danced in his eyes. He stumbled and almost went down. Behind him he could hear the sound of the engines change as they made the turn. Not long now. Soon the engine noise would grow even louder as they made the last turn onto his vector and then the dark would become light. And they'd have him.

Then he heard something unexpected.

A crack and a pop. Then another. He instinctively hunched over.

The sound wasn't loud. The desert swallowed most of the noise, but Max recognized gunshots. He kept going. The shots were not aimed at him.

More shots. Now at a faster clip. Then a new sound. An engine revving but not coming from the direction of the pickup trucks chasing him. It was ahead of Max and getting closer. A shape slowly resolved out of the dark. A big, black Escalade slid to a stop and the passenger door opened.

"Can't you do anything on your own?"

Max climbed inside. The big truck was moving before he had the door closed.

"Never trust those car commercials that show these things going off-road. It's a big lie. It's going to get real bumpy. Here, take this. See if you can make yourself useful."

Lawrence handed him a rifle. It was black with a pistol grip and a curved magazine. Some variant of an AK47.

"It's live, so be careful," Lawrence said as he spun the wheel and hit the gas.

Max was too shocked to question how Lawrence had materialized out of the desert. Max grabbed what Danny used to call the 'oh shit' handle, lowered the window, and fired off a few rounds. He didn't want to hit anything or anyone. He just wanted the guys in pursuit to back off. It appeared to work.

"Don't break an axle; it looks like they might be reconsidering." Max watched the lights slowly fall back. Lawrence slowed down but it was still a rough ride. A minute later, they were behind the ruins and the lights disappeared.

"Need to get the car. Can't leave it," Max shouted.

Lawrence spun the wheel and cut down a space between two of the old buildings. Max looked back. Still no lights. The road, a loose term at best, had not been re-paved like the warehouse approach, but it was better than driving over open desert.

"How did you find me?"

"Tracked your phone. Got an alert that you were moving in the middle of the night. It piqued my interest. Followed you out here. Glad I did."

There was so much more to cover but that was enough for now. "Glad you did." They were coming up on Serrato's Jeep. "Where you staying?"

"Moving around. Mostly hotels outside of town by the main highway. Currently at a Best Western near the interchange for 35 and 44. Next to the Love's truck stop."

"Okay, let's split up. I'll find it."

Lawrence braked hard. Max left the rifle in the footwell and jumped out. Lawrence didn't wait. He was accelerating away as Max raced around the front of the Jeep and jumped in. He was glad he left the keys dangling in the ignition. Ten seconds later and Max was in pursuit. He'd split off later but there was only one way out of this ghost town, and they had to press their advantage while they had it. Max stayed on the bumpy outer roads as long as he could but eventually cut left and found the paved road. He could see Lawrence's taillights in the distance. He looked in the side mirrors. There were lights in the distance. Would they keep up the chase? Max didn't intend to find out. He flipped the headlights on, no use hiding anymore, and pushed the Jeep up to 90 miles per hour. When the road intersected with the state road, Lawrence went left and Max went right.

. . .

It took almost another hour to make the winding, circuitous route north to the Best Western, but Max never saw any cars in pursuit once he turned onto the state road. He called Lawrence when he was in the parking lot.

"You good?" Max asked.

"Just a nice midnight drive."

"What room?"

"214. Park around back."

Max pulled the Jeep around and parked next to Lawrence's SUV. A familiar Cadillac Escalade that he favored. It was covered in dust but otherwise looked no worse for its rescue mission. Max glanced through the passenger window. The rifle was gone. He tapped the hood as he walked past. *Good girl*, he thought.

Room 214 was the second room from the end. The door was cracked. Max pushed through and found Lawrence lying on one of the double beds. There was a single light on and the room was mostly in shadows. Something clicked in Max's head. It was as if someone or something was going through the lost rooms in his mind, the ones that had been blacked out from the accident, and turning on the lights. His head hummed.

"You came to see me in the hospital," he said to Lawrence.

Not a question. Lawrence had been the shadow man at the foot of the bed. "How did you know I was there?"

"I knew where you were tonight from your phone. I knew something bad had happened because of the car."

"The car?"

"There's a sensor in the car that detects any significant impact whenever the vehicle is moving over 25 miles per hour and sends an alert."

Max shut the door and sat on the opposite bed. "Thanks for coming and thanks for tonight."

"It's what we do." Lawrence swung his legs off the side of the bed and faced Max. "So, let's figure this out. Just what kind of trouble did you find this time?"

Max spent the next fifteen minutes filling Lawrence in. He already knew about Blackburn and how it started, so Max took him through Ortiz, the local bank manager killed near the salt house; his visit to Kelley and San Antonio; the social media threats against Kelley's wife and daughter; then his run-in with the two tractor trailer trucks on his way back to Tiendas Reales, the warehouse, and the flash of recognizing the Peterbilt truck at the dock tonight.

Lawrence was quiet when Max finished. "Your memory might be coming back but this thing still has holes."

"Uh-huh. Big ones."

"And that was what tonight was about?"

"You could say that. You've been in TR for a few days now. You've dug into Blackburn. How is he funding the ranch, the real estate, the warehouse? According to Serrato, he also owns at least half the town."

Lawrence reached over and picked up a sheaf of papers. "I was going to send these to you but after you decided to try on another concussion, I thought I'd just bring them to you myself."

Max took the papers and quickly flipped through them. It was a prison file on a Daniel Willeford who spent 54 months, starting in 2002, at FCI El Reno, a medium security facility in Oklahoma, for defrauding his previous employer of almost half a million dollars. There were two photos included. Alex Blackburn had put on some weight and had his teeth capped since he'd been released.

"Mr. Willeford skipped out on his probation. Warrant is probably still good."

"Good to know our instincts for sniffing out a criminal are

still sharp," Max said. "And he went down for white-collar stuff. He's a money guy. A numbers guy."

"Follow the money," Lawrence said.

"I'm trying."

"You think that will lead to the wife?"

"It might not be a direct line, but I think it's related in some way. A lot of Blackburn's plans started up around the same time Rose disappeared."

"So what's next?"

"Two things. First, I want to talk to the driver of that tractor trailer truck."

"If the truck is still there, that shouldn't be too hard. Just gotta be patient."

"If it's not there, I think it's nearby. I don't think he's a traveler. If he was going to disappear for a bit, he would have done it already after he ran me off the road."

"Or he's confident you didn't see him."

"Or heard. I can't remember. These people are plugged in."

"You think they have a line into the hospital?"

"Not hard to imagine. Blackburn could get his ear close if he wanted to."

"That's true. *If* Blackburn is the one behind it."

"You don't think so?"

"Makes the most sense. With what we know. Which has more holes than a screen door."

"I'm not locking in on Blackburn."

Lawrence raised an eyebrow, but only said, "What's the second thing?"

"I want to talk to Blackburn's staff. They provided his alibi on Rose's disappearance and partially for the Ortiz murder. They're all long-term employees. I want to know more about Rose too, if I can. She remains mostly a cipher in all of this. The local girl, the wife, the widow, the disappeared. I have a lot of labels but not a lot of sense of who she is."

"I'll take the warehouse stakeout."

"Be careful. They're going to be on high alert now."

"Still less dangerous than hanging out as a strange Black man in a small town."

"Don't make assumptions."

"No assumptions necessary. Already got the stink eye a few times."

"It might be your charming personality."

"I'm not sure that's translating all that well down here, either."

"Don't give up on this town yet. I want you to meet someone."

CHAPTER FORTY-TWO

"Do I want to see this?" Serrato asked.

Lawrence gave him a look. "She has a point."

Max hesitated. They were both correct. Serrato was a sworn police officer. Even if she agreed with what they were doing, it could still come back to haunt her if everything went sideways. He also shouldn't assume she was as comfortable with treading in gray areas as he and Lawrence were. It could make her liable or an accessory after the fact.

"If you want out or to be kept in the dark, let me know now," Max said.

She blew out a breath and looked across the table at the empty chair. Maybe trying to channel what advice Sam would give her. The three of them were sitting at Serrato and Sam's dining room table. The remains of lunch were scattered in front of them. Empty bowls of leftover soup and the remaining crumbs of bread dotted their plates. Kennedy was not there. She was at the office, which was likely just as well. She might like to hear a good story over a meal, but if she were seated next to Serrato now, she'd face the same ethical quandary. Where would she go to find Rose? How far would she go to protect Angie? To maybe find out what was strangling her town?

Serrato focused back on the table in front of them. "I'm in," she held up a hand, "for now. But I'm not breaking any laws to help you."

"We wouldn't ask you to."

"Don't ask. Don't tell. I'm familiar with that."

Max slid the phone across to her. After their desert escape, they'd crashed for six hours in Lawrence's hotel room and then gotten back to work. Lawrence had enlisted Eddie's help with the photos that Max had managed to take inside the warehouse. He'd already come back with some information while they slept. Serrato picked up the phone and flipped through the various shots of the wrapped pallets. The labels and markings were only partials visible in some shots. Completely obscured in others.

"Does this help?" she finally asked.

"Maybe," Lawrence said. "We're working on it. The technical name for the barcodes found on the pallets is serial shipping container codes or SSCCs. You'll find those on the individual boxes and the pallets. If you can read them, they'll tell you a lot about the logistics of the shipment."

"Can we read them?"

Lawrence smiled. "Yes. Max didn't get the best photos, but what he lacked in quality, he made up for in quantity. We were able to stitch together various shots to get at least one complete readable barcode. There appears to be more than one product in the warehouse, but we couldn't identify the others."

"And?"

"Solvents. Specifically, at least for the pallets in the photos, toluene."

"Never heard of it."

"Not surprised. I had to look it up, too. It's a colorless,

water-insoluble liquid used in any number of legitimate household products like paint thinners, markers, and glue. That smell from paint thinners? It's mostly toluene. It can also be used as an octane booster in gasoline."

"And it's illegitimate uses?"

Lawrence gave a thin smile. "That's where it gets more interesting. You can inhale it or huff it for a cheap high, but it's also a precursor chemical for meth, fentanyl, quaaludes, and PCP."

"Precursor?"

"Precursor chemicals are those that the government regulates because they're known to be used in the illegal manufacture of drugs."

"What's Blackburn doing with it? Is he making it out there?"

"I don't think so," Max chimed in. "I didn't see the whole place, but what I did see appeared to be only for storage. I didn't see anything like a lab or buildings for manufacturing this stuff. I've also seen tanker trucks mixed in with the freight trucks. I think he's shipping it to a facility in bulk, we saw a tanker truck yesterday remember, and then breaking it down into smaller sizes."

"Can't be in containers larger than five gallons or shipped outside a specialized tanker truck because it's classified as a hazardous chemical," Lawrence said.

"On the surface, the operation appears to be exactly what Blackburn's always maintained. A warehouse for import and export. He's a middleman."

"Is this toluene the only thing he's importing and exporting?"

"We don't know," Max said. "It's the only thing we know for sure from the SSCC. And there's a lot of it. A couple of very long rows of it, but we know there are at least two other things in there, too. Plus, I was only in one of the buildings and only in a small part of it. Could be even more."

"Is there that much demand for toluene?"

"I had the same question and did some quick research," Lawrence said. "The short answer is yes. It's projected to grow to $30 billion by 2030. And now is a good time, too, as a lot of the smaller operators were put out of business during the pandemic and the travel bans."

Max watched Serrato take that in and waited for her next question.

"Who is he the middleman for?"

"His buyer could be anyone in the paints and coatings sector. The government oversight will limit the growth, but even a small sliver of five percent a year of $30 billion is a lot of money."

"Or pharmaceuticals," Max added.

"Legitimate or illegitimate?" Serrato asked.

Max held up his hands. "Either way, he's making money."

"Yes, but one way means this town might survive while the other means finding a way to get cuffs on Blackburn."

Max glanced at Lawrence before he said, "We might know more soon."

"Don't ask?"

"Exactly." He wasn't about to tell Serrato their plan to tag one of the trucks with a GPS device. Or that one of the trucks at the warehouse was involved in his accident.

"Okay." She pushed back her chair, stood up, and began clearing the dishes. "This is all interesting and, if Blackburn is involved in the shadier pharma side, it might explain why he's been so quiet about the source of his funding, but there are two problems. One for me, one for you." She looked at Max. "First, we have no proof of anything illegal."

"Agreed. What's the second thing?"

"I think you're getting off track. How does toluene have anything to do with Rose's disappearance?"

"Where there's smoke, there's fire. If Blackburn is involved in the shadier stuff, then it opens up new angles on how and why Rose might have disappeared."

"She went missing more than five years ago. That warehouse didn't start operating until last year."

"Could still be connected. These types of plans don't spring up overnight. It takes time to get everything in place. Renovate those old buildings. If he's really involved with using toluene to manufacture illegal drugs then it would take a lot of coordination to make that happen. Remember toluene is closely watched and regulated. You'd need a lot of coordinated leaks and cooperation to siphon it off and not raise any eyebrows. That takes money and time, so I'm not dismissing it being somehow related to Rose's disappearance."

"Okay, it's farfetched from a timing perspective perhaps, but it brings up another question. If Blackburn is doing this, why would he hire you?"

It was the question he kept coming back to himself and he didn't have an answer. "I don't know. Not yet. Maybe one thing really isn't related to the other. Secrets beget secrets. Maybe he thinks he can find Rose and keep the other parts of his life and business under wraps. I'm not the first guy he's hired. Maybe the others were digging in the wrong sandbox, and he didn't like it."

"So why would he like you doing it?"

"He won't but he also doesn't know we've been digging."

"Not yet."

"True."

"Are you going to tell him at your meeting?"

"Depends on what we find out between now and then. Could be useful to push him, see how he reacts."

"What are you going to do now? Do I want to know?"

"Well, first, I need to, uh, borrow your car again."

She rolled her eyes but nodded. "Okay."

"Then I'm going to talk to the housekeeper. I want to ask her about Rose's life on the ranch. And then ... we have a few other ideas."

CHAPTER FORTY-THREE

Max's mobile vibrated. He was in Serrato's Jeep, borrowed with her knowledge this time, driving out to the Double R. He glanced down at the display. He vaguely recognized the number, it was local, but he couldn't place it. "Hello?"

"Mr. Parish?"

"Yes, who's this?"

"Leslie Halford, Halford Jewelry. I'm returning your call. You left a message."

Her voice was rich and warm but without a real discernible accent. After almost a week trawling the back roads of the state, his ear had become accustomed to the slow honey drawl of south Texas.

"Thank you for returning my call, Miss Halford."

"Please, it's been a long time since anyone called me miss. It's Leslie. Sorry, it took a few days. I was out of town on business."

"Business for the store?"

"Yes, I often take business trips around the southeast to scout for new artists, or pieces, or just unique ... things that I might be able to sell."

"There's enough of that around to make a living?"

"That doesn't seem like a very polite question."

"No? Forgive my impertinence then. I didn't mean to insult you. Just curiosity."

"Well, you know what they say about curiosity, but you are close to the truth. It's a knife's edge. I also do some graphic design and website things to help make ends meet. I wouldn't survive just on local traffic. My store sits out by the highway, so we get some drive-by traffic, but most of my sales are online through Etsy and eBay. But you didn't call to hear about my business, did you? Your message didn't say much. How can I help you?"

Max explained as briefly as he could about Rose and how he'd ended up with her name and number.

"Of course, I remember Rose. It was a terrible thing that happened. Some days it still doesn't feel real. I'm not sure what I can tell you that would help after all this time."

"That's what everyone keeps saying but, in my experience, the best way to find things out is to just keep talking to people. Better yet, listen to people, so anything you can recall might be helpful. Did the police talk to you at the time of Rose's disappearance?"

"No, I've never talked to anyone about Rose."

"But you were friends?"

"I suppose."

"You don't sound so sure."

"A real friend is someone who walks in when the rest of the world walks out."

That sounded too crisp to be spontaneous to Max. "Who said that?"

"My dad. If you needed a bolt, a nut, a screw, or other small metal goods in the Kenosha area, he was your man. And yes, I've heard all the screw and nut jokes by this point, so don't even try."

Max believed her. "How did you get from Wisconsin to Texas?"

"Met a guy at college in Madison. Was stupid enough to marry him after I graduated. Followed the man south for work. Got rid of the man but stuck with Texas."

"You met Rose through the library?"

"Yes. I assume Margit told you we were both on the board."

"Yes."

"A mostly bland and boring job, at least until someone in the community gets it in their head that banning books is a good idea. Then the monthly meetings can get a little spicy."

"Did you socialize outside of the trustee meetings?"

"No. Rose was always busy with that ranch, and she was pretty introverted in general. Our relationship mostly took place in or around the library. We talked about books or the library or sometimes about Angie."

"Do you have any children yourself?"

"No, thank God. I was smart enough to kick the ex to the curb before we doubled down on our mistake with kids."

"Did Rose talk about her husband?"

"Alex? Sure, he'd come up from time to time."

"Did you ever meet him?"

"No, not in person."

"Really?"

"Maybe once in a crowd at a library fundraiser. My impression from Rose was that he was very driven. Very busy."

"Did you get any other sense of him from Rose?"

There was a pause. Max could hear a keyboard tapping in the background. She was either a multitasker or using the time to gather her thoughts. "She seemed mostly relieved."

"Relieved?"

"Do you know about her first marriage? How it ended?"

"Yes."

"That was devastating to her, and I think she was a bit overwhelmed being a widow so suddenly and also being in charge of all the ranch business. Plus, still a relatively new mother. It was a lot, all at once. So maybe it wasn't true love with Blackburn but more of a partnership. She was willing to trade on some things in exchange for having someone around to share the burden."

"Relief is a weird emotion to build a marriage on. Did you get any sense of their marriage?"

"How so?"

Max shrugged and realized that wouldn't translate over the phone. "Anything memorable?"

There was another pause. "If I catch your meaning, she never said anything like that. Nothing to make me worried for her safety, but we really weren't those kinds of friends. She wasn't going to cry on my shoulder. I'm not sure she was the type to cry on anyone's shoulder. I think if anything was happening, and I don't think there was, she was the type that would clam up even tighter. She'd take it until she figured out a solution."

"Did you ever see her with any injuries? Bruises?"

"Rose was an introvert but I'm not. If I saw something like that I would have asked and not taken a story of her running into a doorway as gospel. In fact, now that you mention it, I did see her with an injury once. It was her wrist. She told me it was a minor fracture from falling off her horse when he balked at a creek crossing. She seemed more embarrassed than scared. It happens. Seemed plausible. I didn't even question it. Thinking back on it now, I still don't."

Max could feel the thread running out on the conversation. "Did she have any other friends?"

"None that she mentioned to me unless you count the housekeeper. I can't remember her name, but I remember she would come up occasionally. But her life was mostly that ranch and Angie."

"And books."

"Yes, and books too."

"And you never got any hint that she might ... disappear? Leave Angie? What do you think happened to her, Leslie?"

There was a pause, and her voice was thicker when she answered this time. "I like to think she's still out there somewhere. I don't think she'd leave that girl without a very good reason."

Max tended to agree. It was the one piece of this mystery that bothered him the most. "Thank you for returning my call, Leslie."

Max dropped the phone in the cupholder. He could think of one very good reason Rose hadn't come back for Angie, but he hadn't been crass enough to say the obvious out loud. It was the assumption everyone else had already come to, even if Leslie Halford still preferred to fool herself.

He wasn't sure he'd learned anything new. Or had he? He replayed the conversation and had a nagging sense he'd missed something, but like a cool breeze in the Texas summer, the feeling vanished as quickly as it had come.

CHAPTER FORTY-FOUR

Max parked Serrato's Jeep in the shade under the portico. He knew it was only mildly cooler, but he was determined to take every advantage he could get against the sun. Stetson Hull came down the front steps before Max had a chance to even close the car door. Max had to wonder if there was an early warning system that alerted the ranch to vehicles approaching the house.

Hull wiped his brow with a red bandanna. His gray work shirt showed large rings of sweat at the armpits and neck. With such a small ranch staff, Hull's position wasn't just a figurehead. He worked for a living, and he was not in the mood for small talk. That was all right with Max, but he wanted to find out a little more information on Blackburn's foreman.

"What do you want, Yank?"

"How long have you worked for Blackburn?"

Hull paused and his eyes narrowed as if trying to figure out the trap in the question before he sniffed and stuffed the bandanna in his pocket. "I've worked for the Double R for more than ten years."

"Before Blackburn then?"

"That's right. Chuck, Rose's first husband, hired me on. Blackburn was smart enough to realize he didn't need to change a good thing."

"You from TR originally?"

"No." He left it at that. "You drive all the way out here to play twenty questions? What do you want?"

"I want to talk to the housekeeper. She around?"

"Consuela?" Hull glanced at his watch. "Yeah, she's here. Probably making lunch for her and Jorge. They got a place out behind the barn." He jerked a thumb over his shoulder. "Why do you want to talk to her?"

"She's been around a long time, too, right?"

"Sure, I guess. She was here before me. Just a heads up, she don't speak good English."

Max let that go and started around the side of the house toward the barn. He could feel Hull's eyes on his back. He didn't know if Hull had been involved in the hit-and-run attempt on him, but Max could sense they were headed toward some type of confrontation. Not today. He turned the corner and focused his thoughts on Consuela and what she might know about Rose. He thought she probably knew plenty. You didn't work in someone's home for a decade, help raise their child, and not see and hear things. Maybe things you didn't really want to see or hear.

Consuela opened the door and wiped her hands on a blue apron dusted with flour. She was short, maybe clearing five feet with shoes on, with steel gray hair in a tight braid and the slight rounded hunch of someone who works for long periods on their feet. The smell of tortillas, spices, and cooked meat drifted out of the open door.

Her face was guarded but open. "Yes, can I help you?"

Despite Hull's warning, Max found her English accented but perfectly understandable. "My name is Max Parish. I'm working for Alex Blackburn, trying to find his wife. I was hoping to have a brief word with you."

Something passed across her face at the mention of Rose, but it was there and gone too quickly for Max to read.

Consuela nodded. "I know who you are. Roxy told me about you," she said using Angie's first name. "But Ms. Rose? I'm not sure how can I help. She's been gone a long time."

"I understand but sometimes people know things without really knowing what they know. It will only take a few minutes."

She looked over his shoulder though the barn blocked most of the view of the main house. "I have to get back to work soon."

"I understand. I promise only a few minutes. May I come in?"

After another moment of hesitation, she stepped back and let Max in.

The house was a simple square. Just inside the front door, a set of stairs led up to the second floor. The kitchen was straight ahead past the stairs and an open living room with a couch, an old television, and mismatched chairs was to the right. He followed Consuela inside, past the stairs, and down the short hall. Photographs, almost all black-and-whites, in various sizes were hung on the wall. Max recognized the style and framing from the ones he'd seen hanging in the ranch house near Blackburn's office. Max slowed and took them in. Most showed views of the ranch, the animals, and the surrounding desert landscape, but mixed in were also candid shots of a younger Consuela, not quite as hunched, not quite as gray, and a child whom Max recognized as Angie. There was space remaining on the wall, but, like the hallways outside Blackburn's office, no more photos of the family. A life interrupted.

The home's interior did not have central air conditioning and the temperature increased as they made their way closer to the kitchen. A man was sitting at one end of a simple pine table with a plate of food in front of him. He didn't say anything but looked at Consuela. She said something to him in Spanish. He frowned then looked down and continued eating. Neither of them showed any effects of the heat. Max could feel his shirt sticking to his lower back.

"My brother, Jorge," Consuela said, switching back to English. Max recognized him as the gardener he'd spotted on his first visit to the ranch. She indicated another chair. "Would you like something to drink? Iced tea or water?"

"No, thank you."

She nodded and took the chair opposite.

He started with the same question he'd asked Hull. "How long have you worked for Blackburn?"

And she answered in the same way but without the same hostility.

"I've worked at the ranch for more than twenty years. Twenty-three in Septiembre." A little unconscious Spanish slipping into her speech. Max wondered if that was nerves or just habit.

"So well before Alex Blackburn and Rose were married?"

"Before Mr. Forrest, Ms. Rose's first husband, too. I was hired first by Rose's father when she was just out of high school."

"Your brother, too?"

"Jorge came five years later."

"And you were primarily the housekeeper?"

"Yes, housekeeper, cook, babysitter. Anything they felt fell to a female. Jorge was the gardener. He had no experience with horses but did any of the other manual labor that was needed."

"You've been happy here?"

She smiled but Max wasn't sure it was a truly happy smile.

"Happy? I don't know. That is a hard word to define. What I consider happy, maybe you don't. I am guessing we have lived very different lives and both maybe made some choices we regret. But would you change them? Would they make you happier now?"

Max thought of his wife and daughter and the choices he made that led to their deaths even if it brought down an evil man like Carter and potentially spared other innocent lives. It didn't spare his family.

"I might."

"Then you are lucky to see so clearly."

"I don't know if I'd call it lucky."

"I left my village when I was sixteen. Do you know Tlatelolco? No. I can see in your eyes that you do not. It is a neighborhood in Mexico City. In 1969, government troops opened fire on unarmed civilians protesting the upcoming summer Olympics. La noche triste, it was later called. It was part of a larger protest movement led by labor unions and farmers. It did not stop the unrest. My father was one of the organizers on the farming side. Two days before the opening ceremonies, he disappeared from our house in the middle of the night. The next night my oldest brother disappeared. My mother sent me away after that. I never saw my parents or Luis again. Would I change my father's part in that to spare my family? To keep it whole? Or should I be proud of him for his moral fiber even if it cost him his life and me my father?"

"'Let us all be brave enough to die the death of a martyr, but let no one lust for martyrdom.'"

"Gandhi." Consuela smiled again but Max had no trouble seeing the resignation in the look. "Perhaps I have mythologized him, but who doesn't do that with parents especially after they are gone?"

She set her shoulders and appeared to push the past, at least her past, into the background. It was perhaps a skill she'd become very good at. Could she do it with murder? To save herself from another drastic change? What would happen to her and Jorge if Blackburn was arrested?

She continued, "But that is not what you were really asking, was it?"

"No."

"Let's say I was content. I *am* content. The Robideauxes paid a fair wage and so does Mr. Blackburn. Is it better than the life I might have had if I stayed? I don't know. I'll never know."

"What was Rose like as a child?"

"She was fifteen when I first started at the Double R. She was hardly a child."

"How about Rose? Was she happy?"

"Are any teenagers happy? She was emotional but she kept it mostly under wraps. She was well behaved and polite."

"Did she ever let it out?"

"Only when she was riding. That was when she was her truest self. She loved horses and would ride every chance she had."

"Tell me about her first husband."

Consuela looked past him. "Mr. Forrest. He was a good man. Solid, dependable, and kind. He loved the ranch and the animals almost as much as Rose. It was a good partnership."

"A good partnership is an interesting way to describe a marriage."

"A marriage can take many forms."

"How about her second marriage?"

Jorge had been silently eating up until then, but gave a grunt at the question and pushed his plate back. Consuela glanced at him. "Que?" she said. He stood and responded in a stream of Spanish. Max didn't understand more than a few passing words, but he had no trouble with the tone. Jorge was upset. He walked out of the room. A moment later, they heard a heavy tread going up the stairs.

Consuela called out, "No es nuestra decisión."

"Estoy cansado de no hacer nada."

Pipes rattled, then Max heard the sound of water running. Maybe a toilet flushing. Jorge came back down the stairs, the front door opened and then banged shut. Max looked across the table at Consuela.

"Jorge never had children. Neither did I. We both feel like Roxy deserves better. He blames Mr. Blackburn."

"You don't?"

"For what? He did not expect to suddenly be a single father to a teenager who is not his own. He has continued to provide food and shelter. I think it would be unfair to expect much more. Not all men can be fathers."

Max didn't know if that was true. It had been a long time since he'd been a father, but the bare necessities seemed like a low bar. Still, her answer told him more about Blackburn. "You never answered the question. What was her second marriage like to Blackburn?"

She paused as she gathered her thoughts.

"It was not like her marriage to Mr. Forrest. Chuck. But Rose was different, too. Becoming a mother ... she struggled for a time, but she was back on her feet, if a little unsteady. Then Chuck died and that knocked her back down again. It was a difficult time. Mr. Blackburn was a lifeline. He was helpful. He was kind. He probably saved the ranch from going under."

"It sounds more like a benefactor than a husband."

"It was what she needed at the time."

"Seems like a steep price to pay."

"When you are lost in the dark, you will grab anything you can."

"You said he *was* kind. Did that change?"

She glanced away and that told Max more than her words. She was going to lie. Or varnish the truth. Was she protecting Blackburn or protecting herself? Her small house on this ranch? Her contentment?

"Every marriage has cracks."

"Sure. Periods of tension are common. Did it go beyond that? Escalate from words to actions?"

"I never saw him get violent and hit her."

Max had the sense that she was picking her words carefully.

"Did she ever have bruises or injuries?"

"She worked on a ranch with large animals. Of course, she had bruises and injuries."

"Nothing unexplained?"

"No."

"How about Angie?"

"Never."

Max could tell this was a dead end. Consuela was either loyal, scared, or unwilling to acknowledge the truth of the situation. If there even was a situation at all. Unhappy marriages were common. The odds of ending up in a successful long-term relationship basically came down to a coin flip. Did unhappy mean it was abusive? No. That was a big leap.

Max stood up. "Thank you. I've taken up too much of your time."

Consuela stood as well, and Max saw her face relax a fraction now that the questions appeared over. "Like I said, I'm not sure it will help you find Rose."

He followed her as they retraced their steps to the front door. He looked at the series of photos again as he passed.

"Miss Rose liked to take photos," Consuela said.

"What do you think happened to Rose?"

"I think she is gone. For good. I think if she could have come back, she would have."

Max walked out into the glare of the sun. He paused to let his eyes adjust to the brightness. Max thought of those photos in the hall. Were those photos taken by a mother of her daughter? He contrasted that with what Consuela had told him about Rose and what sounded like postpartum depression. Or were they photos taken by a mother trying to keep her distance?

CHAPTER FORTY-FIVE

He walked away from the little house and around to the front of the barn. He stopped. One of the barn doors was open and he stepped inside, drawn more to the shade than out of curiosity. It was darker but not really any cooler inside. It smelled of leather, manure, animals, and hay. There was a small chicken coop that appeared empty on the right before half a dozen horse stalls, two occupied with the horses he'd seen in the ring previously. The left side held six more stalls, all empty, plus a section with hanging saddles and various other bits of tack. There was a second set of doors at the far end that Max guessed led to the enclosed riding area. The horses stomped and snorted as he walked past, probably unused to his scent. There was a hayloft, about half full of bales, above the closed doors at the far end. A set of stairs along the left-hand wall led up to the loft.

"All done?"

Max turned and found Hull standing in the open doorway. The sun was at his back and his face was in shadow. He was holding a pitchfork, tines down and stuck in the earth. It was maybe a little too on the nose, but Max guessed imagination wasn't Hull's strong suit.

"For now."

"Good. Consuela has work to do."

"You her keeper? What about you? You got any work to do? There's probably some shit to shovel in here, right?"

Hull colored and rocked forward on his toes but then caught himself and smiled. "We'll be seeing each other, Yank. Real soon, I think."

Max thought he was probably right. It happened. Like a broken clock was right twice a day. "Look forward to it."

Hull smiled with those ugly, yellow teeth. He tossed the pitchfork into a pile of tools leaning against the barn wall and walked off.

Max left the barn and headed toward the main house. He walked the fence line of the pool and patio until he came to the back door. He stepped up and knocked. He needed to talk to Blackburn. He knew Consuela and Hull weren't inside. Did Blackburn answer his own door? He peered inside. The kitchen was spotless and empty. So was the large interior living room where he'd waited before. He was about to give up when he heard his name. He stepped back off the step and looked up.

"Hey, stranger," Angie was hanging partially out of a second-floor window, the one directly above the trellis with the flowering vine. Max retraced his steps along the fence to the opposite corner of the house.

"How's it going, Angie? Or should I call you Roxy?"

He saw something pass across her face and then she smiled. Max thought she should do it more often. It softened her features. He thought of the family photos lining the hallway inside the house and, with the smile, he could more clearly see the young woman's resemblance to Rose.

"Angie is good. For now."

"Okay, Angie. Is your stepfather home? I need to talk to him."

"No, he's away for work for a few days."

"You're home alone?"

She gave him a look. "I'm almost eighteen years old. So, yes, I'm alone in the house. But hardly alone on the ranch. Plus, what's going to happen out here? What *could* happen? Absolutely nothing."

Max thought about the body out by the salt house. And of Hull's insinuations the first time they'd met. And Rose's disappearance. Angie might have a hard time getting into much trouble on her own, but bad things could certainly happen out here.

Max thought of something. "Did your mother have a lawyer?"

"A lawyer? How would I know? I was just a kid when she ... left."

"I get the sense that even as a kid, you were observant. You paid attention. You noticed things. Did she?"

Angie thought about it. "I don't know. She might have. I did pay attention. Sometimes watching the adults was the only interesting thing to do. I'm sure she and my dad had an attorney for ranch business, probably somebody in town, but I don't remember anyone specifically."

"Would Consuela know?"

Angie shrugged. "I don't know. You could ask her."

"Were she and your mom close?"

"They were the only two women out here," Angie said. Max thought she was going to stop there, but she continued. "I assume they talked. No, I remember them talking but I don't recall about what. It could have been about making the beds or the week's grocery list. Or it could have been more. It can get lonely out here. I just don't know. I was too young. I'll be eighteen soon, but I don't feel any closer to being an adult.

Does talking about mundane stuff like chores make you close to someone?"

Max didn't have an answer for that. His own life lacked that sort of connection. He thought having someone in your life to talk to about such minutiae was a sign of something, but he didn't know any more than Angie if it meant you were close to someone or just had a collection of people in your life.

"Did she have someone like that? Off the ranch? Someone who she could meet up with or talk to other than Consuela?"

"No. When I think back on it, she had acquaintances. People in town or at the library who she would stop and say hello to but not someone she would call up on the phone to talk about *Real Housewives* or make plans for a girls night." She paused. "Living out here can be ... isolating."

Max saw the sadness on Angie's face as she talked and he wondered if she was thinking about her mother or herself. Then she shook it off with a smile. "What happened to your head? Your face looks like a week-old banana and you walked over here like your joints were held together by Scotch tape."

"Colorful," Max replied.

"I get A's in English."

"I was in an accident."

"Is that what you want to talk to Alex about?"

"That's one thing, yes."

"What else?"

"That's between me and your stepfather."

She gave him that look again. She seemed very practiced at it. "Why do people do that?"

"Do what?"

"Hide things?"

"I'm not hiding anything, but I also work for your stepfather. I communicate with him. What he chooses to tell you is up to him."

"Have you found my mom yet?"

He didn't want to get into his suspicions about Blackburn with Angie, but he didn't see the harm in answering that one. "No."

"Any leads?"

"Ask your stepfather."

He got the look one more time before she replied, "You're no fun." And shut the window.

He walked around the side of the house to the Jeep and thought that being a parent was often likely no fun. If you were doing it right.

He climbed in the Jeep and drove off. He looked at the reflection of the ranch in his rearview mirror and admitted to himself that he didn't like the ranch. Could a place be haunted when it was constantly covered in sunshine? He looked around. He didn't see Jorge, Hull, Consuela, or anyone else. Not even the horses. Maybe it was too hot. He felt a pang of guilt about leaving Angie alone, but what could he do about it that he wasn't already doing? Max drove through the two long mounds that held sentry near the entrance to the ranch and then bumped off the smooth road and onto the rutted dirt. He slowed. Vast emptiness spiraled out in front of him.

Yes, he thought it might be possible. Desolation was its own form of haunting.

Angie walked across the hall to the guest room that faced the front of the house. She watched out the window as Max climbed into the car and drove off. She watched as the car reached the end of the paved section and bumped onto the dirt track. As the Jeep kicked up a rooster tail of dust, she saw two more things. First, Jorge walked around the end of the house. He was carrying a pair of gardening shears and the old feed bucket he used to collect weeds and stray branches. He wasn't looking down at the flowerbeds, however; he was staring after the departing car. Idle curiosity or something else? Unlike Consuela, whom she'd known as long as she'd been alive, and could read her moods and intentions quite easily, Jorge remained an enigma to her. He rarely came inside the ranch house unless there was a minor repair that was needed, and he rarely spoke to her even when they crossed paths out in the barn.

As Angie continued to watch, Jorge suddenly swiveled away from the disappearing car and toward the far side of the front yard. She couldn't hear anything through the pane of glass, but a moment later Stetson Hull rounded the corner and came into view. He, too, was watching Max leave. The man certainly attracted attention. She looked up again but could no longer see the car. When she looked back down again, Jorge was gone. At least, that's what she thought at first. He was still there but had stepped back slightly into the manicured flowerbed. That was something else she'd noticed over the years and now sometimes tried to emulate. Jorge and Consuela were very good at hiding in plain sight.

Hull stood and stared at the road until even the dust got bored and settled down, then he turned and walked toward the house. A moment later, Angie heard the front door open and bang shut and then his boot heels on the wood floor. Jorge wasn't the only one who wanted to avoid unnecessary contact with Hull. She'd seen the way he'd started to look at her, and he'd begun to come up with excuses to come and see her. With Alex gone on business, she couldn't think of why he'd need to come into the house. Other than her. The thought twisted her stomach.

She listened for more movement but didn't hear anything.

She slipped off her shoes and went back across the hall into her own room. She quietly pushed the door closed and locked it. The click sounded loud in the sudden silence. It wouldn't keep anyone out who was determined but it might slow them down. Maybe just enough. She put her shoes back on and looked around. As an only child, she knew every inch of the ranch. She'd spent hours exploring all the nooks and crannies. Was she overreacting? Maybe. Then she heard the boot heels again. On the stairs. Maybe he had a legitimate reason to be in the house but upstairs was off limits.

She ran through her options and made a decision. She needed to find Consuela. Hull wouldn't try anything if she was with her. But first, she needed to get out of her locked room.

CHAPTER FORTY-SIX

Lawrence sat in his SUV in the parking lot and watched the trucks, cars, and foot traffic move past his windshield. He was parked near the restaurant entrance in the sprawling truck stop which also offered a truck wash, mechanical repairs, restrooms, showers, clothing, and sundry items. He watched a guy climb down from his rig and head toward the restaurant. A skinny, younger guy with stringy, shoulder-length hair and dirty blue jeans emerged from between two parked trailers and spoke to him. The trucker shook him off and kept moving. The guy slipped back into the shadows. Drugs or girls, probably boys too if that's what you wanted, Lawrence thought. More likely drugs. Lawrence could see at least three women who had been loitering around the restaurant entrance since he'd pulled in who were obviously offering their own wares for sale without the need for a greasy pimp. A blonde, a brunette, and a redhead. A variety pack. All the colors of the rainbow. He also knew there was a fourth woman with spiky raven-colored hair. He glanced in the side mirror with a view of the red Peterbilt. She was currently occupied.

He thought about Max. World weary and savvy in many ways but hopelessly naive in others. But he did try, and that gave Lawrence some hope for the world at large, but he still moved through a different world than Lawrence.

After they'd left the hotel in the early dawn, he'd taken Lawrence to meet up with a lesbian couple living openly in Texas. A cop and lawyer who were helping Max. The lesson wasn't lost on Lawrence after his cracks about being a lone Black man deep in the heart of Texas. It also wasn't proof of some seismic shift. Yes, attitudes were changing, but it was a slow process. Lawrence got that, but it was still exhausting to deal with all the little things every single day. Living in the land of sin, altered the usual equation. Money and greed pushed race down the priority list. Lawrence was okay with that trade off.

More trucks and panel vans pulled in and got in line for the scale or the gas pumps or grabbed open parking spaces. After five more minutes, the Peterbilt cab's door opened and the raven-haired woman climbed down. She glanced quickly around, adjusted her purple miniskirt, said something over her shoulder, and walked back toward the restaurant. It appeared that each girl had a bit of territory given the way they were spaced out and avoiding each other. Lawrence watched her pass the blonde. The blonde said something and Raven Hair responded with a middle finger. She kept walking until she was near the corner, far from the main doors. She looked to be the youngest, or at least the newest, and that must come with less benefits. Lawrence watched her take out a compact and check herself. Satisfied, she put it away and started hunting the parking lot with roving eyes for her next john.

Lawrence checked the Peterbilt again. No movement.

Two more tractor trailers pulled in. The place was near capacity. Lawrence had passed two similar facilities closer to the interchange. There was definitely money to be made here, legal and illegal. Lawrence had done some research last year when he'd come into some new cash to invest and looked at truck stops and fleet parking solutions. The extremely rapid growth in e-commerce in the last decade had led to an explosion of trucks on the road. And, at least for now, those trucks were all driven by humans and those humans needed a break every ten hours. He still remembered one statistic that highlighted the problem and the potential. For every one parking spot in the U.S., there are 11 truck drivers. Something had to give. Ultimately, he had gone in as a silent partner in some RV parks in Canada and California, but this visit to Texas might make him reconsider the truck stop angle.

He caught movement in the corner of his eye and put his thoughts of future earnings aside as the man from the Peterbilt swung down from the cab and started for the restaurant. Lawrence slid down lower in his seat but as he watched in the mirror, the man never looked in his direction. The Peterbilt driver looked like just about every other trucker Lawrence had seen walking the lot in the last half hour. He was perhaps mid-40s, about six feet tall with shaggy brown hair under a cap with a logo that Lawrence couldn't identify. Jeans, boots, and a checkered shirt or T-shirt seemed to be the unofficial uniform, even in this heat. Maybe the truck cabs ran cold, helped keep them awake. The man ignored the brunette and blonde out front and disappeared through the entry doors. Lawrence tracked him through the windows. He first went left toward the restroom and two minutes later walked back in the opposite direction and took a seat by himself in the truckers' area of the restaurant. Lawrence waited until he'd ordered, slipped out of the SUV and made his way toward the Peterbilt.

This wasn't the first time he'd had to break into a truck. In his standard go-kit, he now had a nice little sniffer device from one of Eddie's online friends which made it quite easy to open electronic car door locks, but he still kept his set of bump keys for when old-school manual methods were necessary. The Peterbilt's cab would require some finesse. He pulled his keyring out. His bump set included a number of keys for International, Freightliner, Peterbilt, and other common rigs. He was confident one of the blanks would work. He did a quick casual circuit, up the row and then back down. The Peterbilt was wedged in, in a diagonal line, with thirty other trucks.

He took care of the easy part first. He walked the length of the Peterbilt and decided the wheel well would work best. The GPS tracker was magnetic and waterproof. He stuck it on the front passenger side wheel well. Not the most secure spot, but it didn't need to last long. Unless they were very unlucky, it would do the job. He moved around to the driver's side and tried to listen for movement in the Freightliner parked next door. It was hard to hear anything over the constant background rumble of the diesel engines. He decided to risk a quick knock. He didn't like the idea of working with his back turned and not knowing if the truck was empty or not. If there was someone inside, he'd find a different way to get the information. Better than being caught and having a gun stuck in his gut. Or worse, looking down and finding a new bleeding hole. Shoot first, question later. He had the idea that truckers might stick together, and he had no doubt there were plenty of guns in Texas. Never mind this parking lot.

He reached up and rapped his knuckles against the Freightliner's window. Nothing. He waited a beat and then did it again. It was an extended sleeper cab. Maybe the guy was out cold. Still no response. Good enough. He grabbed the big side mirror and stepped up on the passenger side of the Peterbilt. He tried an International duplicate first. Put it in the lock and wiggled it gently. Nothing. He tried a Peterbilt next. Same result. He heard boot heels on concrete. He paused and waited for the sound to continue down the row. He never saw anyone. He tried a Freightliner next. This one was looser and after some gentle back and forth, he felt the lock give and turn. He was in. The key was unlikely to start the ignition, but it had gotten him inside and that was enough. He climbed in and shut the door.

The cab was cluttered with detritus from the road: old food wrappers, crushed coffee cups, receipts, bits of food, and other crap. It smelled like sweat, old cheese, and an earthy sweet smell that Lawrence guessed was chewing tobacco from the cans lined up on the dash. This wasn't a sleeper cab, but there was room behind the front seats for light storage or more passengers. Careful to touch as little as possible, knowing what had gone on inside only a few minutes earlier, he settled in behind the driver's seat, tried to ignore the smells, and waited.

Sitting still and waiting was an underappreciated skill. Lawrence had made a lot of money and occasionally avoided a lot of trouble by just sitting still. He did that now and listened to the sounds and the rhythms of the truck stop. No one approached the trucks nearby.

Forty minutes later, he heard footsteps approaching and this time the Peterbilt cab rocked as someone climbed up. A moment later, the driver's door opened and the shaggy brown mop of hair settled into the driver's seat. Before he could put the key in the ignition, Lawrence touched the blade to the inside of the man's ear.

"I'd like to know why you tried to kill my friend."

CHAPTER FORTY-SEVEN

The call with Halford put Max's mind back on Rose. Serrato might be right. Maybe he was concentrating too much on Blackburn. He called Melinda Carson. "Did Rose Robideaux have a lawyer?"

There was a pause as she thought about it. "I don't know. I'm sure she must have used someone for ranch business, but that's not what you mean, is it?"

"No."

"It's a good question. Her will, if there is one, has always been a bit of a gray area because of the lack of a body. It's obviously never gone to probate, and Blackburn hasn't pursued any decision. I've always thought he's just waiting the required seven years before having her declared dead. That's the current law. Like everything else about this case, it's sort of been stuck in limbo."

"That's not that far off now, right? Only about a year. So why is Blackburn pushing it?"

"That's what you're supposed to figure out, Ms. Lansbury."

"Cabot Cove would probably be a lot cooler than TR."

"I think hell itself is sometimes shadier."

Getting back on track Max said, "If she needed a personal lawyer, not for business, where would she go? Any guesses?"

"She wouldn't have a lot of choices. This town isn't big enough to support that many lawyers. If I were you, I'd go down by the courthouse, it's near the center of town, a few blocks from the library. It's big. You can't miss it. You'll find the bail bondsmen and the attorneys cheek-to-jowl. Start knocking on doors. Shouldn't take long."

Melinda Carson was right as Max suspected she was about a lot of things. It didn't take long. Max parked at the curb beside the county courthouse. It was hard to miss. It was perhaps the only three-story building in Tiendas Reales. Three hulking floors spanned most of the block with an arched entryway. It was a neoclassical building that featured yellow bricks and white stone with a striking red mansard roof. The building would have stood out anywhere but felt downright alien in this hot, dusty town with vaguely Old West vibes filled with simple brick and timber boxes. It felt like stumbling across a polar bear on a tropical island. As he strolled past, he noticed a prominent brass plaque near the cornerstone next to the steps. He walked between a row of mature pecan trees for a closer look. Built near the turn of the century, the courthouse had been added to the National Register of Historic Places in 1981. Max thought back to what Serrato had said about the railroad and the early aspirations of the town. Hopes and ambitions that had wilted and died when the railroad pulled up stakes. He pressed a hand against the warm bricks. But the courthouse had stayed.

He continued up the block and crossed the street. He stood on the corner and surveyed his surroundings. There were five storefronts on either side of the street. Both sides of the block were single-story affairs of coarse brick that appeared to cower in the courthouse's grander shadow. On the opposite side of the street was a liquor store, then two lawyers, a convenience store that offered check cashing, and a bail bonds place. He walked the block on his side. Two government annex offices, two more lawyers, and a competing bond dealer. He reached the end and stopped. No one else was out. A truck rumbled past. He was sweating, he felt like he'd been sweating nonstop since he arrived in town, and his shirt was sticking to his skin.

Farther up the next block, he spotted a used car lot, wash-and-go laundry, and takeout food joints. Across the street was a large ramshackle building subdivided into smaller businesses. He was too far away to read the sign posted outside the door. He turned around and walked back. He crossed the street, ducked into the liquor store on the corner, and bought a bottle of water. The clerk was doing inventory and kept to himself after selling him the drink. He lingered inside in the air conditioning while he drank it.

Somewhat reluctantly, but at least hydrated, he waded back out into the heat to start his canvass of the lawyers. The first option was Dunning and Williams who, according to the small sign hanging by the door, offered bankruptcy and corporate law services. Maybe Rose had used them for the ranch, but he didn't think they would offer the type of personal services she might need. He skipped them but stepped inside the next office after reading the gold script stenciled on the glass door. Doyle Stevenson, a sole proprietor offering criminal defense. Not estate planning but in Max's experience, defense lawyers were usually well plugged into the courthouse gossip network. He got lucky. Both Stevenson and his blue-haired assistant were inside. There was no waiting room or reception area. The pair sat at adjoining desks directly inside the small room and turned to look at him when he entered. Max wondered briefly what they did for client conferences. Maybe just locked the front door. Both were well into their 70s and neither desk had a computer on it, though Stevenson held a smartphone in one hand.

When Max mentioned Rose Robideaux, Stevenson brusquely replied, "Never heard of her."

Which Max doubted. The man was in his 70s, but his brown eyes were clear and showed a spark of intelligence. "Really?"

"Of course not. She's the biggest thing to happen to this town since Santa Anna took a leak here on his way to The Alamo. Why are you asking?"

"I'm trying to find her."

"And?"

"Did you have any dealings with her?"

Stevenson frowned. "No, why would I?" This time the puzzlement was genuine.

"No reason, to be honest, but this town isn't that big. I know it says you do criminal law but maybe you do other things, like wills or estate planning."

"No, strictly criminal for me. No moonlighting."

"Do you know who might have handled something like that for her?"

He squinted at Max as if trying to figure out his angle, then looked across his desk at the woman. "What's the new guy's name? Up the street?"

She flipped through a Rolodex on the corner of her desk. "Wallace Carroll."

Stevenson looked back at Max. "That's right. Wallace Carroll. He's a family lawyer but also does estate planning from time to time. I don't know if he did any work for Robideaux, but he would be the best one to ask. He has an office up the street across from the rust bucket lot."

Max frowned.

"The used car place. Wouldn't trust any of Randy's cars farther than the closest curb. You know the types of people who buy there?"

"Thanks for the name," Max said and backed out of the door, not anxious to hear what else Stevenson had to say.

Wallace Carroll's office suite was in the rambling subdivided building that Max had seen earlier on his brief recon tour up and down the block. The building took up the entire block. Max found Carroll's name and office number, 17A, listed on a wooden board posted near a central door. It appeared the name plaques changed frequently. Max entered and found himself in a slim, dark corridor with closed doors lining each side of the hallway. It was clear every inch of space and every rental dollar had been squeezed out of the place.

He could hear air conditioners running behind closed doors but little of the cool air leaked out into the stuffy hall. There was a slightly off-putting smell coming from the carpet, like milk that was about to turn. Max felt the walls creep closer and wished he were back outside. He forced himself forward and walked down the corridor until he hit a T-intersection. Up until that point, the numbers on the doors had been ascending and made some logical sense. To the left were three short stairs upward before the hallway continued. Some of the light fixtures were out farther down the hallway. To the right were no steps but plenty of light. Following the rules he learned by watching horror movies, he avoided the dark end and went right. The numbers immediately jumped up by twenty and he was considering turning around and facing the bogeyman at the other end of the hall when they began descending again. So much for logic.

He found 17A, next to 14X, near the end on the left. He

knocked and heard a muffled reply that he took to mean, "Come in."

The office was small with no exterior windows. Long cardboard legal boxes were stacked around the room. There was a bookshelf on one wall full of more stacked files. Two landscape photos hung on the wall behind the desk. It didn't appear that Carroll was lacking for work. Stevenson had called Carroll the new guy, but you didn't accumulate this much clutter in a few years, let alone a few months. Max could see one box on the floor labeled 2014. Max realized a man Stevenson's age might measure new and old in decades.

Wallace Carroll stood up from behind an equally chaotic desk. The dented industrial desk, which might have come with the office, was full of more paper and various sticky notes. A chunky Dell laptop sat in the middle of the paper storm. Carroll was a few years older than Max with wavy black hair and ears that stuck out just enough to be noticed. "Can I help you?" he asked with a tentative, toothy smile.

"Maybe. My name is Max Parish. I'm working for Alex Blackburn." Max paused to see if there was any reaction to Blackburn's name; he saw nothing but a polite smile. "You know who he is?"

Wallace nodded. "Sure. Not personally, but I know the name. He's a prominent businessman in town."

"So you've never done any work for him?"

Carroll shook his head. "No, I don't do corporate law. I specialize mostly in family law."

"What does a family law attorney do?"

"Typically, contracts or negotiations around divorce or custody, but it can include other domestic or family-related issues including adoption, guardianship, paternity, or child welfare."

"Do you do estate planning? Wills?"

"I've done that occasionally."

"Did you do that for Rose?"

A look of confusion passed over Carroll's face. "Rose?"

"Yes, Alex Blackburn's wife."

"Isn't she missing?"

"Yes," Max replied.

"Well ..." Carroll held out his hands as if to say the answer was obvious, how could he do legal work for a missing person, but it wasn't obvious to Max and he waited. He wanted to hear Carroll say the words. He wanted no confusion.

"Mr. Parish, unfortunately, any client work is confidential and covered by attorney-client privilege."

"I understand that. I'm not asking about case specifics; I'm only asking if Rose Robideaux was a client at all."

"I understand what you're asking and I'm saying even if a client's identity is not strictly covered under privilege, there is also an ethical consideration. I am obligated not to reveal my client's confidences and, if in my judgment, that extends to his or her identity, I must consider that."

Max thought that to be a very lawyerly answer and a sort of answer in and of itself. "You just told me you never did any work for Alex Blackburn."

"In that instance, I thought you were referring to legal matters for his company or businesses. And, in that case, I can say the same for Mrs. Blackburn. I did not handle any corporate matters for them or their ranch."

More legal tapdancing. Max felt the drumbeat of a headache start.

"Are you the only family lawyer in Tiendas Reales?"

"I'm the only one here who specializes but other lawyers might handle certain things as long as they are comfortable. There are other family lawyers in Freer and Encinal, certainly plenty in San Antonio."

"Let me ask you a hypothetical question. What about your employees?"

"I don't have any," Carroll said.

Max held up a hand. "Just hypothetically, if you did, attorney-client privilege would extend to them, right?"

"If they were involved in the casework, then yes."

"So, if you were to hire me for say, a salary of a dollar, you would no longer have any ethical objections to answering my questions or sharing information."

"I'm not sure that removes the ethical considerations. It might only add to them."

"Did you know Rose Robideaux personally?"

If the shift in questions caught him off guard, he didn't show it. "Sure, I grew up here, went away for college and law school but came back. I knew Rose. We went to high school together."

"What do you think of Alex Blackburn?"

"I have no opinion."

"No? It seems like most people I've talked to in Tiendas Reales have an opinion. For better or worse."

"Sorry, not me. I'm not in the habit of judging someone I've never met."

"Very Christian of you. Who is your landlord here, Mr. Carroll?"

"My landlord? I don't know. I know the super. I know the number to call if there's a problem, and I know where to send the rent check every month. Why do you ask?"

Max had a feeling he knew a bit more than that. Lawyers, even family lawyers, liked to know as much information as possible. They were almost pathologically allergic to not knowing an answer. "Do you also know Rose's daughter?"

"Roxy? Sure. I've watched her grow up."

"I'm trying to help, Mr. Carroll."

. . .

Max walked back to his car and tried to stay in the shadow of the low building. It didn't blunt the heat, but he tried to trick his mind into believing it. He was sweating again after half a block. It had been a long shot with Carroll but sometimes you had to take the chance. And Carroll hadn't been a completely dry hole. Max had the sense the lawyer wasn't telling him everything. He thought about how Carroll had used Angie's given name. And the look he'd seen on his face when he mentioned Rose. He'd admitted they had gone to school together, so presumably they were close to the same age. Max guessed Carroll was closer to Rose, at least back then, than he was letting on. Or maybe Max was jumping at shadows. Maybe Carroll only wished he'd been closer to her. Maybe what Max had seen was only nostalgia and the man was still carrying a torch, however small, for an old high school crush that never happened.

Except.

Max reached his car and opened the door. He let the hot air bubble out. He needed to stop by Will's and get a new dashboard shade. Maybe the trip had been a waste of time. He'd scribbled his contact info on a slip of paper and added it to the pile on Carroll's desk. Maybe he would never call. Maybe there was nothing he could tell Max.

Except.

The two landscape photos that Carroll had taken the time to hang up on his walls when the rest of the office remained a disheveled mess were stark, high-contrast shots of the desert at sunrise. Max had seen photos like that before. Recently. He recognized the style.

CHAPTER FORTY-EIGHT

Lawrence's phone pinged. He picked it up from the cupholder and looked at the screen.

"Eddie says the truck made three stops, all at various warehouses outside San Antonio, and then returned to Blackburn's warehouse by 7 a.m."

"All the stops legit?"

"Yes, appear to be. Eddie's digging a little deeper, but all the addresses are registered to businesses that seem to have legitimate cases for using toluene."

Max turned that news over. Maybe Blackburn was really on the up-and-up. Maybe he'd leveraged the ranch, taken a risk, and found an obscure but very profitable niche being an import-export middleman for solvents. Lawrence was always preaching that it was the most overlooked and the most boring businesses that made the most money. Maybe Blackburn had tapped into that.

"There was something a little unusual," Lawrence said as he flipped through more incoming texts from his computer-savant brother. "There was one other stop. According to the

GPS plot data, the truck stopped for seven minutes on the side of Highway 55."

"The state road that leads out of TR?"

"If you say so."

"It's the road that runs past the Double R. Why stop there?"

"No way to know. All we know from the data is that the truck stopped on the side of the highway in the middle of the night. Could have been any number of things. The engine. Tire. Dashboard warning light. Something came loose. Had to take a piss."

"For seven minutes?"

"Okay, maybe not that."

"I get the idea. Still a bit unusual."

"We like unusual."

"Unusual is interesting. Have Eddie drop a pin." Max looked out the windshield. "We're going to be headed in that direction. It's worth a look."

They met back at Serrato's and dropped off her Jeep. She took the keys without comment as they left again. They were parked in Lawrence's Escalade near the center of town on a side street that faced the entrance of a residential neighborhood. The third house on the left, a nice-looking, if modest, brick ranch with black shutters was the home of Bobby Ross. He was a night-shift supervisor at Blackburn's warehouse. He was the guy that the Peterbilt driver, Daniel Montez, had ratted out. Montez had told Lawrence that Ross had approached him with the offer that ultimately put Max in the hospital. Ross had just exited his house and climbed into a navy-blue GMC Sierra that was parked in the driveway. He backed out into the street and drove toward Max and Lawrence. The setting sun was in his eyes, and they knew he had little chance of seeing them waiting across the street in Lawrence's SUV. Ross paused at the intersection, let a dog walker cross, then turned left. Lawrence waited for some traffic to fill in as a buffer and then followed. There was no need to get too close. They ultimately knew where he was going. He stopped once to get a cup of coffee at a drive thru then made the expected right onto 55.

"How do you want to do it?"

"PIT him, I think."

"Risky."

"I want him shaken up. He'll know we're serious. More likely to talk. Have you done it before?"

"Sure, once or twice in my reckless youth. Been a few years."

"You have any other ideas?"

"No, no. That'll work. It ain't rocket science."

"Hang back. Wait for a few miles. Not much out here. Bound to be some empty stretches."

A PIT maneuver was a tactic the police used to end high-speed chases. Max wasn't sure what the letters stood for. He'd heard various incarnations over the years: pursuit immobilization technique, pursuit intervention technique, parallel immobilization technique. Whatever you wanted to call it, it involved tapping the rear quarter panel of the target vehicle and sending it into a spin. Max had a wheelman on a job tell him it rose in popularity in the '80s out in L.A., but Max's pet theory was that it originated in the South with stockcar racing's bump-and-run strategy.

Three miles later, with the sun starting to set off to their right, Max looked back and saw an empty stretch of road. "Let's do it."

Lawrence sat up straighter and put his foot down on the accelerator. The SUV jumped forward and they quickly closed the gap on Ross's pickup. The Sierra was traveling at roughly 50 miles an hour, a couple of ticks over the posted limit. Max thought the low speed would work in their favor. Too much speed could send the pickup into a roll. He wanted Ross shaken, not unconscious. Max saw Ross notice them as he tapped the brakes on the truck. Lawrence kept the speed up and began to drift into the opposite lane as if he were going to pass.

A proper PIT maneuver was a simple demonstration of physics. Newton's Third Law of Motion. When one body exerts a force on a second body, the second body simultaneously exerts a force equal in magnitude in the opposite direction of the first body. As Lawrence inched up alongside, he slowed the SUV to match Ross's speed, then rotated the wheel a quarter turn so the SUV's bumper nudged the pickup's rear end, just behind the wheel well. The pickup slewed in a lazy 360 and then skidded off the side of the road into the dusty hardpan. Lawrence put the SUV at an angle in front of the pickup to keep it from easily driving off. Max jumped out and ran to the driver's side door. Ross could still, if he was with it enough, back up and drive away. Max yanked open the door and pulled the man out. He pushed him against the side of the vehicle.

Ross was not with it. His eyes were soft and unfocused. He was staring at something over Max's shoulder. Maybe something only he could see. If Max hadn't been holding his arms, he thought the man might fall over. His breathing was shallow.

Max slapped him on the cheek. Not hard, but enough to get his attention. "Hey."

"What?" Ross raised a shaky hand and touched his ear. "My ears are ringing."

"Did you hit your head?"

"No. I don't think so."

Max didn't see any blood. Lawrence had executed the PIT

perfectly. Ross's pickup had done a slow, controlled spin. He'd been wearing his seatbelt. Max doubted Ross had a concussion. "Probably just from the stress or adrenaline. From the accident."

The word accident seemed to bring Ross back a bit more. His eyes cleared. He looked at Max. "It wasn't an accident."

"That's right."

"You did it on purpose. You hit me. Why?"

"Not much fun, huh? And my friend took it real easy on you."

"What?" He felt steadier on his feet and Max let go of his arms and took a step back.

"My name is Max Parish." It was clear that Ross didn't recognize the name. "He didn't give you my name, huh? I was traveling on this road right here four days ago in the afternoon in a black SUV, Massachusetts plate 4398JP." He saw that bit hit home. "Yeah, you might not know me, but you knew where I'd be."

"They were just supposed to scare you." His eyes flicked to the stitches on the side of Max's head. "I can't control them. You weren't supposed to end up in the hospital."

"But I did."

"You look okay."

"Looks can be deceiving. What else did he tell you?"

"He? Who are you talking about?"

"The guy that put you on me?"

"It wasn't a he. It was a woman."

"A woman? Not Blackburn?"

"Blackburn? Alex Blackburn? Why would he be involved in this?" Ross looked genuinely confused.

"Did this woman have a name?"

"Heather."

"Heather what?"

"We never got to last names. She chatted me up at Shooters. Two different times. Good-looking woman. About my age. Blonde hair. Nice ... figure. Maybe a bit out of my league. I should have known she wanted something. After a couple of drinks, she started in on a story about a guy. About you." He stood up a little straighter now. "And how you were stalking her and harassing her and how she wished she could get you out of her life."

"Let me guess. She had some ideas on how you could help."

"Yeah. She even offered to pay and I was happy to help. Men who hit women are cowards."

"I agree. She fed you a bullshit story to get you to dance to her tune. None of it was true. I don't even know the woman."

Or did he?

CHAPTER FORTY-NINE

"A woman?" Lawrence said as he drove farther south. "Not Blackburn? Do you believe him?

"Yes. No way he could make up that story on the spot."

"Where does that leave us?"

They'd left Ross by the side of the road. If they needed him again, they knew where to find him. And he knew it. He'd promised to keep his mouth shut.

"Could still be Blackburn. Doubtful that Heather is her real name. Melinda Carson told me Blackburn has a PR woman, Jill something; it's in my notes somewhere. It could be her. I haven't gotten around to talking to her. Don't know what she looks like. She didn't seem important. Need to at least get a look at her. See if she matches Ross's description."

Lawrence was thinking it through and shaking his head. "I don't know. That's risky. If she's legit, why involve her in your thing?"

"True, but we don't know the relationship. We both agree something hinky is going on. Maybe she knows about it.

Maybe she's involved up to her neck. Maybe Blackburn trusts her."

"If she's running PR for Blackburn's interests, she's probably pretty visible, at least around here, so wouldn't Ross recognize her."

"That's a good point. You're probably right. If not Ross, someone in a local bar would likely recognize her." Max thought it all through. "Still missing a piece of this thing."

Lawrence started to reply when the nav system butted in. "You have reached your destination." Lawrence slowed and braked to a stop. They'd been driving along 55 toward the coordinates that Eddie had sent. The roadside stop that the Peterbilt truck had made for seven unexplained minutes. It was only after Lawrence stopped the car that Max looked up and took in his surroundings. He recognized it.

"This is the spot? You're sure?"

Lawrence tapped the SUV's display and then looked at his phone. "Might be off by a few feet, but this is the general area."

"The bank manager, Raul Ortiz, this is where his body was discovered."

Max pointed off to the left. He could just make out the shape of the salt house's roof in the distance. They got out of the SUV and looked around.

"Still can't get used to all the emptiness," Lawrence said.

"'Hell is empty and all the devils are here.'"

"'Modest doubt is called the beacon of the wise,'" Lawrence replied. "Don't think you can quote Shakespeare and call it your own just because I'm a Black man."

Max smiled. "I have plenty of modest doubts, but not about you." Lawrence was the most well-read person he knew. The man didn't so much read books as absorb them. "Why did that truck stop here?"

"Still think it could be a coincidence. Something simple. Something mechanical."

"Maybe," Max said as he started walking along the shoulder. "I'd be inclined to agree if it wasn't so close to the spot where they dropped Ortiz's body. That's too much coincidence for me."

He continued to walk along the shoulder, not sure what he was looking for exactly. The left side of the road was Double R property. The cattle fencing didn't extend this far south, not anymore, though Serrato had told them they'd checked the plat maps and the ranch land's border was still another half mile farther south, beyond the salt house. On the right side was a string of utility poles planted in the parched dirt. Everywhere he looked was a harsh landscape of stubby cacti, crumbling rock, sandstone, dead grasses, and bent trees filtered through the lens of unrelenting sunlight. Max could smell nothing but the baking asphalt and his own sweat.

"You're a hundred yards past the coordinates," Lawrence shouted. He was farther back, walking on the opposite side of the road. "That's probably outside the margin of error for the GPS."

Max waved a hand to show he'd heard and then crossed the road and began walking back in the opposite direction. He spotted it two minutes later at the turnoff. Tracks. Tread tracks. Unique ones. The arid dirt didn't hold a deep impression. It barely held an impression at all. He knelt for a closer look. But it wasn't a mirage. They were there. Faint but distinctive in the same chunky pattern he'd seen before, closer to the salt house, with Serrato the day before. He took out his phone and called her. She answered quietly and he knew she was at the station.

"Did you ever check the reports on those tracks we found out by the salt house?"

"Yes. No mention in the reports," she replied. "So, they likely came after the scene was cleared."

"Thanks," he said and disconnected.

He felt Lawrence at his back. "What do you make of these?" he asked. "They're not from our truck."

"No, definitely not from a truck. Not made for a paved road. Look at that front one. Thick and chunky for traction. One of the wheels is bigger than the other, too. If I had to guess, I'd say it looks more like farm tractor tread." Lawrence looked around. "But why would you need a tractor out here? What are they growing?"

"Nothing. So maybe it's not a tractor, but a forklift."

They drove the SUV parallel to the uneven dirt path that led to the salt house. Lawrence winced at every rock and pothole. "You already destroyed one of my cars and now you're forcing me to damage the struts on another."

"I'm sure you'll find a way to make it a legitimate business expense. I'm probably making you money on this trip."

Lawrence smiled and snapped his fingers. "You are learning, my friend."

They stopped the SUV well short of the shack and walked the rest of the way. The tracks were harder to see. They might have missed them if they weren't looking for them, but they were there and they stopped just short of the door to the salt house.

"So what do you think?" Lawrence asked. "The truck stops and takes on additional cargo? Something that's not on the official manifest."

"Could be." Max walked to the door and pushed it open. He glanced inside. Everything still looked the same as the last time. Old table and broken-down chairs. Empty fridge. Jury-rigged oil drum smoker in the corner. "And they use this as a staging area."

"Why?"

Max waved an arm at the vast emptiness. "Isolated. Empty. Close to the border. Convenient. Take your pick."

"Something is still not right about that scenario though. Why not just time two different trucks to meet out on the road? Do the swap there? Why drive out here?" Lawrence asked.

"The extra step must be worth it to them. It must mitigate the risk somehow. This is closer to your area of expertise than mine." Max still wasn't sure exactly how Lawrence made his money beyond cutting hair at his shop, but he knew much of it was in the grayer areas of the economy. "What do you think? Why would you do it?"

Lawrence walked past Max and into the small house. He glanced around and then walked to the refrigerator and pulled it open. There was no power. No chill of cold air wafted out. It was empty. He shut the door and moved over to the metal sculpture in the corner.

"What the hell is this?"

"Serrato told me it was some kind of homemade smoker. This place is called a salt house. At one point in time, it was closer to the original homestead and was used to cure and preserve meat."

"Huh. Learn something new every day. But that's not what this place is being used for now."

"No. And, up until a few minutes ago, I didn't think it was being used at all."

Lawrence walked back out into the heat. "You notice the door?"

"The hinges."

"Yeah, swing pretty free and easy. You don't expect much oxidation out in the desert with the low humidity, but you'd expect a little. Someone's been doing some maintenance out here."

"Why?"

"You were right the first time. Because it's worth it. It eliminates a risk. Or solves a problem."

CHAPTER FIFTY

Neither of them had anything against The Tin Roof but both wanted a little space from Tiendas Reales and a little variety in their menu options. Lawrence was staying at a hotel to the north, near a highway interchange. It might have technically still been Tiendas Reales or in another town. No one ever stuck around long enough to find out. They kept driving away from the highway and the diners and convenience food and found an incongruous but very passable red-checkered tablecloth Italian joint complete with chianti in straw bottles. Anywhere else Max might have thought they were going for irony but this place played it straight, right down to the entrees. The food wasn't great but wasn't bad either. It was calories and it was different from The Tin Roof.

After slices of tiramisu, they drove back to the chain hotel near the highway. Lawrence keyed open the door and both were surprised to find the message light blinking on the room's phone. Max saw Lawrence's shoulders tense and he felt an energy crackle through his own fingers.

"Expecting someone?" Max asked and looked back into the hallway. It was empty.

"You know me better than that. No one knows I'm here."

Max stayed near the door. Lawrence made a quick circuit of the room, double beds, cheap art, cheaper furniture. All standard hotel fare. He checked the tells that he'd left in place.

"All clear. No one's been in here," he said returning to stand between the beds and stare down at the light on the phone.

"Could just be the front desk checking in. A courtesy call."

"Could be," Lawrence replied.

But a cut-rate hotel a couple of miles off a secondary highway was not the type of establishment that typically called around to check on service. Success was judged more by how often the front desk phone didn't ring.

Lawrence picked up the receiver and after a moment studying the faceplate punched a button. "I have a message," he said when someone answered on the other end. He listened for a moment, his forehead wrinkling in concentration. "Okay," he said and hung up. He turned and looked at Max. "A package was delivered. Addressed to you."

Lawrence went down to the front desk and collected it. He dropped it on the first bed when he returned. They both looked at it but it didn't offer any immediate answers. It was a FedEx box addressed to Max and included Lawrence's room number.

"Not good," Lawrence said.

Max nodded his head in agreement. He felt an imaginary breath against his neck. Someone was watching and he hadn't felt it or seen it. Neither had Lawrence. He felt exposed. Like he was standing out in the desert under the blazing sun. Like he was sitting on a lonely highway while two tractor trailer trucks bore down. It was not a pleasant feeling. He rubbed at his temple which had begun to ache.

"Open it?" Lawrence asked.

"Not sure we have much choice. I doubt it's full of explosives. Clearly, they know where we are. It would be a lot quicker and cleaner to kill us some other way."

"Sometimes it's about making a statement."

"You think it's rigged?"

"No, probably not." Lawrence lifted an end of the box, and they heard something thunk inside as it shifted. "Feels like paper. Like documents. And something else." He slipped a small knife from his pocket and ran it along the edge, then opened the flap and tilted the box again. Two sets of documents slid out onto the mustard-colored bedspread. The first set was thicker, loosely bound with a wide rubber band. The second was thinner, held together by a single paperclip. A third and final item tumbled out on top of the documents: a cheap cell phone. That was it. No ball bearings. No shrapnel. No explosives.

Max picked up the thick stack and removed the rubber band. He flipped through, pausing on certain pages, before moving on. They were in chronological order and covered a period of almost seven years. He'd need to read them again more carefully but the meaning was clear. He handed it over to Lawrence and picked up the other sheaf of papers.

"That's a lot of hospital visits," Lawrence said when he was done.

"To a lot of different clinics and hospitals."

"Abuse?"

"She worked a physical job at the ranch. I'm sure there were some accidents. I'm sure she explained a lot of those breaks and contusions as ranch accidents. But were all of them? Why gather these records if they were legit accidents?"

"She was building a case."

"You notice she switched up her last name. Sometimes it's her maiden name on the intake form. Sometimes Blackburn. Sometimes a combination. She needed the treatment but didn't want any further attention."

"Or Blackburn was right there with her."

"Right. A threat in itself."

"But why did she stop? Why didn't she use it?" He hefted the sheets. "It's substantial. Why not go public?"

"Maybe she did. Or tried to. Blackburn is very tied into the town, in all areas. He could have easily squashed it. Or explained it away as accidents. If there were any domestic callouts or reports, I think Serrato would know. She would have said something. Maybe she was afraid? If we're right, he wasn't averse to hitting her. If he found out she was going to the cops? Who knows what his reaction might be. Plus, she had to think about Angie, too. Maybe she was trying to protect her."

"You think Blackburn abused Angie, too?"

"No, I didn't pick up on anything like that when I talked to her or anyone else. To be fair, I haven't heard anyone say they think Blackburn abused Rose, either. I was thinking more that Rose might be protecting Angie from the knowledge that her mother was being beaten by her stepfather. But who knows? Once you cross that line ..."

They both went silent for a moment. Neither had grown up in ideal situations and neither had ever really known their fathers, but they also didn't have to deal with witnessing abuse of that kind.

. . .

Lawrence dropped the ugly package of documents back on the bed and nodded at the thinner pile that Max still held in his hands. "Do I want to know what that is?"

"It's two legal documents. Both deal with the transfer of ownership of the Double R ranch. The first is a notarized warranty deed from Robert Robideaux to Rose Robideaux. The second is Rose Robideaux's will. It further transfers the title deed to the ranch from Rose Robideaux to her daughter, Roxanne Angela Robideaux on her eighteenth birthday." Max studied the second document. "The will is dated two days before Rose disappeared."

He handed the documents over to Lawrence, who quickly scanned them and frowned. "Angie's birthday is in a week. I wonder if she knows about this?"

"I doubt it. She didn't say anything to me. I get the impression that, other than the horses, she's grown to dislike the ranch."

"Can't blame her. Not a lot of happy memories."

"No. Not at all. Dad dies. Mom disappears. Isolated. Alone."

"What's the point of this first document?"

"I don't know." Max reached over and tapped the area with the signatures at the bottom. "But I know who we might ask in the morning."

Both documents were witnessed and notarized by Wallace Carroll, Esq.

CHAPTER FIFTY-ONE

After some much needed sleep and hot showers, Max and Lawrence grabbed a couple of watery coffees and rubbery bagels from the hotel lobby and headed back toward Tiendas Reales to talk to Wallace Carroll again.

"What are we supposed to do with all of this?" Lawrence said. "Are we even supposed to do something or are we just supposed to be aware of it?"

Lawrence was taking a few evasive maneuvers but neither had spotted anyone tailing them. Max could tell the fact that someone had got the drop on them was bothering him. He'd gone so far as to get down on his hands and knees and check the undercarriage of the car before they left. The car was clean.

"Maybe Carroll will know," Max said.

"If he was supposed to tell you something, why didn't he do it the first time you went to see him?"

"I don't know. Maybe these documents will be the trigger. A sign or something. Maybe I need to ask a specific question."

"Or maybe he won't talk at all."

"Have you ever met a lawyer who didn't like to talk? He might not answer our questions, but I bet he tells us something."

They drove for a few minutes in silence as the SUV's wheels thumped over the seams in the road. They both noticed a large black bird that sat on top of a telephone pole. Its neck swiveled to watch them pass.

"Don't do it," Lawrence said looking over at Max.

"What do you mean?"

"You know what I mean. I can see you want to."

"Well, I do feel weak and weary."

"Don't."

"And I'm nearly napping."

"C'mon, man. You know how I feel about poetry."

"And this," Max hefted the stack of papers along with the burner phone, "feels like a tapping at my chamber door."

"But this is not bleak December weather and I'm pretty sure that was a crow, not a raven."

"Fine, but I think thou doth protest too much. You had that bleak December line pretty handy."

Lawrence smiled. "Poe ain't bad."

Max did not doubt that his friend could recite many more lines of poetry if needed. "What do you think about the phone? Should we power it up?"

"Don't see why not. It was in the box for a reason. At this point, we have more to gain by talking to them than not."

Max powered up the phone. There was one number stored in memory. He raised an eyebrow at Lawrence. He shrugged in return. Max hit the button to dial.

"Hello, Max."

A woman's voice. Texas accent. He sat up a little straighter.

"Hello, Rose." Max saw Lawrence look over at him.

She laughed. It was a dry, brittle sound as if she didn't have much practice. "Oh, I'm not Rose."

"No?"

She sighed. That sounded more natural. "No. She's long gone. I'm just passing on a message. Plus, I don't think we're going to be talking again so names might not be all that necessary."

"You left all these documents and reports about Rose at the hotel?"

"I need a favor, Max."

"And you think you're in a position to be asking for favors?"

"Probably not, but you're still here. I think you want to help. So, I'm asking anyway."

"Can't hurt to ask. I can't make any promises, though."

"I need you to get those documents back into safe deposit box number 239 at the M&P Savings and Loan in TR."

"What?"

"I need those documents back where they belong, and it needs to happen fast."

Max was still trying to process her request. "Why can't you put them back?"

"Because I'm not Rose. I'm not the owner of the box."

"I'm not either."

"Of course not, but I think you might be able to help me."

"Why do you think that?"

"Again, you're still here. You are a stubborn man and I think, really hope, that you might have the necessary skills to help me."

"I think you're making a lot of assumptions."

"Maybe. But I don't think I'm making an assumption about you caring about Roxy."

"How does she figure into this?"

"Her birthday is coming up."

Things slowly started to come together for Max.

"She'll be eighteen."

"Yes."

"And get control of the ranch."

"Yes. The trust dissolves and ownership transfers to her."

"And the deed is filed with the town clerk."

"She said you were smart."

"Who?"

"Doesn't matter. Those documents need to find their way back to box 239. That's where they need to be found."

"How did the documents get out of Rose's box? Presumably she didn't do it."

"No, she didn't. Definitely not."

"Then how?"

"Doesn't matter. I need to get them back *into* the bank."

Not answering questions seemed to be a skill for this woman. But Max already knew how the documents had left M&P Savings and Loan. Raul Ortiz had taken them. He was soon going to be out of a job and was soon going to need some cash. Not a lot of jobs in TR but plenty of opportunity for blackmail. Max now had an idea of why Blackburn had started hiring PIs recently. Pieces were starting to snap together. He focused back on the conversation. "If they're not?"

"Things could get messy. Claims of ownership could be challenged. Or worse."

Max realized that there was one simple solution to Blackburn's problem. If both Rose and Angie were dead, he'd be in line to inherit all the property regardless of when or who had ownership. Another death would bring even more intense heat down on Blackburn but maybe it was better than the alternative. Sometimes the rock is better than the hard place.

"I'm not sure who you think I am, but I can't just waltz

into a bank's vault and do what you ask. Even if I do care about Angie."

"Oh, I don't need you to break into the bank. The federal government has already done that. I just need you to get the documents back to them."

"The M&P Savings and Loan has been bought up by a bigger bank," she went on to explain. "The American way. The local branch there in Tiendas Reales is being merged, or absorbed, by a larger competitor."

Max recalled what Raul Ortiz's sister had said about his job being eliminated and his uncharacteristic anger about it. "I heard about it. You're going to need to drive north to Freer to use the ATM. What do the Feds have to do with it?"

"That's right. The Feds got involved, far as I can tell, because the new bosses got a little worried about some of the paper M&P was carrying. In order to try to stay afloat their threshold for qualified loans is scraping bottom. The buyers aren't hitting the eject button on the deal but they want some assurances, so they called the Feds."

"Is this good news or bad news for you?"

"I told you, it doesn't have anything to do with me, I'm a messenger, but I think it might be good news for you. I hear the Feds will roll into town tonight and will turn the bank upside down, shake it, and see what loose change falls out. If everything is copacetic, it all gets boxed up and moved to Freer."

"If not?"

"I don't know. It might still get all boxed up."

"And you think there might be opportunity in this chaos."

"See, I like that. I don't have to explain everything to you."

CHAPTER FIFTY-TWO

This time they both sat down. It was cramped in the small, cluttered office. Max had to place a teetering pile of folders on the floor to clear a space to sit in one of the chairs. His knees brushed against the front of Carroll's dented desk. Carroll admitted he was the executor of the R&R Trust Company but that's all he would say. So far, anything else Max tried, Carroll asserted client confidentiality.

"What are the property laws in Texas? In regard to marriage?" Max asked.

Carroll paused but then decided the question was vague enough to answer.

"Texas is one of nine U.S. states that is a community property jurisdiction. In general, that means any property acquired by a couple during their marriage is equally owned by both spouses."

"But not before that? For example, if a house is owned before the marriage by one spouse, it would not be considered marital property and therefore equally owned in Texas?"

"That's right. In Texas, property owned before marriage is separate property. Everything else is community property."

"What about something gifted or inherited during the marriage?"

"That gets trickier. It typically would still be considered separate property but might be open to more claims than something acquired before the marriage."

Max now thought he had a better understanding of the first legal document. The one where Rose's father had gifted her the title deed to the Double R ranch. Was it just a wedding gift? Maybe he'd always meant to do it prior, when Rose's first husband, Chuck, had been in charge, but never got around to it, and when he was older saw a proper time to hand over the reins to his daughter and her second husband. Or maybe he knew, or suspected, that Blackburn was not the man he claimed to be. A parent usually has a sixth sense about those things.

"Can you answer questions that are publicly available?"

"Yes, if I can."

"When did Rose and Alex Blackburn get married?"

Max had the notes and clips from his library research on his phone and could find the answer himself, but Carroll could save them all some time. Plus, he was annoyed and wanted to push Carroll a little.

Carroll shifted in his seat. "I'm not sure why you think I would know that."

"You weren't there?"

Now Carroll's cheeks colored slightly and looked down. "No, why would I be?"

"Really? Mr. Carroll can we stop playing these games? I think we're running out of time. You have two of Rose's prints hanging on your wall. You are the lawyer of record on these sensitive documents that Rose put in a safe deposit box. You are obviously a long-time and trusted friend. I'm sure she would have wanted you at her wedding. We just need to know the date. It could be important."

Max thought Carroll might continue with his obstinacy but after a moment he answered, "November 27. The Saturday after Thanksgiving."

And one day after the title of the ranch was deeded to Rose.

Max walked out of Carroll's office and wound his way through the warren of claustrophobic corridors and back out into the superheated late afternoon air of Tiendas Reales. The sidewalk felt sticky on the soles of his shoes. He climbed into the SUV parked at the curb. Even after a week, his body showed no signs of acclimating to this weather. He'd started sweating in just the short fifteen-yard walk between Carroll's office and the SUV's passenger seat. Any time he stepped outside, it was like his body started throwing emergency cooling switches.

He leaned forward and directed a vent at his forehead. Lawrence closed the laptop that he'd been typing on and put the SUV in gear. He drove a few blocks, everything was at least close in downtown TR, two lefts and a right, and then pulled into a parking space with a familiar view. The Tin Roof was to Max's left. He could see the same old couple through the front window seated in their booth at the back reading the newspaper. Looking through the windshield and diagonally opposite was the entrance to M&P Savings and Loan.

"Find out anything while I was with Carroll?"

"Plenty," Lawrence said. "Mostly general stuff about how these things typically go down."

"Anything we can use?"

"The woman was right. The timing is going to be tight.

Unlike most government operations, an FDIC takeover or transfer of a bank is efficient and moves fast. They are in and out. Usually over a weekend or in some cases, depending on the size of the bank, like the M&P, just overnight. Bank reopens the next morning with new management but the customers might not even know. First thing they'll do is an audit and handle the transfer of assets. Buyout or takeover, the process is largely the same. The idea is to move fast and provide as little downtime as possible for the customers."

"Avoid any panics or runs on the bank."

"Exactly. FDIC agents flood in, take apart the bank, and put it back together someplace else or with a new owner or both, in this case."

"What are you thinking?"

"We take advantage of the numbers, all those people milling about, and the speed. We are not going after the money. We are not looking to take anything. The safe deposit boxes are not FDIC insured. They will be inventoried and moved, but security will likely be less. We watch and we pick our spot. I think we'll get a small window to get those documents back into the system when they load the inventoried merchandise and move it to the other bank."

"I'm guessing they might employ private security or armored cars to move the stuff. I don't want to mess with that."

"Probably going to be some video too, if they want to protect the bank and avoid the liability if something were to go missing."

Max studied the front of the bank. It was quiet. Just a couple of cars in the lot, probably the tellers and the branch manager. Whoever had replaced Ortiz. It didn't appear that there were any customers at the moment. The woman had told them the action was scheduled for today, but they couldn't see any government agents about to swoop through the front doors. It looked like any other business day.

"I don't like it. Too fast, too messy. We don't know enough. We'd be walking in blind. Maybe walking right into cuffs," Max said.

"There's always a way. Just depends on how badly you want it. I'm in, you know that, whatever you decide to do."

Max thought about Angie. And Blackburn. And Rose. How badly did he want this? Could he just walk away? Go back to Vermont and Vic and the motel? Keep running somewhere else? He looked back at the bank and saw Angie standing by the front doors all over again. The stress and panic on her face. Now, after the phone call, he understood that he'd been wrong. She hadn't been trying to rob the bank. She had been trying to break-in, to put something back, and Max had stumbled into the middle of it. It had all started with an incorrect assumption. He'd been holding the wrong end of the stick. It still could have ended badly for her that day. And she was still in danger. He wasn't wrong about that.

No, he couldn't walk away.

Then Max thought of something else.

What if his other assumption, the one about Blackburn and his warehouse, was also wrong? He turned that one upside down and suddenly the other side of the equation began to make more sense, too.

"We missed something," he said to Lawrence. "It's not coming in, it's going out."

CHAPTER FIFTY-THREE

"I mean, this is nicer than some of the subways in Boston." Lawrence touched a rail and rubbed his fingers together. "Shiny and well oiled."

The tunnel was five feet in diameter and a little over six feet in height. Both men could stand up without hunching. They'd climbed down about twenty feet via a ladder anchored to the dirt wall.

"How did you figure a tunnel?" Lawrence asked.

"I didn't. Not at first. I was out here twice and didn't see it. I only saw Ortiz's body and an abandoned shack. But we figured Blackburn might be up to something with the toluene, right?"

"Right."

"When I realized I'd had it wrong about Angie, she wasn't trying to rob the bank at all, I turned the equation with Blackburn upside down, too. Maybe he wasn't smuggling something into the country, maybe he was smuggling it *out* of the country. From that perspective, a tunnel here made a lot more sense. You would want something close to the warehouse. Like you said, operationally, the proximity lowered the risk."

"Did the tunnel or the warehouse come first?"

"I think they're tied together. We need to talk to Kelley again about the money. We should be able to figure out how long the warehouse has been operating, but I don't think this tunnel has been here for very long. Everything is still too clean. "

Lawrence lifted his phone light and pointed it down the tunnel. It showed a skinny set of rails running out and disappearing into the distance like a midnight road. "Maybe the walls keep out some of the migrants, but they're doing dick for the war on drugs."

"We lost that war a long time ago. Prescription painkillers are easy to find, easy to use, and relatively cheap to obtain. Oxy is the great equalizer. No one in any demographic is immune. If you want to get high, you're going to get high. The war on drugs is just window dressing and political theater."

"Damn, how cynical you've grown in your old age, Max."

"You think I'm wrong?"

"I didn't say that. We both know plenty of guys in prison for life or strung out on the streets. Not gonna argue with you. Just haven't seen you get that heated."

Max had been thinking about Carter and his sister, Mary. Both were gone and both were victims, in their own ways, of the war on drugs. He would never mourn Carter. The world was better without him, but he often saw the amount of money spent on the drug war and couldn't help but think it would be better spent, if not on the victims, then elsewhere. Maybe it wouldn't have ultimately cured his sister, but maybe she would have had a little more time. A chance, at least.

Lawrence appeared to sense his mood and tried to bring

him back with another question. "You think the toluene came first or the tunnel?"

Max thought about the timing of it all as he reached out and touched the carved walls. The clay-like south Texas soil was very conducive to digging. "I think it was a combination of factors. Have you been listening to the radio at all since you've been here?"

"No, too much twang for my taste."

"The news keeps talking about a new scanning technology going into effect soon at the border. I'm sure all cross-border smugglers write off a percentage. It must be built into their equation. Random checks are bound to catch some product, but this new scanning technology promises to drastically increase that percentage, maybe to an unacceptable degree, so they went looking for a new means to get across the border."

"Tunnels aren't exactly new."

"They're big in SoCal and Arizona where the warehouse districts around the border provide good cover and ample hiding spots, but have you ever heard about anything like this? Serrato told me it's about half a mile to the border. That's a long way. That shows some desperation."

"And ingenuity."

Max gave him a thin smile. "True. The best innovations come from criminal minds."

Lawrence gave a low chuckle. "You got that right, brother. What are we going to do with this information?"

"This is obviously on Blackburn's land. He's got to have some culpability."

"But it's not his land. We just learned that. It's the trust's and then Angie's in a week. You think he can wiggle out on that technicality?"

"I don't know. He can always claim he knew nothing about the trucks stopping and the toluene being offloaded and smuggled out of the country, but I'm not sure how long that's going to hold up. This is not a simple operation. There are a lot of moving pieces. Anyone with half a brain is going to figure that he knew about it. He had to."

"Would help to have some hard proof."

"We're going to have to bring in Serrato."

"Agreed. Maybe her girlfriend, too."

"Gonna have to think about that. I think I could convince Serrato to keep it on the down low for now. Sam might feel the need to get more people involved, she'd have to, and the way Blackburn is wired into the town, he'd probably hear soon after. It would give him time to close up shop and get rid of the evidence."

"So we get the proof and then we take the whole package to her?"

"I think that might be a better way to work it. My primary concern is protecting Angie. If that overlaps with grabbing evidence on Blackburn? So be it. Otherwise, we turn it over to Serrato and let the chips fall. She should be able to make a case. The way you said these chemicals are tracked, they're not sending one big shipment, they're sending a steady drip. Maybe not every night but pretty frequently. Small enough that they can bribe someone to adjust the paperwork or just cover up the difference. Somewhere in that chain is a weak link they can flip."

They climbed back up the ladder and emerged into the salt house from the bottom of the old smoker. The entrance was hidden in plain sight. Max had missed it the first two times he'd been inside. He'd seen only what everyone else had seen. He'd seen what they wanted you to see. An old, out of use cabin that would likely fall down sometime soon. But look a little closer and there were clues. Like the well-oiled door hinges and the tractor treads.

The local cops had probably opened the doors, glanced

inside, found nothing but rust and decades-old grease, and shut the doors again. No reason to look closer. Ortiz's body had been found outside. From their perspective, the salt house was almost coincidental to the Ortiz scene. The police hadn't known about Blackburn's warehouse, the truck GPS-data, and the tractor tread impressions.

Once they knew they were looking for a tunnel, it hadn't taken long to find. The flaking, metal floor of the rusty, old smoker simply covered up the square hole in the ground that led down to the tunnel.

"If they knew this tunnel was here and in use, why did they drop that body here? Almost any other place would make more sense," Lawrence said.

"I might have an answer, but I need to think it through some more."

Lawrence waved an arm. "Think away, Einstein."

They walked back out into a wall of midday heat. The temperature was still pushing near triple digits. Far off on the horizon, Max could see a thin gray smudge on the horizon. Rain clouds. A storm was coming.

"Better get back to the bank. I want to watch some more and get the terrain down. Might have to move quickly if we are going to pull this off," Lawrence said.

As the big beams of the Double R ranch gate popped into view, Max said, "Turn in here."

"We got time?"

"Need to ask a man a couple questions."

"All right." Lawrence made the turn through the big gate and took it slow over the rough approach road. "I know the man has enough money to pave this."

"Pretty sure there are cameras or alarms. I think he likes

that people have to come in slow. There'll be someone waiting."

"What the hell are these?" Lawrence asked as they drove through the makeshift box canyon made up by the berms.

"No idea. Never got a chance to ask. Could be to help redirect floods. Could be decorative."

"These feel as deliberate as the dirt road."

"Could be."

Hull waited by the bench near the portico. He wiped his brow with a red bandanna and stood as Lawrence brought the car into the shaded overhang.

"You want me along?" Lawrence asked.

"Up to you."

"I think this fella and I might have a lot in common. What do you think?"

Max smiled as he got out of the car and thought about Hull trying to figure out his friend.

"Back so soon? Who's your pal?" Hull asked. Max noticed the slight hitch before the word pal as if Hull was overriding his natural tendencies. He was sure Lawrence had heard it, too.

"No one you need to know. Not right now," Max responded.

Hull frowned, not sure what to do with that response, a sliver of stained yellow teeth showing between his cracked lips, then his face cleared, in one ear, out the other. "Mr. Blackburn's still not here. Thought we cleared that up last time."

"I know. Not here for Alex."

"So why *are* you here today?"

"I need to ask Jorge something. He around?"

"Sure, he's around here somewhere. He never leaves. What's he gonna tell you?"

Max ignored the question. "While I'm here, let me ask

you something. Blackburn ever have you work on that shack out by the old homestead?"

Hull spit and then squinted at them. His eyes sliding between the pair. "The old salt house? Where they found that beaner's body?"

"Yes, where Raul Ortiz's body was found. You do upkeep or anything? Maintenance?"

"No. There's nothing out there. Like you said, it's old. No reason to go out there unless you're looking to shoot some border jumpers."

"That something you're into?" Lawrence asked.

Hull looked at him properly for the first time. Lawrence might not look like much, small, thin as a blade, but if you took a good look, you'd see a hardness. Hull backed off. "Nah. Too much real work to do around here. End of the day, I sack out or go into town and have a few pops at Shooters. No reason to go south. Nothing good down there." He spit another stream of tobacco and then turned and walked off.

Lawrence and Max walked in the opposite direction and found Jorge on the far side of the barn working under the hood of a boxy old Ford pickup that might have been navy blue back in the eighties. He dropped the hood and wiped his hands on a rag hanging from his belt.

"Sí?"

"Last time I was here and talking to Consuela, you got upset. Why?"

He shrugged and pulled the rag from his belt and started twisting it. Sweat dropped from his nose onto the hood of the car and momentarily turned the faded blue paint a few shades darker. He looked as if he were about to say something but stopped and only shrugged a second time.

"You said something about being tired of not doing anything. Doing anything about what?"

"To help Roxy."

That was not the reply Max expected.

"Why does she need help?"

Now Jorge looked surprised. "You think she is okay?"

"She seems ..." Max had been about to say okay. That she appeared to be a typical teenager: moody, standoffish, sarcastic, confident she had the world figured out. But then he remembered the girl outside the bank. Was she actually okay?

Jorge spoke again. "She has lost both her mother and father, and she lives here. She spends most of her time alone. Yet we do nothing. I'm told to do my work and let her be." He bit off the last few words and shook his head before continuing again in a softer tone. "She deserves a break. She deserves some help."

"Does her stepfather ... abuse her?"

Jorge's head snapped up. "No, nothing like that unless you count neglect as abuse."

"You never picked up on anything physical?"

"No."

"You're sure."

"Yes."

"What about between Blackburn and Rose? Did he ever get physical with her? Do anything that caused her to get treatment?"

"No," Jorge responded without hesitation. He glanced over his shoulder as if the dirt and emptiness might have ears. "He is a selfish man. He has his ambitions. That is all he sees or cares about."

"Rose never had any unexplained injuries? No casts or wraps or anything?"

"No. Look around. There is a lot of space out here, yes, but we live close. He did not abuse her. Not physically. We would have seen. We probably would have heard."

Not physically. Max thought about Vic and her prairie madness story. A lot of space out here. A lot of history. A lot of ghosts. Maybe Vic's theory was right. If you had time and space, it wouldn't take much to nudge someone's mind over the edge.

"You're sure?"

"Very sure."

CHAPTER FIFTY-FOUR

"What did you make of that," Lawrence asked when they were back in the car on solid pavement and heading back toward Tiendas Reales.

"I think he was telling the truth. I'm beginning to think everyone has been telling the truth. No one I've talked to ever got any sniff of domestic violence between Blackburn and Rose."

"Doesn't mean it didn't happen. A lot of these types of situations are very good at appearing normal and hiding in plain sight."

"I know but if you look at the hospital reports, those injuries would have been difficult to hide. People would have seen. I've only found one person who even mentioned seeing Rose hurt."

"So how do you explain that file?"

"I can't but maybe Serrato can help."

He took out his phone, found her number, and tapped connect.

"You never received any callouts to the Double R for a domestic, right?"

"That's right. I told you that."

"I know. What would you say if I told you I had a whole stack of hospital and clinic reports that suggests otherwise?"

"Without seeing it for myself, I'd say you're probably mistaken."

"There's no way something like this happens and you don't find out?"

"I'm sure there is a lot of domestic violence that takes place behind closed doors and I never know, but what you're talking about? Medical records? We'd know."

"You're sure? How?"

"There are formal and informal ways. Did she pay cash? Or did she have insurance?"

Max flipped through the pages. "Insurance."

"Texas is a mandatory reporting state. All health care providers working in the state have to report certain injury types to law enforcement."

"What if the injuries don't coincide with the reporting type?"

"It might slip through and not get reported but there are informal reports, too. One time might be written off but if these places see you multiple times, we're going to hear about it or someone else will. Actually, hold on. I'll call you right back."

She abruptly hung up but called back less than five minutes later as Route 55 dumped them into the first traffic light in TR.

"There's a women's shelter in town and, as one of the few female town cops, I know the owner and volunteers. I make a point of it. I just called her. She has never heard anything about Rose, either. Not a whiff. If something was going on and she got treatment for it, even if she didn't say it was abuse or coercive or something, between us we would have heard about it."

"Huh," was all Max could think to say.

"Do you have a stack of hospital reports that says different?"

"I'll call you back," Max said and disconnected.

They made the drive back to town and parked in the same spot outside The Tin Roof. The old couple was gone but a few of the counter stools were taken by truckers, none of whom looked like the guys Max had run into previously. A family sat in a booth by the window. A boy of about five with a blond bowl cut looked out and waved. Max waved back and then looked across the street to the bank. The same cars were still in the lot, plus a maroon Toyota Camry near the doors.

"Doesn't look like much is happening," Lawrence said.

"I'm getting the impression that *something* happening is more out of the ordinary in this place."

"Maybe the woman got the date wrong?"

"She didn't strike me as the type to get details wrong."

"Maybe they changed it for some reason she doesn't know."

"Maybe. Always unknowns. Let's give it a few minutes. The way you described it, I don't think they'd do anything during business hours."

It was 4:55 P.M. They sat and watched. Three minutes later, a tall but slightly stooped man, as if he were wilting in the heat, with white hair and pants that he surely called dungarees exited and made his way to the maroon Camry. An employee came to the door next, opened it, looked around, closed it again, and turned the locks.

Two minutes later, a lot was happening.

First, a half dozen dented and scuffed 22-foot moving

trucks pulled up and parked along the street. Guys jumped out of the trucks in twos and threes, maybe 25 in total. They all wore navy workpants and gray T-shirts with a logo on the pocket. It was too far for Max to make out clearly. Probably a local moving company. Or maybe out of San Antonio given the amount of them.

Next, at least a dozen, anonymous four-door sedans came down the road in a line and pulled into the bank's lot.

"That would be the Feds," Lawrence said.

"Yup."

Each car was filled with four agents, probably to satisfy some government expense regulation. Max and Lawrence watched them exit the cars, all wearing similar gray or black suits, some carrying briefcases, some not. They all entered the bank.

Then the muscle arrived. So to speak. Two identical white Hyundais with stick-on decals advertising Armada Security Services. They parked on the street behind the moving trucks. Four men, two from each car, got out and congregated on the sidewalk. They wore gray polyester slacks, thick-soled rubber shoes, and short-sleeve white button-down shirts. Max could see they each had a sidearm and shoulder mics clipped to the breast pockets.

"Retired cops?" Lawrence said.

"Gotta be. Too old to be recent ex-military."

"Too old to still be working a gig like this."

"Probably figure it's easy money."

"Wearing that getup in this heat is anything but easy money."

"Might make them sloppy. Heat will tire an old man out."

"Also might give them itchy trigger fingers."

The movers congregated in a knot on the small patch of grass near the bank's front doors. The security guards hung near the back. It must have been prearranged. After a moment, an agent, this one in a black suit with a red tie, Max was sure he had an American flag pin somewhere on his body, came out and began talking.

"What do you think?" Max asked.

"I think we need some uniforms."

"I might know a place."

CHAPTER FIFTY-FIVE

The door to Will's Hardware was locked but the lights were still on. Max put a hand against the glass and peered inside. He could see Lou behind the counter tallying the day's credit card receipts. Max knocked. Lou glanced up. Maybe he recognized Max from his last late-day shopping trip or maybe he just couldn't pass up a sale. He put the pile of papers down, set his bifocals on the counter, and came around to unlock the door.

"Hello, again." So he did remember Max. A true professional salesman. He opened the door wide and the two stepped inside. "How can I help?"

"Do you carry work clothes? Uniforms? Things like that?"

"We have a small selection. Check aisle seven. Canvas work pants, hospital scrubs, first responder things. Might be some restaurant pants and chef jackets. It's toward the back," Lou called as Max and Lawrence headed down the aisle.

The front half was safety equipment. Vests, reflectors, temporary signs, then came the clothes. It wasn't a big selection, but it was eclectic. Max picked through the offerings.

"Think this will work?" Max asked holding up a pair of

navy pants and a gray T-shirt.

Lawrence looked them over. "No logo, but nothing we can do about that. It doesn't have to fool anyone for long."

"Just long enough."

They paid Lou in cash for the clothes plus a cheap pair of binoculars. They changed right in the store. If Lou was curious, he didn't show it. He let them out and locked the door behind them. They drove down a side street and parked, still with a clear view of the bank, but one that kept them off the main road. Activity had ramped up. Furniture and boxes were leaving the bank. Two of the four guards were outside on the sidewalk. They sipped from paper cups and occasionally looked around. Max assumed the other two were inside.

Max picked up the binoculars and focused in on the guy who had just exited the bank's front door carrying a white bankers box. There was writing on the side of the box in black marker. Max fiddled with the focus. It took a minute but the words came into focus. Small Business Account Records Q4 '21.

"Doesn't look like they've gotten to the deposit boxes yet," Max said.

They continued to watch for another 30 minutes. It was now close to 6:30.

"I've got an idea," Lawrence said as he twisted around and picked up his laptop from the back seat. He tapped the keys, scrolled, read, then closed it and put it back on the seat.

Max put the binoculars down and looked at him. Lawrence was smiling. Max knew that smile. "Am I going to like this idea?" he asked.

"We can thank organized labor for it, so it should appeal to your bleeding-heart tendencies."

Max squinted out at the trucks lining the street. "It's a union shop."

Lawrence snapped his fingers. "Got it in one. I'll bet my

left nut that they'll get at least one mandated break. That's when we get those docs back in there."

"We just walk them onto the truck?"

"You think those two are going to notice? They've been sucking down the coffee. My guess is that they'll use the break time to hit the bathroom."

"Not a bad idea, but we need the boxes to be in the truck already. Specifically, we need her box in the truck. She said there were other things with the documents."

"She assumes the box is still active. That he didn't just dump the rest of the contents and keep those documents."

"True, but I think that's a good assumption. The whole box going missing might bring too much attention. If a claim was made and the box was found with something inside, it would be easier to say the person likely removed the other things and maybe forgot. Hard to do if the box is empty or missing."

"Okay, I'll buy that." Lawrence nodded to the guy exiting the bank. He was pushing a rolling chair with a box on the seat. "So where are we?"

Max pointed the binoculars in that direction. "Still not to the vault but maybe getting closer."

Lawrence looked at his watch. "Closing in on two hours. Figure an eight- to ten-hour shift. Maybe they break in the middle? Gives us a minimum of two more hours. Might work."

Max nodded. "How do you want to do it?"

"Distraction scam could work. Get their eyes looking elsewhere, get on the truck, get the docs in the right place."

Max nodded again. "Okay, which end do you want?"

"Oh, I think I should be the distractor."

Max looked over at him. Lawrence had that smile again. "Why is this making you so happy?"

"Let's just say I'm a fan of irony. Better yet, I can change back into my own clothes."

Time was elastic in moments like this. Max was used to the phenomenon from the long, patient stints of surveillance he used to put in before jobs. He could tell Lawrence felt the same. There was no fidgeting or pointless conversation. They waited and watched. Occasionally, he'd bring up the binoculars and check the labels on the boxes. An hour passed in silence and economical movements. The sun dipped below the buildings and long shadows crept into the street. The far-off storm clouds Max had seen from the salt house rolled closer.

The vault boxes started coming out at ninety minutes.

"Moving faster now," Max said. "Timing might not work. Any ideas for a backup?"

Lawrence thought for a moment. "Might get another chance on the other end. They're not going to leave them on the truck. They must have a plan for them. Probably drive to the consolidated branch and reverse the process. Unload. Inventory the stuff. Put them in new boxes. Doing it there might work even better. Might be a new crew if they don't want to pay overtime. We could slip in and out before anyone on that end gets familiar with each other." Lawrence looked left, out the driver's window. "But I don't think it's going to come to that."

"Why?"

He pointed at a Kia Rio coming up the street slowly. There was a lighted sign on the top from Town Line Pizza. "Here comes dinner."

They talked it over and decided Max couldn't walk straight onto the truck. It would look more natural and believable if he exited the bank with a box like the other movers. He walked around the block and approached the bank from the rear. A back door was propped open; bags of shredded documents were being hauled out and placed in a dumpster that was now close to overflowing. Max didn't pause. He briefly put a hand to the small of his back where he'd stuck the documents then went through the door and into the bank. There were a lot of suits and a lot of activity. He felt the familiar buzzing of white noise at the base of his skull and the coppery taste of adrenaline on his back teeth as he walked. The small vault area was to the left of the customer counter.

Max had the sense that what looked like chaos was carefully orchestrated. The agents were spread out into all available spaces: offices, storage rooms, hallways, the customer lobby. They had taped handmade signs to the doors: Audit, Security, and Investigations. He could hear the hum of a shredder and the thunk of a copy machine. He passed two agents at the teller windows counting cash by hand. One of the security guards stood near the money. Max didn't see the other one. The swinging door separating the back of the bank from the customer area was propped open with a box of printer paper. Max went through without slowing. He kept his eyes up but moving. He didn't linger on anything or anyone. He turned left, went around a bank of four connected cubicles, each with an agent at a computer, turned left again, and passed a moving guy carrying a box as he exited the vault room.

"Pizza's here," Max said, then turned slightly and ducked his chin as the guy passed.

"Thanks," the guy responded. Max nodded and then entered the vault.

There were four suits inside. One drilling the boxes, another pulling and opening them, the third making an inventory list based on the contents, and the fourth filling and labeling boxes like those Max had been watching exit the bank for the last half hour. Completed boxes ready to move were stacked in the corner. The fourth and final security guard stood next to the stack with hooded eyes staring out at the room. At a glance, Max couldn't tell if he was half-asleep or watching carefully. He was tall with close-cropped gray hair and thick shoulders that offset a decent spare tire around his gut. His thumbs were tucked into his belt. This close, Max could see the gun on his hip was a black Glock 42.

Max stepped toward the stack, and he felt the security guard's eyes swivel toward him. Max kept his focus on the top box, but he could see the guard's jaw flex and Max knew he was about to say something. Something that could end up with Max in a boatload of trouble. Then the mic clipped near his shoulder squawked.

"Bob, Jamie. Might have a situation out here."

Other than the brief high whines of the drill biting into the locks, the vault was mostly quiet, with just occasional bursts of conversation as box contents were inventoried. The squelch of the radio was impossible not to hear. Everyone stopped and turned.

The guy reached for the mic, but the other guard inside beat him to it. "What's going on?"

"Single Black male. Appears agitated. Unclear if he's armed ... or on something."

"Roger that. Jamie, I can't leave the money. Can you assist?"

The guard in the vault keyed the mic. "10-4. On my way."

The guy gave him a final look before he hustled out the door. After a pause, the room's activity picked back up. Max grabbed the box on top of the stack and walked out.

Outside, the three security guards surrounded Lawrence. He was across the street, on the sidewalk that ran parallel to the bank and was farthest away from the truck being loaded.

He was back in his clothes and was putting on a good show. He was waving a dog's leash around like a lasso and saying something. Max had no idea where he'd gotten the leash. They briefly locked eyes and Lawrence gave him a small nod and the shadow of a smile. He was enjoying himself. Lawrence had been through plenty of interactions with the police, and Max was confident he could push their buttons enough to keep their interest but not go over the edge. The three guards looked more exasperated than concerned. None of them had their hands near their guns. He left Lawrence to it and walked toward the truck being loaded.

The moving guys were sitting on the sidewalk or the steps of nearby businesses with the pizza boxes and cans of soda spread out between them. He went up the ramp, but the truck wasn't empty as he'd expected. Not everyone had stopped to eat. One guy was still inside stacking and arranging the boxes to maximize the space. The inside was mostly in shadows, the interior lights weak. It smelled like hot cardboard and the fusty wool of furniture blankets.

Max raised the box a little higher so it covered the lower part of his face, but the guy didn't even glance at him just kept shifting the boxes around like it was a puzzle to be solved.

"Just put it there. Grab some food. Take your break. I need some time to get this all sorted. How many more?"

"Maybe fifty. Not more than seventy-five," Max said.

"If it's seventy-five it's gonna be tight."

Max placed the box down on the truck's floor. He had planned to find the right box and slip the documents inside. He realized now that that wasn't going to work. His mind ran through the possibilities. They couldn't guarantee another opportunity at the other end. Could he ignore what the guy had just said, make one more trip, and hope this guy took his break and left him alone in the truck? No, he didn't think

Lawrence could keep up the charade that long, and something about Max had pricked that guard's attention. He didn't want to push his luck there, either. It had to be now. Max turned and started down the ramp. He pulled the papers from where he'd hidden them under his shirt.

"Shit," he said and reversed course back up the ramp.

"What?"

"Found this by the ramp," Max waved the documents around hoping to keep the guy's attention off his face. "Looks like maybe they fell out of a box. Number 239."

"How the hell did that happen?"

"Don't know. Boxes aren't taped. Maybe one got dropped?"

"Shit. Good thing you saw it. Any of those Feds had spotted it, we'd have been canned. What box again?"

"239."

The guy studied the boxes for a moment. "Damn, not this row, but not too far." He started pulling boxes and setting them aside. Max glanced over his shoulder, he couldn't see Lawrence's act from inside the truck, but he could feel time getting tight. The guy had pulled a dozen boxes, making two short stacks, when he said, "Bingo," and pulled one box and set it aside. He popped the lid. "Hand me that." Max gave him the documents and the guy dropped them inside, replaced the lid, and put the box back. "Dodged a bullet there. Hey, tell Bobby to save me at least two slices."

"Will do," Max replied and went down the ramp. Lawrence was gone. The three guards had drifted over to the nearest group of movers and grabbed some pizza. Max went in the opposite direction, cut through an alley, and exited half a block behind the SUV. Thirty seconds later, he was in the passenger seat next to a smiling Lawrence.

"Nothing like a Black man walking alone, minding his own

business, to get everyone's attention. Never been so happy to have Security be so proactive."

They had driven away from the bank after getting rid of the documents. Darkness had come on fast, like a curtain dropping on a stage. Clouds had pushed in during the afternoon, but far from providing any relief; they'd just trapped the heat like a blanket. Lawrence heard a rumble of thunder to the west. He cut his eyes in that direction, but it was just black on black. The thin clouds that had blown in that afternoon were gone and dark thunderheads had taken their place. The heat might break but it wasn't going down without a fight. It was going to be wet and violent.

They were both hungry but driving aimlessly, neither of them wanting to end up back at The Tin Roof again but had yet to make a decision.

"You have any guns or other weapons?" Max asked.

Lawrence looked over at Max. He was staring down at his phone and had gone rigid. He was clearly not seeing the screen but, thinking, hard, the intensity was radiating off him in waves.

"Is a frog's ass watertight? Yes, this SUV has my favorite hidey hole filled with whatever hardware you might need."

"Good."

"Gonna tell me why?"

"Where are we?" Max asked instead as he looked around.

"I don't know, somewhere north of the town center and the bank."

"We need to get back to the Double R ranch. Fast."

"Blackburn's place? Why?"

Max held up his phone. Lawrence could see a text message glowing on the screen. Just a single word: *Help*.

"Because I made a promise."

CHAPTER FIFTY-SIX

"I'm sorry I haven't called in a few days. I've been neck-deep in paper. Virtual paper, at least," Kelley said. Max could hear the fatigue again in his voice.

"Is your family okay? Have there been any more threats?" Max asked.

"No, thank God. They're still moving around, but no more posts or pictures."

"Good. Glad to hear it. I don't think this is going to last much longer. Tell them to hang in there. What have you found?"

Kelley let out a heavy sigh. "I'm glad you're confident because I found a lot of smoke, but no fire."

"What does that mean?"

"It means as far as I can tell Blackburn has ample cash coming in. None of his accounts are in arrears or past due. All his businesses are highly liquid, but I can't pin down the sources of the cash. There are a lot of shell companies and foreign investors. I even called in a marker from a friend who works at the IRS but even she couldn't get any more information. Blackburn's paperwork might invite some scrutiny, but it's all legal and filed appropriately according to the letter of the law."

"Any theories?"

"Actually, yes. Blackburn's motivation has always bothered us, right? Why is he doing this? Why Tiendas Reales?"

"That's right."

"My theory is that Blackburn himself is the byproduct."

"What do you mean?"

"I think the location still matters in some way, but his buying power and influence over the town are secondary. I think spending the money *is* the point."

Max knew the location did matter in one way because of the tunnel but had an idea about what Kelley was talking about. "You think he's embezzling?"

"No, I mean, he's getting paid, but I think he's using the town to wash money."

"Money laundering. Whose?"

"Could be anyone. Take your pick of organized crime syndicates, but given the border location, I'd say one in Central or South America makes the most sense. You'd want to be close enough to keep an eye on someone doing your dirty work."

"Cartels." The toluene and the tunnel.

"They'd be high on my list, but I can't say for sure. The origin of the money is well insulated."

"No way to trace it back?"

"Nothing short of Blackburn giving us a name or a thread to pull on."

"That's unlikely. How does it work?"

"It appears they keep it pretty simple, but that doesn't make it any less effective. Blackburn's unknown foreign partner invests a chunk of cash into one of Blackburn's legitimate domestic businesses, like the warehouse or real estate or any of the other small businesses Blackburn has bought up in TR over time. The important part is that Blackburn has control of that business, often through a shell company, as the primary owner.

"The shell companies are businesses that have large amounts of cash but are not directly involved in any specific part of selling goods or services. Much of the shell companies' cash is used to further invest in other companies, usually by making a loan to another business—typically, another business owned by Blackburn or the original investor."

"Further mixing up the money trail."

"Exactly. The influx of cash from the shell companies appears as an ordinary investment. Blackburn would not disclose he knows the investor. Now, here's the clever part. That company can then—after passing the cash back to the original investor—default on the loan, creating a loss for the shell company that can be used to reduce taxes owed. Having defaulted on its loan, the receiving shell company may declare bankruptcy and go out of business."

"Creating a nice dead end. It's like having your cake and eating it, too."

"And the original investors now have their cash, received from an apparently 'clean' source and the company used to wash the cash no longer exists, which, as you can imagine, makes it very difficult for authorities to have any hope of tracing the money back to its source."

"But it needs a front man."

"And that's Blackburn."

"What's the endgame?"

"Eventually, I think it's the snake that eats itself. The biggest issue these criminal organizations face is what to do with the mountains of cash they generate. I think Blackburn will run out of ways to utilize the cash without drawing serious oversight from the IRS or the FBI. The flow of money that is propping up the town dries up as the bad guys take their laundry somewhere else. Leaving the town high and dry."

"And maybe some people dead," Max said.

CHAPTER FIFTY-SEVEN

It took five phone calls for Blackburn to end up dead, but it started with an email.

Quentin Hoffman was a budget analyst for the Internal Revenue Service. He spent most of his days reviewing PowerPoint or Excel documents for budgetary or financial issues for the various departments and programs within the IRS. When talking to someone outside of the government about his job, he told people he was basically like a cop who worked in Internal Affairs. He audited the auditors. He thought that sounded pretty cool. Quentin's biggest talent in life was self-deception.

He was 39 and unmarried. He wasn't a bad-looking guy and kept himself in shape with a fold-up rowing machine and some dumbbells in his townhouse's spare room. But any potential relationship that stretched past three dates quickly realized, even if Quentin didn't, that he had a mild drug problem and was developing a more severe gambling problem. Any thoughts of a woman fell far below those first two things on his priority list. The smart women moved on after one or two dates. The rest hung on longer, trying to change him but had all eventually given up.

On the government pay scale, he was a GS-9 with experience, and, after his last performance review, he made a salary of $97,387, but if anyone asked, he always said he made six figures. It sounded better and was basically a rounding error. Typically, for an unmarried man living in the suburbs of San Antonio, this would provide a comfortable living. And, for a long time, it did just that, but then he'd had a run of bad luck, starting with the Super Bowl last year, and he just couldn't seem to dig himself out of it. He had been getting pretty desperate when the man had approached him at Legends with the offer. It was a lifeline at just the right time, and he thought maybe his luck was finally changing.

It had taken a month and he'd had to switch after-work bars, but he'd gotten it done. Quentin had barely started his pitch before Roderick Thompson had firmly rebuffed any of his 'hypothetical' requests for help. Maura Pray was the second person he'd approached. Maura worked in IT and did her drinking at The Banshee. Legends and The Banshee were both within walking distance of the downtown government building complex but were otherwise worlds apart. Legends was filled with wooden booths and sports memorabilia. Big, flat-screen televisions lined the walls every few feet. The Banshee was dark and sticky and reminded Quentin of an underground bunker. There were no TVs and definitely no sports. There was a low stage at one end, various alcoves and bars around the edges, and a wide-open dance floor in the middle.

The first time he'd followed Maura inside The Banshee, he'd promptly lost her in the dark, cave-like interior. Maura was a thin, waif-life woman with white hair in a spiky pixie cut with the ends dipped in purple. Quentin thought she looked ridiculous, and he couldn't figure out how he'd lost her. The Banshee was practically empty at that time of day. He ordered a beer and wandered around until it was warm, then he'd left as the crowd started to pick up.

The second time, he stuck a bit closer and caught her disappearing behind a pillar which he'd previously thought led to a service closet. This time, he pushed through and found himself standing in a narrow room full of classic pinball machines. The room was moderately crowded. He watched her settle in front of a red-and-black AC/DC-themed machine. She must have been good because she didn't move for nearly twenty minutes on one play. He tried a few games and gradually worked his way closer until they were playing on adjacent machines, hers an Addams Family one, his Batman. He saw her notice him but he didn't say anything. He quickly ran through his plays and then casually turned to watch her. She really was good. Never appearing frantic or overwhelmed, she just flowed with the game.

When she finally caught an unlucky bounce and lost the last ball down the gutter, she turned to him. "I recognize you. You work for the IRS, right? Or you do something at the building on Hanover. I've seen you around."

"That's right. You there, too?"

"Yeah. I'm in IT. What about you?"

"Cool. I'm in Budget Controls." He didn't offer his Internal Affairs analogy and if she had an opinion on his position, she didn't offer it.

"What brings you in?" She gave his standard corporate casual attire a quick up-and-down glance. "You're not The Banshee's typical clientele. No offense."

He laughed. "I know, and none taken. I think I come in for maybe the same reason you do. I like the classics." He bumped his hip against the brightly beeping machine he was leaning against.

"Really?" Maybe she'd seen his poor play. "Haven't seen you here before."

"No, that's true. Just discovered the place."

"Oh, well, cool." They had hit their limit of polite small talk and she smiled and picked up her glass. "Maybe see you around." She moved off and started talking to two guys playing a Godzilla game. He finished his beer and left.

He found a bowling alley three towns north that also had a small arcade of classic games including two pinball machines. He spent an hour there after work for each of the next two weeks before he went back to The Banshee. He was nowhere as good as Maura but he was getting better. He approached her, and they briefly chatted again but he didn't push it. He moved on and played for another hour before going home. The third time Maura approached him and he knew he'd make his pitch. He was on the Batman machine again and playing well. She stayed until he was done. His score didn't get him on the leaderboard, but it was within shouting distance.

"Nice run," she said.

"Thanks," he replied. "Hey, you said you were in IT, right?" He kept it simple. His brother-in-law had a business. This was his second business. The first had been audited, he'd been caught unaware, he was clean, but it had eaten up the profits to defend himself. He didn't want that to happen again. If he could just get a heads-up if anyone was poking around his business, he would be willing to pay. Would that be something she would be interested in?

She'd given him a long stare before she said, "Five hundred bucks. I'll send you an email if anyone internally searches the business name."

"That sounds fair." He'd been willing to go to $1000, so he felt good when he left The Banshee that night. He wanted to ride the vibe. He'd called his bookie and placed the extra

$500 on the Spurs. They lost, but he didn't let it dent his good mood. Or maybe that was the bump of coke talking. Either way, the guy at Legends had promised $10,000 when it was set up, then $500 a month to keep it going as a retainer of sorts.

That had been 15 months ago. The money had come through and taken some of the pressure off. The $500 had also shown up each month since and nothing else had happened. Until this morning. He'd come into his cube, fired up his computer, and found an email waiting. He'd immediately walked to the elevators, gone back down to the lobby, and walked across the street to the drugstore. He bought a cheap phone and dialed the number he kept on a small slip of paper in his wallet. There was a beep and for a moment Quentin was confused, then he remembered that the man had told him the number was for a pager. Shit, he was nervous. He almost dropped the phone. He panicked for another moment and then it all came back to him. He punched in his new burner number and the code the man had given him the first night. Quentin hadn't needed to write it down. It was his own birthday. It was only as he was punching in the year that Quentin paused to consider how this man had known his birthday and what it might mean. He hesitated over the last digit but then thought of the money. This year's Super Bowl bet hadn't gone any better than last year's. There might be a bonus for this information. He hit the last digit.

The rest of the phone calls went more quickly.

The man who received Quentin's page was the same person who'd spoken to him almost a year and a half ago at Legends.

His name was Hernan Reyes. His pager vibrated as he was sitting in his living room in Scottsdale, Arizona, watching a morning news program. He stood, walked to the kitchen, and removed an ice cube from the freezer, then he walked outside to a shed he kept in the back yard. It was locked with a padlock. He told his wife the lock was because he didn't want the children or the dog getting into any of the pesticides or fertilizers in the shed. But that wasn't the real reason it was locked. He opened the padlock, stepped inside, and closed the door. The shed was larger than it appeared from the front. He walked through the front section with the lawn-mower and gardening supplies. There was a second door and a second lock in the back corner. This one operated with a keypad lock. He entered the code and, after a moment, the door's lock disengaged with a quiet click.

Inside was a narrow office space. Reyes could easily reach out and touch the opposite walls. It was a simple setup. A desk and chair with a laptop computer and printer. The desk had three drawers. All locked. A picture of Reyes's family sat on the corner between the printer and the laptop. Next to the framed photo sat a small aloe plant. It could be any cubicle in any office park in America. Save for one feature. The wall that ran the length of the back of the shed and ran adjacent to the desk and computer was a pegboard filled with cheap cell phones in carefully labeled slots. He used a new phone for each job and kept that phone only as long as the job lasted. There were three boxes of phones under the work-table in the other room.

He took out the phone he'd assigned to Quentin Hoffman and sat down in his chair. He placed the melting ice cube in the aloe vera's pot and then dialed the number from the pager.

A man answered. "Hello?" The voice sounded tentative.

Reyes remembered Quentin. An IRS bureaucrat in San

Antonio. He was constantly licking his lips or wiping his nose. Reyes had a gift for faces and quickly fingering a person's weak point. It was why Reyes was good at his job. It was why he was still alive. But, in Quentin's case, it hadn't been difficult. "Yes, you called," he said now.

Quentin's voice cracked and he had to clear his throat and start again. "Someone at the IRS just queried Double R Holdings."

"Okay, thank you," Reyes said. He disconnected and disassembled the phone. He would dispose of it tomorrow. He swept the pieces into the plastic garbage can that sat on the floor next to the printer. He then unlocked the top drawer and took out another phone. In many ways, Hernan Reyes was like the man in Vegas. He was a cutout, a middleman, set up to backstop any potential inquiries. He was to be sacrificed if it came down to it. He understood and was paid well for this risk. Unlike the man in Vegas, he had just one client. He tapped the single contact in this phone. It bounced off satellites and was answered approximately 800 miles to the south. Reyes repeated Quentin's message and then replaced the phone in the drawer.

The next step didn't require another phone call. The man who answered Reyes's call walked up two sets of stairs inside the large house and, after listening at the door for a moment, knocked. He was told to enter. The man inside sat behind a large antique desk made of oak. The entire desktop might have been larger than Reyes's shed office. Three large, thin monitors and a keyboard sat along one edge of the desk and various piles of stacked paper filled out the rest. Running a cartel involved a lot of cash and a lot of paperwork. Tuaro Ramirez was under no illusions about how his career could, and likely would, end, but he was damned if he was going to be taken out by poor management or a clerical error. He treated the cartel like a corporation and he was the CEO. He put in the necessary hours.

"Yes?" he said without looking away from the screen on the left.

The man repeated the message. Ramirez nodded that he'd heard and the man retreated and closed the door with a soft click.

Ramirez took off his glasses and rubbed his eyes. The project in Tiendas Reales had been both profitable and shown promise for innovative ways to clean money and provide local influence at the same time. It was a newer, more modern version of a company town. He had given Blackburn time and space to see how he'd react. He was disappointed but the next time would be better. They had learned a lot, but it was time to wrap things up. He made a quick note on the pad near his elbow to think more about the lessons learned from the Tiendas Reales venture. It was worth trying again. The toluene was certainly worth saving. He'd need to find another way to get it back across the border. Next, he called a number in Vegas and told the man what he wanted done. The man had a question which Ramirez considered and then agreed. It was a little unusual and not how he typically handled business, but it should be a clean break. No loose ends. He disconnected, dropped the phone on the desk, and went back to the spreadsheet he'd been analyzing.

The man in Vegas took a deep breath. The twins. He knew they weren't actually twins but that was how he always thought about them. A pair working together for this long in this business was unusual. They were dependable, even banal, and maybe that's why these calls, even the routine ones, always made him nervous. The twins were not normal and he would never say it to another person but he could feel the darkness through the phone.

Everyone in this business had a compromised moral compass, he knew that, and everyone dealt with it in different ways, but he sensed it was different for the twins. At some point, long ago, something had changed them. Their moral compass wasn't compromised. It was gone. Killing people had no impact on them. It was a job. Human life had no value other than what the contract paid. They were reapers wearing human masks.

He tapped connect. Better to get it done. It was always better to deal with death quickly.

"Yes?"

That dry, quiet voice, barely above a whisper. The man in Vegas suppressed a shiver and told the man what Ramirez wanted.

"Timeline?"

"As soon as possible."

"Method."

"Whatever you feel is appropriate."

"Proof?"

"None required. Just get it done."

"Okay."

And then he was gone.

CHAPTER FIFTY-EIGHT

The driver's real name was Diego Vazquez. He was a man who was comfortable with long stretches of silence. His sister always invited him to outings with his nieces or gatherings with her friends. She was a social person and couldn't understand that there was a difference between solitary and lonely. He was happiest when he was solving problems or alone. He worked with a partner largely because it made his job easier. It solved a problem. It allowed him to complete jobs efficiently.

As Vazquez sat in the car and watched the street, he didn't think efficient was a word that he would use to describe this current job. Mookie sat next to him and squirmed as the temperature slowly crept up. Vazquez could tell the job and the circumstances also bothered him, but they'd taken the work. In reality, they'd had little choice given the client, and there was nothing they could do about it but see it through to the end. Despite their shared introverted tendencies, they had talked about the situation until the grooves in the conversation were well worn, but Vazquez could see Mookie gearing up to go at it again. This was the longest job they'd ever had, and they'd said more to each other in the last week than they had in the previous 10 years. Vazquez could have done without it, but he knew it kept Mookie calm which Vazquez also thought of as part of the job. Keep the man calm until he was ready to be let off the leash.

But he surprised Vazquez when he said, "Remember the guys in Michigan? Lansing, I think?"

Mookie had told him once, a long time ago when both of them were still young and living in the village, that when he killed he became another person. Over the years, Vazquez had come to believe that Mookie had not been talking figuratively. He didn't block his emotions or tamp them down or turn them off like Vazquez. He became a different person and then when the act was over, he returned to himself. Maybe it was temporary insanity, or a survival mechanism cooked up by a young boy in an impossible situation. They each coped in their own ways but, as a rule, Mookie rarely talked about the past. He rarely remembered it.

Vazquez on the other hand remembered everything. He just didn't let it affect him.

"776 Jolly Road. Acid baths."

One guy, the foreman, had been in workpants and a flannel shirt with a leather toolbelt. The money guy, the one causing most of the problems, had been in a suit. One of his Italian loafers had come off when they folded his body into the barrel. As far as Vazquez knew, the barrels were still in the basement of the foreclosed house.

"That's right," Mookie said. "I didn't like the smell. I had to call a plumber the other day to clear a block at one of my rentals. I went over later to check on the work. The smell hit me like a brick to the face. Reminded me of that job. Never had that happen before. Had to leave the windows open overnight."

The fact that he was talking about a job from five years ago told Vazquez just how far off the rails this current job had gone. All the downtime was affecting Mookie. Vazquez glanced over and watched as his partner's thick fingers twisted the takeout bag from breakfast into a thin white string. The man was getting edgy and anxious. Vazquez couldn't disagree. He felt the same way. While they had tried their best not to attract attention, this town was too small. If they hadn't been noticed yet, they would be soon.

He turned his attention back to the street. He watched as the man exited the building and walked down the sidewalk in the opposite direction. His phone rang. The man from Vegas again.

Vazquez answered and listened, asked a few questions, finished with an okay, and then disconnected. Mookie glanced at him, a question on his face.

"Time to get to work."

CHAPTER FIFTY-NINE

Angie was lying on her bed listening to music. Her stepfather was on one of his endless and never-ending phone calls downstairs in his office. He didn't like her watching the big television in the living room when he was on calls, and he wouldn't allow her to get one in her room. So, the music and the headphones. Occasionally, she flipped through various social media feeds, but mostly it was just the thump of music that pushed her thoughts along.

Even with the big Beats headphones on, she heard the loud bang over the throbbing of the music. It reverberated through the house. She pulled the headphones off and sat up. It had to be the front door banging against the wall. Nothing else could make the house shake like that. Her mother used to complain about it when Angie barged into the house in a hurry and the door ricocheted off the wall and sometimes shook loose the framed photos in the entryway. Her stomach tightened as she thought about Hull, but then she relaxed, he wouldn't try anything, not with her stepfather right downstairs. He might come up and leer at her, but she could handle that.

She was about to slip the headphones back on when she heard the sound of feet moving along the corridor downstairs. Feet. Plural, as in more than one person. Who was it? She swung her legs off the bed and took the headphones from around her neck and placed them on her pillow. She glanced out the window. It was full dark now. Heavy, thick clouds obscured the moonlight. Hull could find an excuse any time of day to come inside the big house, but the various hired hands and Jorge rarely did. Consuela was also done for the day. She'd come upstairs over an hour ago to say goodnight and tell Angie there was a plate of tamales warming in the oven if she wanted it for dinner. She'd be back in her own little house on the other side of the barn. Angie looked in that direction even though she knew she couldn't see anything. The only thing that would bring Consuela back was if Alex or Angie called her. Or if there was trouble. Had something happened to the horses? She glanced out the window a third time, but the barn remained dark and everything appeared quiet.

Who was downstairs and what did they want?

She listened to the sound of the footsteps as they moved through the first floor. She heard the pantry door open and close. No voices and no sounds other than the footfalls and the occasional creak of a loose floorboard. Someone with weight. It was not the diminutive Consuela. She could hear Alex through the floor, his office was right below her room, still talking, apparently unconcerned or unaware of the footsteps. She reached for her phone just as she heard the squeak. She knew each step of the staircase like the bones inside her skin. The second step squeaked if you stepped anywhere other than the far right.

Someone was coming up the stairs. A flutter of panic ran through her body and she froze. Then she heard another sound. A voice. Someone shouting. Hull. Ordinarily, his voice would make her back teeth ache but now it sounded like a choir of angels. "Hey! Who are you? What are you doing?" The only response to the questions was the ear-splitting boom of a gunshot in an enclosed space. A moment later another shot. She was a Texas girl through-and-through. She'd learned to shoot at 10. She knew guns. The second shot was a different caliber. Two shooters. She had her gun, but it was still in her backpack downstairs.

There was a quick series of shots, all in a row, all jumbled together. She thought four, maybe five then the house went very quiet which was somehow much scarier to Angie than the ear-splitting shots. Then she heard the squeak of the second step again. Or thought she did. Her ears were ringing so it was hard to be sure. She decided not to wait around and see. She slid her phone into her pocket and stepped quickly to the window. She popped out the screen and pushed it quickly under her bed and then climbed through before she gently pushed the window back down into place. With any luck, it would buy her some time. She carefully climbed down the trellis and then moved to the left where the old flowering vine was originally planted. She glanced back up but saw nothing. She knelt in the shadows and tried to disappear into the flowers. She tried to think of a plan, something to do other than hide, but her mind was blank.

She glanced up again. The window was still closed but then she saw a shadow move across the wall. She was out of time. She had to get farther away. Then she thought of something. She pulled out her phone. She couldn't risk talking out loud so she simply texted one word then turned and ran into the dark.

Angie looked back once, just as she made it to the barn. She could see a shadow filling most of her window. A head turned, looking left and right. She held still. She'd never been this scared. Not when the ambulance had come for her dad. Or all the police had come for her mom. Those times hadn't felt real. Those things happened to someone else. This was happening to her. That shadow was coming after her. Her legs and arms shook involuntarily. Her breath sounded loud and ragged to her ears. She couldn't hear anything else. She opened her mouth wide, trying to vacuum in enough air to slow her heart rate down. It wasn't working. Finally, she closed her eyes and forced her body to be still for ten agonizing seconds, which felt so much longer, then she opened her eyes. She let out a shaky breath. A little better. The shadow was still there, searching, but she hadn't been spotted.

But it wouldn't last for long. Big, fat drops of rain started to fall and hit the ground with an audible splat. A deep rolling thunder that she felt in her chest rolled across the open space. So much space, she thought. That was the problem. There weren't many places to hide on the ranch. Consuela's house, the barn, and ... under a pool chair on the patio? What should she do? Did she have time to warn Consuela? The door to the barn was half open and the darkness inside was inviting. The dark offered a refuge. She could hide in the dark. But she couldn't leave Consuela and Jorge to face whatever was chasing her completely unaware. She had to try to warn them. She looked over her shoulder. The shadow in the window was gone, but that didn't make her feel any better. She knew it meant it was coming for her. She raced around the side of the barn and banged on Consuela's front door. "Something's happening! Run! Hide!" Behind her, she heard the screech and slap of the ranch's back door as it opened and closed. It wasn't much, but it would have to do. She banged a fist one more time on Consuela's door and then ran inside the barn.

The familiar smells of so many days spent in the barn briefly pushed away her terror. She could hear the soft muffled sounds of the horses in their stalls. The rain started to fall more heavily. She knew the thunder made the horses skittish. She walked over. Bonnie sensed her presence and nickered. Angie reached out a hand and rubbed her chin to calm her. Or maybe calm herself.

She cursed herself again for leaving her gun in her backpack. She thought about trying to find something in the barn to defend herself with, but her mind was frazzled. She couldn't think straight. She couldn't remember where anything was. Surely, there was something in here that she could use but her mind drew a blank. The only thing penetrating the panic was a flashing neon sign in her mind: HIDE! NOW!

She could do that. She could hide. The muscle memory kicked in and she ran for the far end of the barn. To her secret place.

CHAPTER SIXTY

Vazquez searched the second floor. He flung open doors, checked in bathrooms, and looked under beds. This was not how he preferred his jobs to go but this whole endeavor had been off-kilter from the start, and now he could feel it spiraling out of control. He couldn't let that happen. He had to find the girl and finish it.

He stepped into the last room at the end of the hall. Another bedroom. How many bedrooms did one house need? The first floor had been wide open, just the office in the back, but the second floor was a warren, doors and rooms, nooks and crannies. The information they'd received said there would be two people in the house. Both targets. Blackburn and his kid. Maybe a third, older woman, the housekeeper, depending on the time of day. If she was there, she was a target. If she wasn't, that was fine. It was left to their discretion. An hour earlier, Vazquez had tracked her with the binoculars as she exited through the back door and walked toward a small house behind the barn. If she felt death nearby, she didn't show it.

They had not been told about the potential for anyone

else on the premises, especially not someone armed. Now Mookie was bleeding downstairs and Vazquez was playing hide-and-seek with the girl. This needed to end. He slammed the door in frustration and went back and stood in the doorway to the girl's room. Bed, nightstand, matching dresser, beanbag chair, acoustic guitar propped in the corner. The closet door was open. He'd already checked in there. He looked again, checking for a crawl space he might have missed. Nothing. Where had she gone? He went back and lifted the dust ruffle on the bed. Again, he'd already checked but he couldn't think of anything else to do. This time, he didn't look for a body but took in the clutter and noticed the window screen. He stood up and went to the lone window. It faced south with a view of the barn. He lifted the window. No screen. He looked around the window frame. It was covered with a thick flowering vine. There was a wooden trellis ten feet to the left of the window. Could she have gone out the window? He pulled on a vine. It tore loose but only after some serious effort. It might not support his weight but maybe it would hold a teenage girl? And if she made it to the ground, then what? He scanned the surrounding area. It was difficult to see, gathering storm clouds obscured most of the light, but then again, there wasn't much to see. He and Mookie had studied it for four hot hours not that long ago. Big ranch house. Pool patio. Horse paddock. Barn. Small secondary house for the housekeeper. That was it. Beyond that, there was barely a tree or bush to hide behind from here until Mexico. He didn't think she was still in the house. She had heard the gunshots. Her instinct would have been to run. To hide somewhere else. He looked around her room. No phone. Did she have a phone? Definitely. Every teenager in America had a phone. She had called someone and now she'd put some distance between herself and the immediate danger in the house. She'd gone to ground to wait. She trusted in her knowledge of the property to keep her safe and wait for help. That felt right. She hadn't run off for help. The nearest house was miles away. She was still close by. He was sure of it. The ranch was quite a distance from the town and any immediate help. If the police were already on their way, he still had time to make this right.

Even though her great-grandfather had built it, Angie associated the chicken coop in the corner of the barn with her dad. Her real dad. Not only did he let her get some chicks to raise and care for, but he'd also shown her the secret hatch. It had been their secret. The chicken coop was built into the last horse stall in the barn. It had spaces for eight chickens. Four on top, four on the bottom. Her grandaddy had built a clever little button that allowed someone to lift the bottom board on the lower shelf and store valuables underneath. Her dad had told her the chickens were a great distraction for hiding money and gold before cars were common and access to banks was more difficult and time-consuming. She'd been fascinated by the hidden space and often hid her childhood things there. After her dad died, the chickens slowly died off and she didn't get any more. Too many memories she didn't want to revisit. She still came out to the barn for Bonnie and Clyde, but she avoided the coop corner, as she thought of it.

She pulled open the cage and stepped inside now. It was dark, almost pitch-black, in the back corner of the barn, and she moved primarily by feel. She lifted the gate for the lower row of coops and found the button. She pressed it and raised the floor of the lower shelf. She was surprised when it stopped. It only opened a little more than a foot. That had been fine when she was eight, but would it be enough now that she was almost eighteen?

She slipped one leg in and felt her foot touch something

soft and squishy. She clamped a hand over her mouth to muffle the scream as she jerked her leg back. She pulled out her phone and put a finger over the camera flash to blunt the bright light before she turned on the flashlight. She had to risk it. She didn't think she could climb in blind after that. She shined the dim light into the narrow, hidden cavity and then almost laughed. Then almost cried. It was an old Raggedy Ann doll.

Vazquez stood in the doorway to the barn and wiped the water from his eyes. It had begun to rain. It was as if someone had thrown a switch. One step he was hot and dry, the next he was dripping wet. The rain pelted down hard and fast and felt like gritty pebbles bouncing off his skin. He could see his hand in front of his face but not much more. The sheets of rain concealed any moon or starlight. He stepped into the barn. It was dry but dark. He could hear and smell some animals moving around. A light would make him an easy target and, if it had been anyone other than a teenage girl, he might have been worried about getting shot and tried to go by feel. But the girl was on the run and there was a clock ticking. The police were likely on their way. He needed to get this done quickly. He pulled his phone from his belt and turned on the flashlight.

The barn was long and narrow with stalls for animals on both sides. The eyes of two horses flashed back at him from the right when he shined his light in that direction. He walked down the center aisle that split the barn and shined his light into each stall as he passed. All empty save for the two horses. At the far end was an equipment area with saddles, bridles, and grooming equipment along with a workbench and various supplies. Nowhere to hide there. Opposite the equipment area was an empty chicken coop in a converted stall with a thin wire gate to keep the chickens in. If there had been any chickens. He moved on.

In the back corner was a set of stairs bolted to the side-wall leading up. He took them two at a time. Half the upper loft was filled with hay and 50-pound bags of feed for the horses. The other half had been framed out and enclosed. There was a door in the middle. He tried the knob. It was locked but it was a simple push lock, not a deadbolt. He could pick it with a dull butter knife in a matter of seconds, but he didn't have a knife handy. He squared up and kicked the door directly next to the knob. The door flew open. It was a bunkhouse with a bathroom at one end, two sets of bunks against the right wall, and a cheap sofa, armchair, and television to the left. Only one person appeared to occupy the room now. There were no sheets on the other three beds. The room felt empty, but Vazquez quickly searched to be sure. No one under the bed. No one in the bathroom. He went back down the stairs.

Was she hiding in the barn? Had he been wrong? Maybe she'd gone to the house behind the barn. Maybe the house-keeper wasn't going to be so lucky after all. He started to walk back down the aisle toward the door and then stopped. He knew he hadn't thoroughly searched, he didn't have time to do more, but there was another way he could be sure. He turned back toward the work area.

CHAPTER SIXTY-ONE

"**G**oddam you and your ability to wreck my cars," Lawrence growled as he hunched over the steering wheel and tried to avoid the worst ruts in the washed-out approach road to the Double R ranch. Max didn't reply. He was afraid if he tried to talk that they'd hit a bump and he might bite through his tongue. Lawrence might consider that a fair trade for the work that would be needed on the SUV's suspension.

They popped up onto the paved section with a jarring jolt and Lawrence punched the accelerator. He swung the SUV between the two strange built-up berms and Max could now see lights from the ranch house haloing the horizon in the distance.

Lawrence had no comment on the strange built-up berms this time and just pushed the gas and got them through to the other side. The big house sat sprawling and silent in front of them. Lawrence let the SUV coast to a stop a hundred yards from the front door. If there was trouble, there was no use charging in blind. But it didn't look like trouble. The house was lit up on both floors. The outside lights were on too, illuminating the portico entrance and the landscaping. There were no obvious signs of distress.

A raindrop hit the windshield. Then a second and a third. Soon their view of the house and the grounds was shrouded by the sudden rain.

"Now what?" Lawrence asked.

Max pointed to the shelter of the portico. "Let's knock on the man's door."

Her forgotten eight-year-old treasures were pushed into one corner. Raggedy Ann, a moldering notebook, a ball made of rubber bands, a paperclip chain, and a gold-colored heart-shaped necklace that had oxidized to mostly green. The rest of the space was empty if you discounted the spiderwebs and a nest at the opposite end made up of a small pile of straw and debris. She suppressed a shudder. She hated spiders. She hoped during mid-summer, at least, that the rodent nest was no longer active.

Her squeamishness wouldn't matter if she couldn't fit through the opening. She turned the light off but kept her phone in her hand as she put one arm through and then tried to flatten her body. As expected, it was a tight fit. The old wood snagged her shirt in spots and scraped her bare arms and legs but she made it. She lowered the top until it clicked back into place.

She didn't have to wait long.

She could hear, almost feel, Bonnie and Clyde get more agitated. Maybe it was just the storm, Bonnie in particular was easily spooked by thunder, but then she heard the pitch of the rain grow louder and she realized someone had opened the door at the far end.

The boards of the chicken coop were old and warped. She could see slivers of the barn through the cracks. She didn't think she'd be visible unless the guy were to come very close. She had to believe it. She was out of ideas otherwise. She tried to remain still but her entire body was shaking, almost shivering, uncontrollably. She bit down on her lower lip until she tasted blood, hoping the pain might cut through the fear. She listened as the man's feet crunched across the dry hay that littered the barn floor. Then there was a splash of light. He had a flashlight. She squeezed her eyes shut and muttered a prayer under her breath and tried to make a last-ditch deal with God. The light shifted and she was back in darkness. She heard his feet pound up the stairs to the bunkhouse.

She squeezed her hands together to make them stop shaking. He would leave soon. He would come back down and realize she was not in the barn, and he would move on and look somewhere else. She just had to hang on.

She caught a dark glint of movement as the man descended the stairs and moved past the coop and back down the aisle toward the door. Just hold on. Another minute and he'll be gone. But then he stopped and she heard him retrace his steps. Panic spiked in her chest. Had he seen her? Figured out where she must be hiding? No, that wasn't possible. He didn't come toward the coop. Instead, the light bobbed in the other direction. She heard the thunk and clink of items being moved around the workbench. Then she heard a sound that made her heart go still.

They'd each taken a Glock from Lawrence's hidden SUV stash and put them in the waistbands at their backs. But then Max pulled his back out as they climbed the three steps. The door was open.

"Ah, shit," Lawrence said.

They both could smell the slightly acrid scent of gunpowder in the air.

Max pushed the door open with the barrel of the Glock and then went in low and to the left. He felt Lawrence go right. Max slipped behind the grandfather clock that stood in the entryway. "Mr. Blackburn? Alex?" he called. There was no immediate response and Max was about to move forward when he heard a thump and then a low groan. He crouched back down and waited. "Alex?" he called again. No response. He looked over at Lawrence who motioned with his hand. Max nodded. Lawrence moved up to a table in the hallway then Max leapfrogged him to the doorway that led into the kitchen. The smell of the gunpowder was stronger and he noted a small hole in the doorframe. The window over the sink was cracked with a hole in the lower left. Max entered, moved around the large island, and found the first body.

His first thought was Jorge, the groundskeeper, both men were short and squat, but he quickly saw that he was wrong. This man was younger, mid-30s, and heavily muscled in the chest and arms. All the muscles hadn't done anything to stop the three bullets, however. Max noted two entry wounds in the abdomen and a third, higher, that might have clipped his heart or maybe an artery. He hadn't died instantly. He sat in a puddle of blood. His eyes were open. His hands splayed at his sides. A large .44 caliber revolver was near his right hand.

"Gut shot," Lawrence whispered, looking down. "Imagine that's a tough way to go."

Before Max could reply, they heard a thump again. It was coming from the large, open living room to the left.

Max pointed back in the direction they'd come and said softly, "You circle back. Come in from the front entry. I'll go this way. Don't shoot me."

Lawrence nodded and moved off. Max moved around the body, careful not to step in the blood, and then moved toward the open living room with his gun up.

CHAPTER SIXTY-TWO

Vazquez ran the light over the various cans and bags that lined the lower shelf. He pulled a few out, checked the ingredients, and set certain ones aside. Halfway down the row, he realized that was unnecessary. He grabbed an armful and carried it to the center aisle. He used his feet to sweep some of the stray straw into a pile. Then, he unscrewed the caps and emptied the contents onto the ground.

Vazquez had never been a smoker. Smokers were now a distinct minority. It was another thing he believed would mark him as memorable. Plus, it was a potential DNA goldmine if he were to absently leave a butt behind. So, he'd never picked up the habit. But even before he started his career he'd never really been tempted. Cigarettes were far too expensive when he was a boy to ever get him hooked. Food was more important. He'd tried a few times in an effort to look older, but he'd found the taste and the dizziness off-putting.

Cigarettes, no. But fire? Fire was something he'd found plenty of uses for in his career. Fire could kill and destroy evidence all at once. Fire had been Vazquez's friend on plenty of occasions and there was no faster or easier way to get some felony arson started than a plain old lighter. He pulled his out now and flipped open the top. The lighter was brass and stamped with the words 'Good Luck' on one side. It was scratched and appeared old. It probably had a lot of stories to tell. Vazquez didn't know any of them. He'd taken it off of a guy during a job in Winslow, Arizona, in a remote corner of Homolovi State Park. It had fallen out of the guy's pocket when he was going into the hole. Vazquez had picked it up and rather than toss it in on top of the body, he'd slipped it into his pocket. He'd put it to use many times since. And now he'd use it again. He reached down and grabbed a handful of dry straw then flicked the flint knob with his thumb. The flame jumped to life on the first try. It always did. It never let him down. He held the straw to the flame until he was sure it was burning and then tossed it into the puddle of fertilizer and chemicals.

When she was a young girl, Angie went through a phase where she had trouble sleeping. She would wake up four or five nights a week sweating and screaming. It lasted for six months and then stopped happening as abruptly as it had started. She could never remember the dreams or visions, only that they were terrifying. She woke up exhausted. On those nights, one of her parents would come read her a book and lay next to her bed until she drifted back to sleep. After the story, sometimes she still wouldn't be sleepy and she'd ask her parents questions. She remembered one time asking her dad, Chuck, if he ever had nightmares. He said he certainly had some when he was a child like her but he only had one anymore. It was always the same thing. A fire in the barn.

She couldn't see exactly what the man was doing but she

could hear the splash of liquid followed by a strong chemical odor. Her father's long-ago words whispered in her head just as she heard the scratchy click of a lighter followed by a brief yellow glow and then a soft whoomp. The only good thing she heard was retreating feet.

She forced herself to remain hidden in the coop. He was trying to smoke her out. He could be waiting by the door, on the steps, in the aisle, anywhere still in the barn, away from the smoke, waiting and watching for her to panic and bolt from her hiding place. She heard Bonnie and Clyde grinding their teeth and pacing within the tight confines of their stalls. Her heart ached for each of them. She would save them she promised herself. Save herself and then save her horses.

As the fire spread, the smoke became thicker. The pungent smell threatened to make her gag. Suddenly, through the cracks in the board, she saw a line of flame jump from the main aisle toward the coop. The fire nimbly skipped through the fencing fueled by the old, dry hay. She couldn't wait any longer. She'd rather face the shadow man than burn alive. She pushed at the board above her head but it didn't budge. She pushed harder and put her shoulder into it but it stayed fast. Black and oily smoke filtered into the coop and she couldn't suppress a cough and tears leaked down her cheeks. She banged on the board, now desperate to get out and get to fresh air. The board jumped up an inch but snapped back. It didn't open. More smoke poured in instead.

CHAPTER SIXTY-THREE

Stetson Hull lay on his back near one of the fireplaces. Max could see two entry wounds, one near his hip and one higher by his armpit. A chair was knocked over and a vase of flowers was on the floor in pieces. Blood, a lot of it, covered the light wood floor. There was a smear that led from the chair to Hull. It appeared he'd been shot, flipped over the chair, and then dragged himself across the floor before turning back over. Maybe trying to get away or maybe trying to find some cover. Max didn't know. Stetson's eyes were open and shifted toward Max as he neared. Stetson held an old Ruger double-action revolver in one hand. Max saw it twitch, but he lacked the strength to lift it.

"Easy. It's Max Parish. I'm here to help."

The gun barrel drifted away and went still. "Hurts," Stetson said, and small bright bubbles of blood ran over his lips. "Everywhere."

Max scanned the rest of the large living room and saw no one. Where was Blackburn?

Lawrence edged around the doorway at the far end of the room. "Clear at this end," he said.

"Got another body over here. Ranch foreman. Looks like he's the one who had the firefight with the guy in the kitchen," Max replied.

"Is he dead?"

"Not yet. I'm going to call Serrato."

"Is that a good idea?"

"Best case, it's only Hull here who needs help. Worst case, there are others we haven't found yet." He didn't want to put the rest into words.

"Okay," Lawrence replied.

Max approached the last few feet and knelt next to Stetson. He gently rolled him onto his side and found only one exit wound. That wasn't good. He reached back and grabbed a throw blanket off the couch and pressed it to Hull's side, covering both wounds. He took the Ruger out of his hand and tossed it aside and then pressed Hull's arm against the blanket. "Try to hold it here," he said. "I'm going to call for help." Hull didn't reply. Max looked at his face. His eyes were open and staring but he was no longer awake. The blanket fell.

Max didn't want his number on any official record, so he stood and walked down the hallway to use the phone he'd seen in Blackburn's office on his first visit. The office door was closed, and Max realized someone could still be inside. He slowly turned the knob and then flung the door open and ducked back. No reaction. He went to a knee and peeked around the doorframe. He could see a pair of feet seated at the desk. He watched blood drip from the chair onto the floor. He stood and went into the room. He'd found Blackburn.

"Hello?" She didn't recognize Blackburn's number.

"It's Max. Listen, I can't talk long. I'm out at the Double

R. You on duty?"

"Yes." Good, that would speed things up.

"Anywhere close?"

"To the Double R? Not really. And you're making me nervous."

"Blackburn and Hull are dead. One of the shooters is down, too."

"One? What's going on out there?"

"I don't know for sure. I think there are at least two, but I'm not sure."

"Don't do anything stupid. I'm on my way." He heard the sirens kick in as he hung up.

Max returned to the living room to find Lawrence at the wall of windows that faced the barn and the back of the ranch.

"I think we got a problem."

"What?"

"Look to the left. Near the fence."

Max looked, but it was difficult to see through the rain. Then a crack of thunder was followed by a bright flash of lightning and he saw a man standing, half-crouched, half-hidden near the horse paddock gate, just to the left of the barn door. He was facing toward the barn, as if ...

Max started toward the kitchen and the mudroom exit that led out the back and around the patio, but Lawrence grabbed his arm. "Wait, I want to see—"

"We have to go." They hadn't searched upstairs but it was clear, at least to Max, that Angie was outside and that the man was waiting to ambush her. "Angie, she must be out there."

"I know, but what's he doing? If we rush out there, we might just rush into the same trap. Just wait, she's not in danger yet."

Then they both saw the flames and realized that might not be true.

They stood and looked out the mudroom door. "What do you want to do? We can't just run out there. He doesn't know about us. We have the element of surprise. We have to use it to our advantage."

Max forced himself to slow down. Lawrence was right. The pool and patio area were close and would provide some initial cover for any approach, but after that, there was a lot of open ground until the horse paddock and the barn. The driving rain would help a little, and the man's attention was on the barn, but it would still leave them very exposed, especially if the man was armed and, after the scene they just saw inside, Max thought that was a safe assumption.

"I could go back to the car and get a rifle and shoot the guy from here, but I don't think you want that, right?"

"Not yet. Blackburn's dead, Hull is dead, and the guy's accomplice is dead. He's the only one left if Serrato is going to get any answers about what's going on. I want him alive, if possible. But if he threatens Angie. All bets are off."

"I hear you. So, how do you want to do it?"

"I need you to go back to the car, but not for a rifle."

Max waited in a flowerbed by a corner fencepost. The rain showed no signs of relenting. He was drenched. Water cascaded off his head down into his eyes. He remained still and tried to hear over the rain. He knew he would likely hear Lawrence before he saw him. He needed to move and cover the open ground while the man was distracted. Two minutes earlier, he had exited the house by the side door, skirted along the edge of the house, through the patio and pool area and climbed over the fence on the far side, and then made his way up to the corner. He wasn't completely behind the man, but he was now more at the man's back than if he'd tried to approach from the other side of the house. He could still turn and see Max, but he hoped Lawrence would keep his attention.

On cue, he heard the SUV's engine rev loud over the storm and then he allowed himself a quick smile. He heard the music, as well. Lawrence might not love poetry, but he had a strange affinity for opera. It felt oddly appropriate for the moment. A moment later, Max watched the dim glow of the headlights as they came around the opposite side of the house. He then watched as the man turned toward the light and sounds. Max didn't wait any longer. He put his head down and charged forward.

Then, like most plans, it all went to hell.

CHAPTER SIXTY-FOUR

Vazquez turned and watched as the car's headlights approached. Then he heard the music and wondered if he was imagining the whole scene. Had he been stuck on this job so long that he was hallucinating? He knew it was going off the rails and it might not end well. Mookie was shot, hurt badly, and maybe dead in the house. The girl was still hiding, and the police had to be getting close. Plus, it was pissing rain so hard he could barely see. And now this? Not the police, but another unknown party driving a car straight at him while blasting some godawful music. The sound of the job running right into a ditch.

He raised his gun and fired at the headlights. One. Two. Three shots. Even though he was a good shot, he knew he had little hope of hitting anything. But he heard a ping of metal and the lights swerved in response and then slowed. The headlights remained bright but were no longer pointed in his eyes. The car rolled to a stop a hundred yards away. That was good enough for now. He swung his gaze back to the barn.

The car's headlights now provided some light. The rain was doing little to slow the fire. He could see the orange glow pushing against the boards as the flames climbed higher. He could hear it sizzle as they met the rain in the cracks. Smoke poured out of the open door. Where was the girl? If she was in there, she had to come out soon or she'd end up a crispy critter. He glanced back at the car, but it remained still with the doors closed. Should he run over closer and check? He took a step in the car's direction.

Vazquez had always been on the right side of the gun. He'd been the one planning and dictating the moves. He pulled the trigger. He was not used to thinking defensively. By the time his mind caught up and shouted, "Diversion!" and he started to turn around, he was lifted off his feet and slammed into the ground. The gun flew from his hand. He choked on a mouthful of mud as the breath whooshed out of him. He spat and tried to get some air as he struggled to his knees and ran his hands over the nearby ground trying to find his gun. He needed his gun. He was a killer, not a fighter.

He stood and wiped the mud from his face and spun around. It was too dark and raining too hard. Even with the headlights, he couldn't see more than a few feet. The black gun was invisible. He splashed around in the growing puddles. The rain had saturated the arid ground. He tried to keep one eye on the barn but soon gave up. The gun was the priority. If he didn't find his gun, he didn't think he'd live long enough to care about the barn. A shadow moved on his left and then his nose exploded. He stumbled and fell back into the muck. He felt a jarring pain in his lower back as he hit the ground. He thought he'd landed on a rock but then realized it was his gun. He reached back and grabbed it and struggled back to his feet. His face was on fire, and he could taste blood now mixed with the grit in his mouth. His tongue found a jagged hole where a tooth had been. He turned in a circle and tried to find the guy who had attacked him. Goddammit, where was he? He squinted and tried to block out the throbbing in the middle of his face. Suddenly he felt something wrap around his wrist, going for the gun. He spun away and lashed out. The muck was now his friend. He slipped out of the man's grasp, but the shadow burst forward and pushed his arm up and away before he could fire. He kicked out with a foot and felt it connect with bone, but the man came forward again and wrapped strong arms around his chest and arms. He felt the other man's hand scrabbling for his gun as they simultaneously squeezed the air from his chest. Vazquez pulled one arm free and began hammering a fist against the man's ribs. He heard the man grunt in pain and his grip loosened. He kept hammering and tried to drive his fist through the man's chest. He brought his knee up, hitting him now from both sides. They weren't strong blows, but they were consistent and must have had an effect. The man let go and went to a knee with his head bowed. He tried to stand but wobbled and went back to a knee. Vazquez stepped back. This was the position he was most familiar with. He raised his gun.

Her third wracking coughing fit finally shook loose the right thought. She needed to hit the button to release the catch and allow the board to rise. It was the reverse of how she got inside. The smoke was oily and thick and now almost filled the small space. She felt above her head with her hand until she felt the small polished wooden knob. She pressed it and then pushed up. The board rose and she slid out and collapsed on the dirty straw floor.

But she couldn't stay there. The fire continued to spread and the smoke, though still thin on the ground, was building. She rolled onto her hands and knees and crawled to the central aisle. She could see the fire climbing the walls. She flinched at the sound of a loud crack. When the fire reached the stored hay bales in the loft, she knew it would be like a bomb going off. As she watched, it jumped two steps as if it knew there was fresh fuel just ahead. She only had a minute, maybe less.

She crawled toward the main door. The man had left it open to allow the outside oxygen to feed the fire. Bonnie and Clyde huffed and snorted. They were trapped in their stalls in a state of complete panic. She stood to the side so she wouldn't get trampled and opened the stall doors. First, Bonnie and then Clyde. The horses didn't need any directions. They bolted from their stalls and charged down the aisle toward the door and fresh air.

Angie glanced back and saw the fire had reached the bales. There was a roar as the fire consumed them in a rush. She felt the increased heat like a blow to the face. She had to get out, but the smoke was now so thick she could no longer see. Her throat ached. She couldn't stand any longer. She went back to her knees but still couldn't catch her breath. The smoke had filled all the empty space. Her eyes watered. She tried to wipe them but it hurt. She kept them closed instead. She crawled forward and tried to keep the heat at her back. She knew the door was in that direction. Right? It was hard to think clearly. She saw bright pinpricks of light. Were those stars? Was she outside? The smoke was so thick. She needed to get lower. She lay on her stomach. She put her face against the floor.

Then she was moving again. Or being moved.

Maybe this was how it felt to die. You were lifted up and removed from your body.

Still, it felt awfully hot for heaven.

CHAPTER SIXTY-FIVE

Max tried to stand but his legs wouldn't hold him. He fell to his knees. Everything hurt. He needed to get up. He needed to save Angie. He needed to check on Lawrence. He had to hold on until Serrato got here. He had to call Vic. His mind pleaded but his body had simply reached its limit. The crash injuries had left him too weak, too vulnerable. The sprint through the mud and the brief fight had used up what he had left. No matter how long a person lived, it was never long enough. Life always ended a minute too soon. And you rarely saw it coming.

He lifted his head, let the water run down his face, and watched the man raise his gun. He considered the man behind the trigger. Max didn't recognize him. Just a face. Just his time. It was bound to happen. He always knew that one day the impulse that led him into trouble, that made him feel most alive, would ultimately lead him to this moment. The clock had run out.

He felt the ground start to shake and heard thunder in his ears as death approached.

And then it was past him and the man with the gun was gone and the 1000-pound horse ran off into the rain-soaked desert. Max toppled over and passed out in the mud.

He woke up as something jabbed him in his side. Then again.

"Ouch. Stop." He tried to roll away but stopped at the flare of pain.

He opened one eye and looked down the business end of a shotgun. Consuela poked him again. "Did you do this?" She looked like a deranged Mother Goose with the gun and her hair plastered to her forehead in the rain. But neither of them was laughing. She moved to poke him again and he slid back.

"No, of course not."

"Why are you here?"

"Angie texted me."

She thought about that and then moved the barrel aside and stepped back. She made no motion to help him up. He couldn't have been out long. Two or three minutes. Five at the most. The rain had eased up, but the barn was still burning. The flames had breached the roof.

He rolled over onto his hands and knees then pushed himself upright. This time, he was able to stay up.

"Who did this?" Consuela asked. "Who burned the barn?"

"I don't know. It's not just the barn. They shot Hull and Blackburn at the house. There's a guy ..." He motioned off to the left.

"Where?"

Max turned and looked more closely. The man was no longer there. "There was a guy. One of the horses knocked him over when they ran out of the barn."

She looked off into the dark. "Tuaro," she whispered and crossed herself with one hand.

"What's that? Is that a name?"

She ignored the question. "The horses are okay?"

"As far as I know. Scared, but okay. They ran off."

The roof of the barn caved in with a crash. They both flinched, and Max edged farther away from the shotgun and twitchy fingers.

"Please tell me Angie is with you," he said.

"Yes, Jorge pulled her out of the barn, but it was too hot to go back in again for the horses. We thought ..."

She didn't finish.

Max felt a wave of relief at the news. "They're fine. Both of them. I saw them myself. We can find them at first light. Where's Angie?"

"In the house. C'mon. I have called 911. She will be okay, I think, but she needs help. She was in the smoke for a long time."

He wanted to see Angie, but first, he had to check on Lawrence. The way the SUV sat there, not moving, gave him a bad feeling. "Wait, I need to check ..." He waved a hand at the SUV.

He hobbled over. Lawrence was passed out in the driver's seat. Blood ran down his arm. Max opened the door and feared the worst, but Lawrence groaned and opened his eyes. "Burns," he said.

"Where?"

"Shoulder. Lucky shot. Ricochet."

Max could see the entry wound between his neck and shoulder. Max gently moved him forward in the seat. There was an exit wound and a small hole the size of a pencil eraser in the seat upholstery.

Consuela pushed him out of the way. She'd leaned the gun against the SUV and now held a knife. She slit the shirt from his neck to his armpit and moved it aside.

Lawrence hissed.

Consuela tutted and gently probed around the wound. "Don't be a child."

"Pretty handy with that knife, senorita."

"I'm also good with a needle and thread. We need to stop the bleeding. Too messy to do anything right now. You have a first aid kit in the car, yes?"

Lawrence nodded. "In the trunk. On the right."

"Get it," she told Max. "And then get him in the house. I need light and soap."

Max retrieved the small kit and handed it to Consuela and then helped Lawrence out of the car.

"Feels like my arm is going to fall off," Lawrence said.

"I can't believe you left me out there alone and only got shot in the shoulder," Max replied.

Angie lay on the couch inside Consuela's small house. Through smudges of dirt and soot, her face, arms, and legs were scorched pink. Jorge sat in a nearby chair. An open bottle of water was on the table next to her. It smelled intensely like a fire inside the room. Max put the first aid kit on the table and watched her. Her chest rose and fell but her eyes remained closed.

"She's okay?" He wasn't sure who he was asking.

"I feel like I spent an hour licking a barbeque but I'm okay. Or I will be." Her voice was a soft, raspy whisper. She opened her eyes and looked at him. "You came."

"Not fast enough."

She shook her head. "Doesn't matter. You're here."

"A promise doesn't mean anything if it's not kept."

Angie nodded.

"You knew," Max said.

She looked away briefly and then back at him. "I'm sorry. She showed up a few weeks ago. She needed my help." Tears ran down her cheeks. Max put a hand on her arm.

"It's all right. Family can do that to you."

"Suck you in like a black hole." She closed her eyes again.

"Family is gravity," Max said.

Consuela pulled him and Lawrence into the kitchen. "Come. Jorge will sit with her until the ambulance arrives. Bring that." She pointed to the first aid kit. They walked into the kitchen. She disappeared through a different doorway. She returned a minute later with a sewing kit and a lamp with a dangling cord. She removed the lampshade, plugged it in, and placed it on the table. "You," she pointed at Max. "There is a hose just outside the door down that hallway. Go clean yourself up. You," she looked at Lawrence and pulled out a chair, "sit."

Max put the first aid kit on the table and left her to it. As he walked down the hallway, he heard Lawrence yelp as she started to clean his wound. "Don't be una bebita ..." He didn't hear Lawrence's response. He pushed out through the door and found the hose. He was already soaked to the skin so he turned it on and stood under it. The water was ice cold but he didn't flinch away. He needed it to keep himself awake. This wasn't over. It was going to be a long night.

When he had cleaned the worst of the mud off, he shut off the hose and walked around to the front of the house. The fire raged. It would consume the barn. Maybe that was a good thing. Maybe it would spread to the ranch house, too. Too much blood and tragedy had soaked into this soil. Maybe the fire could scour it clean and provide a fresh start. Then he felt a twinge of guilt for thinking it. He turned to Consuela and

Jorge's small house. He didn't wish their house gone. Not everything was bad. Good was resilient.

He watched the red and blue emergency lights approaching in the distance. He looked at his watch. It felt like hours had passed, but it had only been 15 minutes since he'd called Serrato from Blackburn's office.

CHAPTER SIXTY-SIX

"What the hell happened?"

"Remember that question you had about Blackburn? Back at the diner?"

They stood in the living room. She crouched near Hull's body and confirmed he wouldn't need an ambulance. "Blackburn wasn't the devil, not exactly," Max continued, "but he certainly wasn't on the side of the angels."

"I feel like you've been leaving me out of the loop."

"Maybe a little. For your own good. Like we talked about."

"My good or yours?"

"They don't have to be mutually exclusive."

"You're going to have to explain eventually."

"I will, as much as I know, but we still have a problem. There were two guys. It was a team. One of the guys got away in the confusion with the fire and trying to find Angie. It would be ... a lot easier to explain all of this if you were able to take him into custody."

She glanced out the window. "Going to be hard to find him in the dark. That's a lot of ground to cover."

"I might have an idea of where he's headed."

She gave him a long look. "Okay, but I want to see Angie first."

Angie was now asleep on the couch. Jorge was in the chair. Each rise and fall of her chest brought an alarming rattle. Serrato watched her for a moment and then followed the noise into the kitchen.

"You keep crying like a baby and you're going to wake up Angie," she said to Lawrence as she leaned against the kitchen counter.

"You all have to stop calling me a baby. How many of you have been shot before?" All three of them raised their hands. "Really?" Lawrence said. "I need to find some new friends. Fine, you're all serious hard cases. But did you each have your wounds stitched up with no anesthesia, not even a swig of Jim Beam?"

"Okay, you got me there," Max said.

"Morphine is a dream come true," Serrato added.

"That's more like—ow!"

Consuela snipped the black thread and tied off the knot. She took a piece of gauze from the first aid kid and cleaned up the leaking blood then added antiseptic ointment from a small tube, added a new layer of gauze, and taped up the wound.

"Done," she said and began to clean up the used supplies.

Lawrence glanced down at his chest and then gently touched the crisscrossing thread. He winced. "Thank you," he said. Consuela nodded and then left the room carrying a trash bag.

"You fill her in?" Lawrence asked as he carefully pulled on the clean T-shirt that Consuela had left on the table.

"Not yet, but I did tell her we got one guy still out there."

"The guy who shot me. When we catch up to him, I'm going to kill him."

"Hey, you can't say those things with me standing here," Serrato said.

"What happened to the guy who shot you?"

She looked away. "He's dead."

"See?"

"He was an 82-year-old man who discharged his firearm accidentally. I was shot in the toe."

"And then you shot him? Damn, that's cold. But I understand."

"No! Then five years passed, and he died from colon cancer."

"Well, I don't have the patience to wait that long. I want to kill this guy now."

"Stop."

"I've been shot and just had the wound irrigated, cleaned, and stitched like it was still the Civil War. It feels like my bones are on fire. Fantasies of catching and killing this bastard are the only thing making me feel better."

"As long as they stay fantasies."

"We'll see," Lawrence growled. "We gotta find him first."

They drove slowly straight across the land. It would have been easier in Serrato's Jeep, but the suspension of the patrol car held up well and had the added advantage of an LED spotlight mounted on the side mirror.

"Why the salt house?" Serrato asked.

"There's a tunnel under the border."

She gave him a double-take. "A tunnel."

"Yes."

"A tunnel that you didn't tell me about."

"That we didn't tell you about yet." He waved away more

questions. "We'll get to all that. They probably had a car hidden somewhere but maybe not close by and it's isolated out here. Once Lawrence and I showed up, he had to know the clock was ticking. That the police were likely on the way. There are maybe four roads he could use to escape. It would be too easy to get caught in a roadblock. I'm guessing he would think the tunnel is a safer bet. Less than a mile and he's home free."

She didn't look happy with the situation, but she didn't have anything more to say for the moment. She kept her attention on avoiding any sinkholes or snapping an axle in a hidden culvert. Max worked the light with Lawrence spotting. The rain had stopped. The storm had left as fast as it had arrived. The stars poked out between thin wispy clouds. They reached the salt house without spotting him. Serrato braked the cruiser to a stop twenty feet from the open door. She put a hand on the latch when Max spoke up.

"One more thing."

"What?"

"I can't be sure he's not armed. Last I saw him he didn't have a gun, but maybe that changed."

"Of course."

"You got a vest?"

"In the back."

"You can take the lead."

She got out and opened the trunk. She slipped a vest on over her uniform, unholstered her gun, and moved toward the door. She nudged it open and swept the room. She moved inside and they followed. Muddy footprints led to the far corner.

"The smoker?" she whispered.

Max nodded. She frowned but made her way across the room and opened one door. She looked inside and then looked back at Max. He stepped up and removed the loose steel sheet that covered the hole in the floor. Serrato took the flashlight off her belt and shined it down. "Holy shit."

"That about sums it up."

"He's long gone, isn't he?"

Max glanced into the hole. The footprints had faded but could still be seen. There were bloody handprints on the ladder. He knew she didn't need an answer, but he gave her one anyway. "Looks that way, but he's hurt. I don't think he's moving fast."

"Did you follow it to the end?"

"No."

"Even if I go down there and chase him down, jurisdiction is going to get messy.

Max nodded. The law wasn't his problem. Angie was safe. Lawrence would survive. He was done. Or almost done.

"Sometimes evil gets away," he said. "Sometimes standing up in the first place is the best you can do."

"That doesn't make me feel any better."

"It's not supposed to, but it might make it easier to live with down the road."

He could see she didn't believe him. Not right now. Instead, she said, "How long has this been here?"

"Our guess is about a year. Probably not more than 18 months."

"And Blackburn was using this?"

"Yes, trucks from the warehouse were making regular stops. The toluene and maybe other chemicals were going across the border."

"To make drugs."

"More than likely."

"Oh, this is going to be huge." There was a mix of excitement and fear on her face. She would be all right he decided. She held out the flashlight. "Hold this while I climb down. I need to see this for myself before the Feds pile on and shut us out."

They used the road to get back to the Double R. Serrato called the chief and outlined the whole situation. She glanced in Max's direction and he nodded. She had it right.

After she hung up, he asked, "Do you think he knew?"

"About the tunnel? No, probably not. The sheriff's not a bad man, he just likes the easy answer. The tunnel might have been too big for him to ignore. Did he know that Blackburn was straddling the line of the law? Probably. Did he know the specifics? I don't think he wanted to know as long as TR was doing all right and the voters were happy."

"That's a slippery slope."

"That's politics. Just about everything is going to come out now. He knows he can't contain it. He said he's calling the Rangers and Border Patrol which will bring in the Feds. The big wheels of bureaucracy are rolling in our direction. Might take some time, but if he was even a little dirty, we'll know."

"Doesn't sound like you'd mind too much."

She shrugged. "It's going to get ugly and the town might suffer but maybe we need a fresh start." She looked at the barn. "Burn it all down."

Max settled back in his seat. "We'll get you Kelley's financial work. You might not need it. I don't think warrants are going to be a problem, but he's good at numbers. It could help."

"Sounds good. I'd appreciate it."

"After that, it might be better if we were never here."

"Might be."

CHAPTER SIXTY-SEVEN

Max sat in the parking lot with the air conditioning running and watched the orange sun dip toward the horizon. He wasn't in a hurry. Not too much. This story had taken almost a decade to get to this point. A few more minutes wouldn't matter one way or the other.

After they'd left the Double R, he called Carson and tipped her off in exchange for use of Dorothy's guest room for one more night. She agreed. In the morning, he knocked on the sliding glass door and caught Dorothy before she went to work. He showed her a photo on his phone. Then he'd walked across the street to Carson's house. She was arguing with someone on the phone. Might have been the sheriff. She looked twenty years younger when she was chasing a hot story.

"Can I borrow your laptop for a minute?"

She eyed him and waved a hand at the kitchen table where the laptop sat next to a smoldering cigarette. She put a hand over the receiver. "What are you up to Miss Fletcher?"

"Don't worry, I'll give you the good stuff."

He sat down and fifteen minutes later he had as much of the story as he thought he was going to get.

Satisfied, he drove Lawrence to the San Antonio airport. They spent most of the drive complaining about their injuries like old men and talking about anything other than Texas. Max then turned around and drove back south to TR with a promise to keep this latest SUV intact. He ate one last onion burger at The Tin Roof and then drove past the competing dollar stores, the dying motels, and the empty RV park until he reached his destination.

At 4:50 P.M, the last customer left the store. A heavyset woman walked to a GMC Terrain. She wiped her brow with the palm of her hand as she fumbled for her car keys in a large canvas purse that might have been a saddlebag. It seemed like the type of thing that Halford Unique Gifts & Jewelry might sell. He sat in the SUV and watched the Terrain pull out and drive away.

It was time. Max got out and stretched his arms overhead. He was stiff and sore and wanted to do nothing more than sleep for about a week, but first, he had to go inside.

He paused at the store's front door. He could see a woman inside behind the counter, a hard cover book splayed open in front of her. He'd bet ten to one it was a library book. He entered and she looked up and smiled. He flipped the kitschy wooden sign that hung on the door to 'Closed.' He watched her smile falter and then one hand dipped below the counter.

"Can I help you?" she asked.

Max walked closer and stopped ten feet short of the woman next to one of the freestanding display cases scattered across the room that showed off various pieces of turquoise and silver jewelry.

"Leslie Halford?" he asked, though he thought he recognized her voice from their prior calls.

"Yes, that's right. And you are?"

"Max Parish." He thought he detected a twitch, a slight tremor in the smile, but he couldn't be certain. "We spoke on the phone."

"Of course, about poor Rose. I'm not sure I have anything more to tell you."

"Maybe she's not so poor after the last few days. Maybe she's back in the money."

The smile dimmed a little further. It was still there, but somehow told a different story. "I reckon you might be a bit confused. And you're mixing up your tenses, I think."

"See, that was a clunker right there. No farm girl from Kenosha would ever use reckon so naturally. The first time we spoke you said a few other things that stuck in my mind, but I couldn't put a finger on exactly what it was, not at first, but it was like a burr in my head and I got there in the end. As you told me on the phone, I'm stubborn. Here's what I figured, let me know what you think. Dyed-in-the-wool Midwesterners, those who grew up there and spent all their formative years there, who went to college there, would never say their store was by the highway. I've spent time up there. You'd say expressway. And a horse wouldn't balk at crossing a creek. It would get spooked at a crick. You say creek and they'd look at you sideways. If you went to the considerable trouble of adjusting your appearance and coming up with a new backstory, maybe you should have also gone with a vocal coach."

She looked at him. Her eyes were now hard and her smile thinner. "Maybe I fudged my resume a bit. Maybe the fish out of water story gets more sympathy. So what? If we started locking up everyone who did that ..." She lifted the hand that lay on the counter as if to say where would society possibly be.

Max ignored her. "I didn't mix up my tenses. You did. The first time we spoke. Everyone else I talked to spoke about Rose in the past tense. They either assumed she was dead or so much time had passed that it was the natural way to talk about her. But not you. I thought maybe you were just fooling yourself. Hopelessly naive. I've come around to a different opinion now."

"Yeah, and what's that?"

"I think Rose Robideaux is very much alive."

She gave a dry laugh. "And your evidence is my grammar?"

"I'm not a cop. Or a lawyer. Proof is more their thing. I'm just making conversation."

Max took two steps forward. Halford's hand remained below the counter. He wanted to be close enough to make a move if he had to.

"Women do have a distinct advantage in trying to disappear," he continued. "Putting on or taking off some weight and altering their hairstyle, color and cut, can go a long way in altering appearances. When you add modern medicine on top? Cheeks, nose, chin. You could practically live in your hometown, and no one would even recognize you. Tough to change the eyes though. Did you hear about a recent study where an artificial intelligence system was able to identify the biological sex of people just by reading their eyes. They have no idea how it works but it was spooky accurate."

"What are you talking about?"

"Just making conversation. Do you know Melinda Carson? The reporter?"

"Yes."

"She has a sister, Dorothy. She works in the flower shop in town. She never forgets a customer. I mean that quite literally, too. Dorothy has Williams-Beuren syndrome. It's a neurological condition. She never forgets a face. I showed her your picture from the store's website this morning. Do you want to know what she said?"

The smile finally fell and shattered on the floor. It took a little imagination, the surgery really had been good, but if he squinted, Max could see the resemblance like a faint familial echo. Maybe a second cousin. She placed both hands on the counter and Max felt himself relax just a fraction.

"And I think you're taking the long way around to say what you really mean."

Kenosha was long gone. Halford's last sentence was pure southern drawl with a Texas twist.

"Welcome back, Rose. A lot of people have been looking for you."

"I think you got your money's worth. How'd you pay for it? And where'd you go for the new face? Mexico? No, probably not. Too obvious. Too easy to find unless you went deep in country and if you did that maybe the skills you needed, or the skills you could trust, would be harder to find." Max shook his head. "Canada makes more sense. It would be more inconvenient and you'd run a higher risk in being identified in making the long trip north, but the payoff would also be greater and maybe worth the additional risk for you." The shadows outside were growing longer and the lights in the shop seemed dimmer. "That was a neat trick with the library trustees. Establishing Leslie as a real person while preparing to disappear. I went back and looked at all the old minutes. Did you know they post all their meetings online? I noticed Leslie Halford and Rose Robideaux never appeared together in the same meeting."

Standing at the counter in front of him, Leslie Halford had now disappeared for good.

"So what? What's the crime in trading one life that had become unbearable for another?"

"You could have stayed in your daughter's life."

Her eyes flashed at the mention of Angie. Did she understand the toll it had taken? On both of them? Or was it a glint of the crazy that had spawned the plan in the first place? He hadn't liked spending the short amount of time he had out at the Double R, too isolated, too insular. He wondered what spending an entire lifetime there would do to a person.

"Don't try to lecture me," she said. "You've been here a week. Do you really think a divorce would have stopped a man like Alex? It would have been the same set of problems with half the assets. Do you think I did this on a whim? That I didn't make plans? My family made this town. Our blood and sweat are in the ground. Our bones are buried here. In a moment of weakness, I made a mistake. I let a snake inside our house, and I didn't recognize him for who he was until it was too late. Alex was going to take it all away. He was going to destroy my family's legacy."

"So you destroyed your own family."

"It was my job to fix it. By any means necessary. Angie understands that."

Max had to stop himself from taking a step back. That flash hadn't been guilt or remorse. He could feel the rage coming off her in waves. It was the type of anger that could wash away rational thought. The type that might allow a mother to fake her own death and walk away from her daughter.

She continued, almost as if reading his thoughts. "Yes, I left Angie there, but she wasn't alone and it was never going to be permanent."

"Consuela."

"Probably a better mother to her than I ever was. At least back then."

"I can almost understand. Almost. Certainly, I wouldn't want people looking back and judging some of my past choices. But two things bother me beyond just what you put Angie through. First, you sent those two truckers after me and almost killed me."

She ducked her head. "That was not supposed to happen. I'm sorry you were hurt. The intent was not to put you in the hospital. It was to scare you off. At the time, I wanted you out of here. I didn't care where. I just wanted you far away from TR. Things were getting messy. You and that PI from San Antonio were going to screw it all up. I needed you both to back off."

"That was not the way to play it."

"I know that now." She tried for some levity. "I didn't realize then just how stubborn you were."

"I've been told I might have trouble distinguishing between stubbornness and stupidity."

"I was hoping you'd fall more on the stupid side."

"Sorry to disappoint you, but I've had people take their shots at me before and I'm still around. I can't say the same thing about Raul Ortiz. He's the second thing."

She didn't react and after a moment said, "I don't know what you mean. I think those cartel boys who were skulking around town are likely responsible for what happened to Ortiz. Half the town was talking about them. Ortiz ends up dead and now they're gone."

Max shook his head. "That's the easy and expedient answer and I expect the sheriff won't fight it too much, but I don't think it's the real answer. How would those two know about Ortiz?"

"From Alex?"

"How would Alex know? He was being blackmailed. He had no business with that bank. Why would he suspect Ortiz?"

"TR isn't all that big. Not that many banks in town."

"True and you could make up a good story about how they might have gone about finding him, but the simplest explanation is that you were the only one who knew where those documents could have come from. How did you find out?" She didn't answer. "Probably Consuela. Who else was there? Her or Jorge. I don't think she knew what you were going to do but she likely saw the letter or heard Blackburn talking about it. She strikes me as someone who doesn't miss much. Maybe she didn't even know the full impact of the documents. Maybe she just saw your name. But you certainly knew what they were and what could happen if they didn't end up back in that safe deposit box. You knew where to look. Ortiz's access wouldn't be hard to figure out. It wasn't a big bank. Once you zeroed in on him, you tortured him and then killed him to get them back. But then you had another problem. How to get them back where they belonged. First you tried to use Angie. Then, when that didn't work, you realized you had another option. Me. So, rather than try to run me out of town, you doctored up some hospital files to get my sympathy and keyed in on my connection with Angie."

She looked at him and then shrugged. "An interesting theory but you said it: proof is not your domain. This whole thing was a mess. I guess we'll never know all the answers."

"But you'll have to live with it. And so will Angie."

"I made peace with that long ago. When I finally woke up, I was so far down in the hole only the devil was going help me get out." She looked past him and seemed to deflate, the anger ebbing. "And if I let in a snake, then he let in a wolf. Neither one was going to just do what I wanted if I asked nicely."

The final pieces tumbled together. "The cartel. You knew. You left Ortiz's body out by the old salt house hoping someone would find the tunnel and the cartel connection. You knew you couldn't take on the cartel alone."

"Alex was very smart. No, that's not the right word. He was more dangerous. He was greedy and he was cunning. He could hide it behind a facade of charming respectability, that was his special talent. Plus, money will buy you a lot of leeway, but he couldn't hide it from someone living under the same roof."

"You knew and you still left Angie there alone."

The anger didn't reignite. "Yes, but you're not listening. I didn't abandon her. I left, but I was always coming back. I had a plan. And it worked."

"Did it?"

"I've met Alex's partners. Tuaro Ramirez is a businessman. He might get some dirt under his fingernails, but he is not a monster. If Alex screwed up, he would face the consequences. I'm not that naive, but Angie was never in any real danger."

She didn't know, Max realized. Not yet. The gossipy aspects had likely torn through the town and she clearly knew Alex was dead, but she didn't know the true story. She didn't know that her assumptions about Ramirez were wrong. Very wrong. He had talked to Serrato this morning. Angie had been taken to the clinic and would make a full recovery. At least physically. She had been interviewed by different authorities throughout the day. Maybe she hadn't had the opportunity to call her mother. Or maybe she had. Angie was a smart young woman. Maybe she reached the same conclusions that he had.

Max turned to leave. "You should call your daughter, Rose. She needs to hear from you."

The remaining Robideaux family was bent and disfigured but maybe not beyond repair. If you can ask for forgiveness, and you can hold on, things can change.

· · ·

He walked back outside and the heat felt like a relief after the coldness inside the store. He glanced at his watch. His deal with Serrato ended at 6 P.M. He looked down the road. She'd be coming soon. Maybe they'd be able to get Rose for Ortiz's murder. Or maybe her plan would work and she'd walk. But Rose wouldn't get to decide on her own. Ortiz's sister deserved that much.

He climbed into the SUV and brought up the nav system. He smiled. Lawrence. There was only one address programmed in. He could take a hint.

He drove north until the stars came out and the air was cool and crisp. Then he kept going.

This time it was his phone that rang.

"Where are you?"

"Trying to find my way home."

ABOUT THE AUTHOR

Mike Donohue is the author of six previous novels in the
Max Strong series. He lives with his wife, two daughters, and
Dashiell Hammett outside Boston. Dash is the family dog.

Mike doesn't think reading during meals is particularly rude.
Quite the opposite.

You can find him online at mikedonohuebooks.com.

 facebook.com/mikedonohuebooks
twitter.com/miked_mystery

CPSIA information can be obtained
at www.ICGtesting.com
Printed in the USA
BVHW041025090423
662004BV00004B/247

9 781736 829769